"Those who enjoy golf will find *Center Cut* a riveting novel, especially when the duel with Tiger begins!" *—I Love a Mystery*

"Don't start to read the book in the evening and expect to go to bed at your usual time." *—Milford (NH) Cabinet*

"In *Center Cut*, John R. Corrigan has done an extremely clever job of blending murder and mystery with a PGA tour he describes with authority, both behind-the-scenes and on the greens. Credit him with a hole in one." —Robert S. Levinson, author of *Hot Paint* and *The James Dean Affair*

PRAISE FOR *SNAP HOOK*

"Pluses are Austin's complex relationships with his inner-city-project caddy and his CBS commentator girlfriend and his pondering of some splendid passages from the poetry of Philip Levine." *—Ellery Queen's Mystery Magazine*

"Another fun read with an interesting finish." *—New England Journal of Golf*

"Corrigan's second Jack Austin mystery features deft prose, clean plotting, and enjoyable subject matter and will appeal to golf fans." *—Library Journal*

"Corrigan commands a wealth of technical detail to make Jack's every round vivid and exciting . . . Highly recommended for golfers, golf widows and widowers, and everybody who's ever wondered what the fuss is about." *—Kirkus Reviews*

"Imagine a wisecracking Tiger Woods as Sherlock Holmes. That's the sort of lovable hero John Corrigan has created in this new mystery series. Witty and intriguing, *Snap Hook* will delight every mystery reader who loves golf—and every golfer who loves mysteries." —Tess Gerritsen, author of *The Sinner*

"How does a golfer spend an ideal day? Eighteen holes on the links and the evening spent reading John Corrigan's new mystery, *Snap Hook*. Corrigan's Jack Austin is a grand, new hero—sensitive, smart, loyal, and one hell of a fine golfer!" —Roberta Isleib, author of the Agatha- and Anthony-nominated Golf Lover's mysteries

"From sand traps to kidnapping, money laundering to murder mystery, John R. Corrigan is a brilliant story teller. With *Snap Hook*, he hits a hole in one." —Ridley Pearson, author of *User: Unknown*

"John R. Corrigan accurately portrays life on the PGA Tour, and throws in a wonderful twist by adding a mystery and an interesting sleuth in Jack Austin. Anyone who likes golf and mysteries will find the two here." —PGA Tour player J. P. Hayes, winner of the 2002 John Deere Classic and 1998 Buick Classic

OUT OF BOUNDS

OTHER BOOKS BY JOHN R. CORRIGAN

Bad Lie (UPNE, 2005)
Center Cut (UPNE, 2004)
Snap Hook (UPNE, 2004)
Cut Shot (Sleeping Bear Press, 2001)

OUT OF BOUNDS

JOHN R. CORRIGAN

University Press of New England

HANOVER AND LONDON

Published by University Press of New England,
One Court Street, Lebanon, NH 03766
www.upne.com
© 2006 by John R. Corrigan
Printed in the United States of America
5 4 3 2 1

Library of Congress Cataloging-in-Publication Data
Corrigan, John R.
Out of bounds / John R. Corrigan.
    p.   cm.—(Hardscrabble books)
ISBN–13: 978–1–58465–585–5 (alk. paper)
ISBN–10: 1–58465–585–2 (alk. paper)
    1. Austin, Jack (Fictitious character)—Fiction.   2. Golfers—Fiction.   3. Doping in sports—Fiction.   4. Golf stories.   I. Title.   II. Series.
PS3603.O773O94   2006
813'.6—dc22   2006010988

"Starlight", copyright © 1979 by Philip Levine, "They Feed the Lion", copyright © 1968, 1969, 1970, 1971, 1972 by Philip Levine, "I Could Believe", copyright © 1991 by Philip Levine, "The Miracle", copyright © 1991 by Philip Levine, from NEW SELECTED POEMS by Philip Levine. Used by permission of Alfred A. Knopf, a division of Random House, Inc.

This is for my grandfather, George Dumont,
who grew up during the Great Depression.
Gramps, you worked harder than anyone
I know and never once complained.
Thanks for the lessons.

I don't know what justice is. Truth interests me, though.

— Ross Macdonald, *The Drowning Pool*

ACKNOWLEDGMENTS

Many people generously gave time, knowledge, and expertise to assist in the researching of this novel. Without them, this book wouldn't have been written. Therefore, I wish to express sincere gratitude to the following people: First and foremost, thanks to Dr. Charles Yesalis, a professor of Health and Human Development at Penn State and a leading expert on steroids, who answered a blind e-mail with a phone call and shared his knowledge and provided helpful insights. Also, Laura Hayes and Connie Corrigan, who read various drafts and offered insightful criticism; Stacy Jandreau, M.D., emergency department physician at the Aroostook Medical Center in Presque Isle, Maine; Carl Flynn, M.D., of Pines Health Services in Caribou, Maine; Maine State Police Detective Adam Stoutamyer; Andy Pazder, vice-president of administration, Competitions for the PGA Tour; Lori Googins, athletic director at Northern Maine Community College; and Gregory Thompson, life sciences instructor at Northern Maine Community College. These people made the book better. Any double bogies within are the author's errors.

Thanks to everyone at UPNE: Jeff Bukowski, Deborah Forward, Barbara Briggs, Sherry Strickland, and, as always, my editor John Landrigan, who made this book better.

Special thanks to my home team—my wife, Lisa, and daughters, Delaney and Audrey, for their unwavering encouragement and support.

AUTHOR'S NOTE

Although incidental reference is made to numerous real-life PGA Tour players and factual information regarding real PGA Tour venues is offered, all incidents, characters, and events in this book are fictional and exist only in the mind of the author.

OUT OF BOUNDS

I never really knew Ron Scott. In thirteen seasons on the PGA Tour, I'd played only one round with the guy. But there I was, on a winter morning in Chicago, with every other PGA Tour player, paying my last respects.

I sat in the back of the church with my caddy, Tim Silver (a highly emotional sort who looked ready to cry), Brian "Padre" Tarbuck, and Perkins. Padre was coming off his first win in years and was still glowing. It was standing room only. Ron Scott had been forty-three.

"Shitty way to go," Perkins said, his voice flat. He had been a homicide detective with the Boston PD. Now he was a security consultant for the PGA Tour. His aluminum crutches leaned against the pew. He'd made it from the parking lot on them; for longer distances, he needed a wheelchair.

Ron Scott had been killed, a mugging gone bad, the papers said. I guess you said things like "shitty way to go" when you'd been a homicide cop. I'd been home in Maine, lifting weights in my basement gym, when The Golf Channel broke the story.

"The guy worked hard," Padre said. "I never worked out with him or anything, but he was in damned good shape. Re-dedicated himself about a year ago. I'm with the same apparel company, and the rep said he lost four inches from his waist but went from a small to a medium shirt size."

"Must have been busting his ass," I said. "That's how he got out of his slump and managed to win in his forties."

"By the way," Padre said to me, "congratulation on becoming a member of the Policy Board."

I thanked him. After my peers voted me onto the Player Advisory Council, which consults with the PGA Tour Policy Board on all matters affecting the Tour, I was now serving the first of a three-year term on the PGA Tour Policy Board. The Board serves as the PGA Tour's board of directors and has final authority on all matters pertaining to the organization. The Board consists of players, Tour brass, and people outside of professional golf known to be friends of the game. It was an honor and I took my duty seriously.

I turned my attention back to the proceedings. Funerals are always surreal. Yet this time, I really was an outsider. While three of my peers—Hal "Hurricane" McCarthy, a good friend, among them—had made eloquent speeches on Ron Scott's behalf, I hadn't really known the deceased. I was there out of obligation and respect.

At the front of the church, Scott's widow sobbed. She was blonde and wore a long black dress with a black veil. PGA Tour Commissioner Peter Barrett shuffled papers and read a prepared statement. Two young kids sat next to the widow, and I thought of my three-year-old, Darcy. According to my wife, a golf journalist, Ron Scott had been shopping for his kids when his end came. A family man, he'd driven to Chicago from his suburban home and was simply walking store to store at 2:30 on a January afternoon when he was shot to death in an ally.

"You going to Scottsdale?" Padre said, after the service, when we stood to leave.

I leaned to get Perkins's crutches, but he reached past me and took them himself.

"Just trying to help," I said.

"I don't need help," Perkins said.

"Yeah, I'm playing," I said, turning to back Padre. "I'm flying out tonight."

As people filed out of the church, Hurricane McCarthy and Paul Meyers moved past our pew. They were my contemporaries, nineteen- and fifteen-year veterans, respectively. They were whispering and walking slowly. Meyers was animated, his hands in constant motion as he spoke. I called to Hurricane and both men looked startled.

"Sorry," I said. "Just wanted to offer condolences. I know it's a tough loss."

"What do you mean?" Meyers said.

I looked at him. "Ron Scott. He's a tough loss."

"Oh, of course." Meyers nodded and scowled as if upset he'd missed an easy test question. "Yeah, of course he is. Well, see you later." They moved past us.

When we got outside, a tear was running down Tim Silver's cheek.

"You barely knew the guy," Perkins said.

"If you were gay," Silver sniffled and blew into a hanky, "you'd understand."

"It always comes back to that with you, huh?" Perkins said. He was down to 240 pounds from 275 and struggled on the crutches.

"Want a hand?" I said.

"All I want is to throw these goddamned things in the garbage. I was coaching Little League a year ago."

"You still can," I said.

He made no reply.

Across the parking lot, I saw Paul Meyers approach Ron Scott's widow and extend his hand. She lifted her veil and I could see her mascara-stained cheeks. Meyers said something to her. I was no more than thirty yards away, but could tell his remark upset her. Her soft expression vanished. Then she did something that shocked me.

She slapped Paul Meyers's face.

Without another word between them, she got into the back seat of a waiting Lincoln Continental and the car drove away.

Meyers stood looking confused, which I knew wasn't far from his natural state. When he turned around to see if anyone had seen what happened, our eyes met. It was then that his face went from embarrassed to nearly frantic—and left me wondering what I'd just witnessed.

I live and die by my instincts; my profession requires it. So when Hal "Hurricane" McCarthy looked me in the eye a few days later at the FBR Open in Scottsdale and said he'd never felt better, I knew he was lying.

The winds blew constantly that January afternoon and I was working on a semi-respectable, one-over-par seventy-two. Tiger Woods had played that morning, when the breeze was not as severe, and fired a field-scorching sixty-four. Such is life.

"Never felt better, Jack," Hurricane said again and took a pull from a water bottle taken from a cooler on the eighteenth tee.

Throughout the round, Hurricane had spoken little. When we had chatted, he'd asked about my recent ascension to the Policy Board. I'd attended only one meeting to date, but had told him I was looking forward to my term.

"Good to be a decision maker," he had said, back on the fifth green.

"Not so much that," I had replied. "I like having a watch over the game. We all love it, try to do what's best for it," I shrugged. "Now I get to act on that—be a part of the process and help establish policies that protect the Tour, the game."

Hurricane had looked at me for a long time, as if I'd said something offensive. He'd not spoken much after that.

Now he was moving slowly down the eighteenth fairway. He looked like he hadn't slept well. A decade earlier, he'd won the PGA Tour Championship and was once ranked as high as fourth in the world. Those days were gone. His last win had come more than five years ago.

At the season-opening tournament, the Sony Open in Hawaii,

Hurricane three-putted the twelfth green and picked up. I'd heard he snapped his putter across his thigh. Just walked off, withdrawing mid-round. At the time, he was fifteen over par through thirty holes—not within rifle shot of the cut. However, that mattered little to the PGA Tour brass. The Tour doesn't make fines public, but the locker-room buzz had Hurricane's fine at thirty-five grand, a lot of money to a guy who hadn't made a cut in nearly a year. This day, the Tour had little to fear. Hurricane wasn't living up to his nickname. Indeed, he looked ready for a nap.

Hurricane and I watched the third member of our group, Billy Carvelli, hit his tee shot. Carvelli swung like all the young guns seem to now—as if he'd grown up in the arms of swing guru David Renney. A decade earlier, I was consistently in the top three in driving distance. The previous season, I finished fifteenth. The kids hit the ball farther each season. The game was changing and Carvelli symbolized those changes—he stood six-foot-three and, judging from the clubhead speed he generated, six feet of that was arms. He was rail-thin with a classic, fluid motion reminiscent of the late Payne Stewart's. There was a difference between Carvelli and other rookies, though. He was only seventeen years old.

His drive landed near mine, 315 yards away.

"Jesus," Hurricane said, looking down, "chasing you two makes for a long day."

"I've enjoyed it, Mr. McCarthy," Carvelli said.

"'*Mister.*'" Hurricane looked up, grinned, and shook his head. It was the first time I'd seen him smile this day. "Jack, he calls me mister."

"Somebody's got to."

Hurricane chuckled and turned back to Carvelli: "I've got a kid almost your age."

A faint smile formed on Carvelli's lips. He was shy and unassuming and had looked surprised when a fan asked for his autograph, as if he didn't know what the big deal was. *Just golf, right?* But Carvelli was a walking headline. He'd forgone his senior year of high school to turn professional and travel North America with the rest of us.

"You don't smile much," I said to Hurricane, "for a guy putting as well as you are."

Hurricane had battled his putter for more than a year, missing cut after cut. Now he was rolling the ball well. Conversely, his iron game had not been crisp. Five approach shots fell well short, which perhaps accounted for his stoicism. I wasn't about to mention his iron play. Let sleeping dogs lie.

"Like I said," he winked at me as if getting an adrenaline surge, "never felt better. The beer always tastes a little colder after a sixty-six."

The wink was forced. I could tell. Hurricane looked pale and tired and he wasn't close to shooting sixty-six. But after the way he'd finished last season and started this one—eighteen consecutive missed cuts—four over par probably felt like sixty-six. His struggles were tough to watch because no one was working harder. He said he'd hired a nutritionist to go with his caddy/personal trainer. I could see that he'd dropped at least twenty pounds and hit the gym hard.

Hurricane had grown up in Oklahoma and joined the Tour a few years before me, a gap-toothed farm boy standing five-feet-eight with a belly and freckles that now made him look far younger than his forty-four years. He'd always been a hot-tempered redhead and earned his nickname many times over. During my rookie season, I was on the tee with him when, after missing one fairway too many, he'd selected a closer target—his golf bag—and swung his driver through the front of it, just below his name. Then he simply walked off, leaving the club protruding awkwardly from the large leather staff bag, which somehow remained upright like an unknowing but wounded soldier. Over the years, Hurricane made legendary Tommy "Lightning" Struck look like a choirboy, his fines coming so regularly that in the locker room we (only half) kidded him about making "weekly deposits to his PGA Tour account." Yet for all of his antics, Hurricane and I remained friends. He was a family man. As if to illustrate that, wife Sherry stood with his two kids at the side of the fairway and gave him a thumbs-up.

Our threesome had kept our respective tee shots dry, avoiding the lake looming left of the fairway. The tee box on No. 18, a 438-yard par-four, was positioned left of the fairway, meaning you had to hit over the lake. An aggressive tee shot cut significant yardage off the hole. However, you had to judge how much your swing could handle. Instinct rules this game.

"Hear about that Cybett stock?" Hurricane said.

"Who hasn't?" I said.

"Get your money out?"

"Barely."

"Is anyone on Wall Street honest anymore?"

"The more money there is," I said, "the greater the temptation to cheat."

Hurricane cleared his throat and looked away.

"What'd I say?"

"Nothing," he said.

Carvelli followed the conversation, head swiveling back and forth. I tried to include him in our conversations all afternoon, but it wasn't easy. He should have been getting ready for the prom, not worrying about keeping his Tour card. I told him I liked his shirt.

"It's Abercrombie and Fitch."

I nodded.

My caddy and fashion expert, Tim Silver, chuckled. "It's a hip clothing company for twenty-somethings, Jack."

"I've heard of it," I said. "At least it looks better than what Parnevik wears."

"Got that right," Pete Sandstrom, Hurricane's caddy, said. I'd never met him, although I'd heard Hurricane hired a new guy to caddy and be his personal trainer. I didn't know what kind of caddy Sandstrom was, but he looked like everything a personal trainer should be.

"Come on, Hal!" Sherry called from across the fairway. "You can do it!"

Hurricane waved to her, absently.

"How's it working out with Sherry home-schooling the kids?" I said.

"Kids are too old now. Private day schools." He took a labored practice swing. "Sherry takes care of all that. Hell, after eighteen straight missed cuts, the only one not doing his job is me."

"You'll turn it around."

"You got that right," he said, but there was no bite to his words, as if the missed cuts had knocked the wind out of him. He moved to his ball and stood waggling the club behind it. The club waggle ceased and he continued to stand over the ball. Inexplicably, it wasn't a gesture of concentration; rather, he looked tired. The group ahead of us had cleared the green *before* we arrived at Hurricane's ball. Behind us, Sergio Garcia paced on the tee. The day's six-hour round was an anomaly for Hurricane. Usually I had to run to keep up. I glanced at my watch. The Tour's slow-play policy is intricate but basically demands that you stay a shot ahead of the group behind you. Penalties escalate from a stroke to a $20,000 fine.

"Hal," Sandstrom said, "you okay?"

"I'm just taking it slow today. A little tired."

"You should feel great," Sandstrom said.

"Really?" Hurricane said, genuinely confused.

"Hollis said so," Sandstrom said.

"That's right," Hurricane said. "He did say that, didn't he?" He waggled the six-iron one more time before hitting his approach shot.

I figured Hollis to be the nutritionist he'd hired. If that was the case, the meals weren't working. Hurricane swung the six-iron like he was tired—all arms, no legs. The ball drifted right and fell into the front bunker. Still no angry reaction. Maybe he was behaving himself because the kid was with us, but I didn't think so. I'd seen him drive the head of an iron six inches into the sod after a shot like that. This time, Hurricane just handed the club to Sandstrom and we started down the fairway to my ball.

"You can do it!" Sherry called again.

"You can get up and down from there, Dad!" his son yelled.

Hurricane walked on, head down. His family was yelling encouragement and he'd let them down.

The next holler wasn't encouraging. "Billy, stay focused!"

It came from a short squat man with a beard, Carvelli's father. The guy rode him mercilessly all day, hollering directions as if this was a junior event and Carvelli was six. I was watching Carvelli when his father called out, "Don't you *dare* bogey the final hole!" The kid stared at his feet and nodded. His caddy made no attempt to comfort him.

"Sounded like a threat," Silver whispered.

. . .

At my ball, Silver was all business. "One thirty-eight to the center of the green. Hole is cut in the back right. If you can fade the ball, you can stick it in there tight."

"A fade?" I said. "Move the ball *toward* the trap?"

"Thought you had nerves of steel?" Silver said and grinned.

Oddly, Hurricane flinched at the comment.

"Hal, you okay?" Silver said.

"Fine, why?" Hurricane cleared his throat again and looked away.

"No reason," Silver said. The Arizona sun reflected off his shaved head. He had a thick goatee and caramel-colored skin.

"Nerves of steel," I said, and pulled the nine-iron from the bag.

"Par on this hole," Silver said, "would be like picking up two strokes on the field."

"Forget the field," I said. "Woods shot sixty-four."

"Such a realist," Silver said.

I shook my head and went into my pre-shot routine, taking two practice swings, aligning myself, and visualizing the shot. Then I addressed the ball and pulled the trigger. It was one of those rare occasions when the ball did what it was told, moving left to right, hitting the green near the flagstick, and rolling past it. I was putting for birdie from ten feet.

. . .

At the green, Hurricane caught his bunker shot thin and now had forty-five feet to save par. Likewise, Carvelli's approach was long and he had chipped to twelve feet.

"Don't you *dare* bogey this hole, Billy!" his father yelled again. "Keep your focus."

"Yes, Dad," Carvelli said. His voice was a whisper as if the response was automatic.

Silver and I went to the fringe and awaited our turn. Hurricane's putt would run thirty-five feet to my marker, then track to the hole. That meant I could watch the final ten feet of his putt to learn how mine would break.

Hurricane's freckled face was pink now, but his eyes still lacked intensity. The adrenaline kick hadn't lasted long. His teenage son stood behind the green, eagerly anticipating his father's next shot. The boy was about Carvelli's age, maybe younger. Hurricane bent behind his ball like a ninety-year-old. Maybe listening to Carvelli's old man took a lot out of him. Or maybe missing cuts wore him down. Whatever it was, his demeanor belied his new physique. When he finally addressed the ball, he made a long, smooth stroke that resembled Phil Mickelson's silky forward-press. His ball stopped close enough for a tap-in.

"Beauty, Hal!" Sherry yelled. "Way to go!"

"Great putt, Dad!"

Hurricane's head was down, embarrassed, but he tapped in, then tipped his hat and walked to fringe, where Silver and I stood.

"Playing with you is like Father's Day every day," I said.

"I've played so bad for so long, I don't know why they still cheer."

"Yes, you do," I said.

"Yeah, I do. I want to get back to where I was. For them. The past year has been tough. I've put them through a lot."

"Sherry's watched golf for twenty years," I said, "she knows about slumps."

"That's only the tip of the iceberg, Jack."

I didn't know what to say to that. "Well, that was a hell of a two-putt from there. You change your stroke?"

"It's nice now, huh?"

"I'll say. A lot longer and slower. Who's the coach?"

"No coach."

"The Ben Hogan method?"

"What's that?"

"Work your ass off," I said.

Hurricane didn't answer. He looked away, cleared his throat again, and pulled his scorecard from his pocket and tallied his score.

Carvelli was next. He spent nearly two minutes reading the break. This was one of the slowest threesomes I'd ever played in. Hurricane appeared so tired he was moving in slow motion. And Carvelli was terrified of making a mistake, which is no way to play golf. Golf is a game of mistakes. The winner is usually the guy whose mistakes are the least costly.

Carvelli glanced at his father. Old man Carvelli's fat face was red, furious that his son had a twelve-footer to save par. I felt for the kid. He wasn't brash and arrogant—just a high school kid with a gift, a star junior who survived the PGA Tour Qualifying Tournament. Polite and shy. That was refreshing but wouldn't help him endure the pressures and week-to-week grind of the PGA Tour.

Carvelli ran his twelve-footer through the break. Then he hunched, hands on knees. When he straightened, I thought I heard him say, "Five miles."

After he made the come-back attempt, I slapped him on the back. "Nice round. Tough wind."

He didn't answer.

My birdie attempt could get me to even par. I didn't think Woods could shoot sixty-four again in this wind. If I could hang around at even, Woods might come back to the field, and I'd be in contention by Sunday. My practice stroke was short and quick. Awful. I backed off and used a relaxation technique—I squeezed the putter so tightly my knuckles turned white. Then I released and exhaled. I placed the blade of the old Bull's Eye behind the ball and made my stroke.

The ten-footer tracked online all the way, dying into the heart of the cup.

We moved off the green to let the group behind us hit. Hurricane's son, a clean-cut kid in a Green Day concert T-shirt and khaki shorts, approached. "That's my dad," he said, grinning. "Great putting today, Dad."

"I'm doing my best," Hurricane said. When he turned back

11

to me for the customary handshake, his eyes never met mine. He was staring at the ground.

When I reached to shake Carvelli's hand, I noticed his was trembling.

The aluminum crutches were positioned near the bench press and served as a reminder of the recurring nightmare lived by their owner and his family.

At 4:15 P.M., I entered one of Scottsdale's Gold's Gyms, paid my one-day fee, and now stood near the bench press where Perkins lay, his gray T-shirt sweat-soaked. We'd grown up next-door to one another and had been best friends as long as I could remember. Perkins was married, my age (thirty-nine), and father of a six-year-old son, whom he and wife Linda named after me. Young Jackie looked just like him with one difference: Jackie needed neither crutches nor a wheelchair to watch me play golf.

"I see Woods is kicking your ass," Perkins said and sat up, a fine sheen of sweat covering his face.

"And everyone else's."

It was before the after-work crowd. They would arrive in wave and after wave, quickly change to spandex and T-shirts, talk of business or mountain bikes, and barely break a sweat. Near us, a couple gorillas strained and grunted in their tank tops and bike shorts. I wore a T-shirt with "Titleist: No. 1 Ball in Golf" across the front and nylon shorts. Thanks to Perkins and the gorillas, the aroma inside the gym reminded me of the weight room I'd visited twenty years ago when Perkins played briefly for the New England Patriots. He no longer looked like a lineman. Six-foot-six, he was thirty pounds lighter than he'd been a year ago. And every time I looked at him, I felt responsible.

"How's it going today?" I said.

"S.O.S. Been here three hours." He grabbed a towel off the floor.

"You supposed to be pushing that hard?"

"I'm doubling the rehab schedule."

"What's your trainer think of that?"

"Don Perry? He works for the Tour. We meet at five forty-five every morning. After that, he's tied up with players all day."

"So Don doesn't know you're going to a gym in the afternoons?"

He didn't answer. Instead, he leaned back on the bench and did another set. He had 225 pounds on the bench and did twelve reps before straining—impressive as hell. I managed no more than eight reps with that weight. Still, it was a far cry from where he'd been prior to the point-blank gunshot wound.

I moved behind the bench to offer a spot.

"Get away," he said. *"I can do this!"* He forced the fifteenth rep up and let the bar clang onto the supports.

"You might be pushing yourself too hard," I said.

He sat up and looked at me. "I got a six-year-old asking when dad can play tag again, Jack."

My hands felt clammy and something tightened in my chest. I went to the bench next to him and did a warm-up set with 135 pounds. Perkins took his water bottle off the floor, drank, then quickly leaned back and did another set with 225. When I finished my fifteenth repetition, he was still going, fighting fiercely with the weight. He was struggling and I moved to spot him again.

"I don't need help!" he said, face red, eyes blinking away beads of sweat. "I'm going to do this, myself. I'll work my ass off to get better."

Straining with that much weight wasn't safe, but I knew Perkins. I nodded and went back to my bench. As I added plates to the bar, I saw Hurricane McCarthy and his trainer, Pete Sandstrom. Hurricane no longer looked tired and the sight of him in gym clothes—unexpected to anyone who'd known him the past decade—made his weight loss more apparent. I hadn't seen him in anything but baggy golf shirts, the sleeves of which hung to his mid-forearms, and khaki pants. Sandstrom had him doing standing curls with forty-pound dumbbells. He might have dropped thirty pounds, but what was there now was muscle. After my next set, I went over.

"Jesus," I said, "you look ready to fight Ali."

Hurricane looked startled and a little embarrassed. "Oh, well . . ."

"No, really," I said, "I'm impressed. I knew you were working your ass off, but you look great. You'll be in the winner's circle in no time."

"That's what it's all about," Sandstrom said.

"Thanks, Jack," Hurricane said. "Pete's really the one responsible. Pete, you remember Jack Austin from the round today."

"Of course," Sandstrom said. "We're kind of busy here, Jack." His expression fell somewhere between annoyed and distracted. Regardless, it was clear he didn't want me around.

"Oh . . . Sorry . . . Have a good workout." As I turned to go, I caught a fragment of their conversation. " . . . Hollis says you shouldn't be tired," Sandstrom said.

I went back to my bench press and did a set. When I finished, Perkins looked over.

"Who's that?" he said.

"Hal McCarthy."

He squinted. "You're shitting me. He looks like a gymnast now."

"Hired a trainer."

"I guess he did," he said. "How come?"

"He's in his mid-forties," I said, "and hasn't made a cut since last year."

"So practice more," Perkins said.

"We've all practiced for thirty years," I said. "These college kids hit the ball a mile now. And they've got perfect swings, perfect physiques, and the attitude that they can win today. Not next year. Not after gaining experience. Right now."

"Good for them," Perkins said. "What's the problem?"

"There're only a hundred and twenty-five exempt spots. To a guy in the late stage of his career, the Champions Tour is seven, ten years away." I stood to add weight to the bar and shrugged. "You lose your card, you're out—nowhere to play for those seven or ten years."

"Stiff competition," Perkins said.

"And only a win gives you job security," I said. "Hell, when I started, it took me a season to learn the courses and improve enough to really compete. Not these kids. Everyone in my age bracket is working harder just to keep up."

Perkins nodded. "Hard work always pays off." He leaned over, took his water bottle off the floor again, and drank. He started to say something else but stopped short.

"What?" I said.

"You don't know much about the business side of what I do. But private investigations is pretty cut-throat. I'm the Tour's only private security consultant and the money bought our new house in New Hampshire." He paused, his eyes falling to the crutches as if looking at an enemy. He drank more water. His hair had been more white than blond since we were toddlers. It looked almost yellow now, spiked and soaked with perspiration. Our silences had always been comfortable. This one told me something was wrong.

"Got a favor to ask," he said, unable to look me in the eye.

Perkins leaned and grabbed his crutches off the floor, held them upright, and struggled to his feet. I followed him to the leg-extension machine. As he crossed the room, he did so awkwardly, swinging his left leg forward like a sandbag.

At the leg extension machine, he clenched his teeth and began. "Ever think you'd see me struggle with thirty pounds?"

"Never thought you'd get shot and have a stroke."

He'd been my best friend since elementary school. Three years ago, he'd saved my life and I'd named my only child, my daughter, Darcy, after him. That time, he wore a Kevlar vest. Three months ago, a second shot had been fired. This time, there'd been no vest. This time, only I walked away.

"Don't look at me like that, Jack. I hate that look and I've said it before. This is no one's fault. You hear me? The asshole doctor says the prognosis isn't good. I tried to play catch with Jackie and fell over, so the prognosis isn't acceptable."

"You're still a good father," I said.

"Sure. Good at watching movies with my kids. Jackie asked if I'm coaching Little League again this year."

I didn't say anything.

"After I throw this wheelchair off a goddamned bridge," he continued, "I'll walk into the doctor's office—without crutches—and shake his hand." He turned and looked away. His voice was quieter when he said, "Eventually that *will* happen. Everything takes time and a lot of work."

He hadn't told me much about his prognoses or his meetings with doctors, only about his rehab and the hard work involved. But the near-whisper with which he spoke of the future bothered me. Why turn away from me? And why whisper?

I glanced across the room at Hurricane. He was doing curls at the preacher bench now, beads of sweat running down his cheeks. His arms glistened under the lights, his biceps muscles rolling with each curl.

Perkins did a second set with his right leg. "Chicago Homicide told Peter Barrett that a couple things don't jive about the Ron Scott mugging."

Barrett was the PGA Tour commissioner.

"Billy Peters is in Chicago now," he said through clenched teeth, working his left leg now. "He started in Boston . . . we worked together . . . I called him, and he says he'll give me some information . . . and an inch of space." He let the weight down slowly and leaned back, catching his breath. "I think they're swamped and can use the help."

"You don't usually like working with cops."

"I'm trying to protect my job, Jack. A lot of agencies would love my PGA Tour account and a lot are bigger. A couple firms offered to look into the Ron Scott murder."

He was telling me his job was in jeopardy.

"Red, I mean Billy Peters, says he doesn't think this was a mugging, although the case might get closed as one. Says it looks like a sloppy contract job. When I told Barrett that, he said he'd like to put another private guy on it, who would, of course, consult with me."

"And try to take your job."

16

"That's how it works. But it's more than that. I just feel like . . . like I'm not earning my check. And what kind of man doesn't work for his money?"

"Jesus Christ, Darcy, you got shot."

He took a deep breath. "Can you help me?"

Perkins had been kidnapped, taken to the woods of northern Maine, and eventually shot—all in an effort to help me. "I'll do anything you need," I said.

"Legwork," he said, and looked at the floor. "No pun intended. But that's what I need. I know you're busy, Jack."

"You saved my life, twice," I said. "I'm in."

He nodded and went back to his leg curls. I got on the machine next to him. This time, our silence was comfortable. I began my final set, wondering why a contract might have been put on a professional golfer.

At 4:45 P.M., I was back in the locker room at the Tournament Players Club at Scottsdale. Locker rooms on the PGA Tour serve as sanctuaries open only to players, their sons, and officials. Yet while caddies are banned, somehow instructors fall under the "officials" label. In fact, a player whose caddy enters is fined $100, then $250, and $500, subsequently. I never agreed with this policy, and one season I was fined eight times. The locker room is where the Tour gathers to read the paper, play cards during rain delays, talk about fishing or kids or stocks or technology-hyped drivers. It is where we come together, friends and rivals, as what Tour brass calls "a family." It is also where a breakfast buffet is set up, free of charge. So if some $500-an-hour self-proclaimed swing guru is allowed, Tim Silver sure as hell

should be. Tour politics aside, this day the locker room felt more like a morgue than a family room. People were strewn throughout in various stages of dress. No one spoke, and no one looked relaxed.

After Gold's Gym, I'd driven back to the course to shower and now stood before my locker in civilian attire—blue jeans, Adidas Falcon running shoes, and an Izod shirt. Across the room, Fred Couples watched *SportsCenter*. Justin Leonard sat at a card table reading the paper. Beside me, Jesper Parnevik seemed unfazed by whatever was in the air. He pulled two outfits from his locker and held them for me to see: a pink shirt with rose-colored pants, and lime-green slacks with a white short-sleeved shirt with a pointed collar.

"Got to be honest," I said, and shook my head. His attire made Carvelli's look conservative. Parnevik grinned sadly and muttered something in Swedish. Probably felt sorry for a boring khaki-pants-and-golf-shirt guy like me.

Padre Tarbuck approached. He'd won his first event in three years just days before Ron Scott's funeral. Judging from his expression, the party was over.

"Seen Richie Barter?" he said.

"Not since Ron Scott's funeral. What are you pissed about?"

"What do you think?" he said, loudly. "I walk in here this morning and EVERYONE"—his eyes scanned the room; no one looked back—"looks at me like I cheated. *You* flew to El Paso to help me, Jack. *You* know how hard I worked to get my putting stroke back. To hell with Richie Barter. You're on the Policy Board now. You better read Mitch Singleton's column. If you were me, you'd be pissed, too."

I shook my head, confused. Around the room, eyes glanced up covertly.

Padre turned away and said to the room, "Anyone thinks I cheated last week, come see me, man-to-man. And anyone sees Richie, tell him I'm looking for him."

Padre had edged Richie Barter by a stroke, ending his longstanding putting woes and winning the Bob Hope Chrysler Classic. He'd needed only twenty-six putts over the final eighteen holes. He was a former priest and I'd rarely seen him angry.

I walked to the card table and took the discarded sports section, flipping quickly to Mitch Singleton's *USA Today* column:

PGA Tour star claims foes use performance-enhancing substances

Scottsdale, AZ.—Golf's squeaky-clean image took a hit Wednesday when star Richie Barter revealed alleged skeletons in a closet the PGA Tour surely never wanted fans to see.

"I'm sick and tired of losing to guys who are using," Barter said during an impromptu and explicative-laden press conference in the parking lot at Scottsdale's Tournament Players Club, where Barter is entered in this week's FBR Open.

"It's gotten ridiculous," Barter said. "Every guy in that locker room knows who can putt and who can't. And I've had it with the Tour turning a blind eye."

Barter last won a tournament 18 months ago. Sunday, he lost by a stroke after bogeying No. 16 at the Bob Hope Chrysler Classic.

Barter refused to name names but did say, "I know players who've won big-time events recently by using beta-blockers."

Beta-blockers work by "blocking" the body's reaction to hormones produced by the body in reaction to high stress.

"Clearly any substance that might assist in calming one's nerves would in all likelihood benefit a golfer," says cardiologist Thomas Brody, M.D., of the Mayo Clinic. "Professional golfers stand over three-foot putts worth hundreds of thousands of dollars. Anything that might steady your hands would be an advantage."

Barter wants the playing field leveled.

"I'm not saying I would have won every tournament I entered the past two years," Barter said. "But technological advances are one thing. Drugs are different."

With golf clearly on the Olympic horizon, it would seem logical to begin testing for beta-blockers, which the International Olympic Committee classifies as "restricted." Of the 28 Olympic sports, currently only archery, a sport requiring precise fine-motor skills—much like putting—tests for beta-blockers.

Beta-blockers are detectable by urinalysis, according to Brody.

I heard the locker room door open and the silence was quickly disturbed.

"Really cute, Richie," Padre yelled. "I struggle for two years to get over the yips and beat you fair and square, then you pull this? You sonofabitch."

I looked up to see chairs overturned and heard a crash. Padre had gone after him. No first punch; a middle-school fight—tackle and scrum. Padre took Richie down and they rolled around on the floor. I ran over and pulled Padre off. The fact that I was the only one attempting to break it up spoke volumes.

Richie Barter had crossed the line.

.   .   .

Twenty minutes later, on my way to the parking lot, I paused near the practice green. The putting surface was enclosed by a short green wall like a hockey rink. A few players were practicing. One I vaguely recognized and soon realized why—I'd seen him near the eighteenth green earlier. I went to where Hurricane McCarthy leaned on the wall watching his son putt. The boy wore khaki pants and a golf shirt now.

"Looks just like you," I said. The sun was low and only a handful of spectators were around. No one recognized me.

"That's Terry," Hurricane said. "He's fifteen. Wants to be a pro golfer like his old man."

"He's got a good stroke."

"We all did at fifteen."

"True. You don't think about it when you're fifteen. Just walk up to the ball, ram it toward the cup."

20

Hurricane turned to look at me. "Remember when it was like that for us?"

"Sure. High school was probably the last time. I don't think I left a putt short until I was eighteen."

"Terry finished eighth in a junior tournament a couple weeks ago, shoots low-eighties. He stayed here to watch the guys hit range balls while I was at the gym."

"A real golf junkie," I said.

"Yeah. He asked me to help him with his game. Really wants to work hard to improve." Hurricane paused as if suddenly distracted, then said in a near-whisper, "Sometimes it's not that easy."

"What do you mean?"

He shook his head and looked at Terry again. "Son, slow your stroke down a little. The take-away is too quick."

"Thanks, Dad."

Hurricane smiled, proudly. This wasn't like watching the Carvelli family.

"I wish he'd been older when I won the Players Championship. What he's seen of my game lately hasn't been much."

"You'll turn it around," I said. "You're putting better than ever."

"I should be."

"Working hard?"

He didn't reply and we watched Terry make a ten-footer.

"Hey," Hurricane said, "nice stroke, son. A beauty." Then he turned to me again. "I'm reading a book about how to live your life. The guy who wrote it says that a man *is* what he does. You believe that?"

"What do you mean? You are your job?"

"No. Your actions."

"I don't really know," I said, "but it sounds about right."

"And you have a daughter, too."

"What's that got to do with it?"

"A man should never let his kids down," he said, "but it's a catch twenty-two."

"I don't understand."

"Me either," he said.

I was confused.

"Ten years ago," he said, "we weren't playing for the kind of money we are now. If I could win one more time, I could put both kids through college and set them up. You tell someone you play the Tour and they think you're rich. It costs about a hundred grand to play each year. You throw in a couple bad investments and . . . "

"You get burned by the market?" I said. He had asked about the Cybett stock.

"The market?" he said, and chuckled. "I wish. A couple friends."

It wasn't my business, so I let it go. We stood and watched Terry practice. I left a few minutes later.

"The guy's an ass," Padre said, and drank a little more Sam Adams Light. Two beers hadn't calmed him. "I mean . . . to say something like that and point the finger at me—"

"Richie Barter didn't mention you by name," I said.

"He did all but that," Padre said. "After I've struggled for two damned years? What an ass." He looked at my three-year-old, Darcy, seated between us. "Excuse me."

"Potty word," Darcy said, and held out a hand.

"What's this?" Padre said.

"Every time you say a bad word," I said, "you owe her a quarter."

He shrugged, stood, and reached in his pocket. We were in the hotel restaurant. My wife, Lisa Trembly-Austin, was to join us following her duties as CBS Sports' head golf commentator—taping the next day's interviews, reviewing the day's stats, and preparing notes. The restaurant smelled of fajitas and the spices of Southwest cuisine. Around us, people drank "Mega-margaritas" and Tecate. A cacophony of clacking silverware, random conversation, and the drone of the bar's big-screen television persisted. Darcy had spent the day at the PGA Tour's traveling daycare center, playing with other small fries. Now she sat in a booster seat next to me, munching crackers.

"She's attacking those," Padre said.

"Good genes," I said.

A couple rookies were at the bar drinking shots of tequila. Paul Meyers was there, too, but he sat alone, reading the paper, drinking what looked like grapefruit juice. Seeing him reminded me of the scene in the parking lot following the funeral. What had he said to a recently widowed woman to get his face slapped?

I motioned to the rookies. "Remember those days?" I said to Padre.

"Long ago," Padre said.

"Almost fifteen years. We started together, buddy. Everyone knows you didn't cheat last week."

"No. Everyone who *knows me* knows that. There's a difference. Richie said he was tired of 'losing to guys who are using.' I beat him only days before he makes that comment. Come on, Jack. That points the finger directly at me. I'm not making something of nothing here. My agent called, more upset than me."

"Excuse me," a woman said, and stopped our table. She was in her mid-twenties with red hair, sky-blue eyes, and wore a mini-skirt and a blouse with four buttons undone. "Are you Brian Tarbuck?"

"That's right." He smiled, warmly.

"Sorry to bother you, but would you sign this?" She held out a pad and pen.

Padre signed and smiled at her. He'd tucked in his shirt after the fight and looked no worse for the wear.

"I saw you on ESPN's 'Fifty Best-Looking Athletes,'" she said to him.

"Good God," I said under my breath and drank some beer.

Padre grinned at me.

"Are you a golfer, too?" Red Hair asked me. "Are you on the senior tour?"

Padre laughed.

"I'm just distinguished looking," I said.

She shrugged, not getting it, and walked off, glancing at Padre over her shoulder.

"Feel better now?" I said.

"A little."

I was glad when Lisa approached and kissed me on the mouth. She appreciated my distinguished good looks. Darcy got a peck on the cheek; Padre got a smile. After a timely waitress took her drink order, Lisa looked across the table at Padre. He waited. Tour players knew all too well of Reporter Lisa, all five-feet-five, 120 pounds of her—uncompromising and more driven than a paratrooper.

"Thanks for joining us," Padre said, and grinned.

Lisa laughed. "Excuse me, but I invited you. And you know I wouldn't go on the air tomorrow without asking."

"I know," he said. "I already told Mitch Singleton I got over the yips by working my ass off, that Jack, here, flew to El Paso to help me. And that I switched to a belly putter. That's all there is to it."

Lisa gave Darcy a cracker, then took a long, thin notepad out of her handbag and wrote something.

"Richie said players have used beta-blockers," Lisa said, "which in golf, experts agree, *could* classify as a performance-enhancing drug. Is he correct? Are there players using perform-ance-enhancing substances?" Her eyes went from Padre to me.

I reached for my beer. "You sound like you're reading from tomorrow's script," I said, and smiled.

The smile didn't work. She waited stoically. Being married to golf's toughest journalist has its drawbacks.

"Is there any of that going on?" she said.

"I don't know," Padre said.

"Meaning you have no knowledge of it?"

"That's right," Padre said.

"Jack?" Lisa said.

"Padre—"

This time the interruption came from Paul Meyers.

"For what it's worth," he said, "I think the article is bullshit. No one on the Tour cheats."

"Thanks," Padre said.

I watched Meyers walk away. When I turned back, Lisa was staring steadily at me. I was glad the waitress reappeared with her drink. "We're ready to order," I said, and the young waitress smiled.

Across the table, Lisa's drink sat untouched. She was looking at me.

.   .   .

As a rookie, I'd struggled to win enough money to cover gas, let alone a hotel room. Some weeks, I couldn't afford a caddy and Perkins had carried for me. One PGA Tour win and thirteen seasons later, I'd earned enough to afford an oceanfront home in my beloved Maine. It wasn't Tiger Woods-type money, but I saved what I could and, unlike Hurricane, hadn't been screwed out of any.

This week, we were staying in a suite. After our dinner with Padre, Lisa and I were in the main room, drinking Starbucks coffee. She could drink the stuff just before bedtime, but the stuff killed me. One cup had me wired, so I sipped decaf loaded with creamer. It was 8:20 and we were side by side on the sofa. Darcy was asleep in the other room. The television was on The Golf Channel and Jennifer Mills was rehashing Richie Barter's remarks.

"Well?" Lisa said, turning to me.

"What do you know about this Carvelli kid and his old man?" I said, knowing that wasn't what she wanted to talk about.

"Billy Carvelli is a seventeen-year-old former Renney Academy star. He made the finals of the U.S. Amateur Championship last year. A sweet boy."

"Sweet boys don't make it on Tour. What's the deal with the old man?"

"He's the boy's father and his agent."

"I think it's the other way around," I said.

"What's that mean?"

"I just don't like him."

"How nice, Jack. Very reasonable."

Jennifer Mills was reading from Mitch Singleton's article. Lisa looked from the television to me. She'd waited two hours to continue our dinner conversation.

I was torn. I was on the PGA Tour Policy Board now, and thus deeply entrenched in the causes impacting the game and my colleagues. But this wasn't about policy. She was asking me to comment on players. However, I'd accepted my post on the Board and the integrity of the game must be protected at all cost.

"I think Richie Barter's a jerk," I said. "You know I always have."

"I know that. But is what he said accurate?"

"Padre doesn't cheat."

"That isn't what I asked," she said.

I sighed. I was holding my coffee with both hands. It smelled strong (decaf be damned), and the paper cup was hot. The windows were dark and, in the reflection, my face stared back at me, intermingled with the Scottsdale skyline.

"I have no personal knowledge of a PGA Tour player using a substance to cheat," I said. "If I did, I'd start by taking it up with them, personally, then taking it to the Policy Board."

"The media would be last?" she said.

I thought about Padre going after Richie in the locker room. Richie had crossed the line. I nodded.

Lisa drank her coffee. I knew she was morphing into Reporter Lisa, so I turned back to Jennifer Mills, who was asking Stewart Cink what he thought of Richie Barter's remarks. Cink played the question the way he played golf—smartly—talking for three minutes and not saying a thing.

"I know this is a difficult position for you," Lisa said, "and I apologize for putting you in it. But you know I have a job to do." She shifted on the sofa, finished her coffee, and set the empty paper cup on the glass coffee table. When she turned back to me, there was compassion in her eyes and something else I greatly respected. I'd seen it in Mitch Singleton's veteran gaze as well—a determination, not to gain material to humiliate, but simply to find the truth.

There was difference. Often journalists don't know it.

The Golf Channel was always player-friendly, which meant Cink got off easy. I knew I wouldn't be so lucky. I blew out a long breath. "A year ago, I heard a rumor about what Richie said. I didn't take it seriously and wouldn't mention it now, if Richie hadn't started this—because I don't think there's anything to it. And dredging it up can only hurt the game. I'm on the Policy Board, but first and foremost, I'm a competitor. I want a level playing field."

She nodded. We'd been together long enough for her to know that was as far as I'd go.

"I'm tired," I said, and stood up.

"I'll ask around," she said. "On a different note, Perkins left a message saying he'd cover your airfare to Chicago. What's that mean?"

"I said I'd go out there for him."

"And do what?"

I told her.

"You're a golfer, Jack."

"Perkins saved my life," I said, "and got shot doing it. If he asks for help, he gets it."

"And, after all, you've done similar stuff for him before," she said.

I thought about Ron Scott and the possibility of a sloppy contract hit. Just before falling asleep, I remembered Ron Scott's wife slapping Paul Meyers across the face.

. . .

Poet Philip Levine has long been my favorite writer. Having spent the bulk of my adult life traveling city to city alone, reading was an ally. And poetry can be digested in small bites, a good thing for a dyslexic. I'm a slow reader and admittedly I read sixty-foot putts better than I follow all of Levine's nuances. This night, as Lisa slept soundly beside me, I woke and read Levine's collection *New Selected Poems* under the light of a bedside lamp.

Levine wrote of the working class and knew his subject well. In "Starlight," the speaker is a boy recalling his father. The final section reads:

. . . And in that new voice he says nothing,
holding my head tight against his head,
his eyes closed up against the starlight,
as though those tiny blinking eyes
of light might find a tall, gaunt child
holding his child against the promises
of autumn, until the boy slept
never to waken in that world again.

The poem is about a realization, a motif that hit home. Recent days offered one colleague's funeral, while a close friend had been accused of cheating. Worse, Perkins, the most solitary and dignified man I knew, needed help. How long had he agonized over the request? What had it cost him internally to ask? He'd entered private investigations to do things on his own terms, walking away from the Boston PD Homicide after throwing the legal system aside and making sure justice was served on behalf of a young rape victim. The perpetrator spent a week in the hospital. Perkins had always been there for me.

The time had come to repay him, even if it meant cutting into my thirty-event tournament schedule.

Friday at 9:45 A.M., Hurricane McCarthy was tearing up the back nine, needing only seven putts through our first five holes. He was -4 on the day, having clawed back to even par. Billy Carvelli, with father in tow, was two over. I was striking the ball well but not making putts and remained even.

On Tour, Thursday-Friday groupings stay the same. Each group gets one early tee time and one late start, one first-tee start and one back-nine start. Weekend tee times are assigned according to score, in descending order, the leaders playing last. So if you need a wake-up call Sunday morning, you haven't played well. If you clean out your locker Friday evening, you've played worse and, since airfare and hotel are out-of-pocket expenses on the PGA Tour, if you leave Friday you don't break even.

The wind was subdued. Tiger Woods was playing in the afternoon and the benign conditions made me fearful that he'd repeat his sixty-four. Vijay Singh had been No. 1 on the Official World Golf Rankings, Phil Mickelson had won The Masters, and Ernie Els was as gifted as anyone. But Tiger's intimidating aura remained ever present and we all knew no one was better at finishing off the opposition. Moreover, Tiger had a three-shot lead and, with the wind negated, threatened to pull away.

"Got the flat stick going again today," I said to Hurricane.

Despite his putting, he looked worse than he had the day before. His face was pale and taut. Huge sacks hung below his eyes. I'd seen him in the gym and knew he'd dropped a lot of weight and replaced it with muscle, but he acted as if Sandstrom worked him ten hours a day and cut his rations. We were on the tee box at the 431-yard par-four sixth. The degree of difficulty posed by No. 6 was gauged by the wind—if it's with you, it's a birdie hole. This day, there was a slight breeze behind us.

"Come on, Dad!" Terry called from the side of the tee area. His sister was beside him. The girl resembled Hurricane. She was probably eight or nine. "Come on, Daddy, you're the best!" she said.

"Thanks, sweetie," Hurricane said, then to me: "Putting's the name of the game."

He needed to believe that because his tee shot found a fairway bunker. Casually, he handed his driver to Sandstrom—no outburst, no tantrum. Maybe I'd start calling him Breeze.

Carvelli made a long, smooth swing and crushed a drive into the heart of the fairway. "That's the swing, Billy. There it is. Now FOCUS! And don't lose your concentration again!" the senior Carvelli said from the other side of tee box.

Silver looked at Carvelli's old man and shook his head. "Doesn't the idiot realize he's paralyzing his son? Poor kid was shaking over the last putt."

I didn't say anything. I had my own game to worry about, and Perkins's request gave me additional incentive. I wouldn't arrive at next week's event early to practice. I'd probably hop a last-minute flight and sprint to the first tee.

"Bunkers on both side of the fairway," Silver said. "Want driver or three-wood?"

The leader board was bunched—thirty players at even or better—so a couple bogeys could send me packing. "Let's take the traps out of the equation," I said.

Silver nodded and handed me the TaylorMade r7 driver. The sun was bright in the distance. I made my customary two practice swings and addressed the ball, clearing my mind, focusing on my present task. At times, golf offers sensations as pure as any: I brought the clubhead back, pausing just short of parallel, my shoulder turn wide, my back to the target; then I uncoiled, dropping the club inside, clearing my hips, and squaring the clubface at impact. My head was still down when the sensation of crisp contact traveled through my fingertips, up my arms. In my periphery, the tee flew up, dancing end over end. I held the finishing pose. The ball dropped from the crystalline sky to the heart of the fairway, 300 yards away.

"You make it look easy," Hurricane said. "I need more power. The way they're stretching the courses out shot-making is a dying art."

"Nice shot, Mr. Austin," Carvelli said.

"FOCUS, Billy!"

I looked at Carvelli's father and didn't say a word, but I held his gaze a long time as we started down the fairway. "Thanks, Billy," I said. "Putting has always held me back. A lot of weeks turn into putting contests."

Carvelli's father called him over to the ropes. I couldn't tell what was said—the old man's face was placid and Billy offered no reaction. If Carvelli senior was giving instructions mid-round (a two-stroke penalty) it wasn't obvious.

"The past couple years," Hurricane said, "this game sure has felt like a putting contest to me. And the contest hasn't gone well."

"Looks like you've cured that," I said. "I saw the stats this morning. You were second in total putts yesterday."

"Now all I need is a power game," he said, "but second in total putts isn't bad for an old dog."

"Isn't bad for anyone."

Hurricane shrugged. "You take what you can get when you're my age. The nerves just aren't what they used to be." He was my contemporary but sounded much older. "You still love it, Jack, don't you?"

"I love to play," I said, "but that's not what keeps me going. It's competing at this level. I could play at home, but if I lost my card, I don't know if I'd go down to the Nationwide Tour. Trying to beat these guys is what I play for."

"I knew that feeling," Hurricane said. "I had it for a long time."

"If it's gone, what keeps you motivated?"

We were walking in stride.

He drank from his water bottle and looked at me. "You really have to ask?"

"Yeah."

"Money," he said.

. . .

The wheels fall off sometimes.

Hurricane went out in thirty-three, but by the time we reached our final hole, No. 9, he was two-over par. The cut was projected at even. Similarly, Carvelli had grown more nervous as the day progressed, making four consecutive bogeys on the back. He stood at four over. At seventeen years old, he wasn't having fun. He could've been taking all-expenses-paid recruiting trips and planning his future as a can't-miss collegiate star. He should've been nervous about asking a girl to the prom. Not about golf. Not with his talent.

I hit a bomb off the tee, but Carvelli was still ten yards ahead. He and I stood twenty paces away from Hurricane and watched him play his approach shot from 165 yards.

When Hurricane's six-iron fell short of the green, landing in a pot bunker, he turned to Sandstrom and said, "This isn't supposed to be happening."

"It takes a while to see results," Sandstrom said. "Keep your voice down."

"It's been months. I feel like shit. I'm supposed to feel great."

Sandstrom took the iron and slid it into the bag.

"I just lost it today," Hurricane said. "I'm tired."

Carvelli looked at me. I shrugged. His father motioned and he walked over. Tim Silver was looking at the yardage book, preparing for my approach shot. As I started toward my ball, Hurricane was still muttering.

"I finally putt well," he said, "now I lose the rest of my game."

"You need to get stronger," Sandstrom said.

"I'm stronger than ever."

"We'll work on it," Sandstrom said, firmly, his tone no longer typical of a caddy; he sounded like a drill sergeant.

Hurricane was tired and frustrated about his lack of energy. Maybe he was dehydrated, too. It seemed he couldn't get enough water and he was sweating a lot, despite the mild temperature.

"You've got the ship pointed in the right direction," I said to him. "Your emotions are in check."

"You're not swinging through the ball," Sandstrom said. "We'll work on your legs."

Hurricane didn't reply but looked at him the way a high school athlete stood before an intense coach, the older man with his hands on the boy's shoulders, offering instruction, the player nodding, listening intently before entering the game. At that moment, I knew Hurricane was eager to believe Sandstrom. I hoped the caddy/trainer knew what he was doing.

At my ball, I turned my focus to my situation. I was one under par, safely inside the cut. But my approach, from 149 yards, wouldn't be easy. The pot bunker that ate Hurricane's shot loomed in front of the green. Another sand trap protected the right side and any shot that went long and left found a collection area. Once on the green, you dealt with a ridge that added severe break to almost every putt. I drew the nine-iron from my bag.

"That enough club?" Silver said. "The breeze is at us and stronger than it feels."

"A two-club wind?" I said.

"At least one club."

I handed the nine back and took the eight-iron. The shot hit the green like a dart, sticking six feet from the hole. "Good clubbing," I said.

"I am fabulous," Silver said, "aren't I?"

"Good God."

.   .   .

At the green, I was last to putt. Carvelli hadn't spoken in twenty minutes, except for the talk with his old man, and even then only listened and nodded. The more I saw what the kid went through, the worse I felt for him. In the distance, I heard the unmistakable triumphant roar at the par-three sixteenth. The hole was legendary for its raucous crowd, the atmosphere around it always electric. Carvelli was over his fifteen-footer for par when the sound erupted. He backed off and his old man looked ready to charge the sixteenth.

"Somebody made a birdie," Sandstrom said.

"Or bogey," Hurricane said. "You don't know everything."

"Jesus, Hal," Sandstrom said, "stop being negative."

"Why?" Hurricane said. "Everything in life goes to shit."

As if sensing his frustration, his daughter yelled, "You're doing great, Daddy!"

Carvelli hit his putt, the ball breaking hard, running a foot past the hole. He was about to tap in to go five over, when I heard Sandstrom's voice, "Hal, are you okay?"

I looked over. Hurricane was leaning forward, hands on his knees, staring at the ground. He spit. I thought he was going to vomit and started toward him but stopped when he straightened. Hurricane took a step, stumbled awkwardly, and finally regained his balance. When he looked around, he seemed okay.

Carvelli had yet to tap in. "You okay, Mister McCarthy?"

Hurricane waved him off.

"FOCUS, Billy!" his father's voice exploded from the gallery.

Carvelli tapped in. His father shook his head and stalked off, muttering angrily.

Hurricane went to his ball and bent to replace it but didn't. He straightened with a manner that was both sudden and clumsy, like a gasping man who bursts from beneath water. I looked at Silver, my brows raised.

"He's out of shape," Silver said. "Maybe he lost too much weight, but he better get it together because there are hundreds of college kids waiting to take his place."

Hurricane had been doing curls with forty pounds the previous day. There had to be more to it.

"He ought to get a physical," I said. "Something's wrong."

Hurricane had always been a fighter. Now, excluding his recent frustration, he was calm. He bent, replaced his ball, and pocketed the coin. He had twenty feet but never bothered to read the break—just slapped the ball toward the hole and walked as soon as he hit it.

Everyone knew Hurricane was going to miss the cut. That wasn't what bothered me. His rushing the day's final putt did. He'd risen through the ranks with me, when money hadn't been a reason to play, when you had to string season after successful season together (a genuine career) to retire wealthy. We hadn't thought of money then. Some of us weren't thinking about it now.

As expected, his putt missed. He rushed the two-and-a-half-footer like it was a tap-in, never aligning it or asking me if he could finish. Somehow, the second putt fell.

"For Christ's sake," Silver said, "people are paying fifty bucks to walk with him and watch this."

I didn't say anything. I had a putt to make and needed a birdie, and a low score the following day, to have any hope of contending Sunday. My six-footer wasn't going to be easy. The ridge would result in a hard break, right to left, and a quick pace at the hole. I gently placed the toe of the Bull's Eye putter behind the ball, took the putter back slowly, and made my stroke, keeping my head down, listening for the crowd's reaction.

The sound I hoped for, one similar to the eruption at No. 16, never came. Only the sympathetic "Ahhhhh" followed by charity applause. The ball caught the lip and spun out. I tapped in for par.

As was customary, we met in the center of the green to shake hands. Carvelli looked like a kicked dog.

"Keep your chin up, kid," I said. "You've got talent."

He made no reply.

Hurricane took a step closer to shake hands. But when he neared, his eyes rolled upward, and his body fell slack.

I caught him and officials quickly crowded the green.

$\mathcal{I}$ didn't see Hurricane again that week. He was taken to a local hospital and, having missed the cut, had gone home afterward. Yet thanks to Richie Barter's firestorm, on Saturday morning the locker-room rumor mill listed numerous reasons for Hurricane's collapse, fatigue being the kindest. A nervous breakdown and an undisclosed drug problem (which, subsequently, had him checked into the Betty Ford Clinic) were others.

Breakfasted, a light-weight, high-rep chest workout completed, I was going about my business on the practice range when Mitch Singleton approached. Singleton dressed like an old boxing reporter—a cigar dangled from his mouth, a fedora sat tilted on his head, a sports jacket over a white shirt, his tie always at half-mast. If I hadn't seen him do the two-finger shuffle on a laptop, I'd have pegged him for an old black manual typewriter.

"How's it going, Pardner?" he said.

"Hello," I said and waved.

I hit a shot and held the follow-through, studying the trajectory of the ball flying into the wind. I wore a long-sleeved windbreaker that rustled when I swung. Players were huddled on the range in twos and threes. John Daly was at one end waving his hands as he told Joey Sindelar something that had both men laughing. Others warmed up silently, focused on the round.

"The wind is going to change things today," Singleton said. "Blowing the opposite way today."

"What do you need, Mitch?"

He grinned. "Can't I just drop by to say hi?"

"Sure," I said. "Hi." We were both silent; then I said, "You know I don't chat when I'm warming up."

"You don't? Must have slipped my mind. I'm getting old, you know."

"Sure."

"Heard from Hal McCarthy?"

"Not since yesterday," I said.

I handed Silver the five-iron and he wiped it off. Then I drew the six, positioned a ball about an inch ahead of my back heel, and hit a little punch shot, the follow-through abbreviated to keep the ball low. Most Tour events offer at least three models of range balls—Titleist, Nike, and Callaway—and my Titleist Pro V1 flew low, bounced twice, and sat ten yards right of the 150-yard marker.

"He passed out cold?" Singleton had his thin reporter's notepad open now.

"I don't know about 'cold.' His eyes were open. I caught him, though. He's been through a lot."

"He was part of that Nichols Golf Group that went under a couple years ago," Mitch said. "Did you know that?"

I knew of the start-up club-manufacturing venture. A group of Tour pros launched a company about four years ago. I wasn't privy to the details, but Hurricane made it sound like when the ship sank he'd been left aboard to take the financial plunge.

"All I know," I said, "is that the guy's working his ass off to get in shape. He's missed nineteen straight cuts. He's probably exhausted."

"The vultures, of course, tossed Richie Barter a softball," Singleton said, "and he went off about drugs again."

I hit another shot. As amicable as Mitch was, he was no innocent grandfather. He'd been in the top rung of golf journalists for years for a reason. Unless I said it was "off the record," it was on.

"I hear your wife is looking into some rumors this morning."

"Coincidence," I said.

"Most definitely," he said, and nodded, then moved off. I hit another shot.

"Richie Barter shouldn't be airing dirty laundry in public," Silver said, taking the six-iron and wiping it down, "but if there's something there, we're all getting cheated."

That was Silver—"we"—always thinking Team. And he was right. If someone was using a performance-enhancing substance, it was taking money from us. Worse, it was taking trophies. A gust of wind blew. The air felt warm and dry against my face. I hit a three-wood into the wind to see what it would do. My average three-wood flew 280 yards. This one landed at the 200-yard marker. I filed that away for later.

There was more to any potential drug scandal than Silver and I losing money and trophies. There was the game to think about—and my new post on the Policy Board gave that thought additional weight. Since Hurricane's collapse, I continued to recall what he'd said—he was playing for the money. I didn't know much about the now-defunct club-manufacturing company Mitch brought up. I only knew Hurricane's comment bothered me and contrasted startlingly with the seventeen-year-old Billy Carvelli, an awestruck fresh-faced kid.

. . .

"Can I speak to you, Jack?" Billy Carvelli said. "I mean, I know you're getting ready, but . . . "

I was on the putting green twenty minutes before my tee time. The four-foot portable wall still surrounded the practice green like boards around a rink. I walked to the wall.

"I just wanted to apologize for my father. I hope he didn't affect your play. I feel terrible about Mr. McCarthy missing the cut."

"Your father's got nothing to do with Hurricane's play or mine."

He nodded and turned to go.

"Billy."

He paused.

"When are you playing next?" I said.

"The Audi Open."

"Let's play a practice round."

He smiled broadly. "Thanks."

I nodded and Carvelli walked away. I went to where Silver had set up. We'd worked on the same drill for several weeks. The son of a carpenter, I practiced this drill for years: I snapped a chalk string my father gave me against the green, illuminating the line from ball to hole. Then I tried to putt down the line, to the cup. A simple drill, but one that stressed fundamentals—a fluid stroke that opened, came back to square at impact, and opened slightly again on the follow-through. I hit four putts; only two fell.

"Jack, got a minute." It wasn't a question. The voice was familiar and sounded tense, not quite hoarse, but a little winded. My head was down as I listened for the sound of the fifth ball clattering against the bottom of the cup.

Silver answered for me. "We're working on something here, Richie."

No clatter. I looked up. The ball sat short of the hole.

"Just want to say," Richie said to me, "that all the horseshit you hear is wrong. Someone started a rumor."

"You're telling me Mitch Singleton made up those quotes?" I said.

He looked momentarily confused. It didn't take much. "No," he said. "Not that. What's going around the range today. I didn't fail a drug test."

"I hadn't heard a thing," I said.

"Well, it was a misunderstanding." He turned and walked away.

I looked at Silver, started to speak, then stopped.

Silver just nodded. "Don't even get into it. We've got a round to play."

8

At 1:40 P.M., my windbreaker flapping in the wind, I stood on the first tee between Richie Barter and Padre Tarbuck—the guy who felt singled out by Richie's remarks, the same guy who took Richie down in the locker room. If Padre had cooled since their altercation, his face belied his emotions. He stood glaring at Richie and I guessed this threesome wouldn't be like playing with chatty Lee Trevino and funnyman Gary McCord. However, I wasn't there to referee. I had to make up ground. I was –1, eleven strokes behind Woods (–12), ten behind Phil Mickelson.

The first hole, a par four, plays 410 yards. The weatherman on the locker-room television said the wind was blowing ten to fifteen miles per hour. Specifics didn't mean much to me. I only knew that wind meant knock-down shots. Grow up in Texas or England and you learn to play the game on the ground, hitting knock-down shots and bump-and-runs. If you're raised in the northeast, you learn to play the game in the air, hitting fades and draws, striking the ball precise distances, and flying it close to the flag. Nearly fifteen years earlier, after four seasons at UMaine—which had meant winters spent hitting into a net in the field-house and shoveling off patches of the snow-covered football field—I'd somehow survived the PGA Tour Qualifying Tournament (Q School) to earn a PGA Tour card. I'd brought a power game and little else. My putting stroke would never be confused with Brad Faxon's, but after years of short-game practice, I was no longer one-dimensional.

A huge bunker protected the right side of the first green, so I wanted to approach from the left side of the fairway, which created a delicate tee shot. I had a three-iron in hand, the wind at my back. To my left, Padre was still glaring at Richie, his leather glove squeaking as he squeezed and twisted the grip on his driver as if slowly ringing someone's neck.

Richie seemed oblivious, his head swiveled as if searching for someone. "Seen Peter Barrett?"

"Barrett?" I said.

"Yeah," Richie shook his head, exasperated with my ignorance, "the goddamned Tour *Commissioner*, Jack."

Richie Barter's grandfather had founded Barter's Precision Putters, the well-known BPP brand, and I doubted Richie ever stepped foot on a public course, let alone shoveled snow-covered football fields to practice. I stepped close to him. The wind kept our conversation private. Good thing, because most of the gallery was media. Larger crowds were waiting for the leaders to go off.

"I *know* who the commissioner is," I said. "Why are you looking for him?"

"None of your business."

"You know something, Richie . . . "

"Come on, Jack," Silver said. He had the yardage book out. "Take some practice swings and stay loose."

I moved away and swung the three-iron back and forth. I took a deep breath and blew it out slowly. Maybe it wouldn't be so bad to see Padre drop Richie in front of the media. Hell, I might even instigate it. But No. 1 can be a birdie hole and I was eleven strokes back. I didn't want to think about Richie Barter, who, according to him, was the victim of a rumor and, subsequently, now on the lookout for the Tour commissioner.

"Richie," I heard Padre say. Padre was face to face with him and I was too far away to get between them. Several cameras flashed. "Let's get something straight," Padre said. "You don't speak to me today. You got that? Nothing. Not one word." Padre was my size—six-one, 210. Richie was maybe five-feet-eight and 165 pounds. He looked up at Padre, nodded, then started to speak. But Padre raised his finger. Richie closed his mouth and moved away.

"Everything okay?" It was a tournament official.

"Sure," Padre said. He held up his three-iron and studied the clubface. "Sure. Everything is A-okay."

Several more cameras flashed. If Commissioner Peter Barrett wanted to promote the Tour as one big happy family, he should've figured out a way to alter this computer-generated threesome.

"Jack," Richie whispered, "I don't use drugs." Padre was on the far side of the tee box and Richie was back—and looking for an ally. "I hope you know that, Jack."

"I've got other things on my mind right now, Richie."

"Introducing the one-forty tee time," the starter said, and everyone fell silent. "On the first tee, from Chandler, Maine, please welcome Jack Austin."

I tipped my cap at the applause and took two more practice swings. Then I addressed the ball and hit a solid three-iron, 220 yards into the heart of the fairway.

After the others had hit, Richie walked beside me as we moved down the fairway. I wasn't having it. "I think your woe-is-me to Mitch Singleton was piss poor. Your speculation hurts the game."

"'Speculation'?" Richie stopped walking and stared at me. He shook his head and quickly caught up again. "I don't believe this," he said. "You're on the fucking Policy Board. *You* should be the one pushing for drug tests."

"People don't pay to watch us so they can question if we're really this good," I said. "You're dragging the Tour through the mud. If you don't have proof, keep your mouth shut."

"Proof?" he said. "For Christ's sake, Jack, don't kid yourself. Welcome to professional sports in the twenty-first century. All I want is what's fair. I tried to start the ball rolling by offering take the first test. Totally voluntary. Now someone's telling people I failed it."

"Did you?"

"Of course not."

"Then how do you explain the test result?"

"I haven't seen the results yet. But if I failed, something's wrong with the test."

"What are you saying? Someone altered your test?"

"Have a hard time believing that?" he said. "For Christ's sake, Jack, get your head out of the clouds. The game isn't so pure anymore."

It was my turn to stop walking and stare. Richie kept moving and watched me over his shoulder. Then he shrugged with the sincerity of one who'd told someone a truth they didn't want to hear.

. . .

I went out in even-par thirty-five, which, regardless of the wind, wasn't getting it done this day. Taylor Stafford set the pace. He was four holes ahead of me and I had heard the gallery react numerous times to his seven-under-par round. He was −18 overall. Stafford, a journeyman, a winless twelve-year veteran, was scorching the field. He needed only eighteen putts through fourteen holes, according to CBS on-course commentator Dan Ferrin, whom I met on the ninth fairway. "The guy is draining three-pointers," Ferrin said.

As a professional golfer, I should be able to keep my emotions in check and maintain focus at all times. Mental toughness enabled me to forge a career from limited natural ability. However, my mind wandered in and out of this round.

Richie Barter had gotten to me.

How could Stafford, a no-name, putt the lights out? I wasn't naive. Pro sports in the twenty-first century weren't known for honesty or integrity. Yet I'd always believed that reputation due to a very small percentage athletes who grabbed headlines— Kobe Bryant and his rape accusation, Ray Lewis and his murder trial, Jason Giambi and his alleged steroid admission. I'd always believed golf to be different.

Before walking off, Richie had shrugged as if he'd borne bad news. Had he? Where great sums of money are at stake, temptation to cheat exists. Did that include golf? I'd heard the rumors but had seen nothing to confirm them. Accordingly, I'd given golf and its athletes the benefit of the doubt. After all, I was a sports fan, too. Years ago, I'd pulled for Giambi and had been happy for the guy when he'd "earned" his ridiculous $120 million contract with the Yankees. When his alleged admission of steroid use hit the press, I felt betrayed. What I watched Giambi accomplish hadn't been due to ability alone and that left a sour taste in my mouth. Later, after reading reports alleging that upwards of 5 percent of baseball players might have used steroids, I was initially shocked—then outraged; finally disheartened. As a fan, my loyalty had been betrayed.

Could performance-enhancing substances have reached golf? Richie Barter told Mitch Singleton he could name names.

There was a leaderboard near the tenth green. I looked at it. How could Taylor Stafford, a no-name, putt the lights out?

I shook my head. The same damned way Jack Austin had the week he won the Buick Classic—by busting his ass on the practice green for months beforehand. What bothered me most about Richie's published accusations was that I knew people were now questioning everything they saw and maybe even *had seen*, including even my modest accomplishments.

"I *volunteered* to be tested," Richie was saying again.

I was crouched on the fringe at the tenth green looking at the line from my ball to the hole.

"Now there's a rumor that I failed," he said. "That's character assassination."

I nodded toward Padre. "Ask him about that."

Richie's primary concern, as far as I could tell, was Richie—and he went on as if I'd not spoken. "I didn't do anything and here I am looking like the supreme asshole."

Padre was across the green waiting for me to putt. If he could hear Richie, he didn't let on.

"Yeah," I said, "that's how you look."

Silver chuckled at that.

I went to my ball and gently placed my putter behind the Titleist. I pushed all thoughts aside and brought the putter back slowly and steadily. The ball caught the right lip, did a one-eighty, and rolled harmlessly away. I tapped in for a par, remaining −2.

Richie walked to his ball, replaced it, and pocketed his coin. "Your caddy thinks you're a damned riot, Jack. Well, don't forget you're on the Policy Board." He straightened and looked at me. "I approached you as a player seeking help, and you laughed. The game is going to hell in a hand basket," he said, and pointed at me, "and that's happening on your watch."

43

. . .

It was bad enough that I was even par on my round and staring bogey in the face. The golf gods poured salt on my wounds by allowing Richie Barter to stand on the eighteenth green with a birdie putt to shoot a six-under-par sixty-five. I was on the fringe, looking back down the fairway at the lake, which had swallowed my tee shot. Safely in the fairway, Brad Faxon and his caddy went over yardage. Sergio Garcia stayed loose by swinging his club back and forth.

The wind was still blowing. Behind the green, Lisa stood inside the rope, her press credential hanging from her neck in clear plastic. She wasn't alone. Jennifer Mills from The Golf Channel was nearby, as was ABC's Ian Baker-Finch. Richie, despite his round, was still four shots behind the leader. I wasn't close and Padre had struggled mightily, so the media wasn't there because we were breaking scoring records. I looked at Lisa and spread my hands. She shook her head as if to say, *You won't believe this.*

Richie looked up at the press, then at his caddy, who gestured for him to focus on the putt. Richie's birdie attempt was far from a foregone conclusion—a treacherous fifteen-footer. The ball would start on level ground and climb the slope before breaking nearly two feet left at the hole. Richie glanced at the line of reporters again. They could only be there for one reason.

Regardless of how annoying Richie was, the guy was an excellent player. After two practice strokes, he put a nice roll on the ball and it disappeared into the hole. His name was now third on the leaderboard, behind only Stafford and Woods. He handed his putter to his caddy and looked from side to side as if searching for an escape route.

I went to my bogey putt.

"Damage control," Silver said.

"Making the cut and finishing dead last sucks," I said.

"Save par and we can worry about jumping people tomorrow."

When you play thirty events a year, you go to each thinking you can win and trying desperately to position yourself in or near Sunday's final group so you have a chance. But no one wins every week. I'd been called a "journeyman" for a long time. That translates to "survivor" and connotes images of massive struggle, neither of which I deny. I am also a PGA Tour winner, but this week I wasn't in contention. I wasn't playing for the trophy.

Behind the journalists, I saw Perkins leaning on crutches. He hadn't been able to walk the course. Five miles on crutches was out of the question; he couldn't navigate all eighteen holes in a wheelchair and probably had too much pride to sit in a golf cart. He was dressed in a sweaty T-shirt and athletic shorts, his face glistening. He'd come from his second—and self-imposed—rehab workout and looked more exhausted than he had after two-a-days during his football career. *He* was playing for something more important than a trophy—the opportunity to toss a ball with his son again.

I stood over my Titleist and glanced at the hole, ten feet away. When not in contention, some guys withdraw. I looked at Perkins again. When the putt fell, he was pumping his fist.

Sometimes bogey putts are about more than saving a stroke.

On the golf course, life always seems simple: You do your best and do it the right way. If only things were that clear in the real world. They never were, and they were getting blurry fast for Richie. After Padre tapped in, Lisa was the first reporter to speak: "Richie," she said, "would you like to comment on the cocaine rumor?"

9

Hotel life isn't bad, if you can make it feel like home. Padre was with me in the living room of our suite at 5:45 P.M. Lisa was still at the course and, if the media frenzy accompanying Richie Barter's departure from the eighteenth green was any indication, she might be there through dinner.

"We ordering room service?" Padre said. "Or you want to go down to the restaurant?"

He was on the floor in front of a glass coffee table rolling a ball to Darcy. He was staying one floor above us and had arrived dressed like a neighbor appearing for a pool party—in athletic shorts with UCONN on the leg, a gray T-shirt, and black Adidas flip-flops. Similarly, I was in off-duty attire—khaki shorts and a TPC Boston T-shirt. I was barefoot and drinking Heineken from the bottle. Room service sounded fine.

The suite had a bedroom and bathroom off the living space, which had a loveseat, coffee table, television, and sofa. There was a small fridge with miniature bottles of booze and snacks that, if you opened, you bought. Neither Lisa nor I ever opened them. Instead, a plastic cooler of ice lay in the center of the floor with lunchmeat, a six-pack of Heineken, several bottles of water, and frozen yogurt sticks (called "Gogurts") for Darcy. The air was cool and dry from the air-conditioner.

"Kid has great coordination for a three-year-old," Padre said and, again rolled the rubber ball to Darcy, who stopped it and slung it back at him with the side-armed motion of a discus thrower. "Surprising," he said, "given that you make up fifty percent of her gene pool."

"You think Richie does cocaine?"

"I'm not prone to wish ill of people," he said, sounding like the priest he'd once been, "but I must admit I enjoy the irony of him accusing everyone else and now having it come back to bite him."

"You didn't answer my question," I said.

Another irony was that Padre had gone from clergy to the Tour's sex symbol, having recently turned down an opportunity to appear on a calendar with the LPGA's Natalie Gulbis.

"No one really knows what people do behind closed doors," he said.

"He's played awfully well for a long time," I said. "Seems to me, that would be hard to do if he was doing drugs."

A keycard clicked in the door and Lisa entered carrying her laptop. She set it down on the coffee table, picked Darcy up, and kissed her cheek. Then she lifted Darcy's shirt, pressed her mouth to Darcy's belly, and gave her a zurbert.

Darcy giggle-screamed, "Mommy, nooooo."

"I didn't think Lisa Trembley-Austin gave zurberts," Padre said.

Lisa grinned. "Just not on TV."

I dialed room service and took orders: chicken salad for Lisa, steak for Padre, and two tuna sandwiches for me. I ordered Darcy the kids' mac-and-cheese and apple juice. Lisa went to the bedroom and came back wearing a sleeveless blue blouse and khaki shorts. She put Darcy on the floor, sat next to me on the couch, and sighed. Darcy made tracks for the toy suitcase, which lay open near the far wall. Austin family travel consists of two suitcases of clothes, a cooler, a stroller, my golf clubs, Lisa's laptop, my laptop (all Tour players get courtesy computers each season), and two suitcases for Darcy. I'm always surprised the plane gets airborne.

"The press tent is an absolute zoo," Lisa said. "Golfers don't get in trouble, so golf journalists never deal with scandals. Now all hell has broken loose. Kerry Clark from Sportsview Network was caught breaking into Richie Barter's courtesy car."

"Probably makes Richie feel important."

"Now, Jack."

"You're too professional to admit he's a pain in the ass in front of Padre."

"I've known Richie Barter to be slightly full of himself," she said, morphing into the ever-politically correct Reporter Lisa, choosing her words carefully. "However, as you know, a healthy ego is a must for any pro athlete."

"You should be the White House Press Secretary," I said.

She stood and got a water bottle. "This is big news. The American public loves watching people eat crow."

"He said he volunteered to be tested," I said.

"That's interesting," Lisa said, "since he wouldn't speak to the media."

I thought of Richie's comments about my role on the PGA Tour Policy Board. He'd accused me of waving to a sinking ship. "I can't see a Tour player surviving if he's a drug addict. It's a mental game."

"Well," Lisa said, "drugs are a way to relieve stress."

I had nothing to say to that; Padre, apparently, didn't either.

"What about the beta-blocker accusations?" Lisa said. "I hear Richie pointed the finger in the locker room before he ever went to the media."

Last night, I'd said a "rumor" floated around the locker room. She'd apparently done her legwork to come up with a name.

I looked at Padre. He shrugged as if he genuinely didn't know what she was talking about. I did—and couldn't lie to her.

"Last month," I said, "Richie Barter, a world-class whiner and a poor loser to start with, was running his mouth in the locker room about guys making too many putts. He didn't name names. I thought it was foolish. Probably other guys who heard it thought the same thing. But the next thing I know, this week, he goes to the media with his broad accusations. Given today's cocaine rumor, it doesn't seem like Richie has a lot of credibility."

"Was he talking about beta-blockers?" she said.

"He just said guys were making too many putts," I said. "That's all I heard anyway. Probably because I'm on the Policy Board."

"You didn't take it seriously?" she said.

"There was nothing concrete—no evidence, no names—and I figured the game would only get hurt if I said something that sent you digging for what I didn't believe was even there."

"That was for me to decide as a journalist, Jack."

"Maybe I should get going," Padre said.

Darcy was across the room waiving Raggedy Anne about. She turned to us. "This is my baby, Mommy."

"I love your baby, sweetie," Lisa said, then to Padre: "You're not going anywhere." She flashed the smile that could get even Barry Bonds talking about performance-enhancing drugs. "After all, your meal hasn't arrived yet." She turned back to me. "Jack, what exactly did Richie say in the locker room that day?"

"Nothing much. Ranted about guys coming out of nowhere to win."

Lisa sat looking at me. If she'd have tried, she could've bent a spoon. "The Tour had eighteen first-time winners in 2003. The game is global now. There's more talent. That's not 'out of nowhere.' In Mitch Singleton's article, Richie said he could name names."

"I'd like to see that," I said. "He doesn't have the balls. And all he could do, I think, is guess."

"What if he knows something and does name names?" She looked from me to Padre, then back to me. "Beta-blockers might help a player putt."

"Could the Tour test everyone?" Padre said. "After all, we're free agents."

"When you join the Tour," Lisa said, "you agree to follow the rules. If someone refused a drug test, the commissioner's office says they'd be suspended indefinitely."

"But Padre's right," I said. "There's no union. Players are essentially free agents. If someone doesn't want to be tested, that wouldn't look very good. Then again, they could go play in Europe."

"Over there," Padre said, "you can negotiate appearance fees, something the PGA Tour doesn't allow. I don't know much about beta-blockers, just that they relax you. But it's practice, Lisa, that makes you a better putter."

"I'm not discrediting your win last week," she said. "I know Jack went to El Paso to help you. And I believe you worked hard to get your game back. But, theoretically, beta-blockers may very well steady a player's nerves and his hands. That's a clear advantage."

Someone knocked on the door and I got up, relieved by the food's arrival—except it wasn't room service.

Richie Barter stood staring at me. "I need to talk to Lisa Trembley," he said.

10

"You sure you want me to go?" I said to Perkins, who sat nodding.

It was 8:15 P.M. Darcy was in bed, Lisa was still with Richie Barter, and Padre had gone. We sat at opposite ends of the sofa drinking Heineken from bottles. The television was off and he'd just said what my "legwork" consisted of.

"The wife, Elizabeth Scott, won't see me," Perkins continued. "Says she discussed everything with the Chicago cops and is busy raising her two kids."

"She became a single mother overnight."

"Yeah. Billy Peters, my Chicago cop, says she isn't cooperating a hell of a lot with them, either. He went to see her twice. She just cried. Said the second he mentions Ron Scott's name, she sobs. Husband's death is too much for her. She told Peters she doesn't want a long investigation. Wants to move on with her life. Wants to move on for her kids."

"Can't say I blame her."

"I'd want revenge," Perkins said, and shrugged. "Someone killed her husband." He drank some beer. "You'll be able to visit in a more friendly—more relaxed—capacity. You knew Ron Scott."

"Not well," I said.

Perkins would see the widow's predicament that way— avenge the death. I saw her desire for privacy. We were different people but had been close for as long as I could remember. When I was seven and got hurt in the woods behind my house, he carried me home. He'd been helping me ever since. Different worldviews. Best friends, no less.

Perkins told me what he needed. I owed him but knew my limitations. It left me torn. Desire and ability are two different things and I was no P.I. I was a golfer. What he said next left me no chance to object.

"I've got a long way to go, Jack," he said, and looked down at his leg. "I told you the deal. I don't want to get undercut." He didn't look up for a long time. As proud a man as I knew. This wasn't easy for him. Now I felt guilty for having self-doubts. This guy had been shot helping me. "Deirdre Hackney's doing two people's work in my Boston office," he said. "I don't have the money to hire anyone else, and I don't trust anyone besides her." He shifted casually but flinched when something sent a jagged bolt through his leg. "I've thought this through. For what I need, you're a good choice. You worked with Ron Scott. That makes you closer to him and the family than me or any cop. You might learn something—if you ask the right questions."

That was what bothered me. I got up and walked to the door behind which Darcy slept and peaked in. She lay on the bed, eyes shut, arms splayed to each side as if dreaming of flight. I went back to Perkins.

"I'm no interrogator," I said, sitting down again.

"Don't let your head swell, but believe it or not, I actually have faith in you. You've held your own before. Remember Hutch Gainer? Remember the interview you did with Victor Silcandrov? Chicago cops say Ron Scott's death is being listed as a mugging. I don't buy that. And, as the PGA Tour's security consultant, I'm hired to look into any crime involving the Tour."

I heard the determination he'd always had. He wanted to do the things he'd always done, the things his body would no longer let him do. "Are you saying the Chicago cops don't care?" I said.

"They care as much as all cops do. I've been there. You're working eight cases at once. If one's a mugging that went bad, it's a mugging that went bad. Period. Close that file and grab the next one. Peters doesn't buy it but has a full caseload and a guy telling him it is what it is."

"Why do you think there's more to it?"

"It's very likely that Ron Scott followed the killer into that alley."

I sat looking at him. *"Followed* the killer in there?"

He nodded. "Peters told me he'd love it if I could pull enough evidence to force them to keep digging. Ron Scott was shot in the chest with his back to the street. The shooter tried to step over him, left a shoeprint on Scott's jacket. A size ten."

"Maybe they fought and got turned around," I said.

"Maybe. But the shoe print is from a Folsheim. Those are a couple hundred bucks a pair. And it's an upscale, commercial area. Never had a mugging reported there. Plus Ron Scott traveled the world, and he's from Chicago. He'd know better than to get himself in a situation where he could be mugged."

I sipped some beer and considered it all.

"The scene doesn't show a struggle, either," he said. "No fend-off bruises. No skin under Scott's fingernails. Billy Peters thinks Ron Scott knew whoever murdered him, and Peters was a smart cop when I worked with him."

"Think the widow will see me?" I said. "I wasn't close to Ron Scott."

"I know she'll see you," he said. "The Tour is starting a scholarship in Ron Scott's name. Deidre might have accidentally called her and somehow mistakenly said that you're the executor."

"You're shitting me?"

He grinned, impishly. "Miscommunication is a terrible thing. She's expecting you."

.   .   .

A half-hour later, we were watching the NBA. The Celtics were playing the Hawks. Paul Pierce scored fifteen in the first half, but it wasn't enough. The Celtics were down six.

"How's the leg?" I said.

Perkins shrugged. "Hurts like hell right now. Doctor says it'll probably improve."

Probably. Again, I felt guilty for questioning my Chicago trip. "What're your medical options?"

He drank from his bottle of Heineken. "They're not really options. I either become a hell of a crutch user, which I'm not doing, or I bust my ass to see if I can regain full use of the leg."

"Feel okay, otherwise? The shoulder?"

"Shoulder's fine. Just a scar. My overall conditioning is terrible. I feel like a golfer."

I winked at him and drank some beer. We were quiet for a while. The air conditioner hummed as it cycled on.

"How're Linda and Jackie?" I said.

"Fine," he said, staring at the television.

"They coming out while we're in Arizona?"

He shook his head. "I want to rehab."

"What's that got to do with them being here?"

He shrugged. "It's just hard."

"What do you mean?" I said.

He didn't answer me. After a few moments, he changed the subject.

"I'm supposed to interview Richie Barter with Peter Barrett tomorrow," he said.

"Lisa beat you to him."

"To Richie?"

I told him about Barter coming to see her.

"Think she's asking him what crow tastes like?" he said.

"If I know Richie, guilty or not, he's covering his ass. But what confuses me is why he'd volunteer for a test if he was doing cocaine."

"To make people ask that," Perkins said. "It's an ideal cover-up—he sees mandatory drug testing on the horizon, so he volunteers. And when he fails, everyone buys his they-screwed-up-the-test story, because no one would be stupid enough to volunteer if they were using. It's so stupid it's smart."

"I'm not sure the Tour can make us take a test."

"Then Richie Barter truly is stupid," Perkins said.

11

$\mathcal{S}$unday morning, Lisa was up and out of the hotel room before breakfast. I hadn't heard her come in and her pre-dawn description of her date with Richie was cryptic. I knew I'd learn all about it on television with the rest of the world. I had an early tee time, but what's early when there's a three-year-old around? So at 6:25, I was giving Darcy a bath and the process had both of us soaking wet.

Of all the things my PGA Tour career had given me—the chance to compete over and over against the best of the best; financial opportunities my parents never had; the chance to play a child's game everyday through middle age and beyond—I appreciated the time spent with my daughter most of all. With Lisa's career also revolving around the Tour, family life, for us, meant traveling together. And while Lisa had set hours, I had only four (on a good week) set tee times. Otherwise, I made my own work schedule and often that schedule was set around Darcy's needs.

Such was the case this morning. As I bathed my baby girl, I thought of how she would be three only once, how I'd never get these years back, how many of my friends in the "real world," worked seven to seven and saw their kids only on weekends. I may not have Tiger Woods's game, but I had something better.

"Daddy, no shampoo."

"We have to wash your hair," I said. Negotiation with a three-year-old is a learned skill. "Maybe after Daddy's work, we can have ice cream." I felt guilty for the bribe and a little incompetent—Lisa never had to resort to bribes—but Darcy smiled and I rubbed shampoo into her scalp.

Bathing a child, like changing a diaper, is something you do without thought. And it's ironic to recall the days when you were single and realize you're doing something that back then you'd never have imagined. I scooped some water into a large plastic cup. "Tilt your head back."

"Wash cloth," Darcy said. "*Wash cloth!*"

I got her one and she covered her eyes with it and tilted her head back as I poured the water over her. With one hand, I carefully shielded her eyes. I loved looking at her eyes—sea-blue, they reminded me of my father's, my uncles', my own. As I washed her and tickled her tiny toes, I thought of innocence and purity. I thought of golf, a game I'd no doubt share with her in years to come. Like my baby girl, the game represented all that was good in the world—the innocence and playfulness of sport, the thrill of personal growth—but more than any other game, golf represented personal accountability. I recalled my first season on Tour, a season during which I'd been in contention only once. That lone Sunday, one shot off the lead, I'd stood over an eight-foot putt to tie only to have my ball move. I had grounded my putter; therefore, the movement of the ball was a violation. But no one had seen it—except me.

I backed off the putt and called the penalty on myself.

It ended my chance to catch the leader. That was golf. You governed yourself. Whether Darcy excelled in the game or not, I hoped she expressed interest in it. You learn what kind of a person you are when you play the game. Golf teaches life lessons. My mind ran to Richie Barter's beta-blocker accusations and my elected post on the Policy Board.

. . .

Few things are worse than playing in Sunday's first group. I'm a positive guy but there was no way to put an optimistic spin on my 9:34 A.M. tee time. Tiger Woods and Phil Mickelson, the leaders, comprised the final pairing at 2:30. I was thirteen shots off the pace and five hours in front of them.

When Tim Silver and I walked onto the first tee, Kip Capers smiled and extended a hand. I took it and gave a firm shake. Capers was only twenty-five but a four-year veteran. Having attended divinity school before surviving Q School, he'd nearly followed Padre's brazen career path. His career earnings were in the $2 million range, but that belied his struggles. He'd nearly lost his card twice and gutted out the final month of both seasons to finish inside the top 125 on the PGA Tour Money List.

"The List" means everything. A win carries a two-year exemption and a major championship gets you five years. Otherwise, you keep an eye on "The List." You know what happens if you slip to 126 at season's end—a return ticket to the PGA Tour Qualifying Tournament, affectionately known as "The Fall Classic." In 2004, 1,240 players began the first of three stages. Thirty (and ties) earned exempt status on the Tour for one season. Q School is a place no one wants to revisit.

Capers wore his trademark black short-sleeved mock turtleneck with black pants. (I kidded him often about how uncomfortable and hot it must be to make a fashion statement.) His arms were laced with purple tattoos. When he swung, the ropy muscles moved and his tattoos danced.

"Heading back to Boston after this," I said, "or on to California for the Audi?"

"I'm going to Orlando," he said, "to check on Hurricane, after what happened."

"Yeah," I said, "he had a rough week."

Capers was far too polite a kid to ask what the hell I was talking about. But his face gave it away. "Did you see the paper this morning?"

I shook my head.

"Last night, Hurricane collapsed and was hospitalized."

"That was in the papers?"

Capers nodded and glanced absently down the fairway. I did, too. Would've been a great morning to fly-fish. Would've even been a nice morning for a leisurely eighteen holes. This was neither, though. This was the PGA Tour, where the week's best always play last—where this Sunday I was playing first.

"In the sports briefs." Capers pulled his yardage book from his back pocket and glanced at a distant target. "It was on *Sports-Center* this morning, too. He told his wife to call me last night."

"From the hospital?" I said. Nearly 300 yards away, three

Shotlink guys stood with a tripod in the rough and looked like road-survey crew. They'd track tee shots on first hole all day long.

Capers closed the book and turned back to me. "What?"

"Hurricane collapsed," I said, "but he asked his wife to call you?"

"I guess so. Why?"

I shrugged. I hadn't known them to be even associates much less close friends.

"Let's get to it," he said, and went to his caddy.

I did the same. The first hole played only 410 yards. There was no gallery to speak of and no one in front of us. If we had wanted to, we could have played the round in three hours flat. Or I could've taken a mental vacation and just slapped it around for a leisurely four-hour stroll. After all, we were thirteen and twelve strokes back, respectively, clearly out of it. Moreover, this day, there was no wind to keep the leaders at bay. Yet I thought a sixty-five might enable me to climb into the top twenty, a respectable finish.

As the starter introduced Capers and me to no one (Silver was clearly enjoying that irony), a lone kid about fifteen, wearing khaki shorts and a Titleist cap, strolled to the side of the tee box. He stood staring at the big staff bag in front of Silver the way I'd looked at Johnny Miller's clubs at about the same age when I woke up early to follow him.

I took my three-metal back, made a wide arc, and nearly paused at the top as my weight transferred. My hips cleared and the clubhead fired down the line, inside, the clubface coming back to square at impact. I held the follow-through. I didn't need to see where the ball had gone. The swing was well timed and fluid, the contact crisp. Sixty-five was in my sights.

The kid clapped.

"Your one and only fan," Silver said, grinning.

I tossed the kid a ball from my bag. He bobbled it and the ball fell to the ground, but his face was aglow.

.   .   .

Kip Capers hadn't spoken much.

That wasn't uncommon. If you play before every other twosome on Sunday, you made the cut but accomplished little else. Painful to admit, I'd been there before and, accordingly, most of my other leadoff partners seemed less than thrilled to be with me. However, Capers was not any of the other 131 participants. We played practice rounds at least once a month and had dinner at least one other time each month.

On the seventh green, Tim Silver set our large black and yellow TaylorMade bag down, clubs chiming, and took a Power Bar from a pocket.

"Capers isn't much fun today," he said, chewing. "Usually we talk bands, something I can't do with *my* employer."

"What's that supposed to mean?" I said, and moved to my ball on the green. "I offered to take you to a Springsteen show last year. You said no."

"That's retro. I'm talking *current* bands, Jack—Limp Bizkit, Green Day . . . "

"Now hold on. I've heard of Green Day."

"Not an endorsement that'll help their record sales."

"Hurricane McCarthy was hospitalized last night and Kip is going down to see him."

"So he's probably upset. You going, too?"

I shook my head. "I'll be in Chicago the first of the week, but we're still on for the Audi Open."

"Chicago. What are you doing there? Some endorsement thing?"

"No." I examined my line from my ball to the cup.

"You know," Silver said, "on one of these trips to southern California you're going to lose me. With my talent, Hollywood is bound to notice me."

"Notice what?"

"Hell, I can sing, I can dance. Jokes." He spread his hands. "I'm a born entertainer."

I shook my head, marked my ball, and tossed it to him. He wiped it with a towel.

Nearby, Capers was reading his putt.

"You listening to Silver?" I said to him.

Capers crouched behind his ball. "I try not to." It was the first time he cracked a smile all day.

I slapped his back. "How're you feeling?"

"Not so good. This Hurricane thing really has me shaken up." He stood and made a practice stroke.

To our right, the teenage kid gave me a thumbs-up. I returned the gesture. It was 10:45 A.M. Fans were at the course now and some had appeared to watch Capers or me play a shot, then vanished. Only the kid had walked the whole way with our twosome. Capers hit his putt, then tapped in. Then I went to work over my fifteen-footer. I was two-under on my round—a long way from sixty-five—but this could get me going. The seventh was a 215-yard par three, the longest three-par on the course. I'd negotiated the bunkers guarding each side of the green, as well as the collection area in front of the green, and landed safely on the putting surface. But that was only half the battle. Now I was above the hole. My putt would slide right and gain speed. If I didn't judge the speed correctly, I could knock the ball ten feet by the hole.

I glanced at the kid. Next to him, a marshal held up a QUIET PLEASE sign. I set the putter behind the ball, shut my eyes to visualize the shot, and finally made my stroke. The ball turned to the right but held the line, dying into the cup. The quiet sign was down and the kid was leaping. Silver tossed him a Footjoy glove from the bag.

. . .

By the time we reached the eighteenth tee, four hours after we'd begun, we had a gallery. Yet the kid in the Titleist hat had been the sole warrior, having walked all seventeen holes with us. Fans are clearly the backbone of any professional sport and I enjoyed having the solitary kid follow us for a couple reasons: First, it gave me something else to play for. Pride should be enough, but I was tired and needed a challenge in addition to the sixty-five. Additionally, a single fan walking with Capers and me gave me a chance to promote the game, a duty that goes beyond posting sixty-twos, and I had attempted to do so. On nearly every tee box, I talked to young Mike Firth of Scottsdale, the No. 3 player on his high school team. He had PGA Tour aspirations. I offered encouragement—just as a handful of PGA Tour players had done for me when, as a teen, I went to Hartford on a Tuesday during a tournament week to watch them practice.

I lost sight of Firth on the tee box at No. 18, a 438-yard par four. Spectators surrounded the tee, four rows deep. Capers was still even. I was −5 on the day. A birdie here would earn me a sixty-five—and a chance to jump anyone standing still.

"You could've played yourself into the top twenty," Capers said.

"That's what I'm going for," I said. Again, the play was over water. It was a risk-reward hole and, at five under on the round, I was playing with house money. I had the driver out and I hit a long, straight tee shot.

Capers's ball found the lake.

On the green, Capers putted first again and made his parsave. I took a lot of time over my putt. Sixty-five would be a good score, despite the benign conditions. This was a speed putt—fifteen feet, straight. The line was no problem. I had only to gauge the pace. I brought the Bull's Eye back slowly and held the follow-through.

The putt fell.

"When are you leaving for Orlando?" I said, when I shook hands with Capers.

"As soon as I can get a flight," he said, and ran a hand through his hair. His caddy stopped nearby. Kip told him he'd catch up in the clubhouse. "Hurricane's sick, Jack."

"Sick?"

"He's got a heart problem."

12

$\mathcal{I}$f Norman Rockwell had painted in the twenty-first century, she'd have been in his portraits. Her house would have been, too.

Monday afternoon, she told me her name was Elizabeth but I could call her Liz. The late Ron Scott's wife wore jeans and an apple-green cotton shirt with long sleeves. She sat on a tan leather loveseat across a glass coffee table from me in the living room. Her bare feet were tucked beneath her. There was a gold ring on the big toe of her right foot. The long sleeves of her shirt ran to her knuckles and she clutched a sleeve in each hand like a nervous school kid. The pose was cute and she wasn't a nervous woman. She was stunning and she knew it. She sat looking at the wooden fruit bowl on the coffee table, thinking, then blew a strand of blond hair from her eyes and looked up at me.

"This house is something else," I said.

Upon entering, I'd been so taken aback she'd offered a tour— 8,000 square feet, the dining-room chandelier had to be mechanically lowered to be dusted, and the playroom had a drop-down screen and overhead projector. Indoor pool. Workout room. Sauna.

"Oh, thank you. I'm sure your home is just as nice."

"Ah, no."

She looked at me and smiled. "Actually, I know how nice our home is. In fact, it cost more than I ever thought we could afford. This was Ron's dream. He worked for it, designed it, and he was here everyday they were building it. He was meticulous about things."

"I wish I'd known him better," I said. "I respected his work ethic, I can tell you that. He kept himself in great shape."

She nodded. "When he started slipping a couple years back, he rededicated himself. He went to California to train one winter."

"A lot of guys in their forties getting into shape," I said, and smiled.

"Jack, thanks for telling me more about the scholarship. I asked for literature on it when they called. It never arrived. Is there anything else you need?" She glanced at her watch.

I hadn't done much with Perkins's setup. She'd asked about the scholarship and I felt so bad lying to her, I decided to start a small one myself in the guy's name. On the plane, I'd been unable to sleep and went over some questions Perkins had given me. The effort to anticipate the conversation was as futile as trying to play a round shot-by-shot, mentally, before teeing off—too many intangibles. The one time I'd brought up the murder, she started to cry and the conversation steered itself in another direction. But I'd taken a practice day to come. It was time to push.

"I'm on the PGA Tour's Policy Board," I said. It was cryptic. I knew the connotation was that I was there on behalf of the Tour. Hell, maybe I was. After all, despite what Richie Barter thought, I didn't just stand around waving at sinking ships. Mostly, though, I was there because my best friend couldn't be. "Did Ron go into Chicago alone the day he was killed?"

She sighed. "I already went through all that with the police."

"I just have a few questions," I said.

She didn't protest. It made me feel like a little kid—*every lie leads to another.* Now she thought the Policy Board was investigating the murder.

"He went into Chicago alone that day?" I asked again.

"Yes. That's probably why he was mugged, because he was by himself."

"Is that somewhere the two of you go often?"

"Chicago?"

"That area of the city."

"We like the stores there." Apparently, that brought back memories and she started to get emotional again. "Lots of kids' stores."

She pulled a Kleenex from a box on the coffee table. I'd noticed a box in almost every room. I gave her a moment to gather herself. The living room was immaculate. I knew she had two kids, which made me wonder how the place stayed picked up. Darcy had our house in a shambles daily. Then again, our place wasn't 8,000 square feet. The kids' playroom was probably at the far end of the house, in Wisconsin.

"When was the last time the police gave you an update?" I said.

She thought for a minute. "Two, three days ago."

"What did they say?"

She looked at me, blue eyes narrowing.

"I'm going to talk to them, too," I said. "If you don't feel like telling me, I can wait." Finally, a true statement. Maybe I wasn't becoming a pathological liar after all.

"No. I guess it's okay . . . What exactly is this Policy Board, again?"

"A committee of players, Tour officials, and people outside golf who look out for the Tour and the game."

"What does any of the have to do with Ron's death?" she said.

Good question. "He was a Tour player," I said. "The Tour looks out for its own."

She chewed on that a moment, then said, "The police told me there's a chance that Ron followed the killer into the ally."

I nodded.

"You knew that?"

"Yes," I said. "What do you think of that theory?"

"I have a hard time believing it. Ron was very smart. He wouldn't let some creep lure him into an ally. I told the cop, Mr. Peters, that, too. He just nodded and smiled."

"The theory might suggest that Ron knew his killer."

She didn't say anything for a while. She picked a red apple out of the wooden bowl, rubbed it in her hands, and took a bite. Her teeth were very white. She chewed, then swallowed, set the apple down carefully on the glass table, and sat staring at it.

"What's going on here?" she said. "All I know is that my husband is gone. I thought you were here about a scholarship."

I didn't answer. I sat thinking. When you play golf for a living, you trust your instincts. When you've lasted thirteen seasons on the big tour, you know you can rely on them. Something was tugging at me. I didn't get the sense that Liz Scott was mourning. She was angry, not sad. Something about that bothered me. I didn't know what or why.

"Ron is gone," she said, again. "My kids lost their father. Now you show up asking questions that make me think the police aren't telling me everything." She looked up at me, her face deadpan.

The spouse is usually a suspect in a murder. I thought it prudent not to mention that. I spread my hands. "I just heard the theory and wanted to ask about it."

"Well, Ron wasn't stupid."

"That's why he might have known whoever killed him."

"I don't believe that theory."

"Why?"

"Because . . . I just want all of this to go away. I want me and my kids to just move on. My husband's wallet was taken. That must've been why he was killed."

"You're probably right," I said, and told her I had to go.

.   .   .

Liz Scott had been angry to learn one theory had her late husband knowing his killer. That theory originated in the Chicago PD Homicide office. All I needed was for her to call the cops, irate that some golfer knew more about the investigation than she did. I could see the headline now—"Golfer Charged with Hindering Murder Investigation." I treaded lightly when redheaded Billy Peters met me at a downtown-Chicago diner.

"When I knew Perkins, he was a good guy," Peters said, "a guy you could trust. Said he'd do something, he did it. You don't meet many of those, especially nowadays. He didn't tell me much on the phone. What happened to him?"

"Got shot last fall, had a stroke during surgery. Now he can't do much with his left leg."

"How'd he get shot?"

"Helping me," I said.

We were in a booth and I looked down at my white coffee

cup. My coffee didn't need it, but I stirred in another sugar pack and sat watching the spoon move in slow circles. It was better than seeing Peters's expression.

The diner smelled of fried food and the rich aroma of strong coffee, reminding me of small-town Maine where I'd grown up, of the diners where I'd eaten lunch with my father during the summers I worked carpentry with him. Two uniformed cops entered and sat at the counter. The waitress was a big-boned woman with thick hands and crow's-feet at the corners of her eyes. To our left, a television sat on a shelf near the ceiling. The Cubs were playing.

"Sosa's gone now, huh?" I said.

"So you're out here because Perkins got shot helping you?"

"He asked me to come," I said.

He cut his hot-roast-beef sandwich, forked a piece of meat, and chewed. Gravy dripped onto his chin. He took a napkin from the dispenser on the Formica tabletop.

"Nothing personal," he said, "but this wasn't what I had in mind when Perkins contacted me about looking into the Ron Scott mugging. You're no cop. What are you going to do out here?"

"I went to see Liz Scott."

"What did you say to her?" he said, and stopped chewing.

I told him about the visit and about the theory.

"Jesus Christ," he said. "Perkins didn't tell you to keep you mouth shut?"

"Not about Ron Scott knowing his killer."

Peters looked like he'd lost his appetite. "If she calls, the shit will hit the fan."

"Sorry," I said. It wasn't much. I ate some cheeseburger. It was greasy but as good as any diner burger I'd eaten.

"Look," he said. "I like what you're doing for Perkins, but— what was that board again?"

"The PGA Tour Policy Board."

"Yeah, classic." He chuckled. "The *Policy Board* from the preppy sport. How did Chicago Homicide ever survive without you? Listen, this is a police investigation. And with the victim being a public figure, we're hoping the FBI doesn't show up and say, 'Thanks for warming our seats.' So I want this as low profile as can be. If the FBI gets in this, it'll be a horse race or worse."

"Horse race?"

"We'd be racing against them to solve the damn thing, if they even let us"—he held up his fingers—"*assist them*. We'd be working the same case with a tenth of the budget. And it's our case. I took the damned call and was the first homicide guy there. Perkins called me at the right time—I'm swamped. And I know what kind of guy"—he looked at me—"and cop he is. "

"If he was healthy," I said, "he'd be here. I know I'm no cop."

"That's for sure," he said, and shook his head. "I can't believe you told her we think her husband knew his killer."

"She a suspect?"

"She's the wife and she won't say boo to me." He drank some Coke. "I understand why you're here, but this is the deal: Keep out of the goddamned way, keep me informed about what you're doing, when you're doing it, and what you find out."

"Fair enough." I stood, took $15 from my wallet, and put the money in front of our plates. Then I held out my hand. He took it.

I'd just stepped out of the restaurant when my cell phone rang.

"Jack, this is Hal McCarthy."

"How are you?" I moved away from the traffic on the sidewalk and stood near the diner door.

"Oh, fine. Everyone's a goddamned fatalist. But I'm in the hospital in Orlando, Jack, and I was wondering . . . " He paused for maybe five seconds.

"Hal, you there?"

"Yeah. I'm just thinking . . . Look, I'm going home tonight and I was wondering if you could come by." He said it like I was next door.

"Tonight? I'm in Chicago. I'm heading to the Audi Open tonight."

"Did you know Ron Scott?" he said.

"Why?"

"It's about his wife."

13

"*C*hrist, no," Hurricane McCarthy was saying, "Kip Capers is a fatalist, a good kid, but a fatalist. My ticker's fine." He tapped his chest, exaggeratedly. "I sent Capers away. I feel better sitting up than I do lying down, so I think I just got a little tired and fainted. That's all. Same thing happened on the green when I was with you."

I'd changed flights. It was Tuesday at noon and we were at a packed Olive Garden in Orlando near Hurricane's house.

"Where's Sherry?" I said. It was rare to see him without her.

"I sent her shopping," he said. "She didn't want to go, but I told her she can't watch over me forever."

"How serious is this?"

"Oh . . . " He waived that off with a flip of the hand.

At the table near our booth, a young couple had a baby in a highchair. They were trying to get the baby to eat. It made me think of Darcy and of Lisa coercing her with the airplane-to-the-mouth trick.

"What did your doctor say?"

"Oh, I've got a great doctor." He sipped his draft beer. Noon was too early for beer; I was drinking Coke. "The guy understands me, knows what I need."

I'd read the *Orlando Sentinel* and watched The Golf Channel. Reports said only that Hurricane was home but expected to play next week. No diagnosis was offered.

"I lost some weight," he said, and grabbed a breadstick like it was a chicken leg and bit off a chunk. "Getting in shape. Couldn't you tell?" He grinned as he chewed and winked.

"I can," I said. "You look great. What happened at home?"

"Oh, jeez, Jack . . . you know I don't follow all the medical bullshit. I just sort of fainted again." He took a forkful of butter and spread it onto the breadstick.

As dismal as my forte into private investigations had been, likewise, I was no doctor. But I guessed a forkful of butter wasn't helping whatever the hell he had. The waiter reappeared and put a plate of spaghetti in front of me and fettuccini Alfredo in front of Hurricane. I still had Wednesday to practice before the tournament began, but I glanced at my watch. We'd been there twenty-five minutes.

"Hal," I said, "you called me and asked me to come. Said it was about Ron Scott's wife."

"How are Lisa and the baby . . . what's her name, again?"

"Darcy."

"Yeah. How're Lisa and Darcy?"

"They're both well. How's Terry?"

Hurricane drank some beer. "He's always great. So is Jaime, my youngest." He set the beer glass in front of him and sat looking at it. "Christ, so is Sherry. I worked for a long time to give them a good life, you know."

"And you have," I said.

He shrugged. "Things change."

I remembered his money comment and what Mitch Singleton told me about the Nichols Golf Group's failed foray into club manufacturing. I ate some spaghetti and washed it down with Coke.

"You've still got a great family," I said. I almost said, *Money or not,* but that wasn't my place.

"I've got the best family," he said. He made a sound like a sniffle and turned toward the window.

"Hal."

"Yeah," he said, turning back to me. "They are the best—supportive through it all. You know what private school costs for the kids?"

I had no idea and shook my head.

"Thirty-seven grand this year. Three years ago, I built Sherry her dream house. What am I going to do, ask the kids to leave school? Ask Sherry to sell her house? Because of me? You miss nineteen cuts in a row and . . . "

I felt bad for the guy, but I was no financial planner. I was giving up my second consecutive practice day because he'd called and promised something about Liz Scott. "I'm flying to L.A. this afternoon," I said, "for the Audi Open."

"I'm curious to see how that tournament goes. Heard it's some new course and it'll play long. I'll be ready for that one next year."

I ate some more spaghetti. On the phone, his voice hadn't sounded urgent, but it had sounded like he needed to talk. Now I was there and, apparently, the need had passed.

"Liz Scott?" I said, swallowing.

Hurricane exhaled and set his fork down. "I talked to her, Jack. She told me you went to see her." His eyes ran to a table near our booth and fell upon the baby. "When they're that age, you never think things will turn to shit."

I looked at the baby, then back at Hurricane. "What the hell are you talking about?"

"Christ," he said, and sighed, leaned back, and folded his arms across his chest, "some days I feel eighty years old." Around us, people were in various stages of their respective meals. Hurricane's expression contrasted with the looks of other diners, who seemed to be enjoying themselves. "If I can win just one more time, everything would be like it was. They'd never have to worry." He shook his head. "Jesus, I love those kids. Guess how many putts Terry had on a seventy-four yesterday."

He was rambling now. I took a guess.

"Wrong. Twenty-six. How's that?"

"Fantastic," I said, genuinely impressed.

"At least I've got a wife who deserves better and two great kids. You saw Terry. He putts better than I do. He's something, huh?"

I said he was. I'd spent eight of the past twenty-four hours on planes and was laughed at and given marching orders by a homicide detective. The spaghetti was gone and I was drinking Coke. His rambling made me wish I'd ordered scotch. But he sounded like he needed to get something—whatever the hell it was—off his chest. Maybe that was the real reason he'd called me.

"I feel like I'm starting over," he said, and glanced absently around, "at forty-four, and the Champions Tour seems a hell of a long time away. Ron Scott felt the same way."

I waited. It had taken a while, but we were getting somewhere.

"He and I had to keep our cards six more times," he said. "I'm just trying to hold on now."

"You can't play well, just trying to hold on."

"In my situation," he said, "you do what you can."

"You can play this game, Hal. Don't forget that."

"The game is changing, Jack, and I'm not a rookie anymore. I'm trying to win, but I'm realistic. I've got six years. On the senior tour, tournaments are only three days, the courses are shorter, and there are no cuts." He drank some more beer. He'd barely touched his meal. He grinned at me. "It's like a pension plan. But I have to survive six years to get there."

"With the new technology, you can add twenty yards."

"I have. But so have the college kids coming up. Jack, look at the big picture here: Some of these courses we played fifteen years ago had narrow fairways and high rough. Remember when I won in Miami? I hit a three-wood off the tee all week, hit eighty-five percent of the fairways, and won the tournament. Last year they mowed the rough. Who does that favor?"

"The long hitters," I said. "I know."

"Last year's winner only hit fifty-one percent of the fairways. You're lucky. You're built like a linebacker. You can hit it a mile, like the kids."

"I work my ass off in the gym and on the range to keep up," I said. "I'm not in the top five in driving distance anymore. But I'm lifting weights and developing other parts of my game. There's more to winning than hitting a long ball, Hal."

"Yeah," he said, "I know. But maybe not as much as there used to be." He lifted his napkin, carefully folded it, and repositioned it on his lap. "Christ, I've missed nineteen straight cuts. I'm living on borrowed time."

Maybe a scotch wouldn't have been strong enough.

"How come you bothered Liz?" he said, and looked me in the eye.

"'Bothered'?"

"She called me, Jack. You upset her. Please don't go see her again."

"I can't promise anything," I said.

"She's really upset, Jack. Don't bother her."

My eyes narrowed. "I don't like being told what to do, and for the record, I wasn't bothering her. I was asking questions. It doesn't have a whole hell of a lot to do with you, Hal."

"You and I've known each other a long time, Jack. I'm asking you, as a friend. Please don't go see her again."

"Why?"

He shook his head. "Ron Scott was a good friend of mine, a guy I trusted. We understood each other."

"And people are trying to find out who killed him and why," I said.

"Are you going back?"

"I don't know. Why?"

"Just don't," he said. "Let the cops handle it."

"Like I said, Hal, this isn't your business."

"Maybe I'm making it my business."

"What the hell is going on here?"

"I'm trying to help you, Jack. Do what's best for yourself. Don't go see her again."

"That sounds like a threat."

When he didn't reply, I got up and walked out.

The Montville Country Club, outside Los Angeles, was home to the inaugural Audi Open. The title sponsor, having been a mainstay on the European PGA Tour, was apparently branching out, launching a stateside event. As I would soon learn, "launching" was the key word.

Wednesday at 7:35 A.M., I walked into the locker room and took a seat next to Padre Tarbuck. The lockers were pine and hand-crafted and the room smelled of fried ham, potatoes, and coffee—the breakfast buffet. I wasted no time checking it out.

PGA Tour players work hard, sure, but we're spoiled. At the Audi, a guy like me gets spoiled by proxy. Anytime a new event is launched, a primary concern for directors is drawing top players. I'm a career grinder. But other players, guys like Tiger, Phil Mickelson, Ernie Els, pick and choose where they play. Exemptions from major championship wins make the top 125 of little concern for them and in golf guys are free agents. For instance, Tiger can charge a $2 million-per-week appearance fee to play in Europe. By contrast, PGA Tour events can't (legally) offer appearance fees. So events, especially new ones, draw players by other means. Disney makes its tournament a weeklong kid-friendly outing; the John Deere lets players test-drive tractors; another tournament flies players, via helicopter, to a bass lake for a fishing excursion. These are the bennies of the Tour. Guys like me get spoiled by proxy.

Padre didn't look happy to be spoiled this morning. Rather, he was frowning like a brat as he sat looking at the score card. "Ever play this course?"

"No," I said and unzipped my duffle bag. I hung five shirts in the locker. They varied in color, but all had "Adidas" on the right breast and the left sleeve. I put five TaylorMade hats on the top shelf. There were two dozen Titleist Pro V1 balls already in the locker, which I knew retailed for about $50 a dozen (again, spoiled).

"I don't know why I even came," Padre said. "I wouldn't say this to anyone else, but I might be wasting my time. There're probably only ten guys who can win here. Damned course plays eight thousand yards."

"Seriously?"

"Literally," he said. "I'm not shitting—eight thousand and two yards."

In 2005, the average course on the Tour played 7,090. "That's longer than any course on the Tour."

"That's right. And that's how they're billing it. I know a bunch of guys didn't come this week. Billy Garfield came and left. Unpacked, looked at the card, cursed out a few tournament officials, packed up again, and left. I don't blame him."

Billy Garfield weighed 140 pounds. A magician with a wedge and a putter, he averaged only 262 yards off the tee. My three-wood carried more than 270.

"They brought in three chefs from the Culinary Institute of America up in the Napa Valley," Padre said. "The buffet's tremendous. At least I'll eat well this week."

. . .

The rumblings continued on the practice green. An 8,000-yard PGA Tour venue was unheard of, albeit not unanticipated. There will always be a few ways to keep par a respectable score. One is to narrow the fairways and grow the rough. That takes the driver out of players' hands, forcing them to carefully position tee shots by hitting three-woods and irons off the tee and cautiously maneuver the ball around the course. Another way is to build a course near the ocean, where the wind can change directions at Mother Nature's whim. A third way is to lengthen the course. Of late, it seemed courses had been stretched and stretched until, apparently, this one snapped. Eight thousand yards was crazy long, but what bothered people most was that the rough was thin and low.

And maybe, just maybe, that wasn't fair.

Because a long course with little rough is defenseless against long hitters. An average hitter is forced to play par fives by hitting driver, a lay-up, and a wedge to the green. But the Tour's longest hitters can swing for the fences if the rough is unthreatening. Guys reaching par fives in two wasn't new. The difference here was that typically half the field was included in that group. This week—on an 8,000-yard layout—only a handful could hit the ball that far, establishing a major advantage for relatively few. And having little rough only compounded that advantage.

Woods was here this week and it would add instant credibility to the event if he became the inaugural champion. John Daly was here; Mickelson had come; and Hank Kuehne, king of the launchers, the Tour's reining driving distance champ, was also present. Years ago, I'd won that title and felt a little selfish because I knew this layout benefited me as well.

Near the green, Lisa held a microphone up to Richie Barter.

"The Tour wonders why no one's here this week," I heard Richie say. "Look at the score card."

"Actually, the field is strong. Woods, Mickelson, Daly—"

"That's a long-drive contest. That's not golf."

"Those are major championship winners, Richie," Lisa countered. "Those players can do more than hit long tee shots."

"You're missing my point. What about Billy Garfield? He won the damned U.S. Open last year, went the whole week without missing a fairway. What's that get him here? Mark my words, Lisa. The winner this week will hit less than fifty percent of the fairways. He won't need to hit more."

"Well, the golf course is somewhat wide open," Lisa said.

"It's gorilla golf. Anybody can hit it a zillion yards, find it, and hit it again. Precision and accuracy are out the window here. What about the artistry of the game—chipping, controlling your ball flight, and for God's sake, putting? If this is the direction the PGA Tour is headed, there are going to be repercussions."

" 'Repercussions'?" Lisa said. "Could you elaborate?"

"No. And I want to say I'm having a press conference tonight at five."

"About what?"

"I'm not at liberty to say yet. See you at five." He turned and walked away.

. . .

As obnoxious as Richie Barter was, the guy had a point. That afternoon, Padre and I were in the middle of the first fairway. I'd hit a 310-yard tee shot but still had a three-iron to the green. Padre was worse off, standing in the middle of the fairway with a three-wood. The hole was only a par four.

"The shortest par three on this damned course is two-ten," Tim Silver said. "It's going to be a long walk for me this week."

"You'll finally earn your money."

"Better play well, boss. My weekly fee ain't cutting it here. I want that ten percent."

Silver got the PGA Tour standard: $1,200 a week, 5 percent of my earnings, or 7 percent of a top-ten finish and 10 percent of a winning paycheck.

"I figure you're overpaid most weeks anyway," I said. "So I make up for it this week. Besides, what about the Hollywood talent scout who's going to discover you?"

"How can I get discovered here? I won't be able to walk by the end of the week, let alone sing and dance."

"Billy, focus!" It was Billy Carvelli's father, who was following outside the ropes.

Young Carvelli was with us and had hit a monster drive, 322 yards. Exemplifying the problem with the golf course (as Richie had so eloquently pointed out) was that Carvelli pulled his drive twenty yards offline but didn't have to hack it back to the fairway before hitting to the green. Hitting from a gnarly rough had long been an obstacle only the strongest players could overcome and it made most players leery of straying off line. But here, Carvelli had a four-iron out and was waiting for Padre, then me, to hit. We were playing skins—$20 a hole—and I could see some of the fire leave Padre's eyes.

"I'm hitting three-wood to the green." He shook his head. "The scary thing is that, sure, this course is the anomaly, but not by much. We're playing courses that are seventy-six hundred yards now."

"Might be a taste of the future," I said.

"Well, it tastes shitty," Padre said, then hit his three-metal into the greenside bunker.

Padre's caddy, a guy named Dan Dufour, who'd played the Tour for two seasons before becoming a full-time looper, took the three-wood from Padre, slid the clubhead cover on it, and put it back in the bag. We started toward my ball. "Tournaments don't want to give up thirty-two under par," Dufour said. Ernie Els's seventy-two-hole record was −31, set at the Mercedes Championship in 2003.

"Records are set to be broken," Padre said. "The Tour should just limit the equipment. Don't let guys hit three-hundred-and-sixty-yard drives. Control the technology by making a standard PGA Tour ball."

"Equipment manufacturers would never go for that," I said. "Imagine the revenue companies would lose if they couldn't claim their ball as the 'Number one ball on Tour.'"

"That's what it always comes down to," Padre said, "isn't it, money?"

"Golf is big business," I said.

I made a good swing, barely put the ball on the green, and Padre and I walked to Carvelli. Padre was frustrated and I felt for him. Equipment had become so good, so technologically advanced that guys were hitting the ball farther than ever. In the 1980s, if you swung hard, you used a stiff steel shaft. That was the extent of technology. Now computers told you how much spin the ball left the face of your driver with and manufacturers could customize a professional's driver to produce minimum spin, maximizing distance. Those same manufacturers got $600 for a driver after TV viewers watched John Daly or Hank Kuehne hit 360-yard drives, meaning it was too late to control the equipment. As Padre said, money had already taken over.

Thick rough can penalize wayward tee shots of any length. But standing in the rough next to Carvelli, I could see the laces on my spikes. It didn't matter. Carvelli missed the green with his second shot. He was a poster boy for golf's new "power game"—long and wild with a short game that was lacking. Across the fairway, I saw his father take out a pad and pen and write something down.

"Good leave," Silver said to me as we walked to the green.

"Not exactly a realistic birdie putt." I was thirty feet from the hole. "The scary thing is," I said, "that's about as good as I can hit it from that distance."

"Like I said," Silver said, "it's going to be a long week."

Ahead of us, Padre was walking toward the green, his head down.

. . .

The eighteenth at Montville CC was a 237-yard par three over water to an island green. Carvelli had more than kept up with me off the tee all day but was inexperienced and lacked the chipping and putting skills necessary to make scrambling pars. He was four over. Padre had over-swung and was now out of rhythm, seven strokes over par. I'd hit some solid shots but remained one over.

"Wind is at us," Silver said. "It'll be hard to hit a wood close to the flag. Can you reach it with a three-iron?"

"We'll see." I was up five skins and practice rounds are for figuring out club selections.

Only a handful of fans stood near the eighteenth green, including several reporters. This week the PGA Tour was giving the world a glimpse of the future. The media wanted to get the reaction. I figured they were at No. 18 to gauge how the hole would play this week. Any time a tournament ends with a par three, the championship can be decided at that hole, since birdies can be made there. At this par-three eighteenth, given the yardage, just as many bogies would be made.

I took the three-iron and made several practice swings. The breeze made me hesitant. Three-iron might be a stretch. The last thing I wanted was to over-swing and get out of sync. But you can't second-guess. I took the three-iron back slowly, made a wide shoulder turn, pausing at the top. Then I began the descent, swinging inside and down the target line. My wrists turned over at impact, snapping the ball airborne. The contact was crisp. I held the follow-through and watched.

The ball splashed short of the green.

"Lesson learned," I said, and took the five-wood from Silver.

Instead of going to the drop area, I hit my third from the tee box. I wanted to work out the club selection before the tournament. My third shot hit the green, but as Silver initially feared, didn't hold. My Titleist Pro V1 scooted across the putting surface and into the water.

"So what do we hit Thursday?" I said to Silver.

"You got a twelve-gauge?" he said.

15

"I appreciate what you did," Perkins said, "and I still feel awful about asking, especially now with Hal McCarthy threatening you. You guys are friends."

I shrugged and drank some Heineken. It was 7:45 P.M. and Perkins and I were in the hotel bar, his crutches leaned against the bar. Perkins was drinking Jack Daniels and Coke. Across the room, Ernie Els was eating a late dinner with a guy in a gray suit, whom I didn't recognize. It seemed late for dinner, especially with the tournament beginning the next day, but maybe it was dinnertime wherever Els had most recently been. After all, no professional played a more global schedule.

On the red leather bar stool next to Perkins, a small guy in a leather jacket drank draft beer. He wore a biker's jacket with chains jingling. But the guy didn't look like a biker. He had neatly cropped hair and manicured nails. His teeth were polished and even; a businessman who liked motorcycles. He'd come in after us and excitedly watched a basketball game on the television, weaving back and forth with the action. Several times his forearms brushed Perkins's. Perkins had looked over and the guy had given a halfhearted shrug each time. No apology. No "Excuse me." I couldn't remember anyone ever sitting so close to Perkins regardless of how crowded the establishment. Things had changed.

"It was the least I could do," I said.

"What's that supposed to mean?"

I didn't answer but my eyes wandered to the obnoxious guy beside him, then down to the crutches.

I'd arrived at the bar fifteen minutes before Perkins. My Chicago trip hadn't been on my mind. Instead, I'd sipped a beer and thought of the bionic golf course and tried to estimate a winning score. I was betting on −5 for the week. Typically the winning score in a non-major was fifteen to twenty-five strokes under par.

"What's the arrangement with Billy Peters?" Perkins said, and as he spoke, the guy next to him raised a hand in celebration, accidentally spilling part of his drink, some of it hitting Perkins.

I started to tell him what Peters had said but he wasn't looking at me now.

"Cool it," he said to Leather Jacket.

"Hey, man, aren't you a Utah Jazz fan?"

"Cool it," Perkins said again. His voice was low and his stare could've dissolved water.

Leather Jacket was average size, meaning he could sleep in one of Perkins's loafers. But he wasn't sizing Perkins up. He was looking at the metal crutches with forearm braces that leaned against the bar. "Oh, man, sorry. I'll keep it down."

"What are you looking at?" Perkins said.

"Nothing, man . . . I didn't know . . . I'll quiet down."

When the guy turned back to the television, Perkins looked at the crutches. He looked at the guy again, then back at the crutches. He sat staring at them, as I told him about my "arrangement" with Billy Peters. His head wasn't into what I was saying and neither was mine. My mind swept over the past. One time in Lowell, Massachusetts, he and I had been walking down a street when three punks stopped us for our wallets. Perkins hit the first guy. He hadn't knocked the guy out but had sent him stumbling backward. Something else sent them running. He'd been the biggest and strongest for as long as I could remember, but often he hadn't needed that. He'd always had an aura that told people he was wired differently. His actions weren't dictated by the same mechanisms the rest of us have. It was why he hadn't made it with the cops. Yet often it garnered instant respect and fear. The guy next to him had offered something very different.

"Liz Scott wants to move on with her life," I said. "And she's upset that she isn't privy to all that the cops have."

"There could be more to why Liz Scott was upset about not knowing what the cops think," he said. "I made some calls this morning. Ron Scott had an eight-million-dollar term policy. She gets that free and clear now."

I thought about that and about my reaction upon meeting her: Liz Scott hadn't been sad; she'd seemed angry. I said as much to Perkins.

"Angry because you were there? Or because she found out the cops were keeping her out of the loop?"

"I don't know," I said. "Maybe we've both gotten cynical. The lady's husband just got killed. I'd be angry, too. She's left to raise two kids, alone. They were married how long?"

"Fourteen years."

"That's a long time."

"What's Hurricane's stake in her?" he said.

"He was friends with her late husband."

"So why not help catch the guy's killer? And when push came to shove, the guy threatened you. What the hell for?" He finished his Jack and Coke and raised a finger. The bartender got another.

The bar was dark wood, the lacquer nearly a quarter-inch thick. Brass ceiling lights shone down, reflecting off it. It had been a fast few days and my head was spinning. On the top shelf was Perkins's exchange with Leather Jacket. When Perkins had been shot, the doctor had come to the waiting room and said he might never be the same. I was learning what that meant.

"Ron Scott was taken by surprise," Perkins was saying. "No gunshot wounds on his hands. When people get shot in the front, they instinctively shield themselves with their hands and the bullet usually travels through their hands into the body. Scott's hands were clean. He hadn't seen it coming."

"Any luck with the shoe print yet?"

He shook his head.

We sat quietly. Leather Jacket slid off his stool and left. Perkins watched him go and sat staring at the door as it swung shut behind him. For a long time, I said nothing.

"If you need me to go back to see her," I said, "just say so. I'm with you in this—and everything else—for the long haul."

He turned back to me.

"Besides," I said, and grinned, "Hal McCarthy doesn't scare me. To tell you the truth, I'm a little curious about it all now."

"Curiosity has gotten you in trouble before," he said. Then he smiled the same way he had in sixth grade when he'd convinced me to help him fill the lock on the Teachers' Room door with glue.

Around us, glasses clinked and sounds of the television and conversations blended into a symphony of background noise. Perkins's second Jack and Coke was nearly gone.

"Think there's something between Liz Scott and Hal McCarthy?" he said.

"Hurricane's a real family man," I said. "That would be hard to imagine."

"Never say never," Perkins said. "Ron Scott dies. The wife gets eight million bucks and one of his colleagues tells you not to ask questions?"

I ran a hand over the stubble on my cheek, my thumb and forefinger meeting at the point of my chin.

"Didn't think about it like that," Perkins said, "did you?"

"I can't see Hurricane cheating. And I have a hard time seeing someone who looks like her with Hurricane."

Perkins shrugged. "Stranger things have happened." He grinned again. "And give Hurricane some credit. He's lost weight."

"I'm calling it a night," I said. "Got a seven-thirty tee time tomorrow."

"Hit it straight."

"You don't say that here. On this course, just tell guys to hit it long."

He didn't respond, turning instead to the basketball game on television.

I slid off the stool and paused. "Never seen you drink hard liquor before."

"What's that supposed to mean?"

"Nothing," I said.

I waited for a moment but he didn't speak, so I turned to leave. At the door, I glanced back. He was staring at the now-empty bar stool where Leather Jacket had sat. Suddenly he kicked the crutches and they clattered on the wooden floor.

In the hotel lobby, I took the elevator to the sixth floor and stepped out into the empty L-shaped corridor. The hall was well lit, but that didn't matter. I never saw it coming.

I rounded the corner and got hit on the chin by a truck.

.   .   .

"I didn't see anything," I said for probably the fourth time, this time to Perkins.

Two hours after meeting him in the bar, I sat with an icepack pressed to my cheek. Darcy was in the bedroom, asleep on the queen-size bed. Lisa, Perkins, Emilio Rodriguez from the Tour, and a local uniformed cop named Tim Steel sat in the suite's main room with me. I hadn't looked in the mirror, but the lump on my chin felt big enough to need a chair. My wallet had been taken.

"This resort isn't exactly a haven for muggers," Steel said. "How much money was in your wallet?"

"About eighty bucks."

"We canceled the credit cards already," Lisa said.

Steel was maybe thirty with light blue eyes. I'd yet to see an overweight Californian and he wasn't about to break the streak. The guy looked like he'd jumped off the cover of a surfer magazine, donned a dark uniform, and came to see me. Even more annoying—he kept looking covertly at Lisa's bare legs. She was wearing nylon athletic shorts and a T-shirt that read REAL MEN MARRY ATHLETES.

I was on the sofa. Perkins sat across from me on the loveseat, Emilio next to him. Lisa and Steel stood.

"Got a surveillance camera in the lobby?" Perkins said. His eyes were a little bloodshot. Otherwise, he showed no signs of the Jack Daniels and Cokes.

"My partner's checking the tape right now," Steel said. "No one was on the elevator with you?"

I shook my head, which felt like a forklift had dropped on it.

"You rounded the corner and . . . lights out?" Steel said.

"Right. Next thing I know, Tim Neely is shaking me."

"And you know him?"

"He's a Tour player," Emilio said.

"I know him well," I said. "Neely is a New England guy like me. We had a few beers on St. Patrick's Day last year."

"Says he was going for a walk," Steel said.

"Tim Neely didn't jump me. The guy won two million dollars last season."

Perkins sat across the room, noticeably quiet on the two-person loveseat, legs splayed before him, thinking. He held a paper coffee cup in his hands.

"Anything more?" Steel said to me, his eyes on Lisa.

"You talking to me or her?"

He didn't like that. I didn't care.

"You," he said.

"No. That's all of it."

He stood. "Okay. I'm going to lobby to check the tape myself. I'll be back in the morning."

No one would be there. I had a 7:30 tee time and Lisa would be off to the course for pre-round interviews.

"Sounds good," I said.

Lisa looked at me. I grinned.

"Jack, will you be able to play tomorrow?" Emilio said.

"Of course."

"Okay. Get some rest," he said, heading to the door with Steel. "I'll be in touch, too."

When they were gone, Lisa said, "You know no one will be here."

"Affirmative."

A wide smile spread across her face, her head tilting, hands on hips. "You didn't like him smiling at me, did you?"

"Affirmative."

"Can you be jealous at your age?"

I opened my mouth to answer.

"And don't say 'affirmative' again."

"Yes," I said, "I can."

"That's sweet."

"Good god," Perkins said.

Lisa made a pooh-hoo face at him, then went to the bedroom to check on Darcy.

Perkins moved his left leg gently and used his hands to help position it on the coffee table. "Now that everyone's gone," he said, "tell me what happened."

"You heard it."

"No one said a thing to you?"

"No."

"You got jumped in a five-star hotel, Jack. And that comes right after you were threatened. Which, I notice, you declined to tell him."

"My wallet was stolen. Anyone would know stealing my wallet would mean cops. Hal McCarthy wouldn't deliberately involve cops. And he's in Orlando and just got out of the hospital."

Perkins shifted again and flinched. Then he rubbed his leg.

"On top of that," I said, "Hal McCarthy doesn't have Mike Tyson's right cross."

Perkins looked at my cheek for a moment. "The way that basketball's growing, somebody might've hit you with some kind of sap."

" 'Sap'?" I said. "You really are a detective. Can I call you Sam Spade?"

"And I'll name that basketball on your chin Three-putt."

"How was Richie Barter's press conference?" I said to Lisa, who returned from the bedroom. She was shaking her head before I'd finished asking.

"He and his attorney were there with the results from his test," she said.

"I bet the results were negative," I said.

"Surprise, surprise."

"Which means nothing," Perkins said.

"Not according to Richie," Lisa said. "According to him, it should not only squash the rumor but retract it."

"That's the problem with drugs and athletes," I said. "Even speculation can tarnish the player and the sport."

. . .

The call came on my cell phone. I heard it ringing and was out of bed and in the main room by the third ring at 11:45 P.M.

"Jack," a tired woman's voice said. It was Perkins's wife, Linda. Perkins had said she was home in New Hampshire with their son, Jackie. "I'm sorry to call so late, but I need to talk."

"Are you okay?"

"I just need to talk . . . to you. You're his closest friend. Maybe he opened up to you. I just . . . " She sniffled. "I just can't . . . " She started to cry, then fought it off. "I just can't reach him. He's shut me out, Jack."

I didn't have to ask who or what. "What's going on, Linda?"

"He hasn't come home, Jack. It's been three weeks. Usually, he flies home every week or two. I call and he won't talk about his leg. Jackie misses him terribly, so do I. But it's not just not having him here . . . it's emotional. We talk but he doesn't *say anything*. Something's really wrong."

She cried for maybe thirty seconds. When I'd asked him if Linda and Jackie were coming to visit, he said he needed to rehab. I knew him better than anyone knew him, except perhaps Linda. For all of that, there was a side to him neither Linda nor I would ever know. It was what made him different from others. I thought again about the scene in the bar. Leather Jacket had pitied him. The stroke had taken more than mobility and thirty pounds from Perkins. It took an intangible. He'd been as intimidating an individual as I'd ever met—a 275-pound World-Wrestling-Federation frame with white hair and ice-blue eyes. How much of his self-worth was based on that former version of himself?

There was more to him. I wondered if he knew it.

"I can't reach him, Jack," Linda said. "For the first time, I can't reach him. After all we've been through together. This time, he's shut me out."

I couldn't imagine what either of them was going through. Eight years ago, I stood in a hospital maternity ward next to Perkins and watched through wire-meshed glass as his three-day-old daughter, Suzanne, fought for her life. For three days,

85

we'd called her Suzy. She hadn't made it. Perkins and Linda had worked through the pain and tears and two years later Jackie was born. On a lesser scale, Perkins had lost his homicide job after discovering a four-year-old rape victim, locating the perpetrator—the girl's father—and throwing the legal system out to see that justice, in his eyes, was served. The girl's father was hospitalized. Together, Linda and Perkins had gone through it all.

So why was he was shutting her out?

"Let me talk to him," I said. "His leg has thrown him for a loop, Linda. He asked me to go to Chicago for him. In the past, nothing would have stopped him from questioning someone."

"The damage isn't only physical, Jack."

"I know," I said. "I'll get back to you." I hung up.

O n the PGA Tour, Thursday and Friday threesomes are computer generated. Players are categorized into the three flights, according to credentials. Category 1 consists of tournament winners and players in the top twenty-five on the career money list. Category 2 is made up of players currently in the top 125 on the money list, players who have made fifty career cuts, or those in the top fifty in the Official World Golf Rankings. And Category 3 is everyone else—Monday qualifiers, sponsor exemptions, and rookies. A one-time winner, I was in Category 1. The computer paired me with Paul Meyers and at 9:25 Thursday morning, we were on the par-five 605-yard fifth hole.

Meyers was two over par and I was even. My round had been up and down—two pars, a birdie, and a bogey. I'd found the fairway but that was no great accomplishment. It was seventy-five paces wide. My ball had carried the right-side fairway bunker before drawing back and landing. Meyers's tee shot, though, caught the fairway bunker. Now, we stood near his ball.

Meyers wore a bright Tabasco shirt and khaki pants. His golf shoes were traditional black and white. He had a deep tan, neatly trimmed blond hair, and could have passed for a cruise ship's activities director. Without question, he was Californian, born and bred. In the papers, I'd read that we were playing in his hometown. He hadn't spoken much this day, but we'd never been close. He had won seven times in twelve seasons. And, I guessed, at five-feet-nine and 165 pounds, he'd need to call on that experience here. The bunker he stood in was 280 yards from the front edge of the green and Meyers had never been regarded as a long hitter, although he'd sledge-hammered a couple drives this day.

Tim Silver and I stood by as Meyers asked his caddy for a three-wood. I looked at Silver, who raised his brows. "He's going for it?" Silver said.

I shrugged. It seemed illogical. Unless you were John Daly, 280 yards from the sand it made no sense. Meyers couldn't reach the green, so why risk not clearing the bunker's lip or hitting a wayward shot? Hit an iron to the fairway, then a wedge to the green. Meyers waggled the three-wood behind the ball for a few seconds and swung, picking the ball clean. The titanium clubface sounded like a gunshot as it struck the ball. Silver and I both stood slack-jawed when the ball floated softly onto the green.

"Somebody ate their Wheaties today," I said.

Meyers smiled. "Thanks."

Spectators lined the fairway, having carefully selected spots to stake their lawn chairs, perhaps waiting for Tiger to approach. Others, heading to or from other holes, had paused to watch Meyers play his shot. The place erupted. As Silver and I walked toward my ball, I heard one guy say to his son, "Meyers used to be one of the best. Now he's old." He hadn't looked "old" on that swing. Yet the remark made me feel as I often did—like an animal on display. Fans don't realize voices travel over open (and very quiet) spaces. There was nothing to say in defense of Meyers; he'd won one major championship, but that victory was a decade ago. The previous season, he finished 141st on the money list.

"Six hundred yards into the wind," Meyer said, catching up

to me. Either he hadn't heard the remark or was ignoring it. "Ever see a setup like this?"

"It's something else," I said. "You play it much?"

"It's new, but I only live thirty minutes away, so I played it a few times."

"Hell of a shot you just hit," I said. "You carried a three-wood three hundred yards. Into a breeze and off sand."

Meyers smiled broadly. "Lucky shot," he said and motioned to Pete Sandstrom, Hal McCarthy's regular caddy, who was on the bag for Meyers this week. "But I am hitting it better. This guy's getting my old body in shape."

"How's Hurricane?" I said to Sandstrom. It wasn't uncommon for a caddy to work another bag when his regular player was off. The Tour's poor treatment of caddies—no health insurance, no clubhouse access (shower, free meals)—is notorious. And while it costs players around $100,000 to play the Tour (airfare, hotels, meals), it can cost a caddy nearly as much. Therefore, $1,200 a week doesn't go far, especially if your player hasn't made a cut in nineteen weeks, so Sandstrom's appearance was neither disloyal nor out of the ordinary.

"Hurricane's fine," Sandstrom said. "He's home, resting."

To me, Hurricane had seemed anything but fine. However, Sandstrom hadn't witnessed my lunch with him.

At my ball, Silver said we had 275 yards to the green.

"That means my drive was three-thirty," I said, "and I still need everything in the bag to reach it from here. That's crazy."

"Maybe I misjudged the wind," Silver said. "I'd have thought there was no way Meyers could get there. You've got forty pounds on him. Maybe the wind is with you above the tree line."

Silver and I had been together a long time. Occasionally, he might misread a putt. But he didn't misjudge the direction of the wind. Apparently, Paul Meyers was what is known as "sneaky long." He looked too small to keep up with me off the tee, but here we were: He'd reached a mammoth par five in two, from a bunker, no less.

In theory, my best three-wood would reach the green. But it's risky to gamble that you'll strike the ball perfectly. I had two options: I could lay-up to 105—ideal sixty-degree wedge distance—

or try to hit the three-wood of my life. Large sand traps guarded both sides of the putting surface, yet the rough between them was neither thick nor high. If I didn't make great contact, I could stick my chip shot close to the pin from that rough. I chose the three-wood and the ball landed in front of the rough and rolled into the right-side sand trap.

"What happened to your face?" Sandstrom said as we walked to the green.

"I fell in the shower."

"What'd you fall from," he said, "a six-foot ladder?"

I shot him a look.

"Sorry," he said, and chuckled. "That's quite a lump."

He was right about that, and I rubbed Three-putt gently.

.   .   .

By mid-afternoon, the golf course was taking its toll. I'd scrambled to make pars, while Meyers had continued his impressive play, shooting thirty-three. Meyers, at −3, was tied for the lead, meaning the course was playing tougher, perhaps, than even predicted. Yet the other names atop the leaderboard—Woods, Mickelson, Kuehne, and Daly—would only further the argument Richie Barter had made to Lisa the previous day: This was a home run hitter's ballpark. Mickelson was two under par and Woods was one shot behind. Young Billy Carvelli was one over par.

"Well, they got what they wanted," Meyers said, as we stood on the twelfth tee. "The tournament officials, the course designer, the whole lot of them—this is what they wanted." He motioned to the electronic leaderboard near the tee box. "Did you know Daly, who is doing well on this course, made a nine on a hole last week? Boy, that shows a lot of patience, doesn't it?" He snickered. "Takes a lot of precision and course management to do that."

"Well," I said, "you're sure doing okay."

"But course management is out the window here," he said, "and I don't like it."

I looked at the layout before us. The twelfth was a "short" par three. On this course, at 205 yards, it was a birdie hole. A long expanse of wetlands, tall grass, and pussy willows ran from the tee to the narrow two-tiered green, which spanned fifty paces, front to back. Two greenside bunkers guarded the target. Maybe a thousand spectators sat in lawn chairs or stood around the green. Many had probably been there all day, hoping to see someone make a birdie. After all, golf is no different from other American professional sports. Fans want to see the home run, not the carefully placed single hit through the gap; fans want the long touchdown pass, not the well-executed drive that takes four minutes off the clock. Likewise, in golf, fans enjoy birdies made in bunches or the spectacular eagle.

The group in front of us had yet to clear the green, so we were waiting.

"It's dry enough so any ball that lands on the front of the green," Silver said, "will run all the way back." The hole was cut on the back tier. He handed me my four-iron and walked to the cooler, got a bottle of water, and stood near Sandstrom, who was drinking water. Silver looked as if he'd run a marathon already.

"Can I talk to you, Jack?" Meyers said. The spectators lining the tee box stood twenty paces away, waiting to watch us hit.

"I'm getting ready to hit," I said.

"It'll only take a second."

I wanted to focus, to visualize the upcoming tee shot, but I shrugged.

"Thanks," he said. "I don't know if you know this or not, but I was very close to Ron Scott." He leaned casually on a Nike seven-iron.

The club selection caught my attention. Could he hit a seven 205 yards?

"I'm sure you understand how much Liz Scott has been through." I didn't say anything. This was heading somewhere. I kept looking at the seven-iron. "She told me you went to her home and upset her, Jack. I really don't appreciate that."

My focus shifted from his seven-iron. He had my full attention now—and I remembered something. "I'm not the one she slapped after the funeral," I said, "so I guess I didn't upset her as badly as you. What did you say?"

"Excuse me?"

I didn't say anything more. I didn't have to. We had locked eyes after she hit him. And we both knew that.

Meyers inhaled slowly. His head shook back and forth sadly. "You really don't know what you're getting into, Jack. I'm asking you to please stay away from her."

.   .   .

An hour later, I'd fallen to three over par. My favorite poet, Philip Levine, has a poem titled "They Feed They Lion" and, as I walked to the tee at the 237-yard par-three eighteenth, I felt like the poem's cadence had been pounded on skull.

> Out of burlap sacks, out of bearing butter,
> Out of black bean and wet slate bread,
> Out of the acids of rage, the candor of tar,
> Out of creosote, gasoline, drive shafts, wooden dollies,
> They Lion grow.

Indeed, something was growing, but I didn't know what the hell it was. My visit to Liz Scott stirred a pot filled with Hurricane McCarthy and Paul Meyers and God knows who or what else. Hurricane said to stay away from her; Paul Meyers said I was in over my head. In what?

But that was for another time. Meyers, Mickelson, and Woods were pulling away. Mickelson and Woods had finished –5 and –4, respectively. Meyers was tied with Woods with one hole to play. The guy had never been considered a long hitter, but he could really air it out. And that was a huge advantage here, made obvious by the company he was keeping.

If I could birdie the eighteenth and post a low score Friday, I could be in the thick of things heading into the weekend, but it wouldn't be easy. The green was pear-shaped, the pin tucked in the front-right portion—a hole location that meant, to hit it close, I'd have to either cut the ball left to right or go over a deep front-right sand trap. I wanted no part of that bunker, but hitting a gentle fade with a five-wood was asking a lot.

Silver watched as I pulled the five-wood from the bag and slid the head cover off. "That's risky," he said.

"We're eight shots back."

Absently, Silver ran a hand over his shaved head. For the first time I could remember, he had sweated through *both* his golf shirt and the poncho he wore over it. This 8,000-yard track was taking its toll on more than just scorecards. "It's your show, boss," he said, and stepped away.

I'd been around long enough to know tournaments can't be won—and only lost—on Thursdays. However, I was eight shots back already and believed the cut this week would be well over par. Time to gamble. I addressed the ball, exhaled slowly, and brought the TaylorMade rescue club back smoothly. Then my weight transitioned to the front and I drove down and through impact with my left arm and legs. The clubface stayed on plane long after impact, before my right wrist turned over. I finished and held the follow-through. The ball landed fifteen feet from the flagstick. Not great, but a birdie chance nonetheless.

I watched Meyers hit a four-iron to the back-left portion. He'd have to putt across the entire surface, a sixty-footer. "That guy has forearms like Popeye," Silver said. Meyers hadn't spoken to me since our Liz Scott chat.

At the green, I stood on the fringe beside Silver and watched Meyers's ball track to within four feet of the hole. He marked the ball and cleared.

"Eight inches, left to right," Silver said. "It'll be fast. You're putting with the grain."

I placed the pocked face of my old Bull's Eye putter behind the ball (only Steve Jones and I used the Bull's Eye anymore) and pulled the trigger. The Titleist caught the right side and did a three-sixty before falling for a seventy-four.

. . .

Twenty minutes later, I came out of the shower and saw Paul Meyers, still dressed in his golf attire, sitting before his locker, ten paces away. He was hunched, forearms on thighs, when a locker-room attendant brought a shoebox-size package to him.

The locker room was busy at 3:25 P.M. On the television in the corner, Lisa's face dominated the screen and was quickly replaced by J. P. Hayes hitting an iron shot. The locker-room air was a mixture of steam, cologne, and Ben Gay.

"This came, Fed Ex, sir," the attendant said.

Meyers looked at the address and shook his head. "Jesus Christ," he said, ripping the package away from the attendant, stuffing it into a gym bag in his locker. Then he looked side to side, saw no one, and sighed. When he looked over his shoulder, we made eye contact. "What are you looking at?" he said.

Padre had been on his way to the showers. Apparently, he sensed the moment because he paused. I wore only a towel, but had just butchered the back nine in spectacular fashion—and the course should've played to my strengths. I'd visited Liz Scott in an attempt to help my best friend, who could no longer play catch with his six-year-old son and whose wife called me, worried sick about him. Moreover, the Liz Scott visit had cost me one longtime friendship and led Meyers to tell me to buzz off, mid-round, a distraction I hadn't needed. Now he was in my face again.

I walked over. "You say something?"

"I said, 'What are you looking at?' Mind your own business, Jack." He stood up.

"I don't like people telling me what to do," I said. "You've done it twice now in one day."

"That so?" He put a hand on my chest and shoved.

I swayed back, not far enough to take a step, then forward—and hit him with a straight right. The forward momentum added a lot to a punch that traveled only a foot. He went down in a heap.

This time the roles were reversed: It was Padre who grabbed me by the arm and led me away.

The meeting took place that night at 7 P.M. and was held in the casual setting of a hotel room one floor below mine. At least PGA Tour Commissioner Peter Barrett hadn't made me travel.

"Jack," he said, "once again, the reports I'm getting on you are not good."

We sat across from one another at a round table in the corner of the hotel room. Nothing about the room gave me the impression that Barrett was staying there. The beds were made. There was no suitcase, no attaché kit. A circular light hung above the round table.

Barrett looked down at his yellow legal pad and tapped his palm with a narrow silver pen. Then he sighed the way my elementary school principal had many years before.

"Have you ever considered playing the European Tour?" he said, for the second time in as many years. "I mean, really, Jack. A locker-room brawl?"

"I defended myself."

"A Martin Levine, a Chicago-based attorney, called me today. He says you harassed his client."

"Who's his client?"

"Elizabeth Scott, Jack. A recent widow, for God's sake."

"There are two sides to every story."

Barrett held up a hand, shaking his head back and forth. "I'm tired of it, Jack. I don't get calls from attorneys about other players."

"I do my best to promote the game, Mr. Barrett. A lot of guys don't do that."

"Oh, I know you *can* have a very positive impact. You give

balls away during practice rounds. You chat with fans. It's the sideshow I'm sick of. And it's the sideshow that I'm weighing against the good you do."

I sat shaking my head. There was very little to say. I'd been on Barrett's hot seat before. His job was to grow the Tour and promote the game and he was as single-minded in his pursuits as I was in mine.

"Do you know who called me tonight," he went on, "after Mrs. Scott's attorney? Mitch Singleton from *USA Today.* He said he heard you were involved in a locker-room scuffle."

I stopped shaking my head and stared at him. As if by reflex, I said, "Who told him that?" I knew Barrett probably didn't know, but the fact that a reporter had the story bothered me. What goes on in the locker room stays there, a code among athletes. Someone broke the code, hanging me out to dry.

"I don't know how he knew," Barrett said, "but I did some research. I'll meet with the other parties involved as well. You're fine will represent the frequency of your involvement in situations like this over the last few years, Jack."

I waited. I'd put on fresh khaki pants, a blue button-down shirt, and a blue blazer. It paled compared to Barrett's outfit—he looked like he'd just left an investors' meeting on Wall Street. He always looked like that, like a guy you'd trust with your money. He'd been wildly successful in his efforts, landing huge television contracts and noteworthy corporate sponsorships. His success, no doubt, had loads to do with Tiger Woods's impact on the game's popularity, but Barrett possessed the foresight to parlay that into revenue.

"You're fined a hundred thousand dollars, Jack."

I leaned back in my chair and looked at him. "That's a great deal of money, Commissioner."

"We've gone through this before. Trouble seems to follow you and, frankly, Jack, I'm tired of it. I think the amount is justified."

"A hundred thousand dollars for a locker-room disagreement?"

Barrett sighed and shook his head sadly. "*USA Today* is running an article on the front page of the sports section about the fight, Jack. It's time for you to start realizing that all the good you might *think* you do the game is quickly eliminated by a single episode like this. In short, Jack, I keep asking myself why I have these problems with only one player."

I sat looking at him.

"Can you answer that for me?"

"I went to Liz Scott on behalf of a friend."

"A friend? Would you care to elaborate?"

"No, sir."

"Pardon the expression, but that's par for your course, Jack. You're free to go."

There was nothing more to say. Perkins had told me Barrett received offers from other investigators. It was clear that Perkins hadn't told Barrett I was helping him and had gone to Liz Scott on his behalf. Perkins's secrecy underscored his need for help and brought Linda Perkins's call back to me. I stood and walked out, not about to mention Perkins's name.

. . .

That night, I didn't sleep well. At 2:15, I woke and sat before the window, thinking. The fine was enormous. My father was a carpenter, my mother a substitute teacher—$100,000 was more than they'd earn, combined, in two years. I'd been fined before, but this represented more than a punishment. It was a message from Barrett, one that came through loud and clear: Either keep your nose clean or play somewhere else. And the message clashed with my best friend's request for help.

I opened Philip Levine's collection, *New Selected Poems,* and began to read "The Miracle":

A man staring into the fire
sees his dead brother sleeping.

The falling flames go yellow and red
but it is him, unmistakable.

He goes to the phone and calls
his mother. Howard is asleep,

he tells her. Yes, she says,
Howard is asleep. She does not cry.

I didn't finish the poem. Instead, I closed the book. Perkins and I had known each other for as long as I could remember. The time had come to return the favor and I wouldn't let him down. Barrett wouldn't understand that. I didn't expect him to. He wasn't concerned with friendships. However, there was more to life than acquiring the next big television contract.

I thought of Linda Perkins's phone call. Perkins hadn't gone home, nor did he want his family to visit. He was rehabbing twice a day. For whatever reason, he couldn't face his family in this condition. That thought frightened me because aside from full use of his left leg, I knew he'd lost something else. He was more than brawn and balls. I only hoped he knew it.

Weary, I climbed back into bed and shut my eyes.

Then the phone rang. I scurried from the suite's bedroom to answer on the second ring.

"Jack Austin?"

It was a woman's voice, and there was a trace of an accent, which I couldn't place. But I could place the fear I heard.

"Yes," I said. "Who is this?"

"You were right going to Liz Scott, no matter what she say. Her husband's death was no accident."

"He was murdered," I said. I sat in the dark in the main room of the suite. My watch read 2:45.

"But it was no accident," she said.

Then the line went dead. I stared at the phone in my hand. Ron Scott's murder had never been called accidental. What had the woman on the phone meant?

18

"Daddy, we gonna have hang-ga-burgers for breakfast?" Darcy said the next morning.

Lisa had already left for the course and my tee time was 1:20 P.M., so Friday morning I was spending time with Darcy, who, apparently, had food on her mind, which was unquestionably an inherited trait.

"Hamburgers for breakfast?" I said.

She smiled and nodded vigorously. "Mmmm."

Darcy wore purple Disney Princess pajamas, which my mother had sent more than a year ago. She wore them three out of every four nights and they looked like it—faded and frayed. Once they had fit. Now the pants fit like capris, but she loved them. I was still in boxer shorts, the complimentary newspaper spread before me on the coffee table. It was *USA Today* and Mitch Singleton had several articles—one recapping the tournament, the second updating the Ron Scott murder investigation. There was nothing new. The article about the locker-room fight was there, front and center. I didn't bother to read it.

In the sports briefs, I saw Hal McCarthy's name and scanned the three paragraphs. Hurricane had been pulled over for speeding, had disputed the ticket, then, according to the article, "assaulted one officer and was quickly restrained." Now he faced aggravated-assault charges. I wondered what that was about. When I'd played with him, he hadn't the energy to assault anyone. At lunch, though, he'd threatened me and seemed frazzled and frustrated. Maybe he'd tried to take it out on a cop. I wasn't sure what was going on with him. Whatever it was, he didn't want me talking to Liz Scott.

When I'd gotten back in bed the night before, Lisa asked about the phone call. I'd told her about it. To my surprise, her reaction was similar to my own—a long, tiresome sigh. After all, she knew no more than I did. And the events seemed to continually mount: Ron Scott had been murdered; Hurricane McCarthy had threatened me if I didn't leave it alone (apparently, he used the same approach for traffic tickets); Paul Meyers had said likewise; and now a woman called in the middle of the night to tell me the murder hadn't been accidental. What the hell had she meant? No one thought the murder was an accident. To top it off, I was waiting for new credit cards because my wallet had been stolen when I was sucker-punched in a posh resort hotel.

"Waffles?" It was Darcy bringing me back to the present.

She stood before me, thumb firmly in her mouth, clutching one of Lisa's slips, which had once been white but was now faded and grayish, having been dragged—like Linus's blanket—city to city and washed repeatedly.

"You know, those PJs are too small, sweetie. We need to get new ones."

"Noooo."

When dealing with a three-year-old, you pick your fights. It was quarter after seven in the morning. "Are you hungry?" was all I said.

She only nodded, unwilling to remove the thumb to speak.

"After bath time," I said, coyly, "we'll have waffles."

The dreaded "B" word was cause for removal of the sacred thumb. (Unlike me, she found a battle worth fighting at this hour.) "No bath for Darr-ie."

"Talking about yourself in the third person makes you sound like Deon Sanders," I said.

She looked at me, puzzled. The distraction worked. I picked her up and we were in the bathroom before she realized it.

.   .   .

"As opposed to an accidental murder?" Perkins said, after I finished telling him about the phone call. "Is that an oxymoron?"

"I don't know what the hell she meant," I said, and strained to lift 135 pounds on the military bench.

We were at a local gym at 9:25 A.M. Many Tour players will do only light workouts before playing; some only stretch. But lifting weights before a round never bothered me. I lift weights five or six days a week and have since college. I'd read the articles and heard all the theories: Your putting stroke and short-game touch will go if you get too big; your back-swing will become restricted. Those theorists point to one-time PGA Tour star Keith Clearwater who, before the fitness craze, took up weightlifting. According to the armchair experts, it ruined his game. I'm by no means muscle-bound at six-feet-one, 215 pounds. Besides, similar theories once existed throughout Major League Baseball. Not only were those baseball theories disproven, the sport is the poster child for physical *excess*. For me, weight lifting had always been simple physics—the more clubhead speed you generate, the farther the golf ball will travel; and the stronger you are, the less trouble thick rough will give you.

"She asked for you, by name?" Perkins said. He was sitting on the military bench, left leg splayed before him. It looked thin and nearly lifeless. He had bags under his clear blue eyes as if he'd been the one kept awake. "How would she get your cell-phone number?"

I shook my head. "Called the hotel room."

The gym was chrome and mirrors with maroon carpet featuring the establishment's logo, a gold dumbbell. The place was the size of three basketball courts and didn't smell of sweat. A day-pass cost fifteen bucks, so I was sure the clientele wouldn't tolerate stench when it arrived at five, driving sports cars and wearing suits and pantyhose.

Perkins was about to push the bar up to begin but paused and stared at me. "How'd she know where you were staying? Who knows that?"

"No one. But anybody can call the hotel, ask to be put through to my room. Asking for Jack Austin isn't like asking for Tiger Woods." I quickly flashed back to my comment to Darcy about her speaking in the third person. "The desk clerk would say, 'He's not registered here.' So she could've called around until she guessed right. The tournament's being played at a resort, after all. Not a stretch to think the players are staying there."

Across the room, Billy Carvelli was doing dead lifts, a dangerous back exercise if not done under complete control. He was there with a guy in a blue silk sweat suit, who had to be a trainer, and his father, who held a clipboard. After young Carvelli did a set, his old man wrote something down. Then his father turned to the trainer and spoke, his demeanor stern. The trainer in turn said something to Billy. They added maybe thirty pounds to the bar, and the kid strained to lift the weight off the floor, leaning back until it was at his waist, then let go. The bar crashed down, bouncing off the floor.

Perkins saw what I was watching. "Kid could blow a disk," he said.

"The father's a piece of work."

Perkins went on with his shoulder workout, exhaling slowly, pushing the bar over his head, then letting it down slowly. When it was behind his head, at shoulder level, he pushed it up again. He was working out with 185 pounds. Near us, two teenage boys paused to watch—185 on the military press was, after all, quite a sight.

"But she," Perkins strained to finish a rep and held the bar above his head, "asked for you, by name."

I knew where he was going and thought that over. The woman on the phone knew I was getting pressure to let the Ron Scott murder go. How? Did she know I'd been to Chicago? Did she know of Hurricane's threat? Of Paul Meyers's warning?

"How could she know?" Perkins said, and stood up gingerly when he finished his set.

I shook my head, took fifty pounds off the bar, and sat down at the bench. Fighting with 135 pounds on the military press was easier than contemplating it all.

．　．　．

When we met on the ninth tee, Friday afternoon, Paul Meyers looked as splendid as the day—except for the red welt the size of a silver dollar on his cheek. I hadn't grown fond of my own raspberry, Three-putt, and wasn't upset to find it shrinking and now hardly noticeable. Ever vain, Meyers wore a large Band-

Aid on his cheek to cover as much of his mark as possible. The Band-Aid didn't mask much. Unfortunately, the blemish didn't go very well with his look—short blond mane, glistening with gel in the sunlight, a stylish short-brimmed Mizuno visor, a sporty pale-blue mock turtleneck, and khaki pants. I knew he drove a Porsche. Poor fellow. Stepping out of a Porsche with a bruised face just kills the effect.

Some pairings help your game. You play with someone who forces you to step it up a notch or a friend you're comfortable with and you excel. This pairing fit neither scenario. After our scuffle, Paul Meyers and I had little to talk about. I was nearing my fortieth birthday and knew I was too old to be getting into fistfights. But no one shoves me. By now, thanks to *USA Today*, the media knew of the locker-room fight and, like the week before, a group of reporters lined the first tee. The gallery was large. The QUIET PLEASE sign wasn't up yet because we were waiting for the group in front of us to clear. I approached Meyers, extended my hand, and went through the pre-round custom. "Good luck," I said. He shook and said the same.

I went back to the other side of the tee box and Tim Silver. We were starting on No. 9 because the PGA Tour often uses "split tees," where a pairing begins on the first hole Thursday and the ninth Friday or vice versa. Following the cut—when the field is trimmed from 156 players (144 before daylight savings) to roughly the top seventy and ties—everyone begins on No. 1. The ninth hole at the Montville CC was designed, it seemed, to punish anyone who dared shoot a low score on the front—615 yards, a par five. This day, it was playing into a breeze. A pond ran the entire left side of the hole. Two large fairway bunkers were positioned on the right side of the fairway at 250 yards and 280, respectively.

"Anyone reach it in two today?" I said to CBS on-course commentator Dan Ferrin.

"Oh, ten, twelve guys," he said, grinning.

"Thanks," I said.

"Always good to begin the round feeling inferior," Ferrin said, his Irish brogue thick. He'd played the Tour for years and my relationship with him was still more player-player than player-reporter. "Actually Daly reached it. So did Woods. Welcome to golf in the twenty-first century, Jack."

"I liked the century we were in a decade ago," I said.

"When you led the Tour in driving distance?" His smile widened.

"Exactly."

I pulled the TaylorMade r7 driver from my bag and swung it back and forth slowly to stay loose. My warm-up routine never wavered. Forty-five minutes before the round, on the range, I started with a wedge, worked through my irons to my driver, and finished with whatever club I'd hit my opening tee shot with. Then I moved to the practice green and concluded by making a three-footer—head down, listening for the Surlyn cover of the ball rattling the plastic cup.

"You were killing the driver on the range," Silver said. "Hit it just like that."

I nodded. The group in front of us had cleared. A day and a half into the tournament, the bombers were separating themselves from the field. The projected cut was six over par, which was atypical. A difficult course might produce a cut line as high as +2. I'd shot an opening-round seventy-four so, at two over, I needed to get going. My length would allow me to compete on this course. But *knowing it* and *doing it* are two different things.

At least my first swing was solid. The Titleist carried the right-side bunkers and bounded into the center of the fairway. Meyers's ball carried the bunker and then some. It reached my ball on the second hop and rolled twenty yards beyond.

"Holy shit," Silver said.

"Yeah," I said. Paul Meyers hit the ball farther than any 165-pound guy I'd ever seen.

Ferrin noticed it, too. "Paul Meyers," he was saying, as our group moved off the tee, "has jumped from number one-hundred-and-ten in driving distance last year to seventeenth this year. And, from the looks of things, he'll keep rising, folks. A three-hundred-and-fifteen-yard blast here at number nine."

Silver and I walked down the fairway apart from Meyers and Pete Sandstrom. I hadn't told Silver about the threats or my trip to Chicago. Partially, because I wanted to focus on golf, but part of it, too, was that I was acting on behalf of Perkins. And Perkins had never needed help before, let alone asked for it. Out of respect, I was reluctant to talk of Perkins's physical decline and whatever internal conflict it had led to.

"How far to the front edge?" I said, when Silver and I paused at my ball.

"I told you that you could compete here," Sandstrom said to Meyers. They were ten paces away and he spoke in a hushed tone so as not to disturb me. "You maximize your potential and you reap the rewards."

Meyers nodded like an attentive student.

"Two eighty-five," Silver said. His preparation was meticulous.

I drew the three-wood.

"Hitting the three off the deck," Silver said, and motioned to the fairway as opposed to a tee, "seems a little tough. You don't want to lay up? That pond runs all the way to the green."

I shook my head. An electronic leaderboard near us showed Woods at −7 and Mickelson at −6. I was nine shots back. It was only Friday. I went through my pre-shot routine—two practice swings to get a slow, smooth rhythm; then I aligned the shot from behind the ball and finally addressed the Titleist Pro V1. I took a deep breath, the clubhead hovering an inch off the fairway, and tried to clear my head.

This round with Meyers wasn't going to be a chatty affair, but I pushed that aside. I hadn't come here to fight. I hadn't come to miss the cut, either. The sun felt warm on my back, as I took the three-wood away and paused at the top. Autonomy is a word often used loosely. However, it's a state rarely achieved. In fact, few things in life provide even a sense of it. Yet golf requires it. And in the world of professional sports, autonomy is displayed nowhere like it is on the PGA Tour. There's no instant replay to overturn a bad call. No base on balls. No teammate setting picks for you. You're on your own. The PGA Tour is golf's most visible and grandest stage. Every day you play either hero or goat—you either have it or you don't. This day, I had it.

The ball carried onto the front edge and scooted to the back, rolling just onto the fringe.

"That's my player," Silver said, and held up his hand for a high-five. "Perfect. It's a straight putt from there. Fifteen feet away, a great leave."

Meyers played next, hitting a five-wood to twenty feet.

"Jack."

I was walking to the ninth green and paused.

It was Meyers. "I want to apologize for my actions in the locker room."

I stopped short. Silver sensed the moment and moved away; Sandstrom went with him.

"I can see you weren't expecting me to apologize. We've never been close, Jack, so you don't really know me. But Ron Scott was a dear friend and I'm committed to his family. I was just looking out for Liz."

"That's why you shoved me?"

"You upset me."

"That cost me a hundred grand. *That* upsets me."

"That was your fine?" He shrugged. "Mine was only five thousand. I guess you've been in these situations before," he said, and smiled.

Cute—a cute smile to punctuate a cute response. Everything about Paul Meyers was cute—the Porsche, the clothes, the bullshit apology. Everything except the lump on his mug where I slugged him.

It wasn't worth my time. I turned and walked to the green, where Silver was reading the putt. This was the first hole of the day and the difficulty was only judging the speed. The ball would travel the first five feet through the fringe before speeding up once it reached the putting surface. Thousands of spectators surrounded the green. My attempt would be the day's first eagle putt at this hole. I felt the anticipation. Ferrin stood beside the green, microphone in hand, whispering.

Silver crouched behind the ball, cupped his hands over his eyes, and looked through the tunnel, examining the line. "Dead straight," he said.

I nodded, reading it the same way. I was going for the back of the cup. Gently, I placed the old Bull's Eye behind the ball, aligned my shoulders with the target, and made a solid stroke.

105

The ball traveled through the rough, onto the green, and followed the line Silver and I had seen, directly into the hole. The gallery went wild. My fist-pump punctuated the reverberating noise.

Across the green, Paul Meyers looked away and spat.

. . .

I was two under by the time we reached the fifteenth fairway. The sun was bright overhead. No. 15 was a par four, 465 yards. I'd bombed my tee shot and had only a nine-iron to the green. Meyers had already played his approach shot, dumping an eight-iron into a greenside trap.

"Jack," Meyers said, "I want you to realize something about me."

I'd been swinging my nine-iron back and forth, concentrating. It was the first time in more than a decade on Tour someone interrupted my pre-shot routine.

"He's getting ready to hit," Silver said.

Meyers nodded apologetically and moved away.

I began my routine again but in the back of my mind couldn't help wondering if Meyers deliberately forced my pause. I aligned the shot from behind the ball, took two practice swings, and addressed the ball, nine-iron waggling behind my Titleist. My take-away was slow and smooth. I uncoiled and came down, powering the clubface through the turf, the divot flying up and tumbling end over end, landing softly, twenty paces away. But I wasn't watching the sod. My focus was the ball, eyes darting from it to the flagstick. "Be as good as you look," I said.

It landed behind the pin and spun back, settling no more than six paces from the cup. Again, Silver offered a high-five.

"Jack," Meyers said, "great shot. Can we talk now?"

"Yeah. What is it?" We started toward the green. Silver and Sandstrom were in front of us.

"I want you to know I'm a decent human being." When I didn't respond, he went on. His head was down, but he was looking at me like a shy kid peering from beneath hooded eyes. "You must realize Liz Scott doesn't want anyone talking about her husband's death, Jack. You can see why, right?"

"No," I said. "Why?"

"Well, of course, it's a difficult situation, Jack. Would you want people talking about a dead spouse?"

"I'd want to know why my husband was killed."

"She knows why. He was mugged. They took his wallet. Obviously, they were after money."

"Maybe."

" 'Maybe'? What's that supposed to mean?"

"Ron Scott followed his killer into that alley. He knew whoever killed him."

"That's crazy talk, Jack. Ron wasn't stupid."

"Apparently, he was trusting."

Meyers stopped walking. I paused beside him. He squinted against the sun and looked to another fairway where Brad Faxon was playing with Skip Kendall. "Look, Jack, this is none of your business," he said. "So just let it go."

"I've got a better idea," I said. "Let's just finish the round and go our separate ways. But don't tell me what to do again or you'll think that first punch was a love tap."

I walked off, moving ahead of him to the green, where Silver said, "Going to tell me what's going on?"

"Later. Let's worry about birdies right now."

I met Perkins in the bar again Friday night at 9:15. He was drinking Jack Daniels and Coke when I arrived. I ordered a glass of water with a lemon wedge.

He smiled. "That's not too strong for you, is it?"

"It's late," I said, "big day tomorrow."

"You shot sixty-eight, so you won't play until the afternoon."

He was right. At −2, I was paired with Padre Tarbuck in the 1:50 slot, two groups before Woods (−8) and Mickelson (−7), who had separated themselves from the field. The bar was quiet. The hotel was part of a resort but the action must've been elsewhere. The guys who missed the cut had left. The others probably ordered room service and were in their hotel rooms watching ballgames. Most nights, that was my routine. But Linda Perkins had called me.

Perkins took a long pull off his Jack and Coke.

"How long you been here?" I said.

He shrugged, his eyes a little glassy.

"That your first?" I motioned to the drink.

"What are you, my mother?"

"Just curious."

"My third."

"Fourth," the bartender said. He'd been sitting behind the bar on a stool several feet away reading the newspaper classifieds. He was a short squat guy with a full head of white hair and big Fu Manchu. When Perkins shot him a look, the guy just shrugged. He stood and moved casually to the far end of the bar and struck up a conversation with a guy in a dark suit who sat alone.

"Why don't you go home," I said, "and relax for a while?"

Perkins took another drink and looked at me over his glass. "Not bedtime. You can only watch so much TV."

"I mean your real home, New Hampshire."

He set his glass down and exhaled as if a conversation he'd long anticipated was finally here.

"I went home a while ago," he said, his voice as flat as a guy reading a weather report. "Didn't go so well. Jackie doesn't understand. Not his fault, can't expect him to, I guess." He wasn't looking at me; he sat staring at the dark glass on the bar between his hands. His words had a rehearsed quality as if he'd had this discussion with himself many times. "Jackie wants to do the things we always did—shoot baskets, play catch, camp in the woods behind the house. Ever try assembling a tent on one leg?" He looked at me, his face deadpan. When I made no reply, he went on. "I fell, Jack, right on my goddamned ass, right in front of Jackie. The kid was *embarrassed* for his dad. *Embarrassed* for me, tried to help me up, tried to put the tent up *for me.* This," he said, still looking at me but motioning to himself, "isn't the dad he knows." His eyes left mine again and he blew out a long breath and said quietly, "It's not the same one I know, either."

"You are the same man," I said.

He didn't look at me. "Remember my father?" he said.

"Of course," I said. We'd grown up next-door neighbors.

"You never saw him the year he died, Jack."

It was an odd statement. I waited but he offered nothing more. Perkins's father had been diagnosed with stomach cancer during the fall of our freshman year at UMaine. He was dead four months later. I hadn't visited him. Perkins hadn't allowed it. Yet he had gone home each week to spend time with his father.

"How're things with Linda?" I said.

He put the glass to his lips and drank, not swallowing but holding the alcohol in his mouth as he thought. Finally, he swallowed, shrugged, and said, "In bed, I'm like an overturned turtle. She's a saint for putting up with me."

"She loves you," I said.

He nodded. "A saint."

Part of me wanted to urge him to talk to a professional. The other part of me knew him too well to suggest that. He'd opened up to me; that was as far as he'd go. That much I knew. What I didn't know was what to do with what he was telling me.

"You're still the same man," was all I said. "You may have a bum leg right now, but it'll heal. Don't strain family relationships. They may not."

He looked at me, nodded, and hunched. "I know. I know that, but . . . "

I waited. He didn't continue. I drank some ice water.

"There's more to it," he said. "The PGA Tour doesn't pay me to sit home and feel sorry for myself, Jack."

I almost said, *So don't.* But I knew this was more complex than it seemed. This was about a man whose life, professionally and privately, had been built on physicality.

"I'm a security consultant," he said. "I might be pretty useless right now, but that's what I do."

"Your instincts are still there," I said. "In fact, Paul Meyers told me again today to back off Liz Scott. You hit a home run with the Chicago trip. We stirred things up." I smiled. "We just don't know what the hell we stirred."

"*I* should have gone." He took a long pull from the dark glass and looked away. "But I couldn't."

I wondered if he'd meant *wouldn't* or *couldn't* but said nothing. I drank some water.

"Go home, buddy," I said. "Linda and Jackie are what matter. Not work."

"I'll go, when I'm ready," he said and stood. With the crutches, he limped out.

. . .

Apparently, she had a habit of calling at 3 A.M.

This time she woke Lisa and this time her voice wasn't sweet. "Is this Jack Austin?"

"Hello, again," I said.

My recognition gave her pause. "You don't know me," she insisted.

"You called last night."

"But you do not know me."

"Okay."

"You play well today."

My turn to pause—had she watched on TV? Followed on the Internet? Was she here? I tried to place the accent again. Spanish? Lisa was sitting beside me on the sofa, wiping sleep from her eyes. She wore a long gray New England Patriots Super Bowl Champions T-shirt as a nightgown.

"Did you see me play?"

Lisa tilted her head, trying to gauge the conversation.

"You were right to see Liz Scott."

I didn't speak. She said that the previous night. What did she want?

"Liz know everything. She has the answers," she said, then hung up.

I set the receiver in the cradle.

"Was it the same woman?" Lisa said.

"Yeah."

Outside, the pre-dawn sky was black. Stars blinked like rolling whitecaps. Streetlights lit the parking lot and, in the distance, I saw the lights of Los Angeles—those shining bright lights. Jack Austin and movie stars. Mainer goes to Hollywood. This time, the woman with the accent said Liz Scott knew the answers.

To which questions?

The night before, the caller said Ron Scott's death was no accident. Now she said the guy's wife knew all about it. That made her crying to Paul Meyers and Hurricane McCarthy about my visit very curious. But there was something else going on. The caller obviously knew a hell of a lot more than she was saying. She was one of a select few who knew I went to see Liz Scott. Only Perkins, a Chicago cop Perkins trusted named Billy Peters, Liz herself, Hurricane, and Meyers knew I'd gone to see Liz Scott. To have that knowledge, my caller had to be associated with one of them.

"Jack," Lisa said, "what are you thinking?"

I told her.

"She could be a friend of a friend," Lisa said. "Maybe one of the five has a big mouth."

"Thanks for shooting holes in my theory," I said, "but you're right. This is getting more complicated by the minute."

.   .   .

By Saturday afternoon, 8,000 yards simply proved too much for the majority of the field. The leaderboard looked like someone clipped the Tour's driving distance leaders from the morning paper and pasted it in place. Woods (–8) was followed by Mickelson (–7), Hank Kuehne (–6), and John Daly (–5). I was in the top ten, at two under par. The exception was Paul Meyers (–5), who, as Dan Ferrin noted, was previously ranked 110th in driving distance but now was seventeenth. Lisa said she was interested in a how-to piece revolving around the noteworthy change in his game.

The California sun burned bright overhead. The galleries were huge and there was no breeze, but my playing partner, Padre Tarbuck, was having very little fun. This week, apparently, he'd played better than he'd predicted, but hitting four-iron approach shots to par fours finally caught up with him. He lost his rhythm this day, as he had during our practice round. He was five over after eight holes.

"The golf gods turned on me," he said, as we stood on the ninth tee, "and this course only gets tougher." He motioned toward the 615-yard par five.

I didn't say anything. I'd played the first seven holes even par before finally birdying No. 8. I was focused and positive. I made a long, rhythmic swing with my TaylorMade r7. The ball carried the right-side fairway bunker 280 yards away and bounded into the center of the fairway.

"Nice ball," Padre said. "One look at the leaderboard tells you the Tour got what it wanted this week."

I'd heard that before.

"Look at all the big names at the top," he said. "If you can't bomb it, don't come." He hit his drive into the pond that ran the entire left side of the hole.

We'd discussed it during our practice round. Likewise, Richie Barter had called it "gorilla golf" and predicted the winner wouldn't hit even 50 percent of the fairways. Yet the statistics, so far, proved otherwise: Of the names on the first page of the leaderboard, only Daly hit fewer than half. This era had been called golf's "Golden Age" for good reason. The players were better trained and better equipped than ever. And many put in Ben Hogan's legendary hours on the range. Maybe that work ethic was the result of a good old-fashioned competitive spirit. Maybe it was the $5 million purses. Regardless, the stars of the PGA Tour were more than long-drive chumps. For nearly fifteen years, I'd had up-close-and-personal knowledge of that. I still believed I could beat anyone on a given day, but I knew the difference between Woods, Els, and Mickelson and me, day in and day out, was their respective "total" games. No one could tell me those players were just bombers. I thought again of Richie Barter and his parking-lot rant. He'd said some Tour players used performance-enhancing substances, probably beta-blockers, to putt better. The guys at the top of the game were there because God blessed them with ability the rest of us didn't have—and because they busted their asses to develop it. Even Richie must know that.

In the ninth fairway, after Padre hit his fourth shot to the 100-yard marker, Silver and I were considering our options from nearly 300, when I heard someone call to Padre, "Will you comment on the Hal McCarthy situation?!"

I turned to Silver. "Damn reporters. They know we're off limits out here."

"Never seen one do that during a round," Silver said.

Padre ignored the guy. The reporter turned and walked away. I'd never seen the guy before. He was young with neatly trimmed black hair and a liver-colored mole on one cheek and, wearing a navy-blue business suit, looked like this was his first golf event. Married to one of golf's most well-known journalists, I knew most media members. His mid-round question was distracting but he seemed nice enough, pausing to talk to spectators and bending to smile and even make a little girl laugh.

"What's he talking about?" Silver said to me.

"Hurricane was charged with assault," I said. "The paper said he was pulled over and hit a cop."

"What the hell was he thinking?"

"I think he's frustrated on a bunch of levels and something just set him off."

"But that's crazy, Jack. He *punched* a cop?"

"That's what the paper said."

The previous day, this hole played into a slight breeze. This day, the air was still. That meant a quality swing would get me on the putting surface in two. It also meant the leaders would probably shoot low scores, which wouldn't help me catch them, so I pulled the three-wood. I was five strokes back and had made only one birdie. Time to take risks.

"Pin is in the front," Silver said. "Your ball rolled off the back yesterday. Can you hit a high cut?"

"I've got a three-wood out," I said. "Not a damned seven-iron."

"I'm just saying—"

I cursed the course, but I knew everyone was playing the same track. Put up or shut up. I took the three-wood back in a wide arc, shifting my weight, and held the follow-through. The ball didn't cut. It held its line, landed just short, one-hopped onto the green, and stopped twenty-five paces from the hole. I was putting for eagle. The gallery around the green went wild. Padre slapped me on the back. Silver handed me the putter and moved toward the green with added spring in his step.

Twenty-five feet on the ninth green wasn't like twenty-five feet at Augusta National. This green was primarily flat, meaning you only had to judge the pace—a design that gave credence to those claiming the course favored long hitters: Anyone who reached the green in two had a makeable eagle attempt. But putting had never carried my game. When my game went south, the flat stick was usually the smiling culprit.

"No bad thoughts," Silver said, as if reading my mind. "Straight in. Just bang it at the back of the hole."

If only it were that easy. I glanced to the leaderboard. Woods and Mickelson had made no move, remaining at −8 and −7, respectively. The only move was being made by Paul Meyers, who had crept to −6.

"Meyers hits it a hell of a lot farther than anyone gives him credit for," Silver said, looking at the leaderboard. "The guy kills it, especially for someone his size."

I only nodded, returning to the task at hand—twenty-five paces, dead straight. Don't over-read it. Make a good stroke and take whatever comes. All you can control is the stroke. I placed the scarred face of the Bull's Eye behind the ball, set my feet, looked one last time at the cup, and made a good stroke.

The ball caught the lip and spun harmlessly away.

I tapped in for birdie and went to the tenth tee at −4. I was making a move of my own.

.   .   .

On the sixteenth tee, I had it to five under and was on pace for a sixty-nine. Woods had moved to −10, but Mickelson had fallen off and was tied with me. It was Paul Meyers who had the day's best round going. He was −9, four under on the day.

The sixteenth is a long par five, 605 yards, a straight, uphill run. I'd already hit my tee shot safely into the fairway, more than 300 yards away. Padre was waggling his driver, a Cleveland Launcher, behind the ball. He backed off, visualized the shot, made two slow practice swings, then addressed the ball. He swung nearly out of his shoes and the ball settled in the right rough, which wouldn't have been too bad, but it stopped behind a tree. He slammed his driver back into the bag and started down the fairway.

Silver and I followed. To my right, a golf cart pulled parallel to us. Perkins looked over and pointed to a spot fifty yards ahead, away from the spectators. "A heads-up," he said, when we got clear of the fans. "Hal McCarthy has congestive heart failure, Jack. And he got it from taking something to relax him."

"What are you talking about? Beta-blockers?"

"Something different. Finish your round. But I'd avoid the press tent, if I were you," he said, and limped back to the cart and drove off.

"What is it now?" Silver said, as we walked toward my ball.

"Later," I said. I pulled the TaylorMade r7 driver out and handed Silver the head cover.

"Jack . . . " Silver said.

I waved him off. I knew what he'd say: Hitting driver off the deck was risky. A mis-hit could be disastrous, as we'd just witnessed with Padre's tee shot. My head was spinning. Hurricane had said he felt great in Scottsdale when he'd missed the cut and walked around the golf course with the energy level of a wounded fish. In Orlando, he told me his "ticker was fine." Congestive heart failure? Something like beta-blockers? When I'd asked if a new coach helped him with his putting stroke, Hurricane said no. When I'd asked if he'd used "the Ben Hogan method," he looked away. Now I knew why.

All of this would have been distracting enough, but I also hadn't slept a full night in days, thanks to my midnight caller. So course management be damned; I was going for the green with the driver.

I brought the club back slowly and made a wide shoulder turn but, as is my tendency when I over-swing, I came over the top, and the ball went right, an old-fashioned slice—although on Tour, we call it a "fade," just as we tap imaginary spike marks down every time we miss a putt. "Hold on . . . " Silver was calling to the ball. No use.

I was watching the ball rattle around a cluster of pines to our right when I remembered where I'd first heard of Hurricane's illness: Kip Capers.

How had he known?

he PGA Tour Policy Board meets three times each year, typically in March, June, and November. Since my recent appointment, the Board had met only one other time. That meeting had been of the introductory nature, laid back and routine. This meeting wasn't. At 7 P.M., we convened in a conference room somewhere behind the hotel's lobby. Tour Commissioner Peter Barrett had requested the meeting himself, and when I shook his hand at the door, I felt like I had at my initial Policy Board meeting—like Barrett was asking himself how the hell I'd been appointed.

I didn't much care. The respect of my colleagues meant more than the respect of Barrett. Besides, this night, none of it mattered. Something larger was at stake.

The conference room was plenty big for the Board, which was comprised of only four players, one PGA of America official, and four people deemed "public figures with a demonstrated interest in the game." At this meeting there was no coffee, no food. Notepads, pens, and a single photocopied newspaper article had been placed around a long table covered with a maroon linen tablecloth. I took my seat and read the article.

The *Orlando Sentinel* headline read, "Golfer Collapses Under Suspicious Circumstances." After his run-in with police, Hurricane McCarthy, according to the article, went home, complained of a headache, said he couldn't sleep lying down, and finally drifted off while sitting upright. Except it was far worse—Hurricane had congestive heart failure. Unable to wake him, wife Sherry "frantically called 911." In the ER, a Catapres-TTS patch was found beneath Hurricane's shirt. Catapres-TTS is a patch worn to release clonidine, an antihypertensive drug often used to ease narcotic withdrawals. Records indicated the patch had been prescribed and, upon consultation with Hurricane's doctor, the ER physician ordered extensive blood work. The prescribing doctor, a family practitioner named Todd Hollis, said he'd prescribed a mild dosage, much less than what blood tests discovered. Hurricane's health aside, the reported affects of clonidine were particularly disconcerting—clonidine worked by stimulating something in the brain that triggered the central nervous system to decrease one's heart rate and blood pressure.

I set the clipping down and thought of Richie Barter's comments. "This clonidine sounds a hell of a lot like a beta-blocker," I said.

To my right, Bob Daniels, a ten-time winner and former Ryder Cupper, nodded. "You can see why Richie Barter is throwing a fit about this article." Daniels had been on the Board for a year. He was all of five-nine, 175 pounds, but had a short game that drove you bonkers. I'd once played him for $300 on a Tuesday and watched him get up and down six times to save a sixty-eight. Few players were steadier.

"Sure," I said. "Richie looks like a genius today."

"A damned scary thought," Daniels said, under his breath.

Across from us, Barrett cleared his throat. His red silk tie had tiny sailboats on it. "There's much to consider regarding this article," he said, "so I felt it best that the Board meet."

Around the room, heads nodded.

"Richie Barter is demanding that everyone be tested," Daniels said.

"Can the Tour mandate tests on prescription drugs?" I said.

"Look at the putting stats from last season to this one," Daniels said. "Hurricane made a huge leap. That's evidence enough."

Barrett nodded slowly, clearly thinking. "There's a lot to consider here," he said again. "The integrity of the pro game is clearly one of them. However, the game's reputation is another. Beta-blockers are legal in the U.S. Only illegal substances are banned by the Tour. And Hal McCarthy is under doctor's orders to take clonidine. On top of all that, testing is always a touchy proposition."

Technically, Barrett wasn't a member of the Policy Board, although I was fairly certain he didn't care. Typically, the chairman of the Policy Board ran the meetings. But Barrett sat atop the PGA Tour hill and, like a king observing his wares, looked down to see all that was his. And this was a pressing matter.

"Because it was prescribed," I said, "we have to assume it's strictly for medical purposes?"

"Certainly," Barrett said. "The game is built on players governing themselves."

He had a point. I glanced down at the article again.

"What do we know about this doctor," Daniels said, lifting the article, "this Hollis guy who prescribed the stuff?"

"He is licensed and board certified," Barrett said. "No research has ever proven that beta-blockers, let alone clonidine, improves one's golf scores, gentlemen." He put his hands together in front of him, fingertips steepled. "I'm not naive, though. I know what's at stake. But we can't jump to conclusions."

"I played with Hurricane recently," I said. "I commented on his stroke—how much better it is. He couldn't look me in the eye. We need to update our testing policy."

Barrett cleared his throat again. If he'd brought us together to have us agree to calm the players, this wasn't going as planned.

"We should have a banned-substance list, sir," Daniels said.

"As I said, any illegal substance in banned," Barrett said, "and from a PR standpoint, testing is complex."

"'PR standpoint'?" I said.

Two people to my right, someone clicked a pen. I turned to see Chairman Paul Richardson, a honcho with an automotive manufacturer. Richardson was maybe sixty pounds overweight and wore a gray suit. His chin spilled over his shirt collar, and tiny beads of perspiration dotted his forehead.

"There's the good of the pro sport to consider, Jack," Richardson said. "What people *think* about the game."

I leaned forward. Richardson held my gaze. "What exactly are you saying?" I said.

"I'm saying that I see your concerns. You and Bob represent the players and want a level playing field, and rightfully so. But did you know that golf lost as many players as it gained last year?"

Richardson had launched and fostered a youth golf program in Detroit. I knew he cared for the game, but I had the feeling theory and practice were about to collide.

"People stop playing because it costs so much to play," I said. "There aren't many ten-dollar municipal courses being built. Everything's got to be a million-dollar design. Everything is big business."

"Which is an underlying issue here," Richardson said. "Golf is big business. For the game to grow, its reputation must be nurtured."

We sat looking at each other. I knew then precisely why this meeting had been called. However, business or not, Richie Barter, for all his pretension and whining, had been right—I was on the PGA Tour Policy Board; this was my watch.

"When people were worried about 'hot' drivers," Daniels said, "we made testing optional."

The silent Board members nodded in agreement. Daniels was speaking of the COR (coefficient of restitution) test for drivers, which determined the trampoline effect of a driver's clubface. The legal limit for a driver was .830. A few years back, some manufacturers pushed the limit. The PGA Tour had made optional testing, allowing players to continue to "govern themselves."

"With the COR test," Daniels went on, "some of the game's biggest stars were first in line for the optional testing."

"Again," Richardson said, "there's a lot to consider here. Imagine if a test came back positive. We've all seen what Major League Baseball went through."

Daniels was a steely-eyed redhead with a hooked nose. He looked penetratingly at Richardson. "Are you saying what I think you're saying?" he said.

"Gentleman," Barrett said, "the Tour, and the game for that matter, has a certain reputation. I understand your point but, before we panic, we need to know exactly what is going on. Is this for a medical situation? Is this simply one bad apple?"

"I think we need to create a firm list of banned substances," I said, "and to do that, players have to be tested so we have a starting point."

Barrett shook his head.

"Sir," I said, "we're here to defend the Tour's integrity."

"Testing could squash corporate opportunities," Richardson said. "We can't risk what we have because of one bad apple."

Corporate opportunities? I shook my head. "And you think testing might fuel the rumor mill and scare off potential sponsors?"

He nodded.

"Gentleman," Barrett said, "all of us are here because we want what's best for golf. We are all operating with that in mind. As I said, this is a touchy situation. A lot hangs in the balance."

"Sure," I said, looking at Richardson.

"Are you being sarcastic, Jack?"

"I'm just happy to be a part of the team."

Barrett studied my face, opened his mouth, but didn't speak. A well-turned sports cliché can do that. He shook his head almost imperceptibly and moved on, pointing to Richardson.

"I have outlined a procedure here," Richardson said, "that I think is best." He looked down at a typed sheet that lay before him. "The PGA Tour's Media Relations is sending out releases wishing McCarthy and his family the best and saying the Tour is looking into the matter."

"Define 'looking into the matter,'" Daniels said.

"We will continue to remain vigilant," Barrett said.

Testing was out. I exhaled loudly and leaned back in my chair. I sat quietly for the remaining ten minutes. When the meeting adjourned, Barrett stopped me at the door, "Got a second, Jack?"

I waited.

"McCarthy is a friend of yours, isn't he?" Barrett said, and looked at me, eyes narrowed, staring into mine.

"We've been out here together a long time," I said. "But we're not close anymore. Why do you ask?"

"Just curious, Jack, just curious," he said, and turned and walked out.

. . .

I never thought I'd find myself sitting across a booth from Richie Barter. But there I was, a half hour later. Perkins limped into the hotel restaurant on the metal crutches and sat beside me.

"I heard you got hurt," Richie said to him. "How long you going to be laid up?"

Perkins started to answer, but then closed his mouth. "What is this about?" he said to me.

The hotel restaurant was teeming with Saturday-night activity. At the bar, a couple young players sipped iced tea and talked to a female bartender with long blond hair. The iced tea represented changes I'd seen during my career—no longer a trip to the nineteenth hole following a round; now it was the Tour's fitness trailer for a post-round workout. At least the young guys were still chasing women.

"He called me," Richie said, and pointed at me. Then he turned toward me and said, "So you finally want to talk to me." He stirred some Equal into his iced tea and smiled to himself. "People think I don't know anything, but I called it right. I hear Hurricane damned near overdosed on beta-blockers."

Richie wasn't the brightest bulb in the cabinet. "That's not exactly what happened," I said.

"Where'd you hear that?" Perkins said.

"Huh?" Richie said.

"Tell us what you know, Richie," Perkins said. That was the old Perkins. He always heard more than you said. This time, he'd picked up on the insinuation. Crutches or not, he was still Perkins. I wished he knew it.

"You're with the PGA Tour?" Richie said.

Perkins nodded. "We're all ears."

"You work for Barrett?" Richie said, his eyes narrowing, trying to figure it all out. Figuring things out seemed difficult for him, which made me curious as to how and where he acquired his so-called knowledge of performance-enhancing drugs on the PGA Tour.

"I work directly for the PGA Tour Commissioner," Perkins said. He had a small notebook out and was drinking coffee.

"So where's Barrett?" Richie said.

"In a meeting," Perkins said.

A waitress, who acted perky despite her age, appeared. She asked if we'd like anything to eat. All of us declined. She refilled my coffee, which smelled strong, and left. I glanced at my watch. I didn't want to be up half the night.

"Richie, what do you know about beta-blockers?" I said. "You told me the game was going to hell on my watch. Tell me what you know."

"He's here on behalf on the PGA Tour," Richie said, and pointed to Perkins. "Who are you here on behalf of?"

It was a good question. I knew where the Policy Board stood—or where Richardson and Barrett wanted it to stand—but I played the card I'd used previously. "I'm on the Policy Board. This is being investigated."

Richie leaned back in the booth, folded his arms across his chest, and offered another self-satisfied smile. "I was proved right," he said.

"Sure," I said. "How did you know about it?"

Richie's smile faded.

"Richie," Perkins said, "you started this whole thing when you announced your theories in *USA Today*."

"Well, someone had to say it."

"How'd you know?" I said.

He shook his head.

"How much do you know?" Perkins said.

"Probably just about all of it. And my test was negative. This Hurricane thing proves it was just a rumor."

"How?"

"Because, they're out to get me."

"Who?" Perkins said.

Richie looked over Perkins's shoulder at the crowded restaurant and suddenly stood. "I can't be having this talk."

"Sit down," Perkins said.

Richie shook his head. "Can't. But ask Hurricane. He knows it all, too, and he's already ruined. So he might be willing to talk."

"I said *sit down*," Perkins said, his voice as forceful as ever.

"This could be dangerous," Richie said, and looked across the restaurant again. "I can't be having this talk." His eyes drifted to Perkins's crutches. "And you can't force me to stay."

He turned and walked out.

.   .   .

Being "in contention" is a generic term used to describe anyone close to the lead. When I stepped to the tee Sunday, I was ten strokes behind Woods, who was leading the Audi Open. Ten strokes, especially behind Woods, was an enormous deficit. Woods had come from ten strokes back to win but had never given up a ten-shot lead. Truth be told, I wasn't expecting him to this day. I was playing to move up, playing to increase my paycheck. I didn't like that. I didn't like competing and not believing I could win. But Woods was the best to ever play and I'd been around too long to lie to myself about my chances. On a given day, I could beat anyone, including Woods, but spotting him ten shots was simply too much.

Sunday afternoon, when I walked to the tee, the gallery was large. A few spectators yelled encouraging remarks that came over the cacophony like sneezes. But my name was clear and the tone was, too. I wished Barrett was there to hear the fans. Yet their support also sent a jagged-edged spear of guilt through my back. Hundreds of spectators were around this tee to watch golf played at its highest level, some of them even shouting my name.

And Hurricane McCarthy had taken a prescribed medication to calm him.

Why had it been prescribed? His doctor, a guy named Todd Hollis, surely wouldn't say. And why had Hurricane taken more than Hollis recommended? Patches were used to control a patient's intake. How had he overdosed? Worse than the unanswered questions was Hurricane's reaction when I'd asked how he developed his newfound and much-improved putting stroke. He'd turned away, unable to look me in the eye. Apparently, I wasn't the only one feeling guilty.

Someone set a golf bag down on the tee box, the clubheads jingling and clacking. I turned to see Paul Meyers and his caddy, Hurricane's caddy, Pete Sandstrom. I hadn't checked the Sunday pairings, only my starting time. Either Woods, at ten under par, had distanced himself from the field, or Meyers finished Saturday's round horribly to end near my −4 total. The scoring sign, held by an acne-faced teenager, answered my question. The sign read Meyers −5, Austin −4. I shook Meyers's hand and wished him luck.

"I put two balls out of bounds on eighteen yesterday," he said. Then, more to himself than to me: "Got to get used to my distance."

"Well, you're hitting it a ton," I said. It was a forced compliment and Meyers knew as much. He turned back to Sandstrom.

"Let's just worry about our score," Silver said, when I went over and pulled a club from the bag. "He's a jerk and this won't be fun, but let's play some good golf."

I nodded.

. . .

On the par-four eleventh, a 485-yard dogleg, I was −6, having made the turn in two under par. Meyers had reached a par five by hitting driver, then—to my astonishment—a four-iron. On this tee, his length was also an advantage. He hit a draw with a five-wood that carried 250 yards. By contrast, I hit three-wood. The longer the club, the harder it is to move to the ball, and like a hard-throwing pitcher whose curveball won't break, my "draw" didn't bend. The three-wood ran through the dogleg, stopping behind a tree.

"Chin up, boss," Silver said, as we walked to the misbehaving golf ball.

"It always is," I said.

"No, man. You're not used to playing catch-up off the tee. Meyers has you over-swinging. You're out of rhythm. Slow your swing down."

It had been subconscious, but Silver was right. If I don't see the clubface make contact with the ball, I know I'm swinging too hard. It sounds oversimplified, but it's a method I devel-

oped as a junior. And I've always used it to keep myself swinging only 85 percent of full throttle. I hadn't seen the clubface
sweep down and past the ball in several holes. Paul Meyers, all
165 pounds of him, had me swinging for the fences to keep up.
I considered my weight-lifting routine and figured it was time
to reevaluate my workout. I needed to get stronger.

I punched out from behind the tree and then stood in the fairway, 240 yards from the hole. I was still away.

"Five-wood," Silver said, and handed me the club. "Smooth
and slow, Jack. Just ease it up there."

I nodded and made three easy practice swings. *Play your
game. A shot at a time.* The leaderboard told me my –6 was currently in twelfth place. The gallery had thinned. I saw the young
reporter in the business suit. The day before, he'd asked about
Hurricane McCarthy, seemingly before the story broke. To my
left, I heard Sandstrom say, "Ignore him, Paul." I looked over.
Meyers and the reporter were staring at each other.

"What's going on?" I said.

"Nothing," Sandstrom said.

Meyers and I had been cordial, if cool, all day. Sandstrom's
tone indicated a steely dislike.

"Let's go, Jack," Silver said. "Two forty to the pin."

.   .   .

Sunday night, we arrived at the Portland International Jetport
and drove the half-hour home to Chandler, Maine. It was 2:35
A.M. and Lisa and Darcy went straight to bed. I sat behind the
desk in my office, unable to sleep. I had a lot of questions and
very few answers.

Beyond the blackened office window, a distant light bobbed
as a boat moved past our cove. Our two-story cedar-shake home
was built in 1928. In the late-night silence, I listened to the house
creak. We'd gotten the oceanfront house for a (relatively) decent
price, because it needed work. My father and I replaced all
twenty-two windows and upgraded the old linoleum flooring
to floating hardwood. My career enabled me to live in an area
of Maine where, growing up, I never imagined residing. I was
raised in central Maine, which was Chevy trucks and diner

coffee. Southern Maine was Land Rovers and Starbucks. Moreover, Chandler was oceanfront. This week, I'd finished tied for twelfth, earning $80,100—more money than I deserved, considering eleven players beat me. In fact, the money and lifestyle always made me uneasy. I got $2,000 just to show up each week; TaylorMade paid me to play their clubs and wear Adidas apparel. I worked hard and part of me felt I deserved every penny. But the other part considered the more than $300,000 I'd already earned this season and how my father worked nearly a decade to earn that much. Regardless of the fine, that was monopoly money. New clothes and one sun-splashed resort after another—while my father did carpentry jobs in crawlspaces and on rooftops and plowed driveways when it was thirty below.

Outside, the boat was long gone. I saw nothing beyond the black window. Dawn was two or more hours away.

Nothing felt right.

Perkins had said he was staying on tour, simply flying to the next stop instead of returning home. Said he needed to talk to Richie Barter again. I didn't believe that was why he was staying. Meanwhile, Hurricane McCarthy, my one-time friend, had fallen ill in Florida.

I opened my complimentary laptop, logged onto the Internet, and typed in "clonidine." Everything I found supported the *Orlando Sentinel* article. One on-line site listed "dry mouth, drowsiness, fatigue, lethargy" as adverse reactions and under "cardiovascular" listed "congestive heart failure." I thought of Hurricane drinking water by the gallon, trudging as if through knee-deep sand from one hole to the next. I doubted he knew the risks.

The yips are rarely a physical condition. Rather, they are a mental curse, one which all golfers fear. The yips will allow you to put a smooth stroke on the ball from twenty feet, but force a spasm when you go to tap in. Two- and three-footers suddenly become white-knuckle affairs. No study had conclusively proven beta-blockers made golfers putt better. However, the yips have ended many careers. Padre Tarbuck, for one, damn near retired the year before due to his long battle with the yips. Conversely, Hal "Hurricane" McCarthy, who'd earned his nickname ten times over, mysteriously—and seemingly overnight—had turned his putting stroke around.

Clonidine was approved by the FDA in 1974, the article said, and was used to treat hypertension—a description that would no doubt be attractive to the likes of Hurricane. However, it was the final line of the article that kept me awake for another hour: "Clonidine slows the heart rate and lowers blood pressure."

The next morning, I woke at 7:30 to lift weights. Paul Meyers's long tee shots had me motivated. Years before, I'd finished the basement myself, framing and sheet rocking the walls to make a workout room. In the far corner, I'd constructed a makeshift green, using plywood, two-by-fours set on their sides, and indoor-outdoor carpeting. I had six professional-sized golf bags full of old clubs and maybe thirty putters. Various manufacturers sent sets of irons. Some remained unopened in tall boxes leaning against walls. A television hung in one corner. The Golf Channel was recapping the previous day's tournament, which Woods had won; Meyers finished second, earning more than $550,000. That was a lot of money. I did military presses on the bench with 135 pounds. Between sets, I grabbed thirty-five-pound dumbbells off the floor and did quick "super sets."

I was still at it at 9:15, when Lisa carried a small brown package downstairs. "Came for you," she said, and handed it to me, then returned upstairs. The box was no bigger than two sleeves of golf balls and wrapped in what appeared to be the remnants of paper grocery sacks. The block letters had been written in felt-tipped marker. The package had been addressed to me, care of the PGA Tour Headquarters in Ponte Vedra Beach, Florida.

My wallet was inside.

None of my $80 had been taken. In fact, whoever had mugged me had even made a deposit. A handwritten note, in the same block lettering, read: *You can compete until you're 50. If you want to be able to, don't ask about Ron Scott.*

There was no return address.

. . .

After lunch, Darcy was taking a nap, Lisa was across the room reading a book called *The Ethics of Journalism*, and I was in my favorite living-room chair. I enjoyed returning to Maine, following a winter event. I could stoke the fire, sit back, relax, and watch it snow. Snow is easier to tolerate—maybe even enjoyable—when you know you'll soon escape it. This day, winter was still in mid-season form. Shortly after we'd flown in, a Nor'easter had kicked up and three inches were falling per hour.

I read the note again. Kip Capers mentioned Hurricane's heart condition before anyone else.

A log behind the fireplace screen cracked and sap sizzled and oozed out. You don't get that with a woodstove. You also don't get the old hand-crafted wood moldings around the 1928 fireplace with a woodstove. When we'd bought the house, my father had said it had "character." "Character," in this case, meant old and was a euphemism for "money pit." But today I was enjoying it, although somewhat distracted. John Mayer's CD *Heavier Things* played in the background.

Kip Capers had been so upset about his knowledge of Hurricane's heart problems that he'd gone to Orlando to see him. I'd never known the two of them to play even a practice round together. Hurricane was fiery and emotional; Kip was withdrawn and religious. Fire and rain. Hurricane was in his forties; Kip was mid-twenties. Yet, according to Kip, Hurricane had told wife Sherry to phone Kip—from the hospital, no less. None of it added up.

You can compete until you're 50. If you want to be able to, don't ask about Ron Scott. I folded the note and put it back in my wallet.

"That isn't the new wallet," Lisa said, looking up from her book.

I shook my head. "It's the one I lost. It came in the mail."

"The package?"

"Yeah. All eighty bucks still in it, and a note." I read it to her.

"Took your time telling me about this."

"This is your week off," I said. "Besides, Perkins is coming. I called him. He wants to get everything dusted for prints."

"What's the note mean? *You can compete until you're fifty.* They'll allow you to compete, if you stop asking about Ron Scott's death?"

"Maybe."

"What else could it mean?" She closed the book and set it on the coffee table. She had been sitting with her feet tucked beneath her. Now she sat up straight, forearms resting on her thighs. "Do you see something else?"

I did. And I told her.

.   .   .

"So by 'compete,'" Perkins said, "you think they mean *be competitive* on the Tour until age fifty."

"Maybe," I said.

We were sitting in my office. He was behind my desk with his feet up. He'd mixed himself a drink.

"Hairy landing," he said, and smiled. "Takes the edge off."

"Stuff's been in the liquor cabinet for two years," I said. "It would probably take the paint off your car."

He grinned. "Mother's milk."

I was on the leather sofa near the window. Perkins had been on two delayed flights. When he'd reached Logan Airport in Boston, instead of driving to New Hampshire and waiting out the storm, he'd fought through it, driving directly to my house, and arriving late at night. Again he'd avoided Linda and Jackie, this time risking life and limb to do so. I thought of him setting up the tent and falling in front of Jackie, who must have been wondering, in six-year-old terms, what had happened to his dad. I thought about how that made Perkins feel, what it had cost him.

"The letter sounds like part of the conversation I had with Hurricane," I said. "He told me he's just trying to hold on until the senior tour. Said I was lucky I could keep up with the young kids."

"You're really something, huh?" he said, and grinned.

"I told him I work my ass off to do it."

"Anyway," Perkins sipped some more whiskey, "Hal Mc-Carthy didn't take your wallet."

"I know. He was in Orlando when I got jumped."

"But the other guy who threatened you was there."

"Paul Meyers."

"Yeah," Perkins said, and set the short squat glass on the desk. Then he straightened my photos. He was neat, but not as neat as Silver. If Silver had been there, he'd have removed everything and dusted the damned desk.

I leaned back on the sofa and nodded. "Three people—three who we know about, anyway—don't want me talking to Liz Scott. One is Liz herself. The others are Hurricane and Paul Meyers. Only one was there."

"Correct. But the guy's only a hundred sixty-five pounds. Embarrassing to think he dropped you like a," he thought momentarily then broke into a grin, "three-inch putt."

"I didn't see it coming."

Perkins's grin widened.

"And the guy hits a golf ball like he's swinging a sledgehammer," I said.

"Well, I know where I'm off to tomorrow," Perkins said and finished his drink.

"Where?"

" 'Where?' To see Paul Meyers."

"You flew to the East Coast to have a fifteen-minute conversation?"

He shrugged, then looked at the blackened window. Outside, snow was blowing. Occasionally it would scrape like sandpaper against the glass.

"Wait a minute," I said. "We didn't decide anything here. You knew all this before you got here. When I read the note to you on the phone, you added everything up then and there."

He smiled modestly.

"You'll go to Meyers," I said, "but you wouldn't go to Billy Peters. Why?"

"I don't want to get into that tonight," he said.

"The bum leg doesn't have to define you."

He started to speak, then stopped. Finally, he shook his head and said, "You really don't know what you're talking about. Look around us, Jack—this house, your wife, your life. I know who and what I am."

"You're more than your leg," I said.

Neither of us spoke. The house was silent at 11:15. The only sound was the wind-blown snow occasionally scraping the office window.

"I know," he said, and looked at me, "but knowing that and acting on it are two different things." His voice was low, tired. "Can we just drop it?"

"You're only an hour from home," I said. "Give it another try."

"When I'm better. That's who I am to Linda and Jackie."

And Billy Peters. That was why he'd sent me to Chicago.

When he got up, the clanging of the metal crutches shattered the silence.

"Linda called me," I said.

He paused, waiting.

"She needs you," I said. "So does Jackie."

"She used to go to Foxboro to watch me when I played in the NFL, Jack. Now she helps me tie my shoes."

"She loves you."

"That's what hurts so much. You can't understand that," he said. "You got no fucking idea. She's got one kid already and I've got my pride. The best lesson my father ever gave me was when he was dying."

"What do you mean?" I said.

He never answered. When I woke the next morning, he was gone.

22

One time, I was asked why I still do it. The reporter wasn't a sports journalist and the question made it sound like I could afford to retire. But the question also revealed more about the guy who'd asked it than my answer said about me. That's why I was surprised Wednesday morning, as I stood on the first tee at the Omni Tucson National Golf Resort and Spa, when a fellow PGA Tour player asked the same question, albeit subtly.

Young Billy Carvelli was dressed in his bright attire again this day. Several teenage girls stood near the tee box. When he'd signed their programs, Silver said, under his breath, "Like playing golf with one of those boy bands," and moved to the back of the tee box.

"You going to play the Champions Tour, too?" Carvelli said.

"Why do you ask?"

"Just wondering. I mean . . . you've been out here, like, fifteen years . . . that's a long time."

I'd never thought about it like that. But Carvelli was seventeen; fifteen years represented damned near a lifetime to him. "I'm going to play as long as I can compete," I said, and grinned. "Thinking about retirement already?"

His old man had offered detailed instructions about how to begin the practice round, nodded to me, and stalked ahead. Now he stood near the first green. The PGA Tour Championship Course's orange and gold nines played 7,109 yards.

Carvelli looked toward the first green and his father. "No, I'd never consider quitting."

"How many events you play last year?" I said.

As Carvelli thought about it, he made a long rhythmic practice swing. His swing had drawn comparisons to Ernie Els's (a hell of a compliment), and the similarities were unmistakable. They began with tempo. I often swung a pool towel like a golf club to work on my temp, trying to keep the towel long and uncoiled. Carvelli's swing, which I knew to be well over 115 miles per hour, looked effortless, like he was moving in slow motion. It was a swing that made Tour players on the range stop and watch, a gift for which the rest of us would trade a leg.

"Between U.S.G.A. junior events," he said, "and high school . . . like . . . eighteen."

"How many did you win?"

"Sixteen."

His answer came quickly. He'd been asked the question before and I could tell he liked answering it.

"Hell of a winning percentage," I said.

"It was a lot of fun."

"What about this year?"

"It's okay. It was fun being part of a team last year, a lot of friends."

"You live at the David Renney Academy?"

He nodded. I figured even the most annoying roommate was better than traveling North America with his father, but I managed to keep that thought to myself. The first hole was a par four, 410 yards, with a slight dogleg right, a potential birdie hole. Carvelli hit a long, high tee shot that faded nicely into the heart of the fairway, bounding out of sight around the dogleg. I hit a conservative three-wood that landed at the corner of the dogleg. We started down the fairway. After my brief stay in Maine (which had required me to use the snow blower four times in two days), Tucson was a reprieve. At 10:45 A.M., it was nearly eighty degrees. The sun was hot, the air still—and not a goddamned snowflake in sight.

"Laying back?" Carvelli said.

I grinned. "When I was seventeen, the thought never occurred to me, either."

"But you can reach the dogleg. And there's no water or out of bounds."

"Sure, but," I said, turning to Silver, "what are we looking at from there?"

"I'll give the exact distance at the ball, but no more than one-fifty."

"An easy eight-iron," I said to Carvelli. "I'll take that."

"Well, we're inside a hundred yards," his caddy said. "I'll take a sand wedge over an eight-iron any time. Besides, Billy, your father wants you to work on your driving today."

Billy just nodded.

At my ball, Silver said we were 141 from the pin. I could try to jump on a nine-iron or hit an easy eight. I drew the eight. Ahead, the green looked like an island amid an ocean of sand and cacti. My approach shot landed six feet beyond the pin and spun back, settling six feet below the hole. I said nothing to Carvelli's caddy, but Silver shot him a look.

Carvelli had only eighty-five yards to the hole. His drive had been a thing of beauty. Length aside, he had hit a 300-plus-yard fade. The average Tour pro has difficulty hitting a fade or a cut with a three-wood, let alone a driver. And the kid wasn't even eighteen yet.

He pulled what looked like a sand wedge, made two slow practice strokes, and stood behind his ball to align himself. As he addressed the ball, he looked at his father, the solitary figure near the first green. Then he brought the club back quickly and down on a steep angle, his body fighting to catch up with the clubface. It was no use. He hit it fat; the ball fell ten yards short of the green. Carvelli made no show of emotion. He handed the wedge to his caddy and walked toward the ball.

"What was that!?" his father called to him.

He didn't reply.

Silver set my TaylorMade staff bag down near Carvelli's old man. As I drew my putter, I said, "I think you make him nervous."

The bearded man, wearing khaki slacks and one of his son's Abercrombie and Fitch shirts shot me a look of indignation. "Golf requires steely nerves. He'll get used to it."

"It's probably none of my business," I said, "but I think he'd do better if you let him find his own way."

"Find his own way?"

"Yeah," I said, "just let him play. Have a good time."

"Have a good time?" he looked at me for several seconds. I said nothing. Then he smiled and shook his head sadly. "I see that you're serious," he said. "Do you have a stock portfolio, Jack?"

"Sure."

"Do you keep an eye on your investments?"

"Of course. Why?"

He turned away from me and I followed his eyes to Billy.

"I'm doing the same thing," he said, "and you're right, Jack. This is none of your business."

.   .   .

The driving range at a PGA Tour event is many things—a workspace where players warm-up or look for answers; an extension of the locker room where players gather to chat; or a showroom where players compare and try equipment. This afternoon, I needed a workspace. I'd shot seventy-four, disappointing in itself, but my swing was nowhere to be found, even after an hour and a half on the range.

I'd shot worse scores. What bothered me was that I wasn't hitting the ball crisply. You can't win unless you're striking the ball well and I hadn't won in a year and a half. My two-year exemption was up at year's end. Playing privileges can be retained by finishing in the top 125, though I'd never gone into a season thinking that way. I wanted to win. However, this day, as I stood sweat-soaked next to Silver on the range, the search for my swing was more primitive.

At age ten, I'd gone with my father to a nine-hole municipal course, his Chevy pickup bouncing from potholes as we pulled into the dirt parking lot. We shared one set of clubs, a set of 1960 Spalding blades. The course had been squeezed onto a few acres, the greens were far from plush, the fairways and rough indistinguishable from one another. But the hotdogs were great, I'd spent the afternoon with my dad, and I'd hit one shot that was so addictive I was hooked forever.

From a hundred yards out, I'd swung slowly and, for the first time, made pure contact. Dumbfounded, I'd watched the ball rise against sunlight, level off, and drop softly to the green. I can't remember how far the ball stopped from the pin or my score on the hole. The feeling of contact, however, never left me. The sensation ran up the shaft, into my hands, an effortless, pure feeling. My thirst for that feeling brought me back the next week and often kept me on the range until dark as a professional. While dyslexia made school a place of humiliation, I'd found a place that gave joy, a place where I could excel—and I couldn't get enough of it. I was a scratch player by the time I was fifteen.

"Out of sync," Silver said, after I hit a three-iron.

"Brilliant analysis," I said. "Got a swing tip?"

"Sure. Hit the ball better."

I rolled my eyes.

"I'm just the lowly caddy, boss man," he said and pointed to Fred Couples at the far end of the range.

It was late afternoon, and the sun was setting behind Couples. I watched him bring what looked like a four-iron back slowly. From the top, the club seemed to simply fall, sweeping inside on the downswing. His effortless tempo and power couldn't be taught.

"That's not helping."

Silver shrugged and wiped his shaved head with a towel. "Thought watching him might give you good swing thoughts."

"Wrong," I said. "Watching him frustrates the hell out of me." I positioned a ball off my front instep and made an easy swing with the three-iron. I caught the ball thin and it nearly hit the 100-yard marker.

"Jesus, Jack, you sculled it."

I ignored him and hit another. This one wasn't much better.

"There's a bunch of equipment reps," Silver said. "How about I get a hybrid fairway metal? A lot of guys are going to those. Easier to hit than a long-iron."

Behind me, someone set a bag down. Clubs jangled and I turned to see Kip Capers. He wore a towel draped over his trademark black shirt. Tattoos on his forearms danced as he hit an easy wedge shot. He made a face and told his caddy he needed to loosen up. I slid the three-iron back into my bag and moved closer. My caddy had suggested substantial equipment changes. I needed a break. Capers pulled out his wedge, set it across his shoulders, and began rotating his torso, twisting back and forth.

"When did you get here?" I said.

"Why?" he said and grinned. "You see me with a tight back, so now you're looking for a game?"

"I'll take it easy on you."

"Thought you were on the Champions Tour," he said. "You're what, fifty-five?"

I slapped his cheek playfully. This was how it usually was with Capers. He was a good kid, fun to be around, and this interaction contrasted sharply with my previous round with him. Then, he'd been stoic, upset by Hurricane's health, aware of problems before the media. I thought of his mysterious friendship with Hurricane McCarthy. Both men were friends of mine, although I'd never known them to be associates.

"New driver?" I said, and pulled the club from his bag. I took the head cover off.

"Four hundred and sixty cc's," he said. "I'm killing that thing."

I gripped the Nike Ignite driver and set up to an imaginary ball—the 460-cubic-centimeter clubhead was indeed mammoth. "Thing looks like a hockey stick." I handed the driver back. His bag had a Nike logo on the side and contained a set of Nike Slingshot irons, three Cleveland wedges, and a metal wood I didn't recognize, a hybrid fairway club.

"What's that?" Silver said to him. "We're in the market."

"A four-wood."

I pulled the hybrid club out. NICHOLS GOLF was etched on the club's sole. "Where'd you get this one?"

"That's a great club," he said. "I've got a contract with Nike. But that's easier to hit than the Nike three-wood, so I'm sticking with it."

"How'd you get it?" I said. "That was Hal McCarthy's and Paul Meyers's company. It went under."

"You don't have to tell me it went under," he said. He took the club back and slid it back into the bag. Then he pulled the towel from his neck and put it over the club. "I've got to warm up now."

He was about to hit a wedge, when I said, "Heard from Hal McCarthy recently?"

He waggled the club behind the ball. "No. We're not close, Jack."

"You went to see him."

Capers hit the wedge and watched the ball. "I came damned close to becoming a priest." He glanced back at me. "I'm a Christian. I hear someone's sick, I get concerned. Now, I really need to warm up."

I nodded and went back to my practice. He didn't want to talk about Hurricane McCarthy. I hit another ball. The shot was not crisp.

. . .

Lisa, Darcy, and I had eaten at the golf course. Players are allowed to eat onsite, free of charge, and bring family members. Another perk. Following dinner, Lisa and Darcy returned to the hotel. At 6:30 Wednesday evening, I was back on the range, looking for my swing, somewhat reassured by the presence of nearly twenty others. Good to know I wasn't alone. Many caddies were there. It's part of the job and most caddies want to know how their man is doing, what his tendencies are, what the solution is when things head south. But I'd sent Tim Silver home. We'd walked eighteen holes, then spent two hours on the range that afternoon.

To my right, Vijay Singh was drenched in sweat, beating ball after ball with what looked to be a three-iron. Many evenings he and I were the last ones on the range. That put me in good company. I stood my big red-and-yellow TaylorMade bag behind me and dropped two bags of Titleist range balls to the ground. At the far end of the range, the Tucson sun was an orange blaze low and shimmering, dancing atop the 300-yard marker.

I took my sand wedge—the shortest and, in theory, the easiest club in the bag to hit—and made a long, slow swing. The trajectory was too high. The ball failed to travel as far as was customary. Every player has a personal nemesis, a personal flaw they know to look for when the ball gets crooked. My "crooked" shot was the result of an over-the-top swing, a common mistake, one that causes amateurs to slice. I took a glove from my bag and held it against my side with my right arm. I couldn't hold the glove if my right elbow didn't stay against my side. It forced me to bring the club back inside and keep it on plane. I hit three sand wedges that way.

The third one was what I was looking for. The ball flew high and straight and landed softly, dancing around the 100-yard marker. In a half-hour, I hit thirty more, painstakingly going through my entire pre-shot routine for each—lining the shot up from behind the ball; taking two practice swings (careful even on those not to drop the glove); and finally addressing the ball and pulling the trigger. Next, I drew my five-iron. After two bags of balls, I was dripping with sweat. Only Vijay Singh was left on the range. My watch read 8:05.

I pulled the big TaylorMade r7 driver and carefully teed a ball. I brought the club back slowly and made a wide arc, my head steady, my shoulder-turn full. At the top, the club was parallel and, in my periphery, I saw the black clubhead. My downswing was smooth and—I thought—well paced. However, the contact was not flush. The ball traveled 265 yards and bent to the right. I stood watching it, hand on hips, and kicked the tee. Thursday might be a long day.

·   ·   ·

"I take it," Lisa said, when I entered the hotel suite, "it wasn't an easy fix. It's eight-thirty." She was sitting on the floor, her feet tucked beneath her. Her laptop lay open on the carpet before her. She wore a T-shirt that read CBS SPORTS and nylon athletic shorts.

I'd picked up a six-pack on the way back to the hotel and set the Heineken on the coffee table. "I'm working on keeping the club on plane."

"What do you think about tomorrow?"

I shrugged. "During the Maine Amateur one year, I shot sixty-four after having the puking willies until four A.M. the night before. Some of my best rounds have come when least expected."

"Mr. Positive."

"Hey," I said, and shrugged as I opened a bottle of beer, "I'm working my hardest. It's all I can do."

The bedroom door was closed. It meant Darcy was asleep. I sat on the sofa and sipped some Heineken and Lisa went back to work. Statistics were on the computer screen.

"You're ranked twenty-first in driving distance, Jack."

"That used to be my category. Before Tiger and Hank Kuehne."

"Players are stronger."

"I'll say."

"That reminds me," she said. "Paul Meyers said he's too busy to talk this week. I told him I'd like to do a feature on him and a segment on how he has revamped his swing to get longer."

"It's not the swing. He's working out."

She looked at the computer screen. "He went from number one hundred and ten last year to seventeenth. Whatever he's doing, I want to know."

"What's the latest on Richie Barter?" I said.

"I haven't heard." She turned back to the computer, ran a finger down the screen, and jotted something on a notepad beside her.

I sipped some beer. Outside, the sun had set and distant lights twinkled. The only sound was Lisa's tapping. Richie Barter had told me to talk to Hurricane since, according to him, Hurricane was "already ruined" by the clonidine usage. He'd also said people were out to get him. Who? Why?

There was a knock at the door. In golf, not every putt that hits the lip rolls out. Some do a three-sixty and fall in. In life, you get lucky rolls once in a while, too. Richie had told me to find Hurricane. I didn't have to. When I opened the door, Hurricane stood before me.

23

"My pride's in my back pocket, Jack," Hurricane said, when we got to the hotel parking lot and sat in his rental, a Kia Spectra.

He'd asked for a word with me and we'd gone silently to the elevator, down to the lobby. In the silence, I'd leaned against the elevator's glass wall and stared at him, my mind filled with questions and conflicting emotions: Hurricane McCarthy, who had stood before me, tired, his face pale, eyes sunken, was a friend. Yet he'd told me not to talk to Liz Scott. And I was certain his clonidine prescription wasn't medically necessary, which meant he'd cheated me, the rest of the players, and the game. It left him with congestive heart failure, a serious medical condition that would impact his life—he'd never be the player he once was. Additionally, Richie Barter told me they both knew the answers. To which questions? Finally, the last time Hurricane and I spoke, I'd asked questions of my own and he'd threatened me. So why had he come?

Classical music played on the radio. It didn't seem to go with the tense, stilted atmosphere. I was silent. Hurricane sat sweating, rivulets of perspiration rolling slowly down his red cheeks.

"I got very few friends left, Jack. I know I did it to myself." He turned away and looked out the window. The parking lot was still. Street lamps, anchored by yellow concrete islands, cast light over motionless vehicles. He turned back. "They say you learn who your friends are when you're down. I'm down."

I waited. The media had run him over with a paving wheel several times in recent days. And since his doctor continually declined comment, I had no problem with that. But now he sat across from me, defeated. Tough to see. He was a great father and husband, a guy who cared for his family. He didn't have to tell me how the humiliation he caused them made him feel. He wore it on his face like a scar. For a moment, I thought of Perkins, who refused to go home because he thought he was no longer all his family expected him to be.

"I went to three players before coming here, Jack. I didn't want to go to a tournament site, didn't want to be seen. You see your wife's face when you opened the door?"

"She wants to talk to you."

"They all do. None of them will understand."

"Understand what?"

"Why I did it."

"Tell me," I said.

Classical music gave way to an NPR news update. Hurricane looked at the radio. When no sports brief was given, he turned to me again and silently stared at me for several moments. Finally, he took a deep breath and let it out slowly. "Hurricane" McCarthy was gone now. There was no rage. His bearing held the stillness of an aged man, one whom life's winds had blown down. I felt for him, yet I knew he'd done it to himself.

"No one wants to hear my story," he said. "I went to three players' homes. All three threw me out. I'm golf's pariah."

"I'm sitting with you."

"Yeah, you are. How old are you, Jack?"

I told him.

"I'm forty-four. Made some money over the years, but now it's gone. I was good in the early nineties. That was when I was at my best. And that was the wrong time to make your money."

I knew purses had jumped like a Titleist off a trampoline after Tiger Woods joined the Tour in 1996. Not too long ago, $125,000 let you keep your card. Those days were gone. Guys were playing for $1.2-million first-place checks now. If you didn't earn $800,000 by season's end, you found yourself back at Q School. And all that money led to the globalization of golf, which led to competition the likes of which the old guard had never seen—or counted on.

Across the parking lot, two young guys left the hotel and headed to a courtesy car.

"That's Dan Simmons," Hurricane said, nodding toward them. "Kid is twenty-three. Drives a Lamborghini. Remember what we drove at twenty-three?"

"A Chevy Capri station wagon," I said, "with everything I owned in the back of it. Lived out of that thing for a couple seasons."

"Times have changed," he said. "It's why I did it."

"The money," I said. He'd already told me the money was why he played, so I knew it was the money. Yet somewhere inside, I hoped he'd say something else, hoped there was a different reason for his cheating.

"It's not as simple as it sounds, Jack. Remember Nichols Golf?"

"You and Paul Meyers started that club-manufacturing business. It did well for a while."

"It was me, Paul Meyers, Ron Scott, and Kip Capers. And, yeah, it did pretty good for a while. Then the bottom fell out."

"Kip Capers was part of that group?" It explained why I hadn't known them to be friends; they were business associates.

"Yeah. We took him in as a rookie. He was a kid, liked hanging around us, you know? We were older. We'd been on Tour a long time, we'd won some events. I told him the company was going to be big. I believed that."

"You had three well-known names running the show," I said, "pitching the products. I thought it would be big, too."

"Pitching products is one thing. Growing a company is another."

I was quiet. Somehow all this was related to Hurricane's heart failure and clonidine. It was hard to remember he was sick. He put his hands on the steering wheel, his arms thick and coursed with veins. He'd gotten himself into seemingly great shape. He cut the air-conditioner and absently reached for a button on his door, gave a frustrated head shake, then manually rolled down the window. Once, his world had been power windows; now we sat in a rented Kia.

"The company lasted only a couple years," I said. "When I asked why you were getting out, you said you wanted to focus on golf, work on your game."

" 'Wanted,' " he said, "is the key word. That was a lie, Jack. I'm sorry. 'Wanted' had nothing to do with it. Ron Scott ran us into the ground."

"Ron Scott?"

"Yes. And me, he ruined financially. Kip was young. Didn't have much to put into it. What he lost, he earned back quickly."

I thought of what Kip Capers said earlier that day, on the range: *You don't have to tell me it went under.* Now I understood why. He'd taken the hit with the rest of them.

"But I wasn't young," Hurricane continued, "and I was looking to life after golf. I was getting older, the kids were teenagers. My family wanted me home more and my game was deteriorating. I saw what Greg Norman did with Cobra Golf, what some other guys have done with wine and other businesses. I wanted that for my family, you know?"

"And then came Nichols Golf."

"Yeah, I thought I could get that with Nichols Golf. I wanted it for Sherry and the kids, Jack. If Nichols got as big as Ron said it would, Christ, my kids would never have to work. And Sherry, after following me year after year on Tour—I wanted her to have anything she wanted. She deserved it." He looked at the floor. The interior of the car was lit by the green dashboard lights. "Sherry still deserves it. More than ever, now."

"So the company went under," I said, "but that was two years ago."

He nodded. "That's right. Last year, Ron said we could bring the company back, that my four-wood would do it. About a year ago, I started having serious money problems. I got desperate."

"And Hollis prescribed clonidine."

He nodded. "Christ, Sherry doesn't deserve this. My face on TV, the stuff they're writing about me. I've humiliated her. And the kids—what they're going through at school . . . " His voice trailed off. He clutched the steering wheel as if we were moving and he could outrun it all. Pools were forming in his eyes. His family meant everything to him. "I wanted to get the money back. So, yeah, I started looking for ways to turn my game around, fast."

"And putting has always been your weakness."

"Same as you, Jack."

"Sure," I said. "If I putted like I drove the ball, I'd have had a different career."

Neither of us spoke and I thought about how Hurricane had cheated to turn it all around and how fate had somehow evened the score.

"Clonidine," I said.

He nodded. "You're right. Hollis prescribed it. He's a friend, knew I was in trouble, didn't want to see me lose everything. He said he knew doctors who took it before taking oral boards. He said it would steady my nerves."

"It did. You've putted well this season."

"Haven't felt well, though. And this," he pointed to his chest, "wasn't supposed to happen."

"What are they going to do about it?"

"I don't know. He gave me a patch and some pills. I took both, a mistake. Hollis is out of the picture now. But I was told I won't be walking a hilly course in Memphis in July anytime soon. I won't be the same." He sat staring out at the night.

I didn't say anything.

"I'm going to talk to some other doctors. But I wanted to see some guys first, Jack, the guys I'd come up with."

"You cheated," I said. "The game is built on trust. So is friendship."

"Ah, man, Jack, I'd rather have you refuse to see me than say that."

"That's how it is," I said. "If you need something, I'm here. But it's different now."

"Don't worry, Jack. I'm paying a steep price. My lawyer says Hollis is cooperating with authorities, which means confessing. Everyone will know the prescription was bogus soon. I'll pay for what I did, tenfold."

From behind us, headlights cut the darkness. A small Ford Focus entered the parking lot and rolled by slowly, turning to park facing us in an adjacent row. The headlights went out, and the driver's-side door opened.

"But there's more to it," he said.

I looked at Hurricane. "There has to be," I said. "Ron Scott ruined you, financially. Now he's dead. That doesn't look too good."

"Jesus Christ, Jack. I didn't kill him. I'm worried about *ending up* like Ron Scott because clonidine was only the start."

I was staring through the darkness at him. "You're losing me."

"The game has changed, Jack. I was too old to change with it."

A sound like thunder exploded. I had not taken my eyes off Hurricane. In my periphery, I saw the orange flame and was on the floor mat, facing the door, the left side of my face pressed tightly against the glove compartment. Shards of glass from the Kia's windshield rained down. I felt glass on the back of my neck, going down my shirt. Footsteps grew closer. Then I heard an engine and a second set of headlights flashed from behind us, reflecting off the rearview mirror. The footfalls retreated, this time slapping the pavement in a run. Tires squealed. Momentary silence was followed by voices and more running. Then someone was coming from the hotel, yelling for help.

Carefully, I got off the floor.

Hal McCarthy remained seated on the driver's side, hands still on the wheel. But his knuckles were no longer white. Now they were blood splattered.

"What's your connection to the victim?" the cop said.

His name was Jerry Hernandez, but he hadn't told me to call him Jerry. In fact, he hadn't told me what to call him, so I was sticking with "officer." Hernandez had been first to arrive at the crime scene and questioned me there. Then I'd gone to the Tucson Police Department's Midtown Division on South Alvernon Way with him. There, I'd answered more questions, written a statement, and was now answering questions again—many of them repeats.

"Like I said, we've played the PGA Tour for more than a decade together. He came to see me to apologize for cheating."

The room felt like a holding cell—a small wire-mesh window looking down on a busy street, a bare steel desk in the center, concrete floor, and a gray metal door. The overhead lighting was hot and bright.

"Feel like I'm on *NYPD Blue*," I said.

He cleared his throat. "That a joke? I don't do jokes." He was short and built like a bowling ball and had the personality of one, too. "My superior wants to call in a sketch artist. But you say that's not possible."

"I didn't see the shooter. I was on the floor of the car."

"What did you hear?"

"Like I said before, someone walking toward us."

"So shoes, not sneakers, on the pavement?" he said. There was the hint of a Spanish accent.

"I don't know," I said. "Everything happened fast. Like I told you, the car was a Ford Focus, I think. It was dark out. The car was green or blue, maybe black. I saw it pull in, then I went back to my conversation. Then I heard a loud bang."

"A blue Ford Focus was stolen across town tonight," Hernandez said. "We'll go through rental receipts, but that's our best bet. The owner parked the car at a mall, went inside, came out, and the car was gone. More coffee?"

The paper cup he had brought was empty now. It was too late for a second cup. I had an important round to play the following day and was hoping to sleep tonight. I shook my head. Sleep was probably out of the question anyway. Hal McCarthy had been shot, and the shooter had started toward me. Only the arrival of a second car had saved me. The shooter was now at large.

Hernandez reviewed his notes and cleared his throat again. "The victim was part of the same business venture a Chicago murder victim named Ron Scott was in."

"Yeah," I said. "Officer Billy Peters is handling that case."

"How do you know that?"

"The PGA Tour security consultant told me."

Hernandez looked at me as if he wanted to say something. Instead, he glanced at his watch, gave a tiny head shake, cleared his throat once more, and said, "You've answered all my questions. How long do you plan to be in the city?"

Making the cut was never a foregone conclusion, but I'm an optimist. "Through Sunday."

"I'll be in touch," he said and walked me to the door, where Perkins was waiting in the hall.

. . .

Liz Scott answered the phone in a tone that suggested the day before had gone a hell of a lot better for her than me.

I didn't doubt that. At 8:30 Thursday morning, I was still in my hotel room, alone, sitting on the sofa. Lisa had listened to me recall the shooting, ordered me a pot of coffee, and then headed off to work, taking Darcy to the course with her. I'd awoken early, despite getting to bed after 1 A.M. and not falling asleep until three. I sipped black coffee from a white room-service mug. When I told Liz Scott who I was, the upbeat tone vanished.

"What do you want?" she said. Then her voice softened, slightly: "I appreciate the scholarship you and your wife started in Ron's name."

"I'm glad," I said. Lisa had taken that idea and run with it.

"I was under the impression the PGA Tour was doing that. At least his colleagues haven't forgotten him. So what can I do for you?"

"Did you watch the news this morning?"

"I just got back from spin class."

"I'm afraid I've got bad news. A friend of your family passed away last night."

Maybe three seconds of silence, then: "Is that so?"

"Hal McCarthy."

"Hal's dead, too?"

"What do you mean by 'too'?"

"Huh? It's just shocking. First Ron, now Hal. Like you said, he was a family friend."

Her voice was flat, so I didn't have much to go on. However, her pause told me she was thinking, choosing her words carefully. So I changed subjects. "You know, I always liked the Nichols Golf clubs. They still available?"

"The golf clubs?" she said, as if I'd snapped my fingers and she woke. "No that's over."

"What happened?"

She was silent again. I sensed her distrust. I hadn't planned the call, hadn't informed Perkins I was making it. Perhaps that was a mistake. He was better at this, but he was also dealing with his own issues right now.

"Can I get the clubs anywhere?" I said.

"I don't know."

"Who should I talk to?"

"I don't know, Jack. I can't think straight right now."

"Yeah," I said, "he'll be missed."

"Who?"

"Hal," I said. "He'll be missed."

"Oh, yeah."

"Is Nichols Golf out of business?"

"Yes, right now."

"Is the company making a comeback?"

Silence again, then: "No."

"That's too bad," I said. "How did the business go under? I mean . . . the clubs are great."

"Thank you. My late husband would be flattered."

"How did it go under?"

"You know how businesses go. Sometimes risks don't pan out."

"What do you mean?"

"Nothing, Jack. Thanks for calling. And thank you for the scholarship." She hung up.

I closed my cell phone and set it gently on the coffee table. I pushed back, settled deeper into the sofa, and crossed my ankles on the table. I'd have given anything to see her expressions as we'd talked. The call had upset her. She'd become distracted. Yet when I'd said Hurricane would be missed, she'd forgotten who the hell we'd been talking about. What had distracted her?

I got the feeling Liz Scott knew all about Nichols Golf—the company's past, present, and, given her "right now" remark, future. What risks had Nichols Golf taken that hadn't worked out? Two of the four owners were now dead.

Liz hadn't asked how Hurricane died.

I hoped she'd enjoyed the spin class.

. . .

The computer, apparently, had a sense of humor, although I was in no mood for jokes. Perkins escorted me to the locker room after my conversation with Liz Scott, where I learned my computer-generated playing partner was Paul Meyers. It meant I'd spend Thursday and Friday of the Chrysler Classic of Tucson with the same guy who'd threatened me, the same guy the late Hurricane McCarthy said was part of the deal that ruined him financially.

The locker room was busy shortly before 9 A.M. The breakfast buffet was set up and two lines of players made their way through it. The smells in the room contrasted with one another— good cologne, fried ham, potatoes, and strong coffee. Billy Carvelli was on the TV doing an Abercrombie and Fitch commercial. I headed toward the pot with Perkins hobbling to stay by my side. Styrofoam cup in hand, I returned to my locker. They were assigned alphabetically, so mine was in the back-left corner. No one was around.

"She never asked how Hal McCarthy died?" Perkins said. He hadn't gotten coffee or food.

"No. Not a word." I was sitting on the bench in front of my locker. Perkins sat next to me, in front of Woody Austin's locker. My locker door was open. A Titleist rep had left me a week's supply of Pro V1 balls. There were new gloves and several TaylorMade caps.

"You sleep last night?" Perkins said.

"Not really."

"Nightmares?"

"His hands were still on the steering wheel," I said, "covered with blood. But still holding the wheel, like he was just going to drive away."

Perkins nodded. "The murder scene was a bad one."

"He got it in the face. One eye was open. The other was . . . "

"Yeah," Perkins said. "I saw the entry wound. Shooter used a .357. Damn near took the headrest off."

I grimaced.

"Sorry," he said. "I know this is cliché, but focus on the positive. You're lucky to be alive."

My head was spinning—images from inside the car, fragments of my conversation with Hurricane, and Liz Scott's strange reaction. It was ironic that I had told Perkins to appreciate what he had, to go home and be with his loved ones. Now he was giving me similar advice.

The night before, Perkins arrived at the police station on crutches, sat outside the room during my interviews, and waited while I wrote and signed my statement. Then he drove me back to the hotel. And, cliché or not, he was right. Whoever shot Hurricane McCarthy had approached the car afterward, no doubt to shoot me as well. But then the second car arrived and scared the shooter off. So, terrified, sick, and dazed—and with many questions unanswered—I'd gone home to my wife and baby. Perkins had hurt Linda and Jackie by staying away. Like Hurricane, he was ashamed—but unlike Hurricane, he'd done nothing to deserve the shame. Hurricane had humiliated his family and would never get a change to right that wrong. He'd never go home again. I was lucky, indeed.

"How you doing?" Brian "Padre" Tarbuck said, approaching my locker. "You were there?"

"Yeah." I took a sleeve of Titleist Pro V1s and a new glove from the top shelf of my locker. I pulled the glove from its package and folded it neatly into the back pocket of my khakis.

"Did he suffer, Jack?"

I looked at him.

Padre looked from me to Perkins and sighed. "I prayed for the repose of his soul," he said and looked away, awkwardly, aware the question startled me. He'd been a priest, and Hurricane had been his friend.

"I think he suffered a lot recently," I said. "As for his death, I don't think Hurricane felt a thing."

. . .

Paul Meyers acted as if none of it happened, smiling warmly as I stepped to the first tee. "Hey, Jack, buddy," he said, and extended his hand. "Good to see you."

He'd warned me off Liz Scott; I'd dropped him like a two-foot putt and had been fined $100,000 for doing so; and now his former business associate—and my friend—was dead. The smile seemed frozen on Meyers's face. It was 9:18 A.M., and we were the 9:22 twosome. It was only late February in Tucson but already eighty degrees. By the time we made the turn, it would be pushing ninety. Made me almost miss snow.

I shook hands silently, then turned toward Silver.

"Heard you had a rough night," Meyers said. He used casual words with a tragic tone, as people often do when discussing the horrific experience of another.

I turned back. "It was awful."

"I know things haven't been exactly copacetic between us, but some things are bigger than petty disagreements." He clasped my shoulder. "Hal was a good friend. I'm pretty torn up by the whole thing. I was sorry to hear you were there. Let me know if there's anything I can do."

"Thanks," I said. "Hurricane always spoke highly of you," I lied, on impulse, not quite sure why. But I kept it going: "He said you cut him in on the Nichols Golf business."

"Yes, I did," he said, morosely and momentarily looked at his shoes. Then he looked up at me, curiously. "What else did Hal say about the Nichols Golf venture?"

"Not much."

Meyers nodded, satisfied, and went to his caddy, Pete Sandstrom. Ahead of us, the first fairway was clear. Time to go to work. The previous day, I'd spent three hours on the range, beating balls in search of my swing, which had gone on hiatus without telling me. The first hole was a 410-yard par four, a mild opening hole, as PGA Tour venues go. I knew a lot of guys would make birdie here, starting a roll and leading to a low score. I looked down the fairway and selected a target, the white 150-yard marker.

I wasn't hitting driver. The longer the club, the more technically sound your swing had to be. And I needed to find my rhythm and maintain it. Three-wood would get me inside 140. I made two practice swings, bringing the club back slowly and smoothly, pausing at the top, making sure I kept the club on plane. *One shot at a time,* I told myself. Dyslexics are often focused and tend to see the world in black and white. I'd turned slightly above-average ability into a PGA Tour career by virtue of my focus. I needed to call on it here. *Push it all aside. Stay in the moment.*

I addressed the ball and made a slow, smooth swing. I didn't catch the ball flush, but the Pro V1 found the fairway.

"Laying back, huh?" Meyers said, grinning as he bent to tee his ball.

I didn't respond. Instead, I walked to Silver.

"Damn near sculled it," I said.

"I know," Silver said. "But we're one for one in fairways hit. This is still a birdie hole."

At my ball, there wasn't a breath of wind, but I still needed a seven-iron. My tee shot had not been inside 140 yards. Instead, I was left with 155 to the center of the green. My typical three-wood carried 275 yards, so I'd really struck my tee shot poorly, a fact made more obvious by Meyers's drive—a draw into the dogleg, stopping eighty yards from the green. The guy was without question the longest hitter I'd ever seen under 200 pounds.

"We got away with a bad swing," Silver said. "Take advantage of the break. Stick this one close."

I swung the seven-iron back and forth, looking for rhythm. From somewhere, a loud roar went up. Unmistakably, a "Tiger" roar. Woods was on the course and had just done something spectacular. I inhaled. *Control what you can. The here and now.*

This swing was better. But I caught the ball a little heavy. However, a seven-iron was a lot of club from 155 and the ball found the putting surface. Silver gave me a high-five. A smattering of applause sounded near the green.

"Pretty good," Meyers said, walking past me toward his ball, "from way back there."

"I'll take an opening thirty-six after yesterday," Silver said, when I got out of the scorer's trailer.

We'd just completed the front nine and, on Tour, you sign cards for nine and eighteen holes. On the tenth tee, we waited for Meyers, who was still in the trailer. Pete Sandstrom was leaning on their golf bag outside the trailer. I assumed Sandstrom would be with Meyers full time now.

"Woods is five under after thirteen holes," I said, pointing at an electronic scoreboard as I took a water bottle from a cooler on the tee, "and Meyers is three under par."

"Still, even par isn't bad."

"No. Especially after how I was hitting it yesterday."

"And after last night . . . " It was Silver's first mention of the shooting. "How are you?"

"Okay," I said. "Not something I've seen a lot of. Not something you easily forget."

"I bet."

To the left of the tee, Perkins sat in a golf cart. He'd followed us all day, maneuvering the cart slowly to stay between fans, who stood just beyond the roped-off fairway, and me. He wore dark glasses and a blue blazer and was scanning the crowd when I walked over.

"You look like a Secret Service agent," I said.

Perkins glanced to see who it was, then resumed looking at the crowd. "I'm just damned glad you're not Tiger Woods. There're maybe fifty people following you two. I wish like hell you had a description of the shooter."

"I wasn't thinking of the sketch artist," I said. "I was saving my ass."

"If the shooter thinks you can identify him, your ass is still in danger."

"I know where you're heading," I said, "and, like I said last night, I'm not withdrawing."

Perkins nodded. Binoculars lay on the seat next to him. He patted his left side, indicating the shoulder holster. I only shrugged and went back to the tee.

Meyers emerged from the trailer and made his way to the tenth tee. "I still have the honor," he said.

We both knew he did. He'd been courteous at the onset. But that waned and the Paul Meyers I had punched out returned. You can shove the demon in the closet but, eventually, someone opens the door. And as if fans could sense the true Meyers, as Perkins had noted, we weren't drawing a crowd.

Meyers looked at a huge crowd in another fairway. "All the work, all the shit I do, and no one notices," he said in a near-whisper to Sandstrom.

"Poetic justice," I whispered to Silver, who grinned.

"It'll all come," Sandstrom said. "All of it. Hard work, done efficiently, always pays off. And no one's working as efficiently as you right now."

The tenth hole at the Omni Tucson National Resort & Spa was a 501-yard par five. The yardage didn't scare me, but the design did—water left, trees right. Most guys hit a draw off the tee, moving the ball toward the water, but adding distance and shortening the hole. I'd played the front nine ultraconservatively. That strategy wouldn't work here. It was driver or go home. That type of scenario was what made the game great. You learn what people are made of on the golf course. The game illuminates a person's true self. That's probably why business deals get done on golf courses—you find out who you're really dealing with.

And this day, I was seeing what I was made of. I'd worked my ass off since I was a kid to get to the Tour. Mine hadn't been a storied career. Rather, it had been a hard fifteen-season run constructed upon a granite-like work ethic. No one would ever mistake my swing for Ernie Els's or Tiger Woods's. Phil Mickelson wasn't going trade putting strokes with me anytime soon. But I had a Tour win—and had stared down Woods on the seventy-second hole to earn it. In golf, no one ever asks How?; they only ask How many? With Woods standing across the green, I had willed that final putt into the cup, and I had raised the trophy. I knew I had what it takes. I had to bring it out here. I needed a good tee shot. I had to make the swing I hadn't made in nearly 400 practice attempts the previous day.

Meyers hit a 320-yard bomb. He'd reach the par five in two, a birdie almost guaranteed.

I addressed my ball, the head of the r7 waggling behind the ball nearly as long as Sergio Garcia's legendary waggle. Finally, I exhaled then started my swing. I took the club back slowly, making a wide shoulder turn, pausing at parallel. Then I started down, my right elbow sweeping inside, brushing my right hip. The contact was solid. I held the finishing pose and watched the ball drop to the center of the fairway.

I was still thirty yards behind Meyers.

As we moved down the fairway, Silver slapped my back. "We're getting it back."

I'd gone to the range to hit balls after my round, still searching for the magic. After an hour, no discovery had been made and I knew you could make up a lot of shots if the best club in your bag was your putter, so I went to the practice green. I'd finished with a seventy-one, one under par, needing only twenty-six putts to do so. I was five back but within a three-quarter wedge of the leader, Tiger Woods, who was –6.

The temperature had climbed to ninety and, at 3:10, the day would get hotter still. Silver took the chalk line and snapped it on the green, forming a six-foot line to the hole. I hit some putts, working to roll the ball straight down the line. A handful of fans leaned against the green wall, encircling the green. Perkins stood next to Silver, a cane in his right hand. Near them, Woody Austin putted to a hole at the far end of the green. After one putt, he glanced covertly at Perkins. By now, everyone had heard what happened the night before. And Perkins—at 240 pounds, wearing a blue blazer to conceal his shoulder holster, dark glasses and a menacing scowl, head swiveling side to side—looked about as much like a golf coach as an accountant. Everyone knew why he was there. I tried to push it all aside. Tiger Woods, I had read, received death threats. This day gave me even greater respect for the guy.

A kid stood next to his father on tiptoes to see over the four-foot wall the encircled the practice green. I took a glove from my bag and the felt-tipped marker, used to script identification marks on my ball, and signed the glove as I walked toward the kid. He was no more than six and clearly delighted when I handed him the glove. His father thanked me. Near them was a guy I'd seen before but couldn't place. He had neatly trimmed black hair, a liver-colored mole on one cheek, a firm jaw, and wore a pale-blue button-down shirt, open at the throat.

"Hello, Jack."

"Hi," I said, hesitantly. It was easier talking to the six-year-old. After all, I was certain the kid wasn't the guy I'd heard walking toward the Kia the night Hurricane was shot.

"I'm Tom Schmidt. I cover business for the *Los Angeles Times*."

Now it clicked. He was the reporter who'd asked my playing partner to "comment on the Hal McCarthy situation," mid-round. The following day, he'd followed Paul Meyers and me.

"What can I do for you?" I said. Perkins was at my side.

"Can I take you to dinner?"

"What's the *LA Times'* business section interviewing me for?"

"I was working on a story about the collapse of Nichols Golf when Ron Scott died."

"So where do I come in?" I said. "My wife gets first dibs on information I have."

"I know who you're married to. I talked to Ron Scott and Paul Meyers before Scott was killed. You spoke with Elizabeth Scott, correct?"

"How do you know that?"

"Let me buy you dinner. Mr. Perkins, here, is welcome to join us."

"You know my name," Perkins said.

"I'm an investigative reporter," he said. "Look, I'm not asking for any information I assume your wife doesn't already have. I just want to tie what you have with what I know."

Someone wanted me dead less than twenty-four hours earlier. If Schmidt knew anything that might shed light on the shooter, I wanted to know. "We're in," I said.

. . .

Perkins selected the restaurant, a steakhouse in downtown Tucson. The place was spectacular—leather furniture, cherry woodwork throughout, and a stone fireplace in the back with bookcases on each side. Perkins and I arrived before Tom Schmidt and sat sipping Corona with lime in a leather booth. The waitress had put glasses on the table, but we drank from bottles. A light hung above the booth and reflected off the tabletop's heavy lacquer.

"Four players were investors in Nichols Golf," Perkins said. His thin notepad was open and he scanned pages, pausing occasionally to jot additional notes. He still wore the blue blazer.

"Ron Scott, Hurricane, Kip Capers, and Paul Meyers." I sipped Corona. When I set the bottle down, the lime bobbed and tiny bubbles rose to the surface.

"Two of the four are dead," Perkins said. "Tell me again what Liz Scott said on the phone."

"I asked if the company was out of business. She said, 'Right now,' and, 'Sometimes risks don't pan out.'"

Perkins's eyes narrowed as he underlined something in his notebook. We'd gone over what Liz Scott told me three times on the drive to the course that morning. Likewise, Perkins seemed to glance around the room every ten seconds. He'd always been diligent, but now he seemed lost in his work. That scared me a little. I knew players who spent evenings on the range, beating ball after ball, when going through divorces.

"And Hurricane told you Ron Scott was the guy taking the financial risks?"

I nodded.

"And the money was Hurricane's?"

"I think the money came from them all," I said.

"So why was Hurricane's financial hit worse than the others'?"

"I don't know. Maybe he put more money into the company."

"Was he the majority owner?"

I spread my hands and Perkins went back to his notepad. The Corona was good. I'd hit 300 range balls Wednesday to shoot a seventy-one in Thursday's first round, so the beer had been earned. It was closing in on 6:30. The after-work bar crowd had come and gone. Now Perkins and I seemed to be the youngest diners left. Around us, were silver-haired couples. My courtesy Buick stood out in the parking lot full of Lexus SUVs and Mercedes. Regardless of what would be discussed, I expected to at least eat well. I guessed the *Los Angeles Times* wouldn't get out of here for less than two hundred bucks.

Schmidt appeared and sat next to Perkins in the booth. Perkins closed his notepad and put it in the breast pocket of his blazer. A waitress came over and Schmidt pointed to our beers. "My bill," he said. "I'll have a Corona, too."

The waitress nodded and left.

"You're PGA Tour Security," Schmidt said to Perkins, "a consultant from Boston."

"Been doing your homework," Perkins said, once again.

"I saw the cane," Schmidt said. He smiled warmly at Perkins. A little chitchat to start off. "I had surgery for a cycling injury last year. It's a pain in the ass. Rehabbing a knee? Were you on crutches?"

Perkins nodded.

"So the cane is a positive step."

"But not a leap," Perkins said.

"How long will you have the cane?" Schmidt said.

Perkins's eyes drifted to mine. "This is as good as it gets."

"Oh," Schmidt said, his voice tightening a little, "sorry to hear that. And I'm sorry for asking."

I stared at Perkins. How long had he known the cane—and the debilitating leg—were permanent? Why wait until now to tell me? He said he'd come all the way back. When had he learned that wasn't going to happen?

"Jack," Schmidt was saying, "Jack."

"Yeah?"

"You were staring at me," Perkins said.

"Is your wife upset about me taking you to dinner?" Schmidt said.

I shook my head. "She broke the story of Hal McCarthy's murder this morning."

Schmidt nodded. "There was nothing about Nichols Golf in her report."

"Should there be?" I said.

The waitress returned with Schmidt's Corona. He smiled at her politely, took the beer, and leaned back in the booth. No bottle for him. He poured the beer carefully into his glass. Maybe he, too, drove a Mercedes. As he poured, he looked at me contemplatively. Finished, he shook his head and smiled. "So I've been had?"

"What do you mean?" I said.

"I'll ask questions and you won't answer them because Lisa Trembley-Austin is sitting on a major story."

Schmidt wasn't dumb. He wanted to hear what I knew. And I wanted to hear what he knew. However, he realized my loyalty to Lisa complicated this and didn't leave a lot of wiggle room. But I was running on three hours' sleep and hadn't come to discuss the weather with this guy.

"On the range," I said, "you asked if I'd spoken to Liz Scott. That's what you're interested in, right?"

"Yes."

"And we want to know about Nichols Golf," I said.

"Deal."

Perkins had his notebook open again, but he was staring grimly at the metal cane now.

"I read the newspaper accounts of last night's shooting," Schmidt said, "and saw your wife's piece. I keep wondering why you were in the car with him."

"Thirty reporters asked me that when I walked from the clubhouse to the range this morning," I said. "Like I said, Hal McCarthy came to see me to apologize."

"What else did he say?"

"That was about it," I said. I had promised him Liz Scott. I'd keep the rest to myself; I owed Lisa that much.

"Tell me about Liz Scott."

"I went to see her about a scholarship my wife and I started in Ron's name."

"That's it?"

"I asked what happened to Ron. She said she didn't know." Schmidt looked from me to Perkins then back to me. We sat quietly for a long time. Then he turned to Perkins again: "Where do you stand in all this?"

"I'm security. A guy was shot while Jack was with him. The shooter is at large." He spread his hands.

"I don't buy any of this," Schmidt said.

I shrugged. To the guy's credit, he never stopped smiling. I figured that was what you needed to be a successful journalist—a win-some-lose-some attitude. A lot like golf—you make a bogey, you shake it off and move on. The waitress came back and Perkins ordered. I hadn't looked at a menu, so I said to bring whatever Perkins was having. Schmidt ordered and handed the menu to the waitress and she left.

"I've been doing this a while," Schmidt said. "How could a business venture like that collapse so completely? They had brand-name appeal. They had plenty of capital."

"None of those guys had Greg Norman-type money."

"Yeah, the resources weren't unlimited, but they are well known—especially in this particular field. I could see if they were manufacturing cars and needed money. Someone might say, Hell no. But this was manufacturing golf clubs and I hear the clubs were good."

"I heard that, too," I said.

"I want to know what happened. Hal McCarthy walked away broke. Is Paul Meyers broke? Kip Capers? I could see a company owned and operated by four star athletes being sold. That would be like a rock band breaking up, an ego thing—*you don't like my idea, so we'll sell it all.* This is different. What went so wrong? And why is only one guy broke?"

"Liz Scott said a couple things I thought were strange," I said, and told him what I had told Perkins.

"Is the company coming back?" Schmidt said.

"I haven't heard anything like that," I said.

"So Ron Scott was CFO?"

"I don't think any formal titles were given, but Ron did something with the capital."

Schmidt nodded.

"The main question remains," Perkins said. "Who killed two of the four owners?"

"And why?" I said.

"Chicago cops are calling Ron Scott's death a mugging," Schmidt said. "Even today, they're calling it unrelated to the McCarthy murder."

"How long have you been working on this?" Perkins said.

"Since the business went under. You think the deaths are related?" he said to Perkins.

"Yeah," Perkins said, "I do."

"Me, too," Schmidt said.

"Think something illegal went on at Nichols Golf?" I said.

"Not necessarily," Schmidt said. "I think one guy took the financial fall—might be nothing illegal in that; might be something unethical, though. Might be newsworthy."

"And no one will talk to you," I said, "because they don't want bad press?"

"You think Kobe Bryant has a lot of endorsement opportunities right now? Reputation equals money. And, in case you haven't noticed, pro athletes nowadays aren't only playing for the love of the game."

It made me recall Meyers's earlier comment: *All the work, all the shit I do, and no one notices.* He had worked hard on his game and was hitting the ball farther than ever. Yet Lisa wanted to interview him, had in fact sought him out. If he wanted to be noticed, why decline her interview request?

26

$\mathcal{P}$erkins and I left the restaurant, got into the Buick LaSabre, and I pulled out of the parking lot onto a downtown street. At 7:30, the traffic moved slowly. Perkins adjusted the radio and found a sports talk show discussing the local PGA Tour event. One caller said the tournament was over already, that no one could catch Tiger.

I turned off the radio.

"Schmidt say anything that clicks with something you know?" Perkins said.

"Why didn't you tell me the cane was permanent?" I said.

He didn't answer; instead, he looked out the window. It was dark now, the downtown section lit by storefront windows and streetlights. Two kids no older than sixteen walked into a liquor store. I pulled to a red light and stopped. I waited.

"Why didn't you tell me?" I said. "We've been through everything together. I was there when Suzanne passed away. I was there when you had Jackie. I was your goddamned best man."

He didn't turn to face me when he spoke. "I met with the doctor Monday. He said I won't get the leg back to where it was, told me to rest it. It should have responded by now."

"Maybe you're just pushing too hard."

The light changed and I drove toward our hotel.

"No. After the surgery, he gave me a timeframe. When the date got closer and the leg still wasn't responding, I started two-a-days. Nothing worked. I know my body, Jack. He's right. I need the cane."

"Forever?"

He turned from the window. "Forever."

We hit another light. Kids were shouting back and forth on the sidewalk. Music from the car in front of us blared, the bass reverberating like thunder. Perkins sucked in a deep breath and exhaled slowly.

"This doesn't change who you are," I said.

"The hell it doesn't, Jack. I was an All-American in college, not on the dean's list. My whole life, I've been physical. It's who I am, who I've always been."

"You're more than that," I said. "You've made a good living being smart and tough. You're still both of those."

The light turned green and I drove on.

"I've lost something," Perkins said, "part of me."

I thought of the basketball fan in the hotel bar. He hadn't been intimidated by Perkins; in fact, he'd looked at Perkins with pity. His physicality—even the mere threat his size and aura projected—had served him well. He had indeed lost something. But not everything.

"Jackie and Linda still need you," I said.

"Hell of a Little League coach," he said. "And Linda's got one kid already."

"Set your damned pride aside," I said.

Neither of us spoke the rest of the way to the hotel. I pulled into the hotel parking lot and turned to him, but there didn't seem anything to say. I killed the ignition, got out of the car, and walked to the hotel without another word.

Perkins was still in the front seat when I entered the lobby.

. . .

Later that night, I was reading Pulitzer Prize-winning poet Philip Levine's *New Selected Poems* in the light of the bedside lamp, trying to clear my head after the dinner with Schmidt and the drive home with Perkins. "I Could Believe" hit me hard.

> I could come to believe
> almost anything, even
> my soul, which is
> my unlit cigar, even

164

the earth that huddled
all these years to
my bones, waiting
for the little of me
it would claim. I
could believe my sons
would grow into
tall lean booted men

I closed the book and thought of Hal "Hurricane" McCarthy, of the pride I'd seen in his eyes, heard in his voice, when the two of us had watched his fifteen-year-old son, Terry, putt. The night Hurricane died, he spoke of Sherry, of his six-year-old daughter, Jaime, of how none of them deserved the anguish and embarrassment he caused.

The hotel windows were black. I saw my refection staring back at me—a middle-aged man with my father's sad Irish eyes, the same eyes I'd passed on to Darcy. Hurricane had been desperate to recapture the life he once provided Sherry and the kids, desperate enough to cheat and lie to friends. We had come up together—drank beer, laughed, taken each other's money in Tuesday "money matches." We'd attended each other's wedding, shaken each other's hand after our respective first Tour wins. Then he had lied to me, cheated even me. Part of me thought he'd gotten what he deserved. But the part that had looked at him in the car and told him I was still there for him wanted to honor that. I was still here. So were Sherry and his kids. If I could help, I would.

"Darcy's asleep in the other room," Lisa said, sliding into bed beside me. "Can't sleep?"

"Thinking."

"Want to talk about it?" As a nightgown, Lisa wore one of my white T-shirts. This one had "Titleist: The No. 1 Ball in Golf" across the front. She was on her side, elbow propped on her pillow, chin in her hand.

"Hurricane told me he was paying tenfold for what he did. I don't respect what he did, but I understand why he did it. He did it for his family."

"He chose to invest that money, Jack."

"I know. He told me he was just trying to hold on, playing for the money."

"That's despicable."

"I know," I said. "Maybe more than anyone, I know that. I've only won once and my window of opportunity is closing."

" 'Closing'? You've never said anything like that before."

"The rookies are getting younger. Every year, they're stronger, they manage the course a little better, they putt truer, and they're hungrier—and every year they get better. The senior tour can seem a long way away. Hurricane was desperate, willing to try anything. Before he was shot, he'd lost his career. He said he'd never walk a PGA Tour course again."

"So why was he killed? He was certainly no threat on the golf course."

"He was probably killed for the same reason Ron Scott was."

"What's that?"

"I don't know."

"And why would Elizabeth Scott say the company is out of business 'right now'?" Lisa said. "I haven't heard anything about Nichols Golf making a comeback. Have you?"

"No. Nothing."

Lisa was staring at the foot of the bed, thinking.

"Are you still trying to get Paul Meyers to do an interview?"

"I asked again today," she said. "He walked right by me."

"Rude."

"Yeah. I left the newsroom to get away from that."

"I thought you got into golf to chase me."

"Not so much." She grinned.

"Meyers was complaining that he doesn't get any publicity," I said, "that no one notices how hard he works."

"He doesn't let people notice him," she said.

I thought about that, about what Meyers said. Then I thought about Hurricane again, about his wife Sherry and his kids. I envisioned the cops arriving at their home, giving the bad news. Sherry was alone now. The kids' father would never come home. Then I remembered something else. In the aftermath—the questioning at the police station; the phone call to Liz Scott;

the golf round with Mr. Congeniality, Paul Meyers; dinner with Tom Schmidt; and finally the news that Perkins would never be the same—a comment Hurricane made had escaped me.

" 'Clonidine was only the start,' " I said. "That was one of the last things Hurricane said."

"The start to what, a better golf game?"

"No. We were talking about Ron Scott being killed. I said that since Scott had lost Hurricane's money and was now dead, it made Hurricane a suspect. He said he didn't kill him and in fact was scared, too. Someone killed him before he could say of what." I shook my head and exhaled a long slow breath, a breath of exhaustion.

"By the way, you've got a phone message. A Jerry Carvelli is looking for you."

"Great," I said. "That's Billy Carvelli's father."

"I'm going to check on Darcy," she said. "Don't fall asleep."

She went to the other room. When she came back, she closed the bedroom door behind her.

"Are you really tired?" she said.

"Yeah."

She took the T-shirt off and got back into bed.

I wasn't too tired.

By the time I reached the 170-yard par-three fourth hole Friday (my thirteenth because I started on the back nine), I was outside the cut line looking in. The view wasn't pretty—Tiger Woods had gone low and, from the get-go, I'd gone the other direction. I was nine over par for the day, eight over for the tournament. Now Woods (−12) led Paul Meyers by two. Amid gust-ing Arizona winds, they stood five shots clear of the field. We were waiting for the group in front of us to clear the green.

"Never seen you start a round like this," Silver said, and wiped his brow with a towel, then slung it over his shoulder. "Six straight bogeys."

I'd had up-and-down rounds before that included six bogeys, but never consecutively. Moreover, never had I made six bogies without at least a couple offsetting birdies. I'd shot an embarrassing forty-two on my first nine and made three more bogies—so far—on the back. I was staring at an eighty-one, a score only a ten-handicapper could be proud of.

"I'm off today." It was all I could say. Silver and I had been a team for a long time and this day only he was doing his part.

"Off? Jack, you missed that last approach by an entire zip code."

I pulled a six-iron from the bag, walked to the cooler at the back of the tee box, and a got a bottle of water. I drank some and looked at the green. A caddy's role is diversified—swing coach, amateur sports psychologist, green reader, and, as Silver was attempting now, motivator. I usually didn't need additional inspiration. Admittedly, this day I was tired, and during the six-hour round, it had been difficult to remain focused. But the fourth hole got my attention. If my approach shot fell short, it would find the water hazard. Go long and I'd contend with grass moguls. I finished my drink and made several practice swings. It was time to slow it all down—my swing, my walk, my thought process. Typically, I swung no harder than 80 percent. This day, I was going full tilt, the results predictable. Meyers had begun the day with the honor and never lost it. He was −10.

"Don't worry about it, Jack," Meyers said. He pulled the lid off the cooler and took a bottle out. He didn't bother to return the top to the cooler, instead dropping it to the ground.

It was the first thing Meyers had said to me all day. He drank maybe a quarter of his water bottle and threw it in a nearby garbage can. Then he swung a short-iron back and forth. When he stopped, I looked closely. He held it as he folded his thick forearms across his chest. I could see that it was a nine. The guy could hit a nine-iron 170 yards?

"You'll get your rhythm back," he said. "You just seem distracted today. You need to let what happened the other night go. Move on with your life."

"Just move on, huh?" I screwed the top back on my half-drunk water bottle and tossed it to Silver. He put it in our bag.

"Sure, big fella. I mean, I heard you were there. Think how fortunate you are. You ought to forget it ever happened. Just put it in the past."

"Forget it happened? You think it's that easy?"

Meyers's caddy, Peter Sandstrom, was next to him. We were out of earshot of the gallery.

"Well," Meyers said, "maybe not. I was just—"

"The guy was shot, dead. Right in front of me." I could feel something rising in my chest like a balloon of hot air. I inhaled and let it out slowly.

"Look, man, I'm just trying to help."

"You know what he looked like?"

"What do you mean?" Meyers said, and looked to Sandstrom for support.

"I haven't slept through the night yet," I said. "A bullet turned the guy's face into Alpo."

"Jesus, Jack, I'm trying to focus here."

"Sure. You focus. Is that what you guys told Hurricane, when he lost his money? To just *move on?*"

"What are you talking about?" Meyers said.

"That's enough," Sandstrom said. He wore a Nike cap and tinted wrap-around sunglasses, so I couldn't see his eyes. But I heard the challenge in his voice. Then he stated it clearly, "Knock it off, Jack."

"Mind your own business," I said, pointing my index finger squarely at him.

"That's what I'm doing," Sandstrom said. "I'm his caddy, and *we're* still in contention. Let Paul focus."

Meyers's eyes were narrowed and, when I turned back to him, locked on mine. His head tilted as he looked up at me. "I'm afraid I don't even know what you're talking about, Jack."

I wanted to hit him again, but I'd been a taught a $100,000 lesson. So I chuckled. It was all I could do. Too much had happened—Hurricane, Perkins, my swing problems, and the pairing, pitting me with Meyers, the guy I least wanted to play with. I chuckled all the way to the front of the tee box, where Silver waited. I tossed the six-iron back in the bag. Forget 80 percent. This would be as hard as I could swing. Behind the green, Perkins was in a golf cart. He'd been there all day. Now, a redheaded guy wearing a gray suit sat next to him.

I froze at the sight of Chicago homicide cop Billy Peters.

. . .

From a golf perspective, the day had been a strange one. Usually when you play with someone who's burning up the course, you get pulled along for the ride and shoot a decent score. That hadn't happened and, par after par, I came to the ninth tee (my eighteenth hole) at nine over.

Silver took the towel from his shoulder again and wiped his shaved head. Wind or not, it was hot, and the trek had been difficult. "Let's build momentum for the next tournament," he said, and handed me the TaylorMade r7 driver. Translation: *Throw caution to the wind and get your driver straightened out. We're not going to make the cut anyway.*

I nodded and looked behind the tee. Perkins and Billy Peters were still following us. Something was up. Had Peters flown here to talk with me? Or had the Ron Scott murder been linked to the Hal McCarthy slaying? Was the Chicago Police Department finally pulling out the stops? I doubted Peters was here to check on his longtime friend Perkins.

A lake ran down the right side of the ninth fairway, which made a precise tee shot challenging. If I had been in contention, I'd have hit three-iron. However, as Sandstrom had not-so-passively insinuated, I wasn't within rifle shot of the lead. So after Meyers hit his three-iron safely to the center of the fairway, I took two practice swings, and addressed the ball. I widened my stance for balance because the wind was blowing at us now. Hot, dry air poured over me. I inhaled, getting what seemed a mouthful of dust. Finally, I pushed everything aside and made a swing. This time, it was *my* swing, the one I'd been looking for, and the ball exploded off the clubface. It started as a line drive and rose steadily, leveling off, before descending and dropping to the heart of the fairway, leaving only a wedge to the green. Most players would hit three-iron or three-wood and still have 175 yards or more to the putting surface, so my tee shot was a minor success.

We paused in the fairway at Meyers's ball. He had 165 yards to the pin, and it was at least a two-club wind. Meyers was decked out in a new apparel line, head to toe—McNamara designer clothing. His shirt was lime green, white pants, lime-green shoes, and a white visor. The outfit was nothing I'd wear, but I'd seen his shoes retail for $350. Complain as he might, someone, somewhere, had noticed Meyers's improved game—and he was reaping financial benefits. He hit a short-iron that settled within ten feet of the pin.

I looked at Silver. "What did he hit?"

"An eight, I think," Silver said.

"That's a monstrous eight-iron," I said. "In this wind, I'd have hit a six."

Silver shrugged and started walking toward my ball. When we reached my Titleist, I drew the eight-iron. I had 125 yards to the flag, into a stiff wind.

"Sure you want to play the wind?" Silver said. "Or you want to keep it under the wind and run it up there with a low seven?"

"Let's let the wind knock it down," I said.

To my left, Perkins and Peters were still there. They had a manila folder and sat in the white golf cart looking at some papers. I focused on my target and tried to lock in on what I was doing. I went through my customary pre-swing routine—two practice swings, visualize the shot, and address the ball. Then I made my swing. This time the ball flew high and straight, rising over the green. I was about to yell, "Come back," when the wind finally did its job. The ball dropped straight down as if hitting an invisible curtain.

At the green, Meyers was putting for birdie, trying to pull within one of Woods. I had twelve feet for birdie. Silver thought in terms of building momentum; I thought about pride. I was twenty shots behind the leader. I was better than that. From his cart, Perkins gave me a thumbs-up. I nodded and went about my putting routine. When you stand over six-foot putts worth half a million dollars, you don't just walk up and hit it at the jar. You develop an ironclad pre-putt routine you trust, one you can take to the proverbial and non-proverbial bank. I lined the putt up—once from behind the ball, once from behind the cup—made two practice strokes, then addressed the ball. The putt would be slow. Uphill. Only a slight left-to-right break. I set the putter face behind the ball gently, glanced at the hole one last time, and hit the putt. A gust of wind came up as I watched the ball break and roll toward the cup. Sand felt like granules of salt stinging my eyes. But I squinted through it and watched as the ball died into the center of the cup.

As we walked off the green, I headed to the cart, but Peters walked by me without a word. "Mr. Meyers," he said, and introduced himself, "I'd like to ask you some questions about your affiliation with Ron Scott and Hal McCarthy."

.   .   .

In the locker room afterwards, I took my duffel out and packed my Saturday and Sunday outfits, the remaining sleeves of Pro Vis, two gloves, and my after-shave kit. I had learned something. The Nichols Golf venture was a link between Hurricane and Ron Scott—and Chicago Homicide was interviewing the two remaining investors.

Next to me, Woody Austin made plans with a rookie I didn't know to have dinner. Behind me, I heard two guys planning a "family night out" at a local amusement park. I looked over and veteran Tom Leveque glanced awkwardly at my duffel bag then turned away. I didn't bother zipping the bag. I wanted to get the hell out of there. I was going through one of the worst rituals in professional golf—cleaning out my locker after missing the cut. Finally, Padre Tarbuck approached.

"Hey, buddy," he said. "I saw today's scores. Tough week all around, huh?"

"Yeah." I closed my locker.

"I don't say a lot on Black Fridays, but you didn't have much of a chance this week, Jack. Too much to go through. Too much on your mind. Keep your chin up and give me a call if you want to play a practice round next week."

I said I would.

"And don't take this wrong, but relax and enjoy the weekend."

"I'd enjoy trying to kick your ass on the golf course this weekend," I said. "Wish I was getting the chance."

We shook hands and I started for the door, but someone called my name. I turned to see Billy Carvelli and walked to where he sat in front of his locker. He, too, was packing up. The room smelled of cologne, the air damp with moisture from the showers.

"How'd you do?" I said.

"Missed the cut by one damn shot."

"Better than me."

Carvelli took a pair of black shoes off the floor and put them in a small red Abercrombie and Fitch shoulder bag. It reminded me of his situation—he was The Kid, and, apparently, had an endorsement deal to match.

"Saw you on TV the other day," I said.

He shrugged. "That was my father's idea. He's my agent." He tossed some Maxfli balls into the bag. "He's trying to get a hold of you, too. I wouldn't get back to him, if I were you."

"Why?"

Carvelli looked at me as if to say, *Are you kidding?* "The guy's a nut."

"I see. What's he want?"

"I don't know, but he told me to stay away from you. It's probably that."

"Why stay away from me?"

"I never know what that guy's thinking."

"So why'd you call me over, if he says stay away?"

"To see if you want to play a practice round next week," he said, and turned back to his locker. He went on tossing items into the bag.

I didn't know how to respond. I'd never had trouble getting practice-round partners, but this was ridiculous. Always good to be popular—first Padre, now Carvelli—but no way in hell was I getting between a father and his rebellious high school kid, regardless of how good a kid Carvelli was and what an ass his old man was.

"I don't think that's a good idea," I said.

"Why?"

He said it in a defiant tone that made me remember why I'd taken my long-shot chances at the PGA Tour Qualifying School after graduating from UMaine instead of using my English degree to teach high school.

"He's your father," I said. "I'm just a friend."

"And you probably understand me better than he does. I've read about you and the football player, Nash Henley."

I sighed. Lisa and I had taken Nash Henley in when he was eighteen. Now he was twenty-one. The previous year, Nash's biological father had been killed, and I'd honored a promise by helping him find out what kind of man his father had been. The findings hadn't been good and the search led to Perkins being shot and his ensuing stroke. As I thought about it now, whatever Nash had gained, Perkins had lost.

"Nash and I have a lot in common," I said. "We're both dyslexics. I know what it's like to grow up like that."

"I've read five articles about you and Nash. Sometimes I think I have a lot in common with him, too."

I started to speak, to correct him. After all, this kid had a million-dollar endorsement deal. Then I thought about the rest of it. Nash was abandoned by his father, and before Lisa and me, Nash had been taken in by a football coach who saw only NFL potential and the money that went with the realization of that potential. Billy Carvelli wasn't too far from that scenario— I knew as much, after the elder Carvelli's "stock portfolio" comment.

"I played Tuesday and Wednesday alone here," he said. "I don't have a lot in common with these guys." He made an inclusive gesture with his hand. "At least you talk to me. A lot of guys don't like the Abercrombie contract. I almost wish I didn't have it."

I didn't know the particulars of his deal, but he was the youngest guy on Tour, one of two high school kids to ever qualify. That guaranteed hype, and hype guaranteed galleries. The contract was no doubt seven figures, maybe eight. And from a veteran's standpoint, Billy Carvelli hadn't done much to earn that kind of money yet. I didn't doubt the sour grapes.

"You played alone this week?" I said.

"Me and my new fucking trainer. Father fired the guy I was going to and hired some guy who calls himself a 'golf specialist.'"

I remembered seeing him lifting weights while his father charted his progress on a clipboard. "There's a bunch of good trainers in the Tour's fitness van."

"No. This guy is independent. Sandstrom. Peter Sandstrom."

Hurricane's former trainer. One client dies, just add another.

"He a good player?" I said.

Carvelli shrugged. "He didn't play. He walked with me and charted how far I hit each club. Says he'll improve my overall strength by five to ten percent."

"You'll be working your ass off for a long time, then, because that's a lot."

Again, the shrug. "You grow up with my old man, you learn to go with the flow. You playing with me next week or not?"

I looked at him. His "old man" didn't like me because I'd said let the teenager be a kid once in a while. Golfers don't peak when other athletes do, so there weren't a bunch of nineteen and twenty year olds for Carvelli to hang out with. The young guys were busting their asses to get a deal like the one he already had; the older guys had kids his age. He was really alone. And he looked it, amid the locker room teeming with activity—no one stopped by his locker to chat or tell him to keep his chin up.

"Get us a tee time for Tuesday, early," I said, and walked out.

28

"I thought, since Paul Meyers wouldn't talk to me," Lisa said, "that I'd ask his caddy about his improvement. Pete Sandstrom is also his trainer, you know."

I said I knew that. We were in the hotel restaurant at 6:30 Friday evening. I had just ordered steak. I'd been watching what I was eating lately—ordering a lot of chicken—but missing the cut made me feel the weight of entire week. I was exhausted and hoped a little iron would do the trick.

"Sandstrom said he wouldn't discuss Meyers and said," Lisa paused and looked at me, "not to come near him again. I felt . . . threatened."

I had been reaching for a dinner roll and stopped. "Threatened?"

She nodded. Beside her, Darcy opened and closed a cardboard picture book. She paused to point at a picture.

"Cake for dinner?" Darcy said.

"No, honey, mac-and-cheese and carrots."

"Daddy," Darcy said, and tilted her head to look at me with great seriousness, "you're making me nervous at you."

"Sorry, sweetie," I said, and turned back to Lisa. "He threatened you?"

"Not explicitly. Just the look . . . It said, *Back off.*"

Around us, fragments of conversations swirled. A waitress walked by with a tray of steaks, the meat perfectly seared and smelling of Cajun spices, but I was no longer hungry. I leaned back and stared at the bottle of Heineken, which sat untouched before me. I thought about what she had said. I hadn't liked Sandstrom from day one, and the day's golf round certainly hadn't changed that. Yet personality challenged or not, as a trainer, the guy seemed to be going places with his "golf specialist" tag. So his refusal to speak with Lisa made no sense.

"I'm surprised Sandstrom doesn't want to take some credit for his clients' successes," I said. "He's building a training business."

"How big is his business?"

"I don't know. Before this season, I'd never heard of the guy. Billy Carvelli just signed on with him. I guess Billy is taking Hurricane's slot, and he still has Paul Meyers. There are probably others, but those are the ones I know of." I drank some beer. "Lots of guys have people they work with at home. But having a guy traveling on the Tour is something new, so he'll probably do well."

"Meyers doesn't mind Sandstrom working with his competitors? That seems like a conflict of interest, since Sandstrom is also Meyers's caddy."

"Guys who live in the same cities share trainers," I said. "Bunch of guys in Dallas go to Athletes' Center for Training and Nutrition. They share trainers. You want a guy who knows golf, knows the demands of the Tour and your specific needs. Some guys travel to see a particular trainer." I tore a roll in half and gave some to Darcy. "Besides, the guy is a caddy. He probably needs extra money to cover expenses. I don't know any player who'd have a problem with that. Hell, when I take a week off, I tell Silver to pick up another bag, make some extra cash."

"And only in golf," Lisa said, "do competitors give each other lessons."

"A gentleman's game."

The waitress reappeared with our meals. She put the steak in front of me. I got a loaded baked potato with it. Lisa was having a Cajun chicken salad, fat-free vinaigrette on the side.

Darcy looked disappointedly at her carrots. "No cake?"

"Not for dinner, sweetie."

"Mommy, you're making me nervous at you for that."

I grinned and cut a piece of steak. It was good, for restaurant steak. When you travel thirty weeks a year, you cherish what others take for granted. Eating at home is one thing I love, grilling in particular.

"Paul Meyers and Hurricane McCarthy had something in common besides Nichols Golf," I said.

"They shared a trainer," Lisa said.

"Hurricane took clonidine under a doctor's supervision," I said. "Think his trainer knew about it?"

Lisa had been coaxing Darcy to eat. She turned back to me, set the fork down, and took a long, thin notepad from her purse and wrote in it. "I'll be damned," she said, writing.

"Yeah. I should have thought of it sooner."

She looked up at me. "You've had some minor issues on your mind this past week—a crippled friend, another shot while sitting next to you. And," she shrugged as if to say sorry, "your golf game."

"Which sucks right now," I said.

She had missed one. I hadn't told her about Perkins's theory of how I might still be in danger. I figured this was neither the time nor the place.

"Hollis, Hurricane's doctor, prescribed the clonidine. Hurricane got desperate and took too much. Would his trainer need to know what he was taking?"

"It would be much safer," Lisa said, "if he knew. But would Hurricane tell him? You knew him well. What do you think?"

"I don't know," I said. "I don't even think Sherry knew what he was doing."

"You sure?"

"No. But I'll find out."

. . .

The next morning at 10:15, I found myself back at the Tucson Police Department's Midtown Division on South Alvernon Way. I was in Detective Jerry Hernandez's office with Billy Peters from Chicago Homicide and Perkins, there on behalf of the PGA Tour.

"Mr. Austin," Hernandez said, "I appreciate you coming. I know you're taking time away from golf to be here."

Actually, I'd missed the cut and therefore was unemployed

for the weekend. But I didn't feel like telling him that, so I nodded and sipped my coffee. The office was small. The coffeemaker sat atop a gray metal filing cabinet in the corner. The room smelled of strong coffee and cologne.

"Mr. Peters and I are," Hernandez searched for the word then smiled, pleased that he'd found just the right one, "*collaborating* now that there appears to be more to the Ron Scott murder. You're the lone witness to one of the two murders in this investigation."

Hearing that punctuated Perkins's initial warning—as lone witness, I might be in danger.

"And we'd like to ask you some questions," Hernandez said, and cleared his throat. "I'm aware that your wife is a journalist. However, Mr. Perkins assured us you wouldn't compromise a criminal investigation."

"Neither would my wife."

"I'm sure that's the case," Hernandez said, and looked at me with the cynicism of a cop who'd spent an entire career dealing with reporters, "but we're not questioning her. I'm telling you that what is said here, stays here."

"Just like Vegas," I said.

No one smiled.

"See why he was such a hit in Chicago?" Peters said, and turned to Perkins. "Sending him wasn't a good idea. Why didn't you go yourself?"

I was glad to no longer be the focus of the conversation. Peters, Perkins, and I sat across a large gray metal desk from Hernandez. On my previous visit, I'd sat in a small conference room that had felt like a holding cell. This time, I'd made it to Hernandez's office. A step up, albeit a baby step. I drank some coffee and awaited Perkins's reply. Perkins looked at me for a long time before answering.

"I wasn't up to it," was all he said, which was typical Perkins—concise and vague. Was he talking about the leg? No doubt that was how Peters would interpret the comment. I knew that wasn't what he'd meant. Emotionally, he hadn't been ready.

He'd gone from crutches to a cane, but I wondered if he'd made emotional progress since declining the Chicago trip.

Peters turned to Hernandez. "If you hadn't called and tied something to my Ron Scott case, it would've fallen off the front burner. You know how that goes."

Hernandez nodded.

"And, given the budget," Peters said, "if this wasn't high-profile I still wouldn't be here."

We were drinking motor oil from paper cups. Peters finished his coffee, turned in the small office, and tossed the paper cup at the trash can in the corner. The cup hit the can's edge and fell to the floor, spilling the last few drops on the linoleum tiles.

"Shit," Peters said. "Sorry."

"Don't worry about it," Hernandez said, but he cleared his throat, annoyed.

Peters got up and took a napkin from near the coffeemaker. "Perkins and I have talked about this at length," Peters said, and wiped the spill and put the empty cup in the trash can.

I was glad to hear Perkins was still working the case. He sat next to me, expressionless.

"Four guys invested in Nichols Golf," Peters said. "Now two are dead."

"Were they shot with the same weapon?" I said.

All three looked at me. Hernandez cleared his throat once more as if it were a reflex. Then he narrowed his eyes at me. I was there to answer questions, not ask them. I leaned back and enjoyed the stellar Jo. The room fell quiet.

Finally, it was Perkins who answered my question: "Ron Scott was shot with a .357, same as McCarthy. The media hasn't been told what type of gun was used in the Ron Scott shooting."

"Which is how we like it," Hernandez said, his eyes still on me.

"My wife is on the clonidine story," I said, "not the shooting."

"Look," Perkins said, "we called him in because he was there when McCarthy got shot and he knows the players. Give him some information to work with."

Hernandez sat looking at me as he finished his coffee and set the paper cup down on his desk blotter. The room was quiet. As he continued to stare at me, he absently turned his wedding band repeatedly. He cleared his throat when he was angry or uncomfortable. Fiddling with the wedding band was a strange nervous habit. It made me wonder about the state of his marriage.

"Ballistics is running tests to see if the same gun was used in both cases," he finally said. "No footprints were left in the parking lot, so all we have is the single size-ten Folsheim print from the alley where Scott was shot."

"You saw a small car, a Ford Focus?" Peters said to me and tapped a manila folder that lay in his lap. Apparently, it was the case file.

"It was a small car," I said, "something *like* a Focus. I wasn't really looking for details. I was looking at Hurricane and listening to him talk."

"Who's that?" Peters said.

"Hal McCarthy. We called him Hurricane."

"Why?"

"Because of his temper."

"That's interesting," Peters said. "According to your statement, McCarthy claimed Ron Scott took his money. Now Scott is dead. Just how bad was McCarthy's temper?"

"I've seen him break clubs. But I said the same thing to him. He told me he was scared of ending up *like* Ron Scott."

Perkins raised his brows and blew out a deep breath. Hernandez and Peters looked at each other. When no one spoke, I offered the no-shit line: "And now he is." I shrugged.

"Who else lost money in the Nichols Golf deal?" Hernandez said.

"McCarthy, Ron Scott, this Capers kid, and Paul Meyers were the owners," Peters said. "So they all lost money."

I remembered what Tom Schmidt of the *Los Angeles Times* said. "But no one besides Hurricane lost nearly everything."

"Was he majority owner?" Hernandez said. "Or did the others just have more money to start with so they weren't hurt as badly by the loss?"

"I don't know the percentage of ownership," I said. It was a good question, though, one I wished I'd asked Schmidt. "I know Kip Capers was a rookie back then, so I doubt he had much money. Ron Scott had more than Hurricane. But Paul Meyers hasn't done much for a decade, until this season. So Hurricane probably had more than him."

"But you don't know the financial situation of any of them," Perkins said, "investments, stuff like that?"

"No. But I know Meyers won a major. Although, like I said, that was ten, twelve years ago."

"What's that worth?"

"Back then?" I thought about it. "Endorsements and appearance fees? Whole thing would probably have brought a couple million. But it costs over a hundred grand to play the Tour. And Meyers had to go back to Qualifying School five years ago, so he hasn't won much money, hasn't won an event since that major."

"What's Qualifying School?" Peters said. "He got cut?"

"Sort of," I said. "You lose your card, you go back to the PGA Tour Qualifying Tournament and try to finish in the top thirty. Twelve hundred guys try it each year. Four grand entry fee."

"We're getting off topic," Hernandez said. "Let's look at what we have, which are two primary suspects right now—this Capers guy and Meyers. We'll look into their financial records, see where they're at in that regard."

I was a golfer in a room of law-enforcement officials and Hernandez had all but said to keep my questions to myself once already, so I assumed my theories weren't welcomed either. I leaned back in my seat and sipped my coffee. Hernandez was following protocol—when four people go into business together and two get killed, the remaining two are logical suspects, especially when money is involved. But the past four years, I'd spent a lot of time with Kip Capers, on and off the course. He seemed as likely a murderer as I did a trapeze artist. Money had been lost and Hurricane had told me it was Ron Scott's doing. Certainly, money was always a motive for murder, but not the only one. Something was missing from this equation.

"Kip Capers went to divinity school," I said. "I can't picture him shooting anyone."

"We know his past," Peters said. "I don't see him doing those two himself. But if he lost enough money, what's to say he couldn't contract a hit?"

"But what would be gained by killing Hurricane?" I said. "If he lost the most money, isn't he the one with the most motive, the primary suspect? He'd be someone's fall guy."

Hernandez cleared his throat.

Perkins grinned. "I told you he was smart. Good point, Jack. But there's more to it. Aside from revenge, which motivates a hell of a lot of crazy things, there could be some clever financial dance steps here. Like maybe Nichols Golf had some term-life policies naming co-owners as benefactors."

"I can't see Kip Capers as a killer," I said again.

"Look," Hernandez said to me, "we won't get the wrong guy. We don't make those mistakes. No stone unturned."

"Does Scott's widow have an alibi for the night McCarthy was shot?" Perkins said.

"Airtight," Peters said.

"Let's take a coffee break," Hernandez said, still looking at me. "Mr. Austin, thanks very much for your time. That's all." .

I should have gone sooner, but I'd had golf to play.

It wasn't much of an excuse and having spent a lifetime hitting golf balls until dusk or putting until my back ached—in short, working to turn average ability into a solid PGA Tour career—maybe I had said "I have golf to play" too often. At thirteen, I skipped middle-school dances to get thirty-six holes in Friday evenings at the local municipal nine-hole track where, after 3 P.M., $7 allowed you to play until dark. In college, I skipped (a few) team keg parties to practice. Even now, there were days when I felt I didn't spend as much time with Darcy as my father had spent with me. Sacrifices are made to play the

PGA Tour and sometimes I wonder if they are selfish ones. For that reason, I felt guilty as I rang the doorbell of the suburban-Orlando home late Sunday afternoon.

"Jack?" Sherry McCarthy said.

"I wanted to offer condolences in person."

I had told Lisa I wanted to learn if Hurricane told Pete Sandstrom he was using clonidine. Yet that wasn't my only reason for coming. Hurricane had been a great father and he was survived by a fifteen-year-old son.

"The funeral is next week," Sherry said, opening the door and waving me in.

The home was in Gamington, Florida. If golf communities were cars, this one was a Mercedes. Nearly a dozen Tour players lived there. When I had shopped for a Florida condo, where I could practice for several weeks during Maine's horrendous winters, Gamington had been considered, until I saw the prices. From the outside, the McCarthy home seemed huge—stucco with a terracotta roof and plenty of peaks and angles and lots of glass. That estimation was validated when I stood on the tile floor in the entryway. Thirty feet in front of me, a long staircase rose slowly to the second floor. I remembered Hurricane saying he'd built Sherry her dream house. The place had cost at least $3 million.

"This house is really something," I said.

I had told Liz Scott something similar. Liz had said she knew my place was just as nice. It had been insincere and untrue. By contrast, Sherry McCarthy was a stand-up lady.

"It's absolutely spectacular," she said. "We've been here more than a year and I still look around and pinch myself." Then her voice became brittle and low. "Hal bought it for us. This was where we were going to have grandchildren." Her eyes pooled. She stood straight and didn't blink as tears rolled slowly down her cheeks. It was as if crying had become part of her daily routine. She never broke stride.

There was a family room to my left—sixty-four-inch plasma television, leather sofa and matching love seat. Ahead of me, I saw the dining room, the kitchen beyond it, and a glass wall offering an ocean view. A pool lay between the house and the ocean.

"Hal always spoke of having the players over for a big party after Bay Hill," she said, "but we never got around to it. He'd have wanted to give you a tour. Would you like to see the house?"

I told her I would and we walked through the 6,000-square-foot home, across the street from the acclaimed Gamington Country Club golf course. The house had five bedrooms, five full baths, a workout room, Jacuzzi, and a hundred feet of beach. The game room had a drop-down television screen and a bar. One bay of the four-car garage consisted of Hurricane's workshop. Atop the workbench were boxes of metal clubheads and a plastic container of leather grips. On the floor nearby were two barrels of steel and graphite shafts. The workbench was littered with pliers, gloves, epoxy, and white tape. A large canvass sign hung above the workbench that read "Nichols Golf—Move Over Titleist." Terry, Hurricane's fifteen-year-old son, was at the bench.

"Hal spent hours out here, Jack," Sherry said. "He loved golf-club design."

"Was he the designer for Nichols Golf?"

"Oh, yeah. That four-wood some players still use was Hal's idea. He talked about that all the time—such-and-such a degree of loft with a something-or-other shaft and 'bingo!' he would say. He loved that. He wanted that company to be his future."

"What happened to the company?"

Sherry looked at me. Then she looked at Terry, who stood with his back to us. He had the clubface of an iron in a padded vice and was pulling the shaft toward him to alter the angle of the club's lie. Music throbbed from a small radio on an overhead shelf. Terry wore clear-plastic safety glasses and a long white apron.

"The company went under, Jack. You know that."

She turned and I followed her out through an open garage door. We stood in the driveway. It was eighty-five degrees in the late-afternoon Florida sunlight. Overhead, seagulls cawed.

"But how?" I said. "The clubs were great."

"Did you play them?"

"No. I've played the same brand since I was a kid."

She nodded. "That's part of what happened to Nichols Golf. Titleist, Callaway, Nike—those companies are huge and Hal used to say golfers are superstitious; they don't like to change. And then Ron Scott got to thinking he was Charles Schwab."

"What do you mean?"

Sherry looked over her shoulder at Terry. To our right, I heard a young girl's giggle and turned to see young Jaime on a swing set in the backyard. Sherry looked at Jaime, then back at me. She stifled a small moan with her hand and fought the sobs, taking deep breaths.

"Jack, I don't know what's going to happen. Our money . . . "

When she didn't finish, I said, "Sherry, the night Hal was killed, he told me Ron Scott set him back financially. Are you okay?"

"You were the last one to see him," she paused, and turned her back to Terry as she cried quietly. Her shoulders shook this time. "What did he say?"

"Hal told me Ron Scott ruined him financially."

She nodded, still crying. "I'm learning that now."

"You didn't know?"

"I knew we lost money. Not how much. Not all of it." Tears streamed down her cheeks; her mascara ran. "I got a bill yesterday." She covered her face with her hand and shook her head absently. Terry heard nothing over his music. "Stop that," she told herself. "You can't do that. Be strong for the kids." Then to me: "The bill was from a debt-consolidation company. I knew Hal hated Ron and I knew that last year Hal gave some of our savings to Ron. But I didn't know how much."

I had to push and felt bad doing it. "How much did Hal give him?"

"Nearly all of it—more than two million. Hal said it would 'save Nichols Golf.'"

"I don't understand. Nichols Golf folded two years ago."

She shrugged. "I don't know the particulars. Hal handled the money, Jack. I figured they were bringing the company back."

I heard Jaime giggle behind us again. In the silence, the laughter seemed very loud and contrasted sharply with Sherry's cries. I wanted to leave, to allow Sherry to cry with the dignity solitude would provide. But Hal McCarthy had told me he feared for his life only moments before his murder.

And his killer had started toward me.

I needed answers. "By 'Charles Schwab' you mean Ron Scott invested the money. And did it poorly."

"That's an understatement. He told Hal he had a stock tip. 'Can't miss,' he said." She was staring straight ahead as if seeing something I couldn't see. "Well, Ron, it missed."

"What was the stock?"

"I don't know. It wasn't bought in Hal's name."

"The company, Nichols Golf, bought it?"

"I don't know, Jack. I'm trying to put the pieces back together again."

"Will you let me know, if you find out?"

She nodded, but I knew her headaches dwarfed chasing a failed stock.

"What will you do now?" I said.

"Live here for as long as I can."

It wasn't much of a plan. But over the past days, she'd lost the man she loved and to whom she was committed. Sherry McCarthy had traveled with Hal and home-schooled the kids until recently. She had been active in the PGA Tour Wives' Association. For the past twenty years, the Tour had been as much a part of her life as it had been Hurricane's. She'd lost her husband and just learned her money was gone as well. The life she'd lived for the past two decades had been taken from her. Where do you go from there?

"Sherry, Hal was working with Pete Sandstrom, a trainer. What did Hal say about that?"

"He was sore a lot," she said, and tried to smile. "He was working so hard. Why do you ask?"

It was time to ask the question I'd come to ask. I knew the topic wouldn't be well received. "Did Sandstrom know about the clonidine?"

She folded her arms across her chest. "I didn't know anything about that until he got sick. I found out along with everyone else. But he came here the other day."

"Who?"

"Pete Sandstrom. He said he wanted to look around."

"Why?"

She shook her head. "I didn't feel comfortable. I didn't let him in."

"Did you ask what he wanted?"

"Yes. He said Hal borrowed something of his and he needed it back. When I said no, he just left."

I thought about that.

"I hope you realize why Hal had to do it," she said, "why he had to use the clonidine."

I nodded, although I had a problem with her phrasing. Hurricane had not "had to" take clonidine. Cheating is a choice, never a necessity. Yet while condemning his actions, I couldn't condemn the man. I understood why he had done it. He needed money to keep his family in this house, to continue providing the lifestyle he always had. The Champions Tour can seem a long way off when you're in your forties and the young guns are hitting the ball fifty yards past you and rolling it fearlessly on the greens. I would never agree with what Hurricane had done, but I knew Hurricane hadn't acted alone. Todd Hollis, the prescribing doctor, was already in the bag. There was one other person I wondered about. This latest information was interesting.

"Do you think Sandstrom was aware of the clonidine?"

"I don't know, Jack. Why?"

"Hal and some Nichols Golf people shared the same trainer. Two of them are dead now."

"Ron and Hal," she said, "and you think—"

"I don't know what to think, but they had some things in common."

She thought about that for a long time. "A Tucson policeman called and said he wanted to come here with an officer from Chicago. Ron lived in Chicago. That's about this, isn't it?"

I shrugged.

"Once, I heard Hal on the phone with Pete Sandstrom," she said. "They were talking about the workout program and how Hal wasn't feeling good. I got the impression Sandstrom reassured him that it would get better." Her eyes narrowed. "What did I say?"

Guile had never been my forte. I was nodding in recognition. I remembered Hurricane and Sandstrom talking on the course in Scottsdale. The wheels had fallen off Hurricane's round and he turned to his caddy/trainer and said, "This isn't supposed to be happening . . . I'm supposed to feel great." It was Sandstrom's reply that now gave Sherry's remarks credence: "It takes a while to see results. Keep your voice down." Reassurance followed by a plea for quiet. Workout programs don't lead to overnight improvement. So why had Hurricane taken exception? Moreover, why didn't Sandstrom want anyone to hear? And why had he really come to Hurricane's home after his client was dead?

"Hey, Mr. Austin."

I turned around to see Terry. He extended his hand and I took shook it.

"Just the man I wanted to see," I said. "I'd like to talk with you."

"With me?" He looked at his mother.

Sherry looked puzzled. "With Terry, Jack?"

I nodded. "Got a driving range around here?" I said to him. "I want to talk golf."

.   .   .

It was a gated golf community, so the drive to the course was two minutes. I bought two large bags of range balls in the Gamington Country Club proshop. The assistant pro was quiet when he saw Terry. "Sorry for your loss," he said, looking at Terry as he handed me my change. Terry thanked him and we went to the range. In Gamington, apparently supper took priority over practice because at 5:30 P.M. Terry and I were the only ones on the range.

"Everywhere I go around here," Terry said, "people say sorry. It's nice, but I'm trying to forget the whole thing."

"That might not be realistic."

"I know." He took a seven-iron from his bag and hit a shot toward the 150-yard marker. All his clubs were Nichols. He didn't strike the seven-iron well and the ball traveled only 130 yards. "I haven't practiced since Dad . . . "

189

I waited but he didn't finish. Instead, he hit another ball. I hit a pitching wedge.

"You brought your clubs?" he said.

"I don't go too far without them. Besides, my game needs lots of work."

"You're a pro. How bad can it be?"

"Pro or not, it's still golf. The game doesn't change. You never master it and you never know when you'll lose your swing. Mine decided to go on vacation last week, so I'm trying to get it to come back."

I hit another wedge. It wasn't crisp and flew left and long of the 100-yard marker, which meant I'd pulled it. But I hadn't gone to Gamington, Florida, to practice. I had gone to see Hurricane's family. One goal had been completed and I would talk to Pete Sandstrom once and for all. However, there was something else I wanted to do for my fallen friend.

"Your dad told me you want to be a Tour player," I said.

I didn't look at Terry; I hit another wedge shot. This one was better. The sun was descending, but there was still plenty of daylight. In Maine, it was nearly dark already. I heard Terry hit a shot. This time the contact didn't sound heavy or thin. He had struck it well. I turned to flick a ball from the pile between us and glanced up. He was looking at me.

"I loved being out there on the Tour with Dad," he said, "on the range or in the locker room. When I was two, I used to swing Dad's club on the lawn. At three, I played a hole." He smiled as if reliving a fond memory. "Walked the whole way up the fairway and wouldn't let him pick up my ball. I finished the hole. Sometimes I hit a bag before school. When I skip things like going to the movies or stuff like that to come here, people don't understand."

"I do," I said. "And your dad did too, didn't he?"

Terry nodded. "Things changed, though, recently."

"What do you mean?" I was facing him now, leaning on my wedge. In the distance, a man and woman dressed casually left the clubhouse. They'd probably eaten in the bar.

"I mean Dad and I were always close, but the clonidine

thing . . . " He turned away and looked down the fairway. "It was cheating. He was my dad, you know? That's tough to . . . " He pulled a ball from the pile with the blade of his iron, positioned it, and made a smooth swing. The seven-iron traveled 150 yards.

I took an eight-iron from my bag and hit a high fade, working the ball from right to left. When I'm dialed in, I can cut it forty yards and stick it close. This one moved ten and fell short. I knew recent events had not aided my concentration; yet, my swing problems weren't mental. I needed to videotape my swing and review it against past tapes. My setup might be flawed. When I broke from my follow-through, I saw Terry watching me.

"When all is said and done, Terry, your dad was a good man. I want you to know that. What he did was wrong. I guess both of us know that. But he did it out of desperation and he did it for you, your little sister, and your mom."

"Desperate about what?"

He didn't know about his family's financial woes or that they were due to his father's failed business dealings—and failed friendship—with Ron Scott. It wasn't my place to tell him.

"Terry," I said, "what I want you to understand is that if you want to be a golfer, I'll help any way I can. Your father was a friend. As a golfer, I don't like what he did. You're old enough to hear that, so I'll tell you that honestly. But as a husband and father, I understand why he did it."

I understood it; I'd never respect it.

"Would you have done it?"

"No," I said.

"How do I respect him?"

"There's a lot of stuff you'll probably need to work through. That's stuff I don't know anything about. I play golf and I can help you there. You ever need entry fees or clubs or want me to look at a tape of your swing or want to play a practice round together, you call me."

"I won't need clubs or money. We've got that. But I'd like to work with you," he said.

The kid didn't know the half of it. I only nodded.

30

$\mathcal{I}$'d rented a car when I flew to Orlando from Tucson. Now I was driving three hours to Palm Beach Gardens, Florida, where next week's Honda Classic would be played. Green Day's *American Idiot* was in the CD player. My cell phone rang as I pulled out of the McCarthy driveway, so I turned down the music.

"Where the Christ are you?" Perkins said.

"Fine," I said. "And you?"

"The guy who shot McCarthy is still at large. Jerry Hernandez says you might be in danger. So I told him I'd keep an eye on you because he was telling me something I already knew. You left town early. *Where the hell are you?*"

"Heading to I-95 south in Florida. Just left Hurricane McCarthy's house."

"Why?"

I told him.

When I finished, he sighed. "So you're driving to the hotel?"

"Yeah. Lisa knows where I am."

"Just watch your ass, Jack. And next time, let me know when you take off. I thought you were sticking around to practice today."

"Not a hell of a lot of fun watching someone else win after you've missed the cut. I figured it was a good time to go."

There was a pause and then he said, "What did Ron Scott invest the money in?"

"No one knows. Any idea how to find out?"

"I know someone who might. Tom Schmidt, your buddy from the *Los Angeles Times*. Think the caddy, Sandstrom, knew Hurricane was taking clonidine?"

"Why else would he tell Hurricane to keep his voice down when they were on the course?" I said. "And why go to Hurricane's house after he's dead? What did he want?"

"I'll look him up," he said, "and ask some questions."

"Sounds good. Let me know what he says. I'm thinking of going to see him myself."

"Why?"

"He threatened Lisa, told her stay away from him. I don't like the guy. I've got some advice to give back, on Lisa's behalf."

"You're going to tell him if he threatens your wife again you'll punch his lights out?"

"More or less."

"That won't help me get answers from him."

"So talk to him before I do."

"You can be a stubborn son of a bitch."

I didn't say anything.

"One more thing about your visit today, Jack. You've got an adopted son already."

"Nash Henley?"

"Yeah. Now you're taking Terry McCarthy under your wing?"

"Nash has a room in my house," I said. "He spends college vacations with us. This is just golf. If the kid wants to make it, maybe I can help. Hurricane's not around to do it."

"Part of that is Hurricane's own doing."

"Which Terry had no control over."

"Ever see the movie *The Cider House Rules?*"

"Read the book."

"What's the doctor's name, the guy who takes in all the orphans?"

"Larch," I said, "and I have only one kid, a daughter. Nash is like a younger brother. All I've done is offered to help Terry. That's it."

"Nobody else is doing it," he said. "That counts for something."

I was on I-95 and set the cruise control at seventy-five.

"Oh," he said, "I almost forgot. Billy Carvelli's old man is looking for you. Asked me how to get a hold of you, so there's the Carvelli kid, too."

It was my turn to sigh. The Tour wasn't that big. Old man Carvelli would find me. I hung up and continued on I-95. A 1980s Chevy pickup swung wide and rumbled past me, its frame trembling, its engine whining with strain. It might have been my father's Chevy truck—except this one had a gun rack in the rear window.

And a confederate flag painted on the tailgate.

And a skinhead bumper sticker.

I-95 in Florida is not like I-95 in Maine, where your worst-case scenario is hitting a moose at night. They are easy to hit because, unlike deer, their eyes are dark and don't reflect head-lights. I've heard of drunk drivers being scared sober by a near-miss. On I-95 in Florida, however, no moose would dare show his face. He'd be scared of being carjacked or poached.

I turned the Green Day CD up again. I liked it. Not because the entire *American Idiot* album is anti-Iraq War and I'm one of the few Tour players who isn't Republican—a registered Inde-pendent instead—but because the pounding rhythms made for good driving music. I settled in with the flow of traffic and thought about what Perkins had said. I hadn't thought I'd taken a risk by leaving a day early. Maybe I had. I respected his judg-ment on such issues. Someone out there had started toward me once. Would he be back? If he thought I'd seen him, he sure as hell would. Perkins had brought up a second topic as well, Nash Henley. I was no Wilbur Larch, but I did feel for the innocents—always had—and no one is more innocent than kids trapped in adult-initiated problems.

It seemed ironic to be thinking of "innocents" because there is nothing innocent about cheating. But the McCarthy family's problems hadn't ended with Hurricane's death. Only the cheat-ing ended there. Or I was assuming it did. I felt for Sherry. She'd lost it all—her husband and life as she'd known it. She had Hur-ricane to blame. As I'd said to Terry, Hurricane's decision to take clonidine to improve his putting was wrong. Yet it was what had driven him to do so that made the whole thing gray. It ap-peared that he'd trusted a friend with his money. Again, that was Hal McCarthy's poor decision. But it had been a business partner—and a friend—who burned him. Would I have gotten myself in that bind? Everyone would like to say no, but business deals go sour all the time. So in truth, none of us know.

Who killed Hurricane? Ron Scott had motive—Hurricane knew Scott lost his money. But Scott was dead before Hurricane was killed. Paul Meyers had been involved in the same business venture but his career was flourishing, which suggested that his Nichols Golf losses might be inconsequential. I'd never believe Kip Capers could shoot anyone, but he, too, was in this thing. And Pete Sandstrom had trained several of them and might have had knowledge of the clonidine. The more I thought about it, Sandstrom might've had motive to *get* Hurricane to use the stuff. He was launching his personal-training business. If clients were successful, he and his business looked good. On the flip side, what if word got out that he had known about the clonidine? Sandstrom could lose it all. Was that worth killing a client over? But that train of thought was based on Hurricane telling someone or leaking his usage to the media. Hurricane wouldn't do that. Even Sherry had been kept out of the loop.

So I was back where I started. Why had Hurricane McCarthy been killed? Was Ron Scott killed for the same reason? Had tests been done to see if clonidine was in Scott's system as well? And why would Sandstrom go to Hurricane's house following the murder? That looked suspicious. Why would he draw additional attention to himself?

I replayed the Hurricane McCarthy-Pete Sandstrom on-course conversation that Sherry had brought to the front and center. Conversations have lives of their own, living within a listener's perception, which is based almost entirely on surrounding contexts. Hurricane McCarthy had admitted using clonidine to improve his putting. Then Hurricane was murdered, which changed the contexts of prior conversations drastically. He had been exhausted during our first round together and Sandstrom had asked if he was okay. "A little tired," had been Hurricane's reply.

Then it clicked for me. It had been there all along, tugging, urging me to find it.

Sandstrom's next remark had me calling Perkins back.

*L*isa, Perkins, and the rest of the PGA Tour had met me in Palm Beach Gardens, Florida. We were in an Olive Garden Monday evening. Darcy was on my lap attacking a bread stick, Perkins was eating salad, and Lisa was sipping iced tea. I had just finished telling them about my visit with the McCarthy family and about my realization.

"'You should feel great. Hollis said so'?" Perkins said. "That's the statement?"

"Yeah," I said. "Back in Scottsdale, during a practice round, Hurricane was telling Sandstrom how tired he was. That was Sandstrom's reply. Clearly, he knew what Hollis had prescribed."

"Not necessarily."

"What are you talking about?" I said. "Put it with the rest of this and it fits."

"Jack, that's not a confession."

"Look at it in the context of what we know."

"I look at what will hold up in court. Sandstrom mentioned the doctor's name. He didn't mention clonidine. Nothing's illegal about a doctor telling a patient he'll feel better. A good lawyer will say they were discussing some cough syrup Hollis recommended."

"That's bullshit," I said.

"Potty word, Daddy," Darcy said and held up a hand.

I grinned. "Do you take IOUs?"

She looked up at me. I struggled to reach beneath her, into my pocket, to get a quarter.

"You asked if tests were done on Ron Scott," Perkins said.

"None were. There was no need. Cause of death is pretty evident when the guy's been shot with a .357, point-blank."

"So we don't know if he was using clonidine," I said. "What about your sit-down with Sandstrom?"

"He hasn't arrived yet," Perkins said.

I drank some Heineken. Perkins sipped his Sam Adams. I knew Perkins was right. He did this for a living; I was a golfer, not a cop. So maybe the statement wouldn't cut it in court. It cut it for me. My gut told me the statement was proof of Sandstrom's knowledge that Hurricane used clonidine.

The waitress arrived with our dinners. I was having spaghetti and meatballs. She set lasagna in front of Perkins. Lisa got a pasta-and-vegetable dish. I put Darcy in the booster seat beside me and she started eating before the waitress had set her kids' spaghetti and meatballs next to the chocolate milk.

"Kid nearly took the waitress's arm off," Perkins said.

"Good genes," I said.

"Tom Schmidt spent some time researching today. He's coming out here again to talk."

"Does he have something?" I said.

Lisa looked from Perkins to me and back to Perkins, "Am I being scooped by the *L.A. Times?*"

"What do you know about dotcoms?" Perkins said.

.   .   .

"How was the day?" Lisa said, when we'd gotten to the suite after dinner.

We'd put Darcy to bed and were sitting on the loveseat, watching The Golf Channel. Jennifer Mills was talking about the small funeral held for Hurricane. Unlike Ron Scott's ceremony, Hurricane's had not been affiliated with the PGA Tour. I thought of what Hurricane had told me in the car the night he died. Even in death he was "golf's pariah."

"I hit the ball terribly today," I said. "I played two balls, a score ball and a second to try to correct the mistakes. Shot seventy-eight with my score ball."

"You're pressing," she said, and sipped her Starbuck's coffee, which she'd bought on the way home from the Olive Garden.

"You might be right," I said. "I thought it was my setup, so I had Silver tape me on the range today. Then we compared my setup to a tape from the week I won the Buick Classic. I can't see a difference."

"You're putting a lot of pressure on yourself. Whether it's also mechanical or not, I don't know. But I know how seriously you take the game. You're pressing right now."

I shrugged. There wasn't much to say to that. I certainly couldn't dispute it. Golf had been my entire life, until I'd met Lisa. Now it took second place to my family, but in truth it was more like 1 and 1A. I was pressing.

"I'm not within spitting distance of the top one twenty-five," I said.

"You've got all summer."

I nodded but said nothing. I had won the Buick Classic two years ago, the victory good for a two-year exemption. It had taken a decade to win on Tour, so the Buick Classic trophy on my mantle hadn't made me think it would be easy. Yet it had taught me that I could do it, and with that had grown enormous self-expectations. A second win hadn't come (fifty-six starts and counting), and I knew now why so many players claim the second win is harder than the first—you want to prove it was no fluke. You end up trying too hard, thinking too much.

My father took a painting course at the local community college in Maine and told me his instructor said elementary school kids use the whole canvas because they have no fear, but adult beginners often use only a small portion of the surface. When I hold clinics at my home course, the Woodlands Club in Falmouth, Maine, I teach putting basics. Six-year-olds simply ram the ball at the cup. They rarely leave it short or spend time reading a break. They simply hit it. Drop a ball in front of an adult and he lines it up, tries to gauge the speed, and, as has been statistically proven of high handicappers, leaves the ball short, afraid of running the putt by.

"Maybe I am thinking too much," I said. "My exemption runs out this season. And I'd like Darcy to see her father win on Tour."

Lisa sat looking at me for a long time. She shook her head slowly. "Neither of those things have anything to do with hitting a golf ball, do they?"

I looked at her and started to speak. Then I did something smart. I shut my mouth.

.   .   .

A half-hour later, The Golf Channel was replaying a European Tour event from two years ago. I turned the television off. Outside, the Florida sun was a distant orange flame. Maine has little that compares to a Florida sunset.

"Dinner was strange tonight," Lisa said, "a little tense. How's everything with Perkins?"

"He's working again," I said. "Not just rehabbing. It's a step."

"And the cane is forever?"

I nodded.

"He limps badly."

I didn't say anything.

"Has he gone home?"

"Not recently."

"That's too bad," she said, and stood. "I'd take a golf slump any day over that situation."

I considered that as I watched her walk to the bedroom.

.   .   .

At 10:25 P.M., I was standing at the front desk in the hotel lobby.

"Is there a VCR I can use?" I said. "I need to look at a videotape."

The kid behind the desk wore a white button-down shirt and dark tie. His nametag read TIM. He looked young, probably a business-management major interning.

"Is this for a corporate outing, sir?"

"No. Private. It's a golf tape."

"Oh, you're here for the tournament."

I said I was. He made a phone call and the manager appeared and led me to his office, where there was a TV-VCR setup.

"What's it like to play golf for a living?"

"Best job in the world," I said, and thought again of Lisa's last statement.

"Take as much time as you need, sir. We could've sent a VCR to your room."

"No, this is fine."

He left and I slid the first tape in. I watched my swing in slow-motion from two years ago. The setup was fine—knees slightly bent, left shoulder higher than the right one, my grip looked perfect, and the take-away was low and smooth. The club rotated back and stopped just before parallel. The descent was on plane and my weight transfer seemed perfectly timed with the impact.

I exchanged that tape for the video shot that morning. The setup seemed fine again. I pressed Pause and looked at it carefully. Everything looked aligned well. My grip was the same. I took it off Pause and watched the take-away. I stopped the tape again at the top of my backswing. I studied my clubhead in relation to my swing plane.

There was an inconsistency I hadn't seen earlier.

The swing plane, the angle and arc of the golf swing, is the imaginary circle the club should follow back and through. Most players try to remain "on plane" throughout. But at the top of my swing, I was moving the club away from my body, coming over the top slightly.

In the elevator on the way back to my room, I made an imaginary swing in front of the mirrored wall, freezing at the top, checking the club's location in the reflection. Again, it was slightly askew. It wasn't something Silver would pick up watching me swing. I had to stop at the top and look at myself from behind to see the flaw.

I got off the elevator and started toward my room. This time, my pause was not calculated. This time it had nothing to do with golf.

Two men stood near my hotel door. The smaller one, I recognized.

"I've been waiting for you," he said.

"*L*ast time I saw you," I said, "you told me you couldn't talk and sent me to Hurricane. Now he's dead."

Richie Barter didn't speak for a long time. He looked like he hadn't slept in a week and fidgeted like a guy awaiting a verdict. He ran a hand slowly through his hair. Then he cracked his neck with a long, slow roll. When a dull thud came from the room above us, Richie flinched. He was sitting across the coffee table from me in the main room of my suite at 10:45. Hands motionless in his lap, he stared down at the leg of the coffee table. He wore khaki pants, black loafers, and a black T-shirt that had the cover of Bruce Springsteen's *The River* on it. The shirt wasn't tucked in, which gave him the disheveled weekend-preppy look. It was always interesting to see a guy my age who was still single. I went to The Wiggles concerts; a guy like Richie still saw The Boss.

"Who's your friend?" I said. Richie had left the other guy in the hall, saying he'd "be right out." The guy was African-American, wore dark glasses, and stood at least six-feet-five. He had to go 300 pounds. He wore a navy-blue sports jacket and stood silently, only nodding in reply.

Richie ran a hand through his hair again. "That's Brian," he said, still looking down. "He's a personal security specialist."

"A bodyguard?"

He didn't answer. The only sound was the fan Lisa had going in the bedroom. We brought it with us because we liked the sound when we slept. When you sleep in thirty-five different beds a year, anything adding consistency is welcomed.

"I heard you were with Hal when it happened."

"That's right," I said, and waited for him to go on. He didn't. Had the bodyguard been hired in response to the second murder?

The bedroom door was closed, so Lisa and Darcy were asleep. I had tried to convince Richie to go to the hotel bar to talk. He wouldn't and in fact rushed to get into my room.

"About ten years ago," I said, "I'd have taken a triple bogey to have *a woman* want to get into my hotel room half as bad as you did. What the hell's going on?"

Richie didn't speak and continued to stare at the floor. He hadn't waited for me at quarter of eleven to come here and sit in silence. So I waited. As I watched him, I realized he wasn't staring at the coffee table's leg. Rather, he was looking at a small rubber Polly Pocket doll Darcy left under the table. I got up and went across the room for a bottle of water, which sat on the windowsill. I opened it, drank, and looked out at the parking lot below. Rows of bright street lamps, anchored by yellow islands, illuminated the lot. People walked to and from parked vehicles. The view paled compared to the sight from my living room at home—the endless expanse of ocean—but that's life on the road. And it's a life I'm damn lucky to have. When I turned around to walk back to the sofa, I was startled.

Richie stood two feet away.

"Jack, man, I'm not with them. I just invested."

"Don't sneak up on me, Richie," I said, and sidestepped him and went back to the sofa and sat, "or you'll need your bodyguard. What did you come here for? You told me and Perkins you knew 'just about all of it.'" I made quotation marks with my fingers. "But you told us nothing. Now things are worse. Hurricane's dead."

"Jack, I—"

I sensed a line of bullshit and waved him off. "It's late, Richie. Either talk or leave."

He walked to the sofa and stood in front of me, staring down for a long time. I felt like he was looking at me but seeing something else. He was thinking, clearly distracted, his mind in overdrive. Then he sat and blew out a long breath.

"I was part of Nichols Golf, too," he said. "I don't want to end up like the others."

"So you hired the bodyguard?"

He nodded. "Nothing permanent. I hope they catch the killer soon, so I can let Brian go. But I'm not taking chances."

I clasped my hands atop my head and closed my eyes. I was tired of it all—Hurricane's death; his cheating; what poor Sherry was going through and what her future held; Perkins's internal struggle and what it was doing to his family; and my piss-poor golf game. There were still five months remaining in the season, yet I felt like it was late August. Richie had started it all with his public accusations. Then all hell broke loose. Now he was back.

"What's your connection to Nichols Golf?" I said, and crossed my ankles atop the coffee table. I leaned my head back against the seat cushion. I had an 8:10 A.M. tee time.

"I invested in the company, wrote Ron Scott a check for a hundred grand, and lost it all."

"Who else was an outside investor?"

"No one else was stupid enough," he said. "That's not why I'm here, though, not about Nichols Golf. Only what it led to."

I sat up straight, forearms on my thighs, and looked at him. "Do you know who killed Ron Scott and Hurricane McCarthy?"

"Not who. Maybe why."

I repeated his words, shaking my head slowly. "For Christ's sake," I said. "Tell me why."

Richie looked at me, thinking. Then he glanced at the door like a child making sure a parent is still there before taking a step alone. I saw fear in his jittery mannerisms. Like him or hate him, the guy was a world-class athlete. This night, his movements were stilted, no coordination apparent. Fear was also present in his eyes. Weeks earlier, this same guy held an impromptu press conference in a parking lot, pointing fingers and making sweeping accusations that turned out to be true. That brash athlete was long gone. He fidgeted under my gaze. His feet were flat on the floor, and dark half-moons were under his eyes.

"I'm not here for me," he said, and motioned to the door behind which stood the bodyguard. "I've got Brian. But Billy Carvelli listens to you, Jack. Tell him to stay away from Pete Sandstrom."

"Why?"

"Sandstrom is no good."

"Did he know about Hurricane using clonidine?"

"What did Hurricane tell you?"

"He admitted it."

"Admitted all of it?"

"He said he used clonidine to improve his putting."

"Oh," Richie said. The tension seemed to ease from his shoulders. He looked at me, head tilted slightly. "What else did he say?"

"He told me why he thought he had to do it."

"That's it?"

"What else is there?"

Richie stood. "Look out for Billy Carvelli, Jack."

"His father does that. Why are you saying this to me, anyway? Why don't you look out for him yourself?"

"I'm looking out for us all," Richie said.

"By going to Mitch Singleton? By calling people out in the press?"

"I'm the only one looking out for us, Jack."

"Bullshit," I said. "Do you know who killed them?"

"No."

"Why'd you come here?"

"For Carvelli," he said, and turned and walked out.

I was still seated when the door closed behind him. I leaned back, closed my eyes, and blew out a long breath.

. . .

At 7:45 the next morning, I called the clubhouse to have a note left in Billy Carvelli's locker canceling our practice round. I dialed Liz Scott's number again. Richie Barter had lost $100,000 in the Nichols Golf fiasco and Sherry McCarthy had told me Ron Scott thought he was Charles Schwab.

"Good morning," a familiar voice said, answering the phone. "Scott residence."

"Liz," I said, "it's Jack Austin."

"Oh, I—I get Mrs. Scott for you."

"Who's this?"

"I get Mrs. Scott."

I was sitting on the sofa in boxer shorts, sipping coffee. *SportsCenter* was muted. Lisa had gone for a run, and Darcy was on the floor playing with her Polly Pocket dolls. "You're 'poseta do it like this," Darcy said in a most serious voice; she was the ventriloquist as dolls spoke to one another. It was Tuesday and many players would be arriving, so I could go to the course a little later and catch someone for a practice round. Hopefully, I would see Pete Sandstrom, too.

"Hello?"

"Liz, this is Jack Austin."

"Oh . . . how are you?"

"Fine. Who answered the phone?"

"The maid, Jack. Why? It's very early."

"Just curious. Last time we spoke, you said the Nichols Golf group took some investment risks."

"No, I didn't."

"Sure you did. What did they invest in?"

"I have no idea."

"Your husband did the investing and he lost some of your money. You must know."

"No. I don't."

"How can that be, Liz?"

"Who handles the money in your house, Jack?"

I was silent.

"My point exactly," she said. "What else can I do for you at the crack of dawn?"

I tried to think of something else to ask that might lead to investment information. I was no private investigator. I was the world's ninety-ninth-ranked golfer—and slipping.

"You still there, Jack?"

Nothing came to me. "I appreciate your time," I said.

"It's quite all right," she said. "Have a pleasant day." She hung up.

The receiver was a ten-pound weight. I sat staring at it. Why had she denied her previous comment? And where the hell had I heard the maid's voice before?

"I hope you understand my position on all this," Peter Barrett, the PGA Tour commissioner, said. "And I hope you are fully aware of your responsibilities, too."

I had arrived at the golf course at 9:15 A.M., gone to the range, and hit exactly two practice shots before Emilio Rodriguez, a former CPA, now Barrett's right-hand man, approached. He looked like a Secret Service agent on his lunch hour—jacketless, dark slacks, starched white shirt with a dark tie, and sunglasses. He informed me that I was to meet with Barrett.

Now Barrett and I were in the clubhouse, in a back office, just the two of us. All cozy. I had no idea what my "responsibilities" were but was starting to feel like Tiger Woods—people waited for me where ever I went: first, Richie Barter and his "personal security specialist," now the Commish.

Apparently, Barrett thought I knew what my "responsibilities" were. We sat in awkward silence.

Barrett cleared his throat.

I looked at him.

He raised his eyebrows.

I nodded encouragingly.

Still silence.

"How 'bout them Red Sox?" I said.

"Excuse me?"

This day, Barrett's silk tie was red with tiny blue sailboats. He angled the leather desk chair as if he was going to prop his feet atop an open corner drawer. I knew that wasn't about to happen. Instead, he leaned back and crossed his legs, the toe of one winged-tipped loafer bobbing effeminately. The office smelled of Barrett's musky cologne. He had a fresh legal pad positioned squarely in the center of the desk blotter and his trademark gold pen lay atop it. No coffee, the computer screen behind him dark. I wondered if the hotel had lent vacant offices to PGA Tour brass. Or had Barrett had simply thrown the hotel manager out and taken the guy's workplace?

"I'm confused as to why I'm here," I said.

"Hal McCarthy was a friend of yours, wasn't he?" Barrett said. He'd asked that same question as I left the Tour Policy Board meeting, at which he'd attempted to play spin doctor. His accusatory tone remained.

"Yes," I said.

Barrett nodded as if my answer explained a lot. In fact, the answer oversimplified my emotions. Minutes before his death, I had told Hurricane he'd violated our friendship. I wouldn't let a grudge follow him to his grave.

"It's a tragic situation," I said. "His family is left financially strapped. His kids have no father. His wife lost her whole life. It's going to take a long time for them to pick up the pieces."

Barrett's eyes narrowed and focused on mine. He sat like that for almost ten seconds. Then he nodded to himself as if he'd just figured something out. "Jack, Hal McCarthy's victories are being wiped out—taken out of the Tour's press materials and off the archives of PGATOUR.COM. Trophies are being made and will be presented to the players who finished second in those events. The money lost by the players who participated the weeks Hal McCarthy won will be paid out with every player moving up a spot."

"You're sending a strong message."

"Yes," Barrett said, and leaned closer. "The PGA Tour is not as forgiving as you seem to be."

"I don't condone what he did, Commissioner. Remember Hutch Gainer?"

"He's still suspended for his involvement in gambling on Tour events."

"And I kicked his ass for him," I said.

Barrett didn't like my choice of words. I didn't care.

"I didn't do it because he gambled," I continued, "but because he was throwing strokes. He dishonored me, every other guy out here, and the game. Nobody works a lifetime to have Hutch give him strokes so some guy can win a bet."

"This is different, Jack. Hal McCarthy was *excelling* because of what he was doing."

"It's not so different," I said. "Both scenarios disgrace the game."

"And you sympathize with him?"

"No. But circumstances drove him to the edge and beyond. He was broke because a friend betrayed him. And that left him desperate. I don't condone what he did. I don't like what he did. We were friends and he cheated me."

"But you still feel for the family? I think the wife had to know about it. Those putts that were suddenly dropping made her money as well."

My "responsibilities" were becoming clear: Tow the company line, Mr. Austin. "I don't think Sherry McCarthy knew a thing, Commissioner. Regardless, yes, I do feel for the family. This whole scenario bothers me. Sure, Hurricane made some putts he might not have made. But look at what that cost him. He was finished before he was murdered. He told me he'd never walk another PGA Tour course."

Barrett smiled at me the way a parent does a child who just doesn't get it, a sad-but-friendly smile. I thought he might pat my head.

There had been a time, when, as with Hurricane, I had respected Peter Barrett. Now I saw him as a cold man more concerned with the game's reputation than the people involved in it. I wanted to tell him to go to hell. But after a $100,000 fine, that would surely get me suspended. And given my place on the money list, I couldn't afford not to play. So I leaned back, crossed my legs, and sat looking at him, letting things settle.

Like many dyslexics, I'm prone to seeing the world in black

and white. Often that leads to tunnel vision. Never had there been a time when I didn't know what I loved and wanted.

Yet there was no black and white in Hurricane McCarthy's situation. There might have been. If I had simply shut that hotel-room door on Hurricane the night he'd asked me to sit in his car and listen, everything would have remained the way I liked it—a perfect square, no rough edges, and I could've carefully boxed the whole mess up, tied the lid on it, and heaved it. After all, being just a golfer is a hell of a lot easier than being a friend. If I had distanced myself, never heard his story or talked to his wife and son, I might have been able to shut the complicated view out and simply condemn the actions and the man. But I had agreed to sit in the car with Hurricane that night. And I had heard a man beaten by a game that had left him behind, beaten by friends who turned out not to be, and by his own desire to remain what he'd always been to his wife and kids—the provider, the father.

I could condemn his actions, but try as I might, not the man.

Hurricane McCarthy's was not the typical story of professional-athlete-turned-cheater. It was about money—Hurricane had even said so—but it had little to do with greed.

"Jack," Barrett said, "I'd like to sit down with you and Mr. Perkins later and go through this, top to bottom. What time would work for you?"

.   .   .

I returned to the range to find Silver regaling a three-player audience with Jack Austin tales of woe. "Two in the water?" Padre Tarbuck said, and burst into laughter. "That's like *Tin Cup!*"

"Whatever the story is," I said, approaching them, "I'm sure my caddie gave me the wrong yardage. Happens all the time."

Silver grinned and we went back to my station. JACK AUSTIN was on a sign in the center of the range. TIGER WOODS marked the station next to mine. Silver went to a small stand at the end of the range and asked the man behind the counter for two bags of Titleist Pro V1 balls.

"How was the chat?" he said, when he returned.

I shook my head. It was time to work. "I reviewed the tapes last night. I think I saw something. Watch me at the top of my backswing. I'm coming off plane."

"I didn't notice that yesterday."

"I don't think it's obvious, but I think my hands are getting away from my body a little bit." I hit a pitching wedge that traveled my standard 120 yards. The trajectory and distance were ideal. Maybe seeing the video had been enough. I hit a second wedge. This time the ball drifted left to right and fell twenty yards short of the 100-yard marker.

"Yeah, sure," Silver said. "There it is. Hold your club at the top."

I brought the club back and paused.

Silver moved closer and pulled my hands away from my body. "This was where the club was on that last swing, before you started down."

It was a drastic change. When on plane, I couldn't see my hands at the top of my backswing. The club was set parallel to the ground and not there very long before I began the downswing. My hands were somewhere behind my right ear, out of my periphery. However, when Silver moved my hands away from my body, I could see them out of the corner of my eye. I told him as much.

"Take a few slow swings and stop if you see your hands."

"It's no way to play," I said, "looking for my hands. I'll have to take my eyes off the ball."

"It's just practice," he said.

I brought the wedge back again. It felt awkward, but at the top, I glanced quickly to check the club's positioning. It worked. I saw my hands and stopped. Then I did it again. This time I saw nothing, refocused on the ball, and finished my swing, hitting a solid wedge shot. I made a practice swing, looking for my hands, saw them, and stopped. I did this two more times, saw nothing, and then hit a shot.

"Bingo, Jack," Silver said. "I deserve a raise."

"You're overpaid as it is," I said, grinning.

"One of these days, when I get noticed, you'll be sorry to see me go. What do you think of this idea? I sent an e-mail to

Queer Eye for the Straight Guy and told them about an idea for a show where they would come to the Tour and give you a make-over."

I looked at him for a long time, shook my head, then hit another shot.

． ． ．

At noon, I was in the clubhouse eating lunch with Lisa and Darcy. Silver wasn't with us because, while players are issued no less than four clubhouse passes per event, caddies receive none, and I had already given my passes to Lisa and Perkins, who'd requested the remaining two. So Silver was at Caddie Central, a PGA Tour-funded mobile caddy shack parked near the range. The "Caddy Wagon," as we call it, provides caddies a place to relax and get a home-cooked meal for a nominal fee. Not bad. But the contrast between the two facilities—one a Mercedes, the other a rusted Pinto—is symbolic of the treatment of caddies on Tour. The salaried loopers working for Mickelson and Woods can earn more than I do. Yet the other caddies, the guys who stand in the parking lot as the players arrive and ask if anyone's looking for a looper, live a tough and often desperate existence—no room, no meals, no health insurance.

Lisa was eating her chicken salad and reviewing interview notes. I was trying to eat a tuna sandwich and get Darcy to eat her PB&J. I have difficulty enough multitasking, but this job was way out of my league. Like most parents, my wits were no match for a crafty three-year-old and Darcy had purple jelly on herself and a large spot on my khaki pants. She found it more interesting to push down on the top of the sandwich and watch the jelly ooze out the side than to actually eat the thing.

"Who'd you interview?" I said, chewing a quick bite of tuna while wiping Darcy's hands with a white linen napkin.

"Paul Meyers actually approached me," Lisa said. She held her fork with her right hand. With her left, she flipped a page, and then waved the hand, palm up, in a *Who knew* gesture. "He said there had been a misunderstanding that led to his caddy being 'slightly abrupt.'"

"'Slightly abrupt'?"

"Paul told me about an equipment change that added twenty yards to his tee shots. It's interesting. He says a stiff-tipped driver made so much difference that he replaced all his shafts to match the one in the driver."

"The guy hits a seven-iron two hundred yards," I said, "and he weighs what, one sixty-five? A stiff-tipped shaft made that much difference?"

"That's what he said—twenty yards on every club."

I sipped some ice water and chewed a cube. A stiff-tipped shaft accomplished what one expected—it eliminated the flexibility at the bottom of the club; it was like swinging a two-by-four. Some guys liked that; others claimed that final little whip just before impact added distance. I hadn't seen any hard statistical data to prove one theory or the other. However, the guys I knew who used stiff-tipped shafts swung the club 120 miles per hour and used them for control. Paul Meyers, all 165 pounds of him, didn't fit that image.

On the table between us, my cell phone rang. I grabbed it as Darcy took the bread off the top of her sandwich and put her hand in the jelly.

"Jack," Lisa said, "I thought you were watching her. I'm trying to work."

"Hello?" I said pinching the phone between my shoulder and ear as I pulled Darcy's hand out of the jelly and wiped it with the napkin again.

"Mr.—Mr. Austin." The voice cracked and shook with uncertainty. "You gave me your cell phone number. I—I hope it's okay that I called. This is Terry McCarthy."

"Terry," I said, "you okay?"

Lisa looked up from her notes. "Terry McCarthy?" she whispered.

I nodded. Beside me, Darcy dropped her sippy cup to the floor. I grabbed it and wiped the mouthpiece with my napkin. "What's going on, Terry?"

"I—I'm in the workshop, and, well, like, the athletic director at school brought in a guy to talk about this . . . so I know a little about this because he mentioned this one by name."

"Terry, slow down."

I heard him inhale. Then he continued: "I—I opened a pocket on a golf bag Dad never used anymore—it was behind, like, three others—and the guy who spoke at school, well, he said this stuff is banned and dangerous. I found it in the bag. Mr. Austin, I'm scared. I don't know what to do. The cops are here, talking to Mom."

"You're in your father's workshop?"

"Yes."

"What did you find, Terry?"

"It's one of those orange pill containers. It says *stanozolol* on the side."

"I'll be damned," I said, and looked at Lisa.

Her notebook was closed now. She stared at me intently.

"Terry," I said, "listen to me very closely. You take the bottle to those police officers. You can trust them."

"But it looks"—his voice cracked; I knew he was fighting tears—"bad for my father."

The kid was holding anabolic steroids, caught between a dead father's legacy and two live cops in his living room. Goddamn you, Hurricane.

"Terry," I said, "you have to do it. Take it to them now."

He said he would and we hung up.

"Now I know why Pete Sandstrom went to Hurricane's house," I said, and dialed Perkins.

*L*ife presents itself in a series of realizations.

I couldn't return to the range after lunch. For the first time in my life, I didn't feel like playing or practicing. Instead of taking Darcy back to the day care, I went back to the hotel with her and sat on the loveseat and watched her play with Polly Pocket dolls. Occasionally, she asked me to change a doll's clothes by pulling one rubber outfit off and replacing it with another. Mostly, though, she just played and I sat on the couch silently watching, noticing everything about her: Her knees and ankles were pressed flat against the carpet, a pose that would cripple any adult. Her expressions varied with the voice of each character—eyes flickering then growing wide, mouth curving up, then drooping suddenly. An adorable spot of grape jelly I'd missed was still on her chin. Once, she looked up, saw me watching, and fell silent. I pretended to look away. She went back to her game, once more the ventriloquist giving voice to each doll. She was absolutely perfect in her purposeful innocence.

As a kid, I had discovered golf because my father introduced me to the game. He and my mother were far from the "country-club set," so Dad didn't start playing until his mid-thirties. But he loved the game and saw something in it that could be passed on to his only son. My first round was played with him at a nine-hole municipal course in central Maine. It was late fall, bird-hunting season, but this was a Sunday and Dad asked if I wanted to try golf.

My father stood only five-feet-ten but had the broad shoulders and thick callused hands of a laborer. Wrinkles like small map lines creased the corners of his eyes. He looked weathered but not tired—life had never beaten him. Rather, the gleam in his pale-blue eyes told you he knew the journey was to be enjoyed. His beard was white now but had been brown back then. The sky overhead was gray and we had just putted out on a par-four. I'd lost two balls on the hole. Dad asked my score.

"Five," I said.

"Five, huh? That's a really good score on that hole, son."

I smiled, a fourth-grader proud of the recognition.

"A great score, really," he continued, "on a tough hole like that. I made six."

"Six?"

"Yup," he said. "That was the best I could do. Next time, I'll do better."

I only nodded, considering the statement. After several moments, as we walked to the next tee, I said, "Maybe I had an eight."

"Let's sit down on the bench," he said. We had reached the tee box and the foursome in front of us was still in the fairway. He had his arm around me. "You know why I like golf, Jackie? Because it lets me judge myself against the course."

I looked at him.

"And most of all, I like it because I can judge myself against just me."

"Just you?" I said. "But you were playing against me."

He shook his head. "I was playing *with* you. I'm playing against myself."

He was quiet and I thought about that for a long time.

"And you've got to be honest to do that," he said.

I continued to look at him, silent, but nodding.

I had been ten that day and I never took another mulligan. Even now, during practice rounds, I play one "score" ball and count everything, hitting second shots only to correct the mistakes. I fell in love with golf shortly thereafter and, although dyslexia slowed me, struggled through books on Ben Hogan and Bobby Jones. I read of their lives, learned of men who practiced until their hands bled, of men who chipped balls into hotel-room chairs until three in the morning—men of dignity and integrity. In doing so, I came to further understand my father's lesson.

Darcy held up another Polly Pocket doll and I helped her change the clothes.

"You're my besta buddy, Daddy," she said.

I grinned. "You're my besta buddy, too, sweetie."

Outside, the early afternoon sun shone brightly. I knew guys were playing and practicing hard. But they didn't know what Perkins, Lisa, and I now knew. Soon Barrett would know. Then Lisa would break the story, blowing the scandal wide open. First, clonidine, now stanozolol.

On the PGA Tour.

Richie Barter had put performance-enhancing drugs in the public eye less than a month earlier with his tirade about putting. I'd heard the beta-blocker whispers, but that was all they were—unfounded rumors. A face-to-face admission to using clonidine and a bottle of stanozolol tablets in a guy's golf bag was another matter. I'd read enough sports pages to know stanozolol was an anabolic steroid. And I'd followed the Raphael Palmira scandal, so I knew there could be no mistake. Hurricane McCarthy hadn't been reaching for a Power Bar in GNC and accidentally grabbed the steroid. He had told me "the game was changing." This was his attempt to keep up. "'Clonidine was only the start.'" I said it aloud, repeating what Hurricane told me the night he died.

Darcy looked up from her game. I smiled and shook my head. She returned to her Polly Pockets. Hurricane's remark had come on the heels of me pointing out that since Ron Scott had taken his money and Scott was now dead, the situation didn't look too good for Hurricane. He had countered, saying he too was scared because clonidine "was only the start."

Stanozolol came next.

Who was Hurricane scared of?

And why?

· · ·

At 6:35 P.M., Perkins sat across from me at a table in the clubhouse dining room. Fred Funk was with his wife and a table full of kids at the far end of the room. J. P. Hayes and wife Laura were near us. J. P. asked what I thought of the course. I answered and asked how things were in El Paso. Perkins and I were waiting for *Los Angeles Times* reporter Tom Schmidt. A waitress moved past our table with a two-inch-thick steak. Perkins nearly salivated.

I snapped my fingers, getting his attention. "You were telling about this afternoon."

"Local cops picked Pete Sandstrom up at the golf course for questioning," Perkins said. "I was there. Quite a sight. I thought Paul Meyers was going to shit himself."

"They went onto the course?"

He shook his head. "Two homicide cops, plain clothed, walked right onto the driving range, up to where Meyers was hitting, and flashed the tin." Perkins sipped some Bud Light. I had taste.

I was drinking Sam Adams. "Meyers starts giving them crap about this being a practice day and him being a taxpayer," he made quote marks with his fingers, "'in the fifty-percent bracket.' Then they explained, quite eloquently, that his ass could be hauled in, too. He zipped it and Sandstrom went with them."

I shifted and took my credential, a PGA Tour money clip, off my belt. It was digging into my side. I set it on the table. "You saw all this?"

"I was right behind them." Perkins shrugged and smiled, devilishly. "And enjoyed the view."

"I'm sure," I said. "You just happened to be there?"

"Jerry Hernandez—"

"The Tucson cop?"

He nodded. "He's kind of running this thing, since Hurricane was killed in his city. So when the McCarthy kid gave him the steroids, he called the local guys here and they've been pretty good about keeping the Tour in the loop. They called me. Peter Barrett wants the whole world to know the PGA Tour will get to the bottom of this."

"So he made sure you went with them."

"And wore my PGA Tour pullover. I felt like one of those FBI guys you see on a TV raid—navy blue with PGA TOUR STAFF across the back."

"Barrett wants people to know this is an isolated situation."

"It better be," he said, and raised his brows.

I didn't touch that. "How's Linda and Jackie?"

"Fine."

"You talked to them?"

"Every night."

"Why not go ho—"

He shook his head before I finished. "I'm working right now."

"Fly them out."

He sighed. "When I'm ready." He shook his head. "I know that sounds selfish. Christ, I know it is selfish, but they deserve better. They had better. I need to be ready."

His family had always come first. I was surprised by what he said and had half a mind to tell him it was selfish indeed, that it wasn't only about him.

"The cane is a step up from the crutches," was all I said, "and the crutches were a step up from the wheelchair."

When he didn't say anything, I let it go.

"Were you in on Sandstrom's interview?"

He shook his head. "No. Only the cops. I was outside the box, listening."

"'The box'?"

"The glass interview room. Jerry Hernandez is pretty good at being a prick when he wants to be. Billy Peters is back in Chicago. He's got a case load and Chicago PD doesn't have the budget to send him flying all over the country. But if Jerry can shake something loose from Sandstrom about the Ron Scott murder . . . "

"They might send Peters back?"

"That's what he said. Right now, the Ron Scott killing is getting to be a cold case. Ideally, you solve a murder within the first forty-eight hours. After that, the odds get bad. Sandstrom denied everything today. He said he worked with Hal McCarthy and is very sorry if McCarthy decided to use any performance-enhancing drugs, since he'd never suggest that to a client. Says he 'has no idea' how someone would acquire stanozolol. Says he absolutely knows nothing about either murder."

"He's full of shit."

"About the stanozolol for sure. Probably the clonidine, too."

"The murders?"

Perkins drank some Bud Light without making a face. Iron will of a monk. Then he looked around the restaurant. Tom Schmidt was nowhere in sight. A little girl in a yellow dress walked past our table to where Sergio Garcia was eating with an older man in a navy blue suit. She held out a piece of paper and a pen and Sergio signed and smiled, chatting lightly with the girl.

Perkins set his glass on the table. "Like I said, Hernandez is good. I sat behind the mirrors and watched. He dragged Sandstrom back and forth over the coals for three hours. He's got alibis for both murders. They're solid and he didn't flinch. The steroids, though"—he shook his head—"no one bought his story."

"What did he say?"

"He says he went to Hurricane's house to see if McCarthy still had his weight-lifting belt."

"You're shitting me."

"Sure, Jack, that's what we said, too. Except when Hernandez called Sherry McCarthy, she said the belt was there."

"That doesn't prove he didn't give him steroids."

"He wouldn't have," Perkins said. "Todd Hollis, the doctor, has admitted to getting clonidine for Hurricane. He'd be the guy who got them, but Sandstrom would have been the brains behind it—how much, when to take it, all that shit."

"Hollis admitted to the clonidine. What's he say about stanozolol?"

Perkins shook his head. "His official story was that he thought Hurricane's stress level might," he made the quote marks again, "'put him at risk of a heart attack and therefore felt Mr. McCarthy needed them.' So far he denies knowledge of the stanozolol. He's probably holding out for a deal from the prosecution."

We both finished our beers. The waitress returned and we ordered two more.

"Sandstrom's such an arrogant prick," Perkins said. "I'd love to get him alone for about twenty minutes. He'd be singing steroids."

"Sandstrom's training business is growing," I said. "He had a lot to lose if anyone found out Hurricane was using steroids."

Perkins considered that for a while. He shifted and grimaced, then moved his leg as if he needed to do so to keep blood flowing through it. "I don't think Sandstrom killed those guys, Jack. The alibis are airtight. He was in California at a conference—in a goddamned room with a hundred people—the day Ron Scott was murdered. He used to work out there." He shook his head. "I watched him answer those questions. I don't think he was lying."

"Well, someone killed two people," I said, "and then started toward me."

When the waitress put down our second beers, Schmidt was right behind her. He looked at Perkins's Bud Light. "I'll buy, if you want something decent."

"Cute," Perkins said.

"Beck's," Schmidt said, and the waitress went to get one. "You guys just get here?"

"We're not on Hollywood time," Perkins said. "In Maine, quarter to seven doesn't mean seven-fifteen."

Schmidt grinned. He didn't look like a business reporter this night. He wore khaki shorts and a T-shirt that said FIGHT CANCER BIKE-A-THON 2005. He had legs like Priest Holmes's.

"You into that?" Perkins said.

"Biking? Yeah. I love it. After my knee surgery, the doctor said no more running or squats. I tried this. How about you? You said the cane was permanent. Biking might be something for you. It's great. Early in the morning—peaceful and quiet, just you and road."

Perkins shrugged. "Christ," he said, and glanced at me. "I haven't gotten that far yet. The last two months, I've been an asshole to everybody who loves me."

Schmidt didn't know what to say to that. I didn't either. I wanted Perkins to go home and had just listened to him explain why he couldn't. I didn't fully understand his thinking; maybe I couldn't—I hadn't been the one who was shot. Now Perkins sounded as if he didn't understand it himself.

The waitress returned with Schmidt's beer. He thanked her and she left.

"I think I have what you guys were interested in," Schmidt said. "What do you know about dotcoms?"

"Computer businesses?" I said.

"No. On-line businesses," he said. "Let me start at the beginning. Paul Meyers, Ron Scott, and Hal McCarthy got the idea that they could use McCarthy's club designs and their collective name recognition to launch a line of golf clubs. There's a problem, though. Callaway, Titleist, TaylorMade, Nike—these are the big boys and they have all kinds of money."

I knew Tiger Woods and the Nike design people spent days on end trying to match him to a driver and ball, Woods hitting shot after shot in a T-shirt and nylon athletic shorts, until they found the right combination. Likewise, I'd read that Taylor-Made had sunk thousands into a custom-made left-handed set of irons for Mike Weir. Certainly, a start-up company couldn't immediately compete.

"I'm with TaylorMade," I said. "I played Maxfli forever. Then TaylorMade bought them."

"That would have been the best-case scenario for Nichols Golf," Schmidt said. "Took three months, but I finally spoke with the guy who oversaw Nichols's portfolio"—he looked from me to Perkins—"anonymously and in confidence. I will sit in jail before I give up my source."

"We get it," Perkins said. "It goes no farther."

"Best-case scenario for Nichols Golf and all parties involved within would have been a sale to a large company, but that didn't happen. The company folded."

The waitress returned and we ordered. Perkins got something called the "pepper-jack steak," I asked for the halibut, and Schmidt got chicken Parmesan. We ordered another round of beers.

"Richie Barter invested a hundred grand," I said, when the waitress was gone, "and somewhere along the way, Kip Capers got involved."

"That answers the question I had for you," Schmidt said. "I wondered where the additional capital came from. How do you know that?"

"Hurricane told me they took Kip in. How much money did Nichols Golf take in?"

"I don't know the exact amount," Schmidt said. "'Hurricane'? Is that McCarthy?"

I nodded. "I don't know how much Kip invested or lost. Richie told me he gave a hundred grand himself."

"The start-up was two million," Schmidt said.

Perkins was listening intently, writing information in a small notepad. His beer sat before him untouched now.

"They bought a facility in southern California, near Meyers's home. My source doesn't know what they paid for that, although that'll be fairly easy to track down."

"Had to be a lot," Perkins said, "if it's California."

"They started off making full sets of clubs immediately, which is unusual. Typically, you make one club—a wood or a putter—to establish your product and build a following. Except Ron Scott and Meyers were convinced the company already *had* a following because the *golfers* had a following."

"Name recognition," Perkins said.

"Except in golf," Schmidt said, "it doesn't always work like that. Nike has Tiger Woods. But Nike isn't overtaking Titleist in sales. Why?"

"Phil Mickelson answered that," I said. In 2004, Mickelson, in an attempt to compliment Woods, said it was a testament to Woods's talent that he could play "inferior equipment" and still dominate. Nike did not take it as a compliment. Schmidt had never heard about the remark but nodded when I told him.

"A lot of guys are like you, Jack. Grow up playing one brand and trust that company. Or a company throws huge endorsement dollars around. Nichols Golf wasn't about to match Woods's hundred-million-dollar Nike deal. Name recognition goes only so far."

I drank some beer and added things up. "So Ron Scott thought if he could invest well he could generate additional capital."

Perkins looked up from his notepad, glanced to see Schmidt nodding, then said to me, "How do you know that?"

Schmidt didn't wait to hear. "That's right. Apparently, he thought that since he'd done well investing on his own, he could bust the market. The end result was predictable."

"Lost his shirt," Perkins said.

"Collectively—his, McCarthy's, and Meyers's."

"What did he invest in?" I said.

"I'd assume many things," Schmidt said. "I wasn't given access to the portfolio."

"So once the market started to turn on Scott and he started losing," I said, "they needed more money. It becomes like gambling. You go to Vegas, lose more than you expect on the first night, don't want to go home and tell the wife you lost two grand, so you get desperate to make it back."

"Which leads to larger bets," Perkins said, "and losses."

"Sure," Schmidt said, and drank some beer.

"This is where Kip Capers and Richie Barter must come in," I said.

"Yes. And Scott told Darw—my source—that McCarthy agreed to put more into the kitty—"

"And now his wife and kids are flat broke," I said.

"That would make sense. He put over a million more into it for a total of a million and a half." Schmidt shook his head sadly and set his glass down.

"And Ron Scott kept investing?" I said.

"And apparently doing it poorly."

I leaned back in my chair and ran a hand through my hair. Perkins scribbled furiously, catching up.

"Why would Hurricane give a million if the first half million or so wasn't enough?" I said. "And why only him?"

"I can't answer that," Schmidt said, "but remember that Richie Barter invested, too."

"He gave a hundred grand," I said, "a drop in the bucket. Hurricane threw down his family's future. You never knew him. One thing I can say about him is that he was a family man. It makes no sense."

The waitress returned with our meals. It would be a late night because the Tour Policy Board was to gather later, but I didn't eat. I looked out the window and watched the sun fall quickly. Sherry McCarthy had told me Hurricane wanted the company to go, that he loved golf-club design. We had all watched Greg Norman make millions away from the course. But Norman was a world-class businessman. Most of us were not—and we knew it. Moreover, Hurricane knew his game was in decline. He'd told me as much. In the car, the night he was shot, he'd said he peaked in the 1990s, before Tiger Woods brought huge weekly purses. So why would Hurricane risk his family's future? I had no answer. However, I sure as hell knew what his gamble resulted in—total desperation. And that led him to cheat. As courses were lengthened and young kids brought a power-ball mentality to the game, Hurricane took desperate measures to make back the money he'd squandered.

"You going to eat?" Schmidt said.

"I wish Ron Scott was alive. I'd like to ask him why Hurricane invested more than anyone else."

"I've been covering this stuff for twenty years, Jack. People make bad investments every day."

"Hurricane would do a lot of things," I said. "He'd put his reputation on the line. We know he'd cheat. But he wouldn't risk his family's future. I don't buy that."

"Well," Perkins said, "he did."

I nodded. The question remained why.

The gang was all there. After Hurricane's admission and murder, I had requested the meeting and Policy Board Chairman Paul Richardson obliged, calling the last-second gathering. All but one Board member had been able to make it. Peter Barrett looked perturbed when he arrived.

"Eight-thirty is an absurd time for a Policy Board meeting," Barrett said, taking his seat.

"I want to thank you all for coming," Richardson said, "and to apologize for any inconvenience. I spoke to our playing members yesterday. Hal McCarthy's admission could have serious ramifications—from both a playing and a financial standpoint. I agreed that we needed to meet."

He was the automotive industry exec who'd been so concerned about PR issues the last time we'd met.

"Jack," Barrett said, turning to me, "I'm told you requested this meeting of the full board."

I nodded. We were seated around a long boardroom table at a hotel banquet room; notepads and pens were before each man. Coffee and water had been provided. There were no windows, only a high ceiling. Generic landscape paintings, typical of all hotels, hung on the white walls.

"The Board needed to meet, sir," I said.

Bob Daniels was next to me. "I agree with Jack," he said. "I was pleased the Board could meet." He looked around. "Thank you all for coming."

"We have definitive proof that steroids have reached the PGA Tour," I said. "We need to initiate a list of banned substances, a firm testing policy, and a testing schedule. This has to be done."

"When we spoke before," Richardson said, "we were speaking hypothetically, talking about rumors. Commissioner, we have evidence now."

Barrett leaned back in his chair and looked at Richardson, momentarily surprised to have lost an ally. Then he became suddenly downtrodden. "I know. It pains me greatly. I love the game, believe in the values it represents, and seek to protect its reputation constantly. Things have changed since we last met."

I looked at Daniels. Maybe this would be easier than I'd thought.

"I fell in love with golf for the same reasons all of you did. I know full well what is at stake here." Barrett shook his head sadly and stared at a wall hanging for several moments.

"Yes, it's a difficult position," Richardson said. "I haven't slept well for several nights. We have to balance the integrity of the game against possible damage to the game's reputation."

"That's precisely why I'm so glad we have an effective substance-abuse policy already in place," Barrett said. "Any illegal substance is banned. If we have reason to suspect someone, we ask him to be tested. Anyone who refuses—and no one ever has—is suspended indefinitely."

No one spoke for several seconds.

Then I said, "That's not good enough, sir."

Barrett looked at me. Across the room, someone poured a glass of water from a pitcher. Ice cubes splashed into the glass.

"The PGA Tour is not going to panic because of one bad apple," Barrett said. "I have thought about this since the shooting. We all have responsibilities. Mine include protecting the game's image for our corporate sponsors. Golf is the last untarnished pro sport. The Tour can't afford to lose that image."

Richardson looked torn. For the next twenty minutes, he spoke about both sides of the issue. He offered examples of corporate sponsors who had told him they wanted "excellent role models" when they "pay for a television ad." Then he explained things from Barrett's point. At the end of that analysis, he said, "Will those same sponsors put their money elsewhere if we overreact?"

"Updating our testing isn't overreacting," I said.

"Changing the testing procedure now," Barrett said, "in the wake of the Hal McCarthy situation, would send the wrong message."

"Maybe we should let things die down," Richardson said, "and come back to this issue."

Barrett liked that. I didn't. It wasn't good enough.

"Commissioner, we don't have a union to stonewall testing like other pro sports," I said. "Now is the time to implement a serious testing policy. That is how to protect the integrity of the professional sport. And it would reassure the public, possibly attract sponsors."

"You don't consider our policy serious, Jack?" Barrett said, one eyebrow raised.

"It sure as hell looks like Hal McCarthy didn't," I said, and looked at Daniels for support.

He sat silently.

The meeting went that way for another twenty minutes. No agreement could be reached. Finally, Richardson found a lull in the discussion and adjourned the meeting.

Then Barrett cleared his throat. "I'd like to apologize to everyone who flew in today. Some people may be panicking, when clearly there is no reason for it. The PGA Tour can't panic over one bad apple. That could ruin the Tour's image."

. . .

When I returned to the hotel room, Lisa looked up from her laptop. I assumed Darcy was sleeping. Lisa wore shorts and one of my button-down shirts.

"They took Pete Sandstrom in for questioning this afternoon," she said.

Her voice was filled with excitement and her eyes danced. It was probably the same look I had on the back nine on Sundays when I was in contention. She looked beautiful. The coffee table before her was covered—the laptop, a teacup, a small carafe, and two notepads; a discarded room-service tray was on the floor next to her with the remnants of a chicken salad.

I nodded. "Yeah. I ate dinner with Perkins."

"Thought you were practicing all afternoon."

I shook my head.

"Was Perkins in on the questioning?"

"No," I said. "Just listening."

"I've got to call Perkins," she said. "I spent the afternoon working on this story. Tomorrow I go to the primary source."

"Sandstrom?"

"Yeah."

"Be careful."

"What's wrong? You sound exhausted."

"This situation gives you a rush. It knocks the wind out of me. This isn't supposed to happen in golf."

"Jack, this is a big-money professional sport. And this is the twenty-first century."

I knew all that. I'd heard it before. I still didn't like it. Not *my* game. Not golf. I didn't feel like talking, so I went to bed with my Philip Levine collection. After twenty minutes, my head was pounding too hard to read.

Steroids had reached the PGA Tour.

Originally, Richie Barter placed his performance-enhancing-supplement theory in the public's collective eye by spouting off to Mitch Singleton. Richie was a spoiled brat, a loudmouth, and no saint himself, but he had been right.

It made me recall Hutch Gainer. Hutch had dropped strokes to allow gamblers to win bets. I had been outraged and felt betrayed. I hadn't busted my ass since age ten to compete against the world's best players only to have a guy give me strokes. So I took matters into my own hands. I'd dragged Hutch into a dark closet and hit him with every ounce of uppercut I had. That was years ago. I was a different man now. I had a wife and family. And this situation was different. Then, I had known that only Hutch Gainer was involved.

Was Hurricane the only golfer using steroids?

In Tucson, Richie made me doubt the validity of Taylor Stafford's excellent round. That was the risk. It happened to baseball. When even one player is caught cheating, the integrity of the game is questioned. All performances are doubted.

Lisa planned to break the story the next day. Peter Barrett would no doubt deem Hurricane the lone user and continue to paint him as the only bad seed. I wanted desperately to believe that, but I wasn't sure. Pete Sandstrom had entered golf through a single client—Hurricane. Sandstrom's denial notwithstanding, I knew he was cognizant of his client's use of clonidine and stanozolol. I'd heard enough while playing with them to know about the clonidine. And the weight-lifting belt was bullshit—Sandstrom had gone to Hurricane's house to locate the steroids and cover his ass.

Outside, a siren slashed through the night's silence. It was only 9:25. I wasn't going to sleep anytime soon. I got out of bed, pulled a T-shirt over my head, and threw on a pair of blue jeans. Then I took a walk.

. . .

I was in the hotel lobby, holding a paper cup of coffee I'd gotten from the bar, when he caught up with me.

"I looked for you all day," Billy Carvelli said. "What happened Tuesday morning?"

"Sorry," I said, and sipped my coffee. I hadn't expected to be recognized. I wear khaki pants and a collared shirt so often that the jeans and "Life is Good" T-shirt amounted to a disguise. By contrast, Carvelli wore red breeze pants and a form-fitting white long-sleeve shirt. His hair was matted to his forehead. The shirt stuck to him like a wet tissue.

"Been running?"

"No," he said. "Lifting."

I thought of Richie Barter's warning to get Carvelli away from Sandstrom. We were near the revolving lobby door. A gust of cool night air hit me as two players in their mid twenties walked past us, a twosome dressed for a night on the town. One wore distressed jeans and a starched button-down shirt, not tucked in, beneath a blue blazer. The second guy I recognized as a rookie who'd had a top-three finish already this season. He wore blue jeans, a Dave Matthews Band concert T-shirt under a black leather jacket, and headphones. A white cord ran from the earbuds to a hand-held iPod. Their laughter carried the energy of anticipation as they went out the revolving door into the night. I watched them go. They were young, by Tour standards, but Carvelli looked like a baby next to them—and the contrast was startling.

"Who were you working out with?" I said.

"My trainer."

"Sandstrom?"

"Yeah. My father says he can get me"—Carvelli shook his head, disgusted—"'to the next level.'"

I didn't say anything. There was always a "next level." Golf is the dog chasing its tail. You can't master it. I had strived to get to that elusive "next level" since I'd begun playing. Even now, I wanted desperately to win again, to prove the first no fluke. Satisfaction in golf is fleeting at best. The game does that to you. I stood looking at Carvelli. Or the game does it to your old man.

"Pete Sandstrom is an asshole, Billy. And he's standing in the eye of a storm. Get the hell away from that guy."

"Billy," someone said, coming through the revolving door. It was Carvelli's father. He was no more than five-nine with a face shaped like a pear. He held a clipboard and a scorecard. "You made two bogies today," he said. Momentarily, his gaze swung to me; he made no attempt to hide his scowl. "You know what that means," he said, turning back to Billy.

"Two miles," Billy said.

His father didn't answer. He looked at me again. "What's going on here?"

"I was going for a walk when Billy came in. I hear you've been trying to reach me."

He looked at Billy. "Go change into running shoes and meet me back here in five."

"You make him run for every bogey he makes?"

"We had this talk once, Jack. It's no concern of yours. In fact, *none* of his training practices are your business."

"That why you've been looking for me?"

"To tell you to stay the hell away from my son."

A handful of people were in the lobby, some in business attire, others dressed casually. Fred Couples moved past us and went outside.

"There must be more to it than that," I said. "We had that talk once already."

He looked at me, a penetrating anger in his eyes. Billy had not left.

"Billy shouldn't be working with Pete Sandstrom," I said.

The senior Carvelli was shaking his head before I finished saying it.

"If you give a shit about your son's reputation—and I know you do because endorsements ride on it—you'll get him away from Sandstrom."

He made a fluttering movement with his hand, dismissing my remark. "Accusing and proving are two different things, Jack."

"So you know?" I said.

"I know athletes are younger now and they get bigger and stronger every year. That's what I know. And there's one personal trainer who honestly evaluates that situation." He turned back to Billy. "Go change into running shoes."

"Dad," Billy said, looking at the floor, "I don't like Sandstrom."

"Billy, DO IT NOW!"

We were suddenly the center of attention. The elder Carvelli didn't seem to care. Billy slumped away. I wanted to crawl under a rock. But Richie Barter had dragged me in from the start and recently returned, mentioning Billy by name. I couldn't walk away.

"Sandstrom is going down," I said. "Get Billy away from the guy. He's going to ruin Billy's reputation. Or worse."

"Worse?"

"Billy's a teenager. He's not even finished growing yet."

"You don't get it, do you? This is about keeping up."

"It's about cheating."

"Yeah, I heard that about you—Mr. Provincial. A little self-righteous, aren't you?"

I didn't deny it. We stood looking at each other. Then he laughed at me and repeated what I'd said: "'It's about cheating.'" He looked me in the eye, chuckling, and shaking his head sadly.

I stood, watching him, listening to him laugh. I'd been laughed at before. That wasn't why I hit him. It was his expression—the way his eyes narrowed viciously, the way his grin swelled on his face and his head shook back and forth, a sympathetic gesture, as he chuckled. If you grow up dyslexic, you know what it feels like to be pitied for your lack of comprehension. No one calls me dumb—and when my right cross landed flush on his chin, his chuckle was shattered. The only sound remaining was my own rasping breath ringing in my ears.

He went down and Billy Carvelli rushed to his father's side. "What are you, crazy?" he yelled at me.

I didn't say anything. I pushed through the revolving doors, out into the night air, holding my right hand and wondering for myself.

I couldn't see past ten feet in front of me, but that didn't matter. At 6:10 Wednesday morning, I was alone—with my game, my thoughts, and a bag of balls, as heavy fog pressed down on the range. For the first time in what seemed a long time, I didn't care where the ball went.

Maybe I hadn't seen past ten feet all along.

My right hand was stiff from the shot I'd landed on the senior Carvelli's cheek, the first and second knuckles slightly swollen. I had iced my hand for an hour the night before, although you couldn't tell by my first swing. When the pitching wedge sent the four-inch divot leaping end over end, I felt like someone had parked a Goodyear on it.

I hit a second shot, trying not to hesitate, trying to keep the clubhead moving through the ball. This time, I felt like I'd barehanded a flare. I dropped the wedge, clasped my right hand with my left, and hunched. I stayed like that for several seconds, thick fog pressing all around; a crow cawed loudly overhead. Tee times had been pushed back to allow the fog to lift. The golf course had not yet awoken. I didn't hear the rumble of mowers or fragments of distant conversations or car doors shutting.

My throbbing hand was an unrelenting reminder of everything I had come to the range to escape: Hurricane's fall and death; Pete Sandstrom and what I believed he'd introduced to the game; and my own lack of self-control, which, as I continued to hunch, clutching my hand, obviously threatened my participation in this event.

Behind me, I heard the tinkle of golf clubs as someone approached.

"Sprain your wrist, Jack?" It was Kip Capers. He, too, was caddy-less. He stood his bag up and moved closer. Two fairway woods with pale blue clubhead covers leaned against his bag. Each said NICHOLS GOLF. "Want me to run back to the clubhouse, get someone?"

"No. I'm fine." I straightened and opened my hand, spreading the fingers wide; then I made a fist. I did this several times. Each time hurt like hell.

"Try one of these," Capers said.

I took a fairway metal from him and hit one. The graphite shaft gave, cushioning the impact of the clubhead striking the turf, easing the pain I felt in my hand. The ball traveled low, a nice line drive that carried 250 yards.

"It's a four-metal," he said. "Stick it in your bag this week, if you like it."

I slid the cover on the club and did just that. "You an equipment rep now?"

"I still think the company made good clubs. And," he said, grinning, "I'd like to make back some of the money I lost." Capers took a pitching wedge out. It was in the seventies and humid, but he wore a dark pullover that concealed his tattoos. A cross dangled from a short chain off his ear. If the PGA Tour had a Dennis Rodman, Capers was it. He was ten feet away and looked at my hand. "Knuckles look swollen—nothing too bad, though."

"How long were you in Nichols Golf?"

"Still am."

"I thought the company went under."

"It did. Doesn't mean I think it's dead forever. Like I said, I believe in the equipment."

"Is Nichols Golf making a comeback, Kip?"

"How should I know? I still think the clubs are as good as any. I invested so I'll stand behind them. You know, Jack," he said, put out, "business deals are confidential."

"That's the slogan for Nichols Golf, isn't it? You guys should have it printed on your cards."

"Man, what's with you this morning, Jack? I don't ask about your business deals."

"People aren't getting killed in mine. I've had it with Nichols Golf and everyone involved. You and I have been friends for years, but I want answers. And I'll get them. Two investors are dead, Kip." I was staring at him through the fog. "The night Hurricane got shot, he told me he got screwed. Now he's gone and his family is broke. I want to know how and why."

"You're telling me he was killed *because* of Nichols Golf?"

"How well do you know Pete Sandstrom?"

"The caddy? Not at all. Why?"

I didn't answer. Knowing your weaknesses can be your best asset. Guile had never been my forte and I'd run my mouth enough. I took the four-wood out again and hit a second shot with it. The result was consistent with the first. I didn't see my hands at the top of my swing. The motion felt taut and controlled and the graphite shaft again cushioned the blow, despite my hand feeling stiff, my fingers as brittle as ice-covered twigs.

I believed Kip. When he was a rookie, Padre Tarbuck and I played practice rounds with him, ate meals with him. He was a good kid. Investing was no crime. And to my knowledge, he had no contact with Pete Sandstrom.

"I don't know what your problem is this morning, Jack, but I know only one good thing came out of that company— McCarthy's four-wood, the HURRICANE. Keep the club."

"You and Meyers are still on your feet," I said, unsure why.

Capers's expression changed—anger to pain to exasperation. He shook his head. "Keep the damned club. Like you said, we've been friends a long time. So I figured you knew me."

"I do."

"No, Jack, apparently you don't. I have no idea why those guys got killed. I invested. That's all I can tell you—and that I lost a half a million bucks. Paul Meyers and I are still here. Hell, he's playing better than ever. But I got involved because I really liked the clubs. I thought the company would do something. I was a rookie and half a million bucks was a hell of a lot of money. I had to sell my damned house when I lost it all. Yeah, Jack, I want you to have that club. In fact, do me a favor. Shove it."

He slid the wedge back into the bag, slung the bag over his shoulder, and walked away. My hand wasn't the only thing throbbing. Now my head was, too.

Deservedly so.

.   .   .

By 7:15 A.M., I was on the third green. Silver was on the bag and we were playing alone. A new fad on Tour was to play practice rounds before the media arrived. Tiger Woods had started it, going off around 6 A.M. to do his work and leaving Dodge before interview requests mounted. I didn't have the same problems—no one lined up to interview me; fans weren't following my every move—yet, this day, I sought solitude.

"You haven't said a word since we started, Jack," Silver said. He took the flag out and walked to our bag, which was on its side on the fringe, and put the flag atop it, careful not to set it on the putting surface.

"I was an asshole to Kip Capers this morning." I was making practice strokes, speaking to my feet.

"Kip?" he said. "Word in the Caddy Wagon was that you didn't treat Mr. Carvelli too well."

I looked up.

"Heard you popped him," he said.

"Things are getting to me," I said, and crouched behind the ball. The twenty-footer would move six inches, right to left. No. 3 at the Mirasol Sunrise Course is a monster—a 246-yard par three.

"What are you mad at Capers for?"

"I'm not." I straightened, made my customary two practice strokes, then I addressed the ball, carefully placing the putter blade behind it. I made my stroke.

Misread. The ball broke the other way, coming to rest four feet right of the cup.

"Hold on," Silver said, and tossed me a second ball. He crouched behind the hole to look at the green. "What were you looking at?"

I just shook my head.

"Clear your mind, boss. That's left to right, no question. Hit a second putt."

I did. When this one stopped at tap-in distance from the hole, Silver grabbed the balls and replaced the flagstick. We moved toward the fourth tee.

"Going to be a tough week," he said. "All the big boys are here and we've struggled a little. Want to get things off your chest?"

"I don't like Mr. Carvelli."

"No shit. There's got to be more to it."

"There is. But I don't want to talk about it."

"Does you hitting Carvelli have anything to do with Lisa working before seven today?"

"What are you talking about?" I said.

"I saw her this morning as I was leaving the hotel to run. She was in the parking lot doing an interview. No camera or anything, just her and a guy."

"Who? Peter Barrett?"

"No. A caddy, Pete Sandstrom."

"Did she have Darcy?"

"No. What's wrong?"

"Who else was there?"

"No one. They were at the far end of the parking lot. I wasn't close to them."

"Got your cell phone?"

He looked at me. They were banned from the course. That hadn't stopped him before and we both knew it.

"Ringer's off," he said.

"I don't care about that right now." I rummaged through the bag, found it, and dialed.

Lisa didn't answer.

I called the daycare. Darcy was there. I hung up and handed him the phone.

"Jack, you're getting frantic. What's going on?"

"We need to cut this short," I said.

She wasn't where she was supposed to be at 8 A.M.

Each morning, hours before going on-air, Lisa went to the CBS trailer to prepare. Often, I would break from hitting range balls or putting, get Darcy from the daycare, and stop by to visit. An intern once told me Lisa was her hero. "The most driven woman I've ever seen," the kid had said. It was that drive that frightened me now. She'd met Pete Sandstrom at the end of a parking lot, alone—and no one in the CBS trailer knew where she was.

I went to the clubhouse, moving room to room, my mind racing. Lisa was to break the story this day. She'd spent the previous day gathering background information. Yet it wasn't like her to schedule an interview, no matter how newsworthy the story, before 8 A.M. Had Sandstrom figured the story was on the horizon and contacted her? After all, Perkins had been there when Jerry Hernandez, the Tucson cop running the Hurricane

McCarthy murder investigation, had brought Sandstrom in for questioning. And my friendship with Perkins was well documented.

The clubhouse dining room was packed. I moved table-to-table. Lisa wasn't there.

I went to the clubhouse's one-room library. The door was closed. I opened it, looked among the floor-to-ceiling dark-wood bookshelves and leather furniture. Not there. I went outside and walked to the driving range. Often, she conducted pre-round interviews there. Not this day.

But Pete Sandstrom was.

The driving range was lined with players and caddies. Some stood in groups, talking. Others were working, ironing wrinkles from their swings before the event. Others were hitting one club then another, trying to find the right utility wood or short-iron for a particular shot they anticipated playing this week. Just a typical Wednesday. Sandstrom was at the far end of the range, standing behind Paul Meyers, his hands clasped behind his back like a patient football coach watching his quarterback.

A rookie named Tim Simmons, who weighed less than the bag his caddy carried, walked past them. Simmons had made only four cuts and wasn't within rifle shot of the top 125. He saw Sandstrom's jacket and stopped to ask about his business. It was much too hot for the windbreaker but the logo on Sandstrom's back—LEFT COAST TRAINING above the words "Golf Specialists" and a picture of a dumbbell—stood out like a billboard. Sandstrom handed Simmons a brochure. I could feel my neck redden. The kid said something I couldn't hear. It must have been a compliment, because Sandstrom played it modest: "Oh, he's the one swinging the club," he said, pointing to Meyers. "I just help him work out." Simmons read the brochure as he moved to his spot on the range.

I walked closer. "Where's Lisa?"

Sandstrom turned around. He wore sunglasses, khaki shorts, and running shoes. His hair was jelled, his chiseled jaw clean shaven. Fresh as a May afternoon.

"Where's Lisa?" I said again.

"How should I know?"

"Jack," Meyers said, and leaned casually on a club, "there some kind of problem? We're trying to work here."

"She interviewed you this morning." I took a step closer to Sandstrom.

"Yeah. Then she left."

"Who initiated the interview?"

"Why are you asking me these questions? Talk to your wife, man."

"Jack."

I turned to see Lisa approaching. I looked back at Sandstrom, who stood grinning like the cat who ate the canary. I didn't like his grin one bit.

"I heard you were looking for me," Lisa said.

I nodded and walked toward her. Sandstrom waited until I was the proper distance, then shouted my name. I turned back. His sunglasses were off now.

"She's a big girl, Jack," he said, dragging the words out. "A big girl and, from here, she looks like she can *really* take care of herself." He put the earpiece of his sunglasses in his mouth and bit down on it.

The fog had burned off. I felt the eyes of my colleagues on me as Sandstrom and I stood glaring at one another.

"I try to accommodate interview requests, Jack."

I walked back to him.

"Jack," Lisa said.

"I'm fine." I stopped when we were face to face. "You're a sick son of a bitch. Stay away from my wife."

"Just trying to grow my business, man. A guy like you, you can compete until you're fifty. Other guys, they hit forty or forty-five, and they need something extra."

Lisa was next to me. Her face held a vague recognition; behind her eyes the pistons were firing. She knew something significant had been said. I knew exactly what.

"I work my ass off, shithead," I said.

He went on, as if I'd not spoken: "A specialized workout routine is what I'm talking about," he said and cut the tension between us with a casual shrug. He turned and went back to Meyers.

As I started away from him, he glanced over his shoulder at me and grinned.

.   .   .

Lisa and I walked directly to the dining room and took an empty table. I looked around—white linen tablecloths, china, and silver flatware. The refined setting clashed with my earlier emotions, which had sent me through the building, room by room.

"I looked all over for you," I said. "You scared me half to death. What were you doing alone with that creep?"

It was condescending and I saw the flames leap behind Lisa's eyes. She raised one brow, but the waitress approached and saved me. Lisa turned to her, smiled, and politely asked for coffee. So did I. When the waitress was gone, Lisa cleared her throat. I braced.

"Good morning, to you, too, Jack. Yes, I heard you were look-ing all over for me. Pete Sandstrom called very early and said, if the offer still stood, he would 'be delighted to do an interview before leaving for the course.' He was polite and courteous on the phone." There was an edge to that last line that said, *Unlike you, right now.* "When I met him in the lobby, he waved me out-side and started walking."

"And you followed him?"

"Yes."

"Across the parking lot?"

"Yes."

"Alone? Before seven A.M.?"

"I thought I might get him to say something about the mur-ders, Jack. I am a reporter, or did you forget?"

"All I know is you're the mother of my child."

She let out a slow breath and tilted her head. Her tongue ran along her upper lip, something she did only when furious. The coffee arrived before she could launch. And I know a lucky bounce when I see one. I spoke before she could.

"I know what your career means to you," I said. "And I know I jump before I look a lot. I've been putting my foot in my mouth all morning. I'm sorry."

"I don't know what else you've done, but you know damned well Darcy is my top priority. You also know that you're not the only one with something at stake here."

"You want the story."

"Yes. So I asked Sandstrom about the murders. He declined to comment. I asked about clonidine and stanozolol. He said, 'It's disheartening to hear that a client would use those things.' He kept trying to focus on the success of his clients—Paul Meyers in particular and Ron Scott."

"Ron Scott?"

Perkins sat clumsily onto one of the two empty chairs, the salt and pepper shakers overturning. My coffee sloshed onto the saucer. He had once moved with the agility of a speedy defensive end. Now he propped the cane against the side of table and positioned his leg carefully.

"Richie Barter came to the clubhouse," he said, shaking his head in disbelief, "and said Pete Sandstrom is a disruptive influence on the driving range and should be forced to leave it. I went out there and was told you and he got into it—that *you* caused the disruption."

I didn't say anything.

"That true?" Perkins said.

"Kind of."

"Jesus Christ. Well, at least you didn't hit *this* guy. Barrett caught wind of whatever the hell took place in the hotel lobby last night. He's asking people what they saw."

I drank some coffee. We all claim to know ourselves better than we do. The restraint I'd found this morning, standing face to face with Sandstrom, hadn't been there the night before. I didn't understand it all. Only that it had something to do with having been laughed at as a kid. The previous night, the laughter had triggered my temper and my fist had followed.

"Sandstrom said something important this morning," I said.

"Pertaining to . . . ?"

"To this whole thing—the steroids and the murders. He said, *You can compete until you're fifty.* Remember the note in my wallet? *You can compete until you're fifty. If you want to be able to, don't ask about Ron Scott.*"

240

"Same phrasing," Perkins said. "And you think the note came from whoever killed Ron Scott?"

"It's only one sentence," Lisa said, "and it's not at all a unique phrase. It could be a coincidence. He's a trainer, and everyone your age is concerned with playing until they're fifty."

"Put yourself in my shoes," I said, "and you wouldn't be talking about coincidences. I go to Chicago to ask Liz Scott some questions, then I get sucker punched in a five-star hotel and my wallet gets stolen. I get the wallet back in the mail with my eighty bucks still in it. And there's even a bonus, a note warning me not to ask questions. Now Sandstrom says something I read on that note? I don't believe in coincidences. Put yourself in my shoes, and you wouldn't either."

"Jack," Perkins said, "I told you, Sandstrom was in California when Hal McCarthy was shot. There were over a hundred people with him at a conference banquet."

"He could have had it done."

Perkins shook his head. "I don't get that from his interview with Jerry Hernandez."

The waitress returned and offered Perkins coffee. When he nodded in reply, she filled his cup. Lisa sipped her coffee and made a face. I knew it was too weak for her. At home, she made newsroom-strength diesel; restaurant coffee wouldn't cut it.

"Maybe Sandstrom hit me, took my wallet, and sent the note," I said, "but paid to have the killings done."

"That works for Hurricane, but Ron Scott knew whoever killed him. Everything about the crime scene indicates that." Perkins drank some coffee. "Look, Jack, Jerry even got warrants for both Sandstrom and Meyers. They were clean."

I hadn't heard about the searches. That news made me more frustrated.

"For Christ's sake," I said, and blew out a long breath. I should have been practicing—Lord knew my game needed work. My wife was dedicated to a fault and had scared the hell out of me before 8 A.M. But I was also dedicated to a fault and therefore could say nothing. Except, stupidly, I *had* said something and, for the second time that day, had offended somebody. Kip Capers had left a four-metal but stalked away from his brief encounter with me. No one was lining up for practice rounds now. Which reminded me of Billy Carvelli. He was only seventeen and had seen me hit his father. Rightfully, he had been outraged. Frustration had my decision-making skills clouded. Something had to give.

"Maybe Sandstrom killed Ron Scott but hired out the Hurricane murder," I said.

"Why would he do that?" Perkins said. "That doesn't fit the profile. Once you do one, why stop? That's taking an unnecessary risk. The hire could talk. And you've proven to yourself you have what it takes."

The three of us sat in silence, drinking coffee. Across the room, Adam Scott ate with Sergio Garcia. I waited for a horde of single women to storm the place. Next to them, a group of men in their fifties, dressed in business suits, ate and spoke intently. The one leading the conversation, a fat guy whose neck spilled over his tie, waved his fork as he spoke between bites of scrambled egg. A family was eating beside them. I didn't recognize the man, although he was clearly a golfer—maybe a local club pro who'd gotten in as a Monday qualifier. If so, this week could be the highlight of his career. All in all, the PGA Tour world seemed to revolve as usual.

That would change the moment Lisa broke her story.

"When is your steroid piece airing?" I said.

"Just before nine this morning. I'm going on *The Early Show* with Terry McCarthy's finding and the PGA Tour's statement."

"Which is?"

"The standard one-bad-apple denial."

"You agree with that?" Perkins said.

"I don't know," she said.

"I was asking Jack."

I looked at him. Since our conversations about him going home, he seemed lost in his work. I knew it was his alternative—to going home and facing his family. His voice and expression told me he was working now.

"When I told Carvelli's old man to keep Billy away from Sandstrom," I said, "his father told me golfers are getting younger, bigger, and stronger and that Sandstrom was the only

242

personal trainer 'who honestly evaluates that situation.' That thought process scares me."

"You didn't think golf was above the problems of other sports, did you?" Perkins said.

"I don't know what I thought," I said. "Since the game is based on integrity, I guess I hoped the professional sport would always be that way, too." I shook my head. "Lord knows, there've been enough examples in other sports for me to know better. The bigger the money, the bigger the greed."

"That's the way of the world," Perkins said.

"But there's more to it. Like Lisa said, everyone wants to play until they're fifty. That's hard to do."

"You're saying Hurricane might not have been alone," Perkins said.

Lisa sat very still, listening and thinking.

I picked up the coffee cup but didn't drink. I sat staring at it, collecting my thoughts. It was a complex question, a complex issue. I knew why Hurricane had done it, so I knew it could happen again.

"I'm not denying the Tour's one-bad-apple statement," I said. "I don't think the Tour is overrun by guys using. But testing is the only way to know for sure, because a guy like Sandstrom is a creep, but the scary thing is"—I set the cup down again—"he's also a dime a dozen."

Neither of them said anything. They sat looking at me.

I wanted to be there. She was, after all, my wife. I was also on the Policy Board and much of my involvement in this mess was because of that. So I wanted to be there when the story broke.

I anticipated an uproar as I sat before my locker pretending to try on new shoes and glancing constantly at the television that hung suspended in the corner of the room. The locker room smelled of cologne, not sweat, a fact Perkins often commented on after two seasons with the New England Patriots. Around me, guys were in various stages of a typical Wednesday: Tiger Woods was tying his spikes, getting ready for a pro-am. The World's No. 1 player had no doubt been selected first in the weekly draft by some guy who'd paid no less than $1,500 for the honor. I was chosen about half the time. John Daly and Hank Kuehne were in the field this week, so I was off the hook. They would play, chat, have fun, and all the while try not to watch the amateur's swing because the shanks are contagious—and anyone who says otherwise has never had them. Justin Leonard was across the room sharing the sports page with Brad Faxon. Jim Furyk was reading Mitch Singleton's column in the USA Today.

Paul Meyers was on a bench, reading Golf World. He was decked out in McNamara designer clothing. This day, his shirt was white with hot orange sleeves and pants the same color. His belt buckle was the size of a softball in the shape of a large M. I wouldn't be caught dead in the outfit, but no one had asked me to wear it either.

On television, Charles Donald, host of The Early Show on CBS, was sitting on a stool, hands clasped in his lap, in the New York studio. Beside him, a large-screen television monitor projected a live shot of Lisa standing outside our locker room, near the eighteenth green. She wore a headset and held her notepad.

"This morning, we're following a breaking story from the PGA Tour," Donald said. "Lisa Trembley-Austin is live from Palm Beach Gardens, Florida, where the Honda Classic will begin tomorrow."

The camera cut to Lisa.

Padre Tarbuck was across the room at a card table, reading the paper. He set the paper down. "Jack, what's this?"

I wasn't about to feign ignorance. I'd started the ball rolling by going to Liz Scott's home—half because I was a member the Policy Board and half because I was Perkins's best friend—but I'd been part of it from the start and I wouldn't lie about that. I sat staring at the screen with maybe fifty colleagues who'd stopped in various stages of dress and activity to watch.

"Good morning," Lisa said. She wore a sleeveless CBS golf shirt; her hair was done, her makeup artfully applied. If I hadn't been waiting for the earth to shake, I'd probably have thought she looked like a million bucks. "CBS Sports has obtained evidence linking a former PGA Tour star, the late Hal McCarthy, to the anabolic steroid stanozolol. The steroid was recently discovered in McCarthy's home. McCarthy's physical transformation this season is noteworthy."

"Did McCarthy fail a test?" Donald said.

"No. The PGA Tour does not conduct random drug tests. And a routine blood test, say one you would get during a physical, will not turn up stanozolol. There're only a handful of labs in the nation with the capability to test for anabolic steroids. And since the cause of death in McCarthy's case was clear, no autopsy was conducted."

"Golfers don't look like what I envision steroid users to look like," Donald said.

I couldn't tell if he was speaking genuinely or aiding the report by tossing Lisa softballs. It didn't matter. Lisa had done her homework.

"Yesterday, I spoke with several notable experts who agree that if a golfer worked with a trainer, a nutritionist, and took a steroid like stanozolol, he could lose weight"—she glanced quickly to her notepad, then back at the camera—"one expert said as much as thirty pounds, and still improve his overall strength by up to ten percent in only eight or nine months." She paused briefly. "I understand what you're saying, Charlie. Hal McCarthy didn't look like a lineman but, like many players, he favored golf shirts with sleeves that hung to his mid forearm, so a physical transformation wasn't apparent. A ten-percent improvement in overall strength, in golf, would be a remarkable gain—and a potentially huge advantage."

"Does golf require that much strength?"

"The game is changing. Courses are longer, the rough is thicker. The stronger you are, the shorter the course will play and the less bothersome the rough becomes."

She'd summed it up perfectly.

"What will happen?" Donald said.

"PGA Tour officials are adamant that steroid use among golfers is not common. As most golf fans know, McCarthy was recently murdered. Tucson police are still investigating that and looking for a connection between the stanozolol and the murder. The Tour released the following statement: 'The PGA Tour demands the highest integrity of its players and will conduct an internal investigation.' CBS Sports will continue to follow this story."

The screen cut to Donald in the studio. He said, "And coming up after the break . . . "

Someone hit the clicker and the locker-room television went black. Everyone turned to look at me. I got to my feet slowly and stood on the bench in front of my locker. The questions seemed to blend. I raised my hands and shouted, "Hold on and listen!"

The room fell silent.

"Hurricane did it," I said. "You've all heard about the clonidine by now. Add the steroid to the list." Billy Carvelli sat directly in front of me. I looked straight at him. "As a member of the Policy Board, all I can say is that I urge you to be vigilant against this and report anything you see."

Carvelli looked away.

"*This is golf,*" Richie Barter yelled.

"That's right, Richie," I said, "and the game is changing."

The room fell silent once more. I got down, the soapbox lecture over. Players broke off in pairs and threesomes; the cacophony of frantic discussion was loud. A locker-room attendant walked to where Meyers was seated and handed him a package. Meyers looked at the return address, then looked at the box as if it were ticking. He took out his cell phone, opened it, barked something into it, and closed the phone. Finally, he glanced around the room once and quickly left. I'd seen a similar delivery once before. That time, he'd turned on me and asked what I was looking at. Our fight had ensued.

This time, I simply followed him.

. . .

I felt bad leaving the locker room after getting on my high horse and telling players to be vigilant, but I had to see what Paul

Meyers had received—and see what he'd do with it. Meyers went to the parking lot near the clubhouse. It was private parking for those associated with the event. At 8:55 A.M., the day before the tournament started, the lot was full of nearly identical Buick courtesy cars. Meyers walked to a LaSabre at the end of a row. He beeped the locks and got in the driver's side.

I went to my car, which was parked two rows behind Meyers, and sat, waiting to follow him, my car idling.

Nothing happened.

Through the windshield, I could see the back of Meyers's head. He was looking down. His shoulders jerked and I could see a piece of white packaging he'd torn off. I got out, moved between the cars, and walked up to his driver's-side window. I got lucky. A car entered the lot, so Meyers looked up at it instead of checking his driver's-side mirror. I stopped when I was just behind his left shoulder.

Behind me, I heard the slap of shoes on pavement and turned to see Richie Barter. Richie stopped walking when he saw me before continuing to his car.

I turned back to Meyers. He'd torn the box open, tape and white cardboard scattered across the passenger's seat. He was holding an orange prescription container.

"What the fuck are you doing!?"

I turned to see Pete Sandstrom running toward me.

"What are you, a fucking peeping Tom?!" he yelled.

I had turned completely around and he was in front of me. Behind me, I heard the driver's-side door open.

"Stay there," Sandstrom shouted.

The door closed.

"You're digging the fucking hole deeper and deeper," Sandstrom said.

"I know what you're doing," I said, "and you're going down."

Across the lot, a car door slammed.

"Ron Scott was in the best shape of his career when he died, so was Hurricane. It was stanozolol."

"You're crazy," Sandstrom said.

"Maybe their consciences got to them," I said, "and they

247

started talking about blowing the whistle. You couldn't have that."

Sandstrom was quick. I only saw his fist the moment before impact.

I was out for only a few seconds. When I got to my feet, the car, Meyers, and Sandstrom were gone. I hadn't been able to make out the orange container's label.

But I didn't need to.

. . .

"That's a hell of bruise," Perkins said, titling his head as if admiring it. He sat across the coffee table from me.

The icepack had done little. My right cheek made a good date for my swollen hand. On the coffee table, my laptop was open, the screen displaying the PGATOUR.COM website. Next to it, Perkins's notebook was open, his pen atop it. He had finished writing the statistics down.

"You know that this," he motioned to the computer, "doesn't prove a thing."

"Proves something to me."

"Not to the courts."

I shrugged.

A keycard rattled on the outside of the door and Lisa entered at 4:45 Wednesday afternoon. When she put Darcy down on the carpeted floor, the toddler ran to me—"Daddddy!!!!"—and leaped into my arms. I caught her and leaned back on the sofa. Two minutes later, Darcy had forgotten about me and was rummaging through her toy bag.

"What a day," Lisa said, and flopped onto the loveseat beside me. "Oh, God, what happened to your cheek?"

"It's been a long day," I said, "and it might be just starting."

"It is for me," Perkins said. "I'm going to talk to Jerry Hernandez about more search warrants for Meyers and Sandstrom." He got to his feet slowly and bent to get the cane that leaned against the sofa. "I'll be in touch." He started toward the door.

"You call home lately?" I said.

He turned back to me. "I told you once, Jack, every night. And it's none of your business."

"Fine," I said, my eyes locked on his.

Lisa cut the tension by blatantly clearing her throat.

"I'll see you later, Lisa," Perkins said.

She went over and kissed his cheek. Then he left.

"What's going on?" she said, and sat back down on sofa. "I've got an interview with the Tour's media relations director tonight."

I pointed to the screen.

"Driving distances?" she said.

"Yeah," I said. "In the dining room this morning, you said Ron Scott worked with Pete Sandstrom. I knew there was a connection I was missing. When I went to Liz Scott's home, she told me Ron went to California to train. I didn't get it then. Seeing Sandstrom try to recruit new business on the driving range triggered it. California is where Sandstrom's company started. Ron Scott was Sandstrom's original link to the PGA Tour, not Hurricane. Scott went to train with Sandstrom in California. I just got off the phone with Liz. She verified that." I pointed to the computer. "And Scott's driving distance improved by almost twenty yards the year after he started working with Sandstrom."

"What are you saying?"

"We can point to the doctor, Todd Hollis, all we want to. But *this* is how steroids got to the PGA Tour—Sandstrom and his Left Coast Training, starting with Ron Scott. After Scott, Sandstrom moved on to Hurricane. Both of those guys are dead now, both shot with a .357."

She brushed her hair over her ears and made a face. "First off, you don't know that Ron Scott used steroids. Technology and a workout could be good for twenty yards."

"*Twenty* yards?"

"It's been done."

"Not often."

"Second," she said, continuing, "McCarthy and Scott had another connection besides Pete Sandstrom. They had Nichols Golf, too."

I shook my head. "Everybody in Nichols Golf, with the exception of Kip Capers, shared the same trainer. I think Scott and Hurricane got ready to blow the whistle, to come clean, so Sandstrom killed them, or had it done."

Lisa thought about that. She stood, went to the windowsill, got a bottle of water, and returned. "In the dining room, Perkins told you he doesn't agree, Jack. You don't trust him on this?"

"Yes and no. He's working more than ever, but he's not himself right now."

"Because he won't go home?"

"Yeah," I said, "he went home and it didn't go well. Now he says he has to be ready to go home. He feels inadequate. That's why he sent me to Liz Scott to begin with."

"All of that's neither here nor there," she said. "If the authorities could prove Sandstrom killed Ron Scott or Hal McCarthy, they'd have arrested him. They searched their houses and found nothing."

"Well, I found something this morning." I told her about Paul Meyers's orange container in the parking lot. "Sandstrom and Meyers took off. Jerry Hernandez was looking for them when I came back here with Perkins. Hernandez wants that orange container." I held out my hand and she passed her water bottle to me. I took a drink. "This morning, on the range, Sandstrom was handing out brochures. The guy's a parasite. And Billy Carvelli is his new client."

"You think Sandstrom will have him using stanozolol?"

"I think Carvelli's own father would see to that. But Sandstrom will get it and be happy to help."

Across the room, Darcy was playing with her Polly Pockets. She held two and they spoke back and forth, Darcy's voice changing as each talked.

"Jack, you know what you're like when you get blinders on. Dyslexics are often single-minded. Sometimes it's a good thing— you hit balls for hours to work out of slumps. But this situation," she shook her head, "is different. Billy Carvelli's actions are out of your hands."

"I know that."

"And, like you said this morning, whatever Pete Sandstrom is, he's a dime a dozen."

"And, like you said this morning, whatever Pete Sandstrom is, he's a dime a dozen."

"That's why I want him gone. Send the message."

She looked at me, brows furrowed. "Well, Perkins doesn't even think Sandstrom killed those men."

"That doesn't make Sandstrom completely innocent," I said.

"Listen to yourself, will you? You don't have control over who can work as a trainer. This is bigger than you, Jack."

"That's exactly what I mean. And it's why I want him gone."

The clonidine had been bad enough. Hurricane probably made some putts he wouldn't have by using it to steady his nerves. However, no study had conclusively proven clonidine made someone putt better.

Steroids, though, were different. They would undoubtedly help a golfer. And the world knew a PGA Tour player had used stanozolol. It only got worse from there. Now I knew how Paul Meyers—at 165 pounds—launched a nine-iron 170 yards. And I'd bet my last dollar Ron Scott had also used stanozolol. The statistics pointed to that; so did his trip to train with Pete Sandstrom. Ron Scott, Hurricane, and Meyers, a threesome.

And two of the three were now dead. I thought about that as I walked into the locker room Thursday morning.

Once steroids infest a professional sport, everything changes. Accomplishments are doubted. Physical fitness is questioned. Whispers follow. Then finger-pointing starts and that spills over to the locker room. On Tour, the locker room is usually a sanctuary. This day, the place was damned near empty. No card games. No fathers with sons. No chitchat in front of the television. No talk of fishing or stocks or politics. Lisa's story had already changed things.

Richie Barter sat alone at the card table and looked up from his paper. "You and I are the eight twenty-two," he said. He had dark-blue bags under his eyes and a two-day growth on his cheeks.

"Yeah, I saw the tee time," I said. Richie looked like he'd joined the rookies for a rough night on the town.

The golfer I'd seen but hadn't recognized in the dining room the day before approached and introduced himself as Jim Milton. He spoke with a British accent, said he played the European Tour, and that he "rounded out" our threesome. We shook hands and I went to my locker. I took off the jeans and T-shirt I wore and pulled a new shirt off a hanger. I stepped into khakis, put on dark socks, and took a new glove and TaylorMade cap off the top shelf. After changing into soft-spiked Adidas, I went to the range.

Judging from the amount of players there, you'd have thought every guy on Tour had the work ethic of Vijay Singh. I went to my practice station, designated by a small sign with my name on it, and hit a slow, smooth sand wedge that carried no more than eighty yards. After several more, I moved to my eight-iron, then finally my four-iron. My hand was okay. Silver stood behind me, watching for my flying right elbow. It was happening less frequently now. I would lapse once in fifteen shots and the ball would start like the others but bend right. That was progress, but concentrating on your elbow (or any component of your swing) is no way to play tournament golf. You want to think only about where to hit the shot. But I'd been a grinder for fifteen seasons and knew to take what I can get.

Billy Carvelli walked onto the range with his caddy. His father was neither caddy nor coach and remained outside the ropes.

"Jesus," Silver said, "you see the look Carvelli's father gave you? Man, that bruise on his cheek is something."

I hit another shot. This time, the ball broke like a slider, tailing to the right. I handed the club to Silver and walked to where Carvelli stood with his driver across his shoulders. He rotated his torso back and forth, loosening up. When he saw me, he paused.

"I want to apologize," I said.

Carvelli was facing me and glanced past my shoulder at his father. He turned to stand beside me so he could put his back to his old man. "You shocked the hell out of both of us," he said.

"Yeah, well, I was wrong."

The grandstand behind the range was filled and John Daly was playing to the crowd, hitting one-handed wedge shots. He walked to his bag and pretended to reach for his driver. There were hoots and hollers from gallery. He pulled his hand away quickly and grabbed the sand wedge. Boos. He turned to the fans and grinned. Finally, he took the driver, pulled the big lion headcover off, and tossed it to his caddy. The gallery roared. Through it all, Carvelli's father squinted and hollered to Billy, who ignored him.

"Your father wants you," I said.

"I'm sure." He turned to his caddy. "Stan, give me a couple minutes."

The caddy nodded and moved away.

"I turn eighteen in two weeks, Jack. I'm legally an adult then and I'm going to start making the decisions that affect my career. The first thing I want to do is hire an agent, a real agent. Not my father. Know anybody?"

I had just apologized for interfering. Now he was asking me to do it again. I told him the truth. "I don't have an agent."

"No?"

"I'm ranked ninety-ninth in the world," I said, "and pushing forty. There's not a lot of negotiation in my deals."

"Oh," he said, and looked away uncomfortably.

It reminded me of how young he was. He thought everyone had companies knocking down the doors with endorsement offers. "Look," I said, "I've got a lawyer. Maybe he can recommend somebody."

"That's okay. A bunch of agencies have called. My father keeps chasing them away, saying he's my agent. I'll call one back."

"An agent shouldn't be your number-one concern right now."

"What then?"

"Get the hell away from Pete Sandstrom," I said.

"I hate that guy. He was supposed to meet me here," he looked at his watch, "ten minutes ago."

"I think he's behind a lot of shit, Billy," I said. It was vague, but it was all that was needed.

Billy nodded. "He was McCarthy's trainer."

"Get away from him."

"I will. Like I said, I'll be an adult in two weeks."

"You already are," I said. His agent/father/micro-manager had seen to that by pulling his childhood out from under him like a scatter rug.

He looked at me and nodded slowly. I didn't say anymore. I turned and went back to Silver.

.   .   .

On the first tee, Jim Milton and I had to wait for Richie Barter. Missed tee times on the PGA Tour are not taken lightly. Miss one, and you can be disqualified; if you're late, you face a two-stroke penalty. The starter was a man in his fifties wearing a blue blazer. He held a clipboard with names crossed off and glanced at his watch. "Jack, where is Richie Barter?"

"I saw him in the locker room."

"He's got about thirty seconds."

I shrugged. We weren't a brand-name grouping—no Mickelson, Woods, or Els among us—so only a handful of fans stood around the first tee. I had my new four-wood out, my glove was on, and had marked my Titleist Pro V1 with a red dot under the 1. I was ready to go. I heard golf clubs jingle and turned to see Richie and his caddy approach. He still looked weary when he stepped to the first tee. The starter gave him a look, then checked his watch.

"Don't worry about it," Richie said. "I made it."

"Please welcome the eight twenty-two starting time."

The small group applauded.

"On the first tee, from Chandler, Maine, Jack Austin."

I tipped my cap acknowledging the light applause. No. 1 played only 383 yards, a dogleg to the right. I didn't need my driver. I made two practice swings keeping my elbow tight against my side. After address, I made a smooth swing, the ball flying straight and stopping in the mouth of the dogleg.

Silver took the club and gave me a low-five. "There's the swing, boss. It's going to be a good week."

Richie was next to hit. He had his driver out. A par four under 400 yards was considered short on the PGA Tour. But Richie had never been a long hitter. He brought the club back and took a rip at the ball. He couldn't have executed the shot any better. The ball started down the middle, then faded to the right, into the center of the dogleg, bounding out of sight, leaving a short approach to the green.

Milton was next. He also hit his driver, but with much less success. His tee shot started right and never came back, finding the right-side woods. His caddy told him it was still in bounds. "I hate looking for balls in Florida," Milton said. "I always feel like I'm about to get eaten by something."

We all chuckled and moved down the fairway.

"I've got one of your clubs in the bag this week," I said to Richie.

"One of *my* clubs?"

I nodded and reached across Silver to pull the four-wood from the bag. I passed it to Richie.

"The Hurricane," he said.

"It's carries farther than my rescue club and is just as consistent."

"That was McCarthy's baby."

"Poor sonofabitch," I said.

"Why do you say that?"

"Why do I say that? The guy was shot to death."

"Didn't you see your wife on TV yesterday?"

"Are you saying he got what he deserved?"

"Damned right. At least your wife is looking out for the sport."

I thought about Lisa and what she would say. "She's reporting the facts, Richie, that's all."

"That's what you think? And you're on the Policy Board?" He shrugged. "I'm just glad someone's looking out for the game."

"Haven't we had this conversation?" I said. "You heard what I said in the locker room. I urged players—"

"Yeah, yeah. I heard your 'vigilant' rah-rah bullshit. What's that do? Not a thing."

"What do you want from me?" I said. "That's all I can do, Richie."

I watched him go and shook my head. He still thought I had failed the game and the Tour. I didn't have time to worry about what Richie Barter thought of me. And I sure as hell had no desire to seek his approval. We had reached my ball. Silver set the bag down and I pulled the nine-iron. He took his yardage book from the front pocket of his poncho, flipped it open, and started calculating the distance to the back-left pin placement.

"Nine-iron or wedge?" I said.

"Slight breeze at us. It's one twenty-five to the center. One thirty-three to the flagstick—a three-quarter nine."

I couldn't feel a breeze but trusted Silver. I moved behind the ball, made two practice swings, and visualized the shot. I addressed the ball, carefully placed the clubhead behind it, and swung.

This time my right elbow did what it wanted—and the ball missed the green to the right. It was a bad miss because it "short sided" me, meaning I'd missed to the side where the pin was, leaving me little green to work with. The pitch shot would be difficult. It was a play TV announcers call a "mental error." Out of the corner of my eye, I saw a golf cart on the tarred path. Perkins was behind the wheel. When he waved me over, deliberately interrupting my round, I knew something was wrong.

And things quickly got much worse.

I never thought it would end with Hurricane's death, but I sure as hell hadn't expected what Perkins told me.

As we moved to my ball, which lay in a bunker to the right of the eighteenth fairway, Richie Barter said, "Tough break," and pointed to my Titleist.

I saw the ball and shook my head. "No. Just another piss-poor swing. I've made a lot of them today."

The eighteenth hole had given me fits for years. It played uphill, a heavily bunkered 424-yard par four that forced a player to be straight off the tee. I hadn't been. Now my ball lay in a sand trap 145 yards from the green—and Richie, of all people, was consoling me.

Silver set the bag down at the edge of the trap. "An eight-iron should be enough," he said. "The ball is far enough from the lip so you can hit an eight."

I nodded. Usually, I play an eight from 150 yards. But on a long bunker shot, I don't use my body. I choke down and swing only my arms, attempting to pick the ball clean and hoping it stops when it lands. The wind had picked up and the sun was gone from the sky. It was overcast now, the Florida air heavy and hinting of rain.

"You okay, Jack?" Richie said.

"Why do you ask?"

He shrugged. "Don't get offended. It's just that since your buddy showed up the first time, you haven't been the same."

"The first time?"

He nodded and pointed to Perkins who sat in a golf cart beside the fairway.

"Jack seems okay," Milton said.

"You don't know him," Richie said, as if we were close friends.

I hadn't seen Perkins return. Nearly three hours earlier, he'd departed immediately after telling me who was missing and who was dead. When I looked over now, he waved for me to continue.

I took the eight-iron from Silver and made a long practice swing, using only my arms, no torso. David Toms had scorched the field, posting sixty-four (−8). My name wasn't on the leader board. Worse, my back-nine performance validated Richie's question. After playing the front in thirty-four (−2), I was three over on the back, on pace for a seventy-three. Richie was right. What Perkins told me had distracted me, although that was no excuse. A professional should be able to tune everything out.

I made a second practice swing. Milton had gone to the far

edge of the fairway, where he'd hit next. Richie stood near Silver, his legs spread wide apart, arms folded across his chest. Sunglasses covered his weary eyes. He'd been upset with me from the very start, saying the sport was going to hell during my tenure on the Policy Board. This day's discoveries would surely get him off my back.

"Pete Sandstrom, the trainer, never showed up today," I said.

"No?" Richie said. "So what?"

Lisa usually made at least one appearance during my round, especially if I played before she went on-air at 4 P.M. This day, I'd yet to see her. It made me think the media already had the story.

"Paul Meyers killed himself," I said. I had thought Hurricane's and Ron Scott's consciences had gotten to them. Apparently, Meyers had more integrity than I'd known. Poor bastard.

"Really?" he said, his voice flat.

I couldn't see his eyes behind the dark glasses. I hadn't expected the news to upset him. After all, he'd stood in a parking lot in Scottsdale and brought performance-enhancing drugs to the forefront of golf. But I hadn't expected his next statement.

"That's good. Now they're all gone, so the game is clean again."

"Jesus, Richie."

"What?"

"We're talking about life and death here."

"I'm not. I'm talking about golf."

I just shook my head. As callus as his remark was, it reminded me of what I said to Lisa—"I want him gone." Something dropped in my chest. I'd been referring to Sandstrom. According to Perkins, Meyers had used a .357 to blow his brains all over his Buick LeSabre courtesy car and Sandstrom could not be located. I had wanted the whole lot of them away from golf. I hadn't requested brain matter be left in their wake. The image of Meyers in his car—the same one I'd seen him in only a day earlier—had disturbed me since Perkins first arrived nearly three hours before to inform me.

I stepped into the sand trap, wiggled my feet back and forth for stability, and swung. The sound should have been a *click*.

Instead, it was a *splash*. From 145 yards, you don't want to hear anything except the clubface striking the ball.

The ball fell ten yards short of the green.

I cursed under my breath and handed the club to Silver. When I got out of the trap, Richie was already walking to his ball. Milton was next to hit. Then Richie took very little time and, from only 120 yards, hit to the center of the green instead of playing toward the difficult pin location.

"What's the rush?" Silver said. "He in a hurry to celebrate the guy's suicide?"

On the green, Milton putted first, lagging to two feet from thirty-five feet away. He putted out and moved to the fringe. Richie went next, quickly rolling his fifteen-footer three feet by. He didn't ask me if he could finish. He quickly hit his three-foot come-back attempt. It caught the edge and fell. I was next, having chipped to four feet. I lined up the par putt carefully but the attempt missed. I tapped in for a seventy-four.

Milton met me in the center of the green. We shook hands. When I turned toward Richie, I saw only his back. He was already headed to the clubhouse.

. . .

It was 4 P.M. by the time I caught up with Perkins in the clubhouse. Jerry Hernandez, the Las Vegas homicide detective, was with him. Hernandez wore a conservative suit again. If Hernandez had any sense of humor at all, I'd have said he dressed like an FBI agent. This day, he looked more stressed than usual, his face pinched into a perma-scowl. I controlled my urge.

When the waitress appeared, Hernandez wasted little time.

"Scotch," he said, "on the rocks. A double."

"Just a big glass of water," I said.

Perkins shot me a look, then to the waitress: "A Sam Adams." She smiled and left. However, Perkins wasn't finished with me. "Water?" he said, and shook his head. "Trying to embarrass me in front of my friend?"

I shrugged. "You guys are starting a little early, aren't you?"

"No reason not to," Hernandez said. "The local guys want to

investigate their own murder. We're background information now."

It had been a long day already—up-and-down golf rounds wear you out—so it took a second for it to register. Across the room, a little girl in a pink dress ran circles around her parents' dinner table. The mother, visibly embarrassed, tried to the get the girl to stop. Finally, she stood and collected her daughter. I watched the showdown, feeling a combination of smug pride (my kid would never do that) and luck (I might have been there once or twice). Then, slowly, I turned back to Hernandez. "Murder?"

"That's right."

"Paul Meyers killed himself," I said, "so you're saying they found Sandstrom."

"Not before Meyers did," Perkins said. "Sandstrom's body was two miles away from here, in a wooded area. Something got at him in the woods, but the cause of death was still apparent."

"Three fifty-seven?" I said.

"Yeah. Meyers left a note that said he, Scott, and McCarthy got stanozolol from Sandstrom and that Meyers felt he had to end the whole thing by killing the others. The note rambled on and said Billy Carvelli was the final straw."

"Meyers couldn't let Carvelli get dragged in?" I said.

"That's right," Hernandez said.

I leaned back in my chair and looked around. When I'd entered, I spotted Richie Barter having a beer with *USA Today* columnist Mitch Singleton, the aged reporter. Now I knew why. Across the room, Mitch asked Richie something. Richie shook his head and drank from his glass. Then Richie spoke and Mitch jotted something down. This thing had started with a Richie Barter headline. Apparently, it would end that way.

"Beautiful," I said, and motioned to them.

"What?" Perkins looked over. "Oh, Richie Barter, the prince of the PGA. That the old *USA Today* guy with Barter? The columnist?"

"Yeah. Mitch Singleton. Richie just told me he's glad they're all gone. 'The game is clean again.'"

"That'll make for lively reading," Hernandez said.

The waitress returned with our drinks. I drank my ice water. Hernandez held up his glass and Perkins clinked it to "closed cases."

After one beer, Hernandez stood and tossed $20 onto the table. "This round's on the Las Vegas PD," he said, and extended his hand. "It was good meeting you both. But I hope I don't see you when you come to Vegas next year."

"Going back?" Perkins said.

"Those are my orders. Meyers has no alibi for Ron Scott's murder or McCarthy's. And when the powers that be get a chance to close a case like this, they slam the door and throw away the key. Besides, taxpayers don't want me hanging around Disney World for a few days. This case broke our budget weeks ago."

Perkins and I stood and we shook hands all around. Then we watched Hernandez go and sat down again. I drank some ice water and glanced out the window at the players working on the practice green.

"It's time for you to go home, too," I said.

"You want to let up about that?" he said. "I've got some loose ends to tie up."

"Like what?"

"Like why McCarthy gave Ron Scott $1.5 million."

"Tom Schmidt said there was a good chance no would ever know that," I said. "He said that when the players were still alive. Now they're all dead. No one will ever know."

"I don't get paid to quit."

"You are quitting," I said.

"No, I don't quit."

"You're quitting on your family."

His head turned slowly toward me and I saw the anger in his eyes. I had pushed him.

"Mind your own goddamned business," he said. "I'll take care of my family, Jack. You worry about yours."

"I am," I said.

He looked at me for a long time. Then he tried to stand up. His bum leg made the motion awkward and he slammed the table, knocking over my glass. He sat back down.

"I'm sorry," I said, "for interfering."

"That's part of who are," he said. "You always stick your nose where it doesn't belong. Usually, it's to help somebody and I appreciate that. Right now, I don't."

"I don't know what you're going through," I said. "So I won't say I do. But I know your family is hurting. It's not about you."

He opened his mouth to speak, then closed it. He got up again, grabbed the cane, and limped away.

I drank some water and sat quietly. He'd sent me to Chicago and had spent one night at my house instead of his own. Across the room, the kid in the pink dress was back. Now she was sitting and eating happily. Perkins hadn't been home in close to six weeks. Linda hadn't called me in days. What was she going through? How much more could she take? How much more would she take? Perkins had to reconnect soon. It was getting to be now or never.

Perkins's involvement in the case was over. The participants were dead. Any security detail now would involve only funeral arrangements. I flipped open my cell phone and called a second-grade teacher in New Hampshire.

. . .

At least I wasn't the only guy who needed practice. The practice green was mobbed. Tiger Woods had posted a modest seventy and was stroking four-footers as caddy Steve Williams stood beside the hole and gently kicked the balls back to him. Phil Mickelson was alone, ten feet from a hole, stroking the ball with his smooth forward-press. Around one cup, three guys discussed the new "claw" grip that had so inspired American Presidents Cup star Chris DiMarco.

Since my swing was being held together with Duct tape, putting would be paramount. I dropped three balls and stroked them from fifteen feet. The line was straight. The first two missed to the right. I adjusted my stance and the third fell. Two more missed below the cup from ten feet on a side hill. I realigned myself again. The third ten-foot bender dropped. Next, I moved to a straight three-footer. I took my normal stance and then I rechecked it. Too far right. Somehow, my alignment had gotten skewed. When you play often and lose confidence in your putting, you put enormous pressure on your long game. Maybe that explained my flying elbow. I adjusted my alignment and all three short putts fell. Lesson learned.

Padre Tarbuck walked out of the locker room, down the roped-off walkway, to the practice green, which was enclosed by a green four-foot wall to keep spectators away. He went directly to a group of three guys who were putting near the edge of the green and said, "Hey, listen, Paul Meyers . . . "

I refocused on my putting stroke and positioned three balls from five feet. Again, the line was straight. I rechecked my alignment. Once more, the putts fell. As Lisa said, my black-and-white worldview is oddly suited for golf, a game where things really are as they seem. After all, the ball is either in the hole or it isn't. Unfortunately, it's always the other aspects of life that throw me for a loop.

As I walked off the practice green, I saw two women—one of whom I recognized and hadn't expected to see again. What was Liz Scott doing here?

"I really don't have time to chat," Liz Scott said, and then she checked her watch and looked around. She pursed her lips and narrowed her eyes, clearly put out by something.

We were near the practice green. I leaned on my putter, my hat in my hand. People moved past us on both sides. She looked differently than she had at her suburban home. This day, she wasn't dressing Talbot's. Her blond hair was cut Dutch-boy style and worn shoulder-length. She wore a wide-brimmed hat, rimless blue sunglasses, and a short yellow sundress. If she'd worn gloves and carried an umbrella, I'd have called her Scarlet.

"We wait twenty minutes already, miss," the maid said. "You like for me to call cab?"

The maid was a tiny woman, no more than five-feet-two, and looked too fragile to clean the 8,000-square-foot Scott home. I'd seen few real-life maids, so I didn't know what they wore. But this lady had on a white long-sleeved blouse, black pants, and black leather flats. She had dark eyes that matched her short raven-colored hair and spoke with an accent. When our eyes met, she immediately turned away. She knew I'd recognized her voice.

Why had she called me? Had she known Paul Meyers killed Ron Scott? If that was the case, why hadn't she gone to the police? Why had she urged me to question Liz?

"What brings you here?" I said to Liz for the second time.

"Jack, I'm certain that's none of your business. But if you must know, I'm here for a business meeting."

"The Nichols Golf Group?"

"Why do you ask?"

"I need ten minutes of your time."

She took the blue tinted glasses off and titled her head slightly. "What's wrong?"

"Something happened and you'd rather hear it from me than on TV."

She stood staring at me through a long pause. Then she looked at her watch again.

"Miss," the maid said, "maybe he not coming."

"Who are you waiting for?" I said.

"Where the hell is Paul Meyers?" Liz said. "Gabriella, he did call last night, correct?"

The maid nodded. "At eight-thirty."

"You won't be meeting Paul Meyers." I was looking at my feet when I said it.

"What?" Liz said.

"Paul Meyers won't be meeting you."

"How do you know? You don't know my business dealings, Jack."

"I know you won't be meeting Paul Meyers," I said, and looked up. "He's dead, Liz."

．　．　．

"Paul?" Liz Scott said, ten minutes later. "A killer? That's preposterous. He and Ron started the company together."

I almost said, *And started doing steroids together, too.* But I didn't. The time for pointing fingers had passed. Lisa and I were in a small sitting room in the bowels of the clubhouse with Liz. Above burgundy wainscoting, the walls were white and covered with photos of golf royalty. I sat under the collective gaze of my heroes and studied Liz's face. She sat across a glass coffee table from me, dark streaks of mascara lining her cheeks. Her reaction to Meyers's death had been stronger than I'd anticipated, so I'd called Lisa in to offer a woman's touch. Maybe I should have anticipated Liz's reaction. Her husband was shot to death only weeks earlier. Now Paul Meyers's suicide note scandalized her late husband's legacy. In fact, the note damaged the reputations of the late Ron Scott's business associates as well. Moreover, whatever business meeting Liz had come for was canceled—permanently.

Lisa handed her another Kleenex. "Thank you," Liz said, and quietly blew her nose.

I looked out the window. Near the corner of the building, Gabriella, the dark-haired maid, stood alone on a tarred cart path leading from the clubhouse to a driving range. She dipped a hand into her purse, looked around nervously, and withdrew a cigarette. She lit it, glanced covertly around once more, and took a long drag. When she held the cigarette away from her mouth and exhaled, she had the expression of one who'd quenched a thirst. I excused myself and went outside.

Gabriella didn't hear me approach and jumped when I said, "Hi."

"Oh, er, I—"

"Don't worry about it," I said, and pointed to the SMOKING IS NOT PERMITTED ON THE PREMISES sign. "I won't tell."

We stood in silence for maybe five seconds. She looked at me. I smiled. She smiled back and raised her eyebrows. "So . . . "

"So," I said.

"What I can do for you?"

"You tell me," I said. "After all, you called me, remember?"

"Sir, I no know what you talking about."

"How long have you been in this country?"

"Six year, since I eighteen."

"Always with the Scotts?"

"No. For two year with family in California."

I nodded. "Gabriella"—she seemed surprised that I knew her name—"we both know you called me twice in the middle of the night, so let's not waste time arguing about it. Why did you say Ron Scott's death was no accident and that Liz knew something about it?"

"I no know what you talk about."

"Listen!" It had been the worst day in the history of the sport—any hope that only Hurricane had done steroids had been lost with Meyers's note implicating Scott and himself as well.

She heard the frustration and anger in my voice and stepped back.

"Four people are dead. You know something about one of the murders. Tell me."

"Four?"

I nodded. "Ron Scott was the first. Hal McCarthy, Pete Sandstrom, and Paul Meyers. Meyers killed the others and then shot himself."

"Mr. Meyers? That impossible."

"That's what happened, Gabriella. What's your last name?"

She looked at the clubhouse, then back at me. "Martinez . . . Gabriella Martinez."

"That's what happened, Gabriella."

Her head shook side to side again. "That not possible. I mean, I guess it possible, but he would no do that. They have plan."

"Who?"

Again, she looked at the clubhouse.

"She's inside," I said, "and we're out of view. You can talk to me."

She took another long drag, exhaled slowly, and looked at me for maybe five seconds. I watched her eyes as she thought long and hard about what she knew and what she wanted to say.

"You called me twice and asked me to look into Ron Scott's death. I did that. Now I want to know why you called. Why didn't you go to the cops?"

"I need this job," she said. "You no understand. I know how professional golfer live."

"You know how *some* professional golfers live," I said. "My father's a carpenter. My mother's a substitute teacher. I live within my means."

Her eyes narrowed and a momentary grin formed on her face, then vanished. "You no idea. My mother get hurt in vacuum factory. She no work now. I send money back to her in Juarez. I need this job."

Suddenly, she turned her back to me, dropped the cigarette, and crushed it beneath her shoe seconds before a golf cart driven by a rules official in a shirt and tie rolled by. She must have thought the cart was a threat. I knew the rules official didn't have time to stop. Somebody on the course needed a ruling. I felt like a heel and was glad for the interruption. Gabriella was right—growing up middle-class in America made me no expert on her Third World life.

"I shouldn't have said what I did. You thought if you went to the police you'd jeopardize your job?"

"Of course."

"Our conversation stays private," I said.

She thought about that. Then she nodded to herself and said, "Then you come to Mrs. Scott and I know about them. She no know that, still don't know. But I put thing I see with thing that happen to Mr. Scott and . . . "

"What did you see?"

"Mr. Meyers and Mrs. Scott."

"Together?"

She looked at me, confused by the idiom. Finally, she shrugged. "She fucking him," she said, as if describing the weather.

"How do you know that?"

"Mr. Meyers come, meet Mr. Scott about golf clubs. When Mr. Scott leave room, Mrs. Scott and Mr. Meyers like teenager when the parent leave. I outside cleaning a window and see them. She say this trip for business. I know better."

"You said they had plans. Did they murder Ron Scott?"

She spread her hands and shrugged. "She sleep with her husband friend. Now her husband dead. How it look to you? I think within three year they be married."

"That's a pretty bold assumption for someone worried about losing her job."

"That is why I tell you look into it. There something else. At funeral for Mr. Scott, I see her slap him. It make me think he told her what he do—kill Mr. Scott—so she slap him."

I thought about that. I'd seen the same slap. Gabriella's take made sense.

"Beside, I like Mr. Scott. He send my mother five thousand dollar when she get hurt. I didn't like what his wife do. And then you come to ask about it. So I know you looking into it. I just call to . . . " She searched for the right word. "How you say . . . *encourage* you."

Lisa and Liz Scott walked out of the clubhouse. As I watched Gabriella Martinez walk briskly toward Liz Scott, a single question tugged at me: Why would Paul Meyers kill himself if he planned to be with Liz Scott?

*W*hen I caught up with Liz Scott, just before dinner, her demeanor and mascara-stained cheeks gave credence to Gabriella's claim of a relationship with Paul Meyers.

Her hotel-room door caught on the safety chain and she peered at me through the two-inch opening. "It's been a tough few weeks," she said. "I'd like to be alone right now."

"I understand. I won't take much of your time."

She considered that. I could hear the dull voices coming from a television behind her.

"Well," she said, "your wife was very nice to me." Then the door closed, the chain jangled, and she held the door open.

I thanked her and entered. I pulled the straight-backed desk chair out and sat. Liz took the remote off the bed and turned the television off. Then she went to the window and leaned against the sill. Still wearing the sundress, she leaned back until her shoulder blades were against the glass, and crossed her ankles. Her legs were long and muscular. The air in the room was cool and smelled of heavy perfume.

"I can't imagine what there is to talk about," she said.

There was only one thing I'd come to ask. I wouldn't waste her time or mine. "Why did you slap Paul Meyers across the face after Ron's funeral?"

She paused just long enough for me to know the question took her by surprise. "I don't know what you're talking about."

"Liz, Paul told me all about you and him," I lied.

She chuckled but her eyes narrowed and never left mine. "I'm in no mood for sick jokes, Jack. My husband was murdered."

"Which leads us back to what Paul Meyers said about your affair."

"He said no such thing," she said, and shifted her weight so she could cross her ankles the other way.

"I saw you slap him. Did you do it because he told you he killed Ron? Or were you in on that from the start?"

"What?" she said, her hand covering her mouth. "Good God, Jack, is that what you think? You haven't told anyone that crazy theory, have you?"

"It makes sense." I leaned back in the chair. "Things get much easier for you and Paul with Ron dead. Was that the original plan, before Paul felt guilty and killed himself?"

"Good God, Jack. Oh my God. No!"

She was no longer leaning against the sill. Now she stood ramrod straight, both hands on her hips, staring at me. Jerry Hernandez had gone back to Las Vegas. I had seen to it that Perkins's home had come to him, and I'd given Gabriella Martinez my word that our conversation would stay private. That might prove a hard promise to keep, but I wanted to be sure I had something concrete if I had to break it. It meant that if this was going further, I'd have to push it there. So I'd pushed Liz Scott—and she was reeling.

"You can't think I had anything to do with Ron's murder."

I just looked at her.

"I can't explain the suicide note," she said, "but it doesn't even make sense. Not one bit. Paul didn't kill Ron. I know that. I flat-out know it, so you can't say I had anything to do with Ron's death. Have you told the police this half-brained theory?"

"How do you know Paul didn't kill him?"

She turned away from me and stared out the window. In the distance, the Met Life Snoopy blimp floated over the golf course. It was 5:25 P.M. The blimp was taking aerial shots.

"I would've been Paul's alibi," she said, "if he needed a real one."

"'A real one'?"

Still back-to me, she nodded. "He was questioned, like everyone associated with Pete Sandstrom, and he had another alibi, like I did. Gabriella saw me at one that afternoon and at three-thirty, so she told the police I was home all afternoon. That's what she thought." Liz turned to face me. Behind her, the sun was bright in its early evening descent, entering the room over her shoulder, highlighting her blond hair. "Paul must have trusted you," she said, softly.

I didn't deny her inaccuracy. And I didn't feel guilty, either. It was now or never for more than Perkins's marriage.

"I slapped Paul because he wasn't at all upset. In fact, he was like a kid, excited about how much time we could spend together now that Ron was gone."

"Didn't that make you suspicious?"

"No. It seemed callous and upset me, so I slapped him. But I knew where he was when Ron was killed, so the thought that he might have killed Ron never crossed my mind."

"Where was he?"

"With me," she said, looking at the floor. "Paul and I spent the afternoon that Ron was killed in a Chicago hotel, together."

I knew Ron Scott was murdered around 2:30. She had just accounted for herself and Paul Meyers from 1 to 3:30.

"You wanted to know," she said, and shrugged. She brushed a tear from her cheek. "I hope you'll vouch for me, if you told anyone about your theory."

Perkins had said the suicide note had not been typed. I wondered if a handwriting analyst was being brought in. In theory, Paul Meyers could have paid to have the murder committed, except the crime scene indicated that Ron Scott knew his killer.

"Besides," she said. "Paul understood our situation and my relationship with Ron. I've got two kids."

"What does that have to do with anything?"

"I'm a good mother. Paul knew I'd never disrupt my family. Even after Ron's death, Paul understood that we'd never live together."

"Why?" This wasn't consistent with Gabriella's estimation.

"My children were extremely close to Ron, and my children come first. Paul knew that." She said it matter-of-factly and I believed her. "Besides, Ron had his own little flings."

"An open marriage?"

She made a motion like a flutter with her hand, dismissing my remark. Her eyes avoided mine. "Nothing we talked about. But we both knew. And we both knew that the kids came first. Each of us did what we needed to do to keep the family together."

"Family, huh?"

"Yes. We weren't the Cleavers, but no family is."

"Did you love Paul Meyers?"

"Love him? We had fun."

"What about Ron? Did you love him?"

"Do you believe in love, Jack?"

"Yes."

"That's nice," she said. "I love my kids."

I didn't say goodbye. I didn't thank her. I simply turned and left, taking a splitting headache with me.

．　．　．

"A plane ticket for my wife?" Perkins said. "Very cute. But I can handle my family affairs."

"I'm guessing Linda arrived," I said.

Twenty minutes after leaving Liz Scott's hotel room, I had

called him—and cut him off before this same tirade began over the phone. Now we sat in front of the hotel on a cement bench. A tall stainless-steel cylinder filled with sand was next to the bench. I smelled cigarette smoke and saw the orange glow of a butt. On the other side of the bench was small palm tree.

"She arrived," he said, "with Jackie."

"You spend time with them?"

"Since eleven this morning," he said. He paused and picked up the cane, which leaned against the bench, and examined it closely as if looking for a tiny scratch. "I just want to say you're an asshole for going behind my back—"

"It's been two months. It was now or never."

"—and to say thanks," he said, and finally turned to look at me. "Thanks."

"No one gives a shit about your cane," I said.

"I do."

"You're still a husband and a father."

"Haven't been a good one lately."

"It's not too late to make amends," I said.

He nodded.

"And you're still very good at what you do," I said.

"All of that's easy for you to say."

"I know that," I said, "and I didn't like getting involved, but I'm your best friend. And I thought it was now or never."

"Do you understand why I've been . . . ?" His words trailed off.

"As well as I can understand it all," I said, "based on what I know of you and based on never being in that situation. It might all boil down to pride."

"Pride got me everything I have."

"True," I said.

"Pride's not a bad thing," he said.

"I know," I said, "and I know you want to be what you were—for them."

He nodded. "Physically, that's not going to happen and that's tough." He blew out a deep breath. "You know why I never let you visit my father after he got cancer and they told him he only had a few months?"

"I always wondered."

"Because I didn't want you to see him that way—I didn't even want to see him that way myself."

"Sick?"

"No, not that—mean, bitter, angry. He felt like he got dealt a bum hand and he spent the last four months of his life angry at the world. I don't like remembering him like that."

"Hard to imagine him being that way," I said.

"Well, imagine it," he said. "My mother and I lived it. I drove home every week just to see how she was holding up. She had no family around there. I had no brothers or sisters. I didn't like him, at the end."

I'd known him all my life but we'd never gone here before. Perkins hadn't spoken of those four months when his father was sick. At the time, during college, a routine question yielded unmistakable anguish and I always dropped the subject. In the ensuing years, we'd moved on. The subject hadn't come up.

"He taught me everything about life," he said, "how to be in-dependent, how to act, how to be a man. But those four months taught me something, too. And one day I woke up feeling sorry for myself and angry and I knew I couldn't go back like that. My plan was to come all the way back, then go home like nothing had happened. When the doctor said that wasn't happening, I got really screwed up."

A car parked and Phil Mickelson got out the passenger's side and walked by us and into the hotel.

"I didn't know what to do after the doctor told me that," he continued. "I just knew I didn't want my son to see me the way I saw my father. What an idiot I've been. Not even rational."

"Don't be too hard on yourself," I said. "You've been through a lot—some major physical and psychological changes. And your parents never really leave you."

A man walked out of the hotel lobby past us, and headed to-ward a car in the parking lot. He wore a navy blue suit and looked tired, as if this was the final leg of a long business trip. Perkins and I watched him go, neither speaking for several mo-ments.

"Thanks," he said, "for doing what you could, when you could."

"Thank Linda and Jackie, not me."

Bob Guilford, a four-time winner, walked out of the hotel and paused when he saw me. "Jack, how's it going?"

"Fine, Bob. Your son still playing for Florida State?"

"Shot sixty-six last week," he said, and nodded a greeting to Perkins. "Good thing Richie Barter pushed the drug issue, huh? What a mess."

"Richie didn't do much to help the outcome," I said. "Four guys are dead. It's up to the Tour to provide the solution, which is testing, and Richie's got nothing to do with that."

"Yeah, I guess," Guildford said, and continued on. I watched him go and shook my head.

"You said you had something to tell me about Liz Scott," Perkins said.

I told him what I'd learned in her hotel room.

"Did you tell her that someone called you twice to implicate her?"

"No."

"I wish we knew who it was. Seems like it must be someone close to her."

I didn't say anything. I'd given Gabriella my word.

"If what Liz says is true," I said, "Paul Meyers had nothing to gain by killing Ron Scott. He and Liz weren't getting any more involved than they already were. Hurricane had motive—all that lost money—but he didn't do it. And you've said Pete Sandstrom was in a ballroom with a hundred people when Ron Scott was killed."

"We still don't know why Hurricane gave more money than the others," Perkins said.

"I think he was desperate. He knew his game was in decline and he saw the Nichols Golf business as a chance to hold on to what he had. When he lost the money and then the business collapsed, he turned to clonidine and stanozolol."

"Let's get back to Paul Meyers. We have a .357 with his prints, an entry wound consistent with a suicide, and a goddamned note saying he killed Ron Scott, Hurricane, Pete Sandstrom, and then himself."

"I believe Liz Scott," I said.

"I'll get the name of the hotel and find out whose name the room was supposedly under and check that alibi."

"The note says Paul Meyers killed them because he wanted the steroid ring ended. He wanted it stopped before Billy Carvelli got sucked in."

"Which makes sense to me," Perkins said. "It all adds up."

"Except for Liz's story."

"Except for that."

"But look at this from a golf perspective," I said. "Paul Meyers was having a great season. He's up for comeback player of the year. Why would he kill himself? The Tour isn't on the verge of testing."

"You know that?"

"I'm on the Policy Board."

Perkins shifted his leg and grimaced. "We had this fucking case closed. I was relaxing with my family."

"If this isn't a murder-suicide," I said, "someone got away with four murders."

. . .

The next morning, I sighed, sipped more coffee, and reread Mitch Singleton's headline in *USA Today:*

"Golfer Richie Barter, a Prophet?"

Palm Beach Gardens, Fla.—Richie Barter has long been among the game's best at reading greens, but the golfer may have saved his best read for off the course.

"I'm glad I could help the game," Barter said Thursday on the heels of the steroid scandal that ultimately led to the deaths of three PGA Tour players and one trainer. "I feel badly about" the deaths "but the game has to come first. And at least golf is clean again."

Barter's accusations of performance-enhancing drug use among PGA Tour players initially raised eyebrows and, according to him, drew the wrath of several players.

"I had Jack Austin, a member of the Tour's Policy Board, tell me to keep my mouth shut," Barter said. "Some guys buried their heads in the sand. I couldn't do that, not when the game was in jeopardy."

Austin could not immediately be reached for comment.

Now Barter is seen by many as the face of those who opposed cheating in professional golf.

"Someone had to stand up to them," Barter said. "I've tried to get on the Policy Board for years. You have to jump through hoops and it's a popularity contest. And no one wins popularity contests by ruffling feathers. Maybe my peers will take me seriously the next time they vote for the Player Advisory Council."

Players elected to the PGA Tour Player Advisory Council usually transition to the Policy Board once their three-year advisory term has ended.

Tour Commissioner Peter Barrett announced today the PGA Tour is stepping up its substance-abuse policy and initiating random tests.

"I'm proud to have had something to do with that," Barter said.

Barter says he's considering telling his story on a larger scale.

"I've been approached to write a book about my season. It would inspire kids to stand up for the truth. The country needs leaders who aren't afraid to tell it like it is and fight for integrity."

I set the paper down and sipped my coffee. Coffee wasn't strong enough. The PGA tour was "stepping up" its drug testing? Perfect. And, of course, Richie Barter and Peter Barrett were taking turns patting each other on the back for that. Worse, Richie was using *USA Today* as a forum to campaign for the Advisory Council and to pitch his book. He was also using the article to criticize me by name.

I'd known Mitch Singleton for years. He was the kind of reporter who would have actually tried to reach me. He didn't have my cell-phone number and I hadn't checked my e-mail. I still didn't appreciate the column running without my version of events.

It was 7:15 A.M. and I was seated on the bench before my locker. The breakfast buffet of honey-baked ham, eggs, French toast, and warm rolls smelled mouth-watering. But I wasn't hungry. I hadn't slept well the night before. I'd lain awake until 3 A.M. trying to decide what to do with Gabriella Martinez's and Liz Scott's stories.

Something didn't jibe.

Paul Meyers had a new endorsement deal with a hip apparel company. Lisa was featuring his improved game on CBS. And he had a love interest, even if they'd never be together full time. Yet Meyers killed Ron Scott, Hurricane McCarthy, Pete Sandstrom, and then himself. Why would a candidate for the PGA Tour Comeback Player of the Year Award kill himself? His suicide note claimed the guilt he felt for bringing steroids to the PGA Tour was simply too much and he couldn't bear to watch young Billy Carvelli make the same mistake.

Had Paul Meyers's conscience gotten to him?

Liz Scott said he couldn't have committed the first murder because he was with her at the time of the shooting. Would Meyers have hired someone to shoot Ron Scott? When I'd asked the same question about Hurricane, Perkins told me that MO didn't fit a killer's profile—either someone hired hits or did them himself. Regardless of who killed Ron Scott, the crime scene indicated that Scott knew his killer, which limited the suspects and made Meyers a logical choice.

Would Liz lie to protect him?

Socks and a new pair of Adidas shoes lay on the floor before me. I sat barefoot in jeans and a white Titleist T-shirt. Will Arlington, a five-time winner on Tour, sat down next to me. "You might have a slander suit against Richie," he said.

I didn't reply. I thought back to Ron Scott's funeral and the scene outside the church. Liz had slapped Paul Meyers. Hard. At least I now knew why. Meyers was pleased to be able to spend more time with her. His giddy reaction upset Liz, so she smacked him. His reaction didn't contradict Gabriella's estimation that Liz and Meyers would be together permanently in three years. If Meyers had believed that, he had motive to kill Ron Scott. What if Liz had led him to that conclusion—intentionally or unintentionally? Or what if Liz's version of the slap was a lie and Meyers had in fact told her after the funeral that he killed her husband? If that was what happened, Liz Scott had heard a confession and had not reported it. Too bad I couldn't get Paul Meyers's side of the story.

I stared into my locker and shook my head. I'd shot seventy-four the day before. My focus should have been on golf. After all, according to *USA Today*, I didn't even care about what took place on the PGA Tour. Hell, maybe I should call Richie Barter and let him handle it. After all, he'd called me out in the article. I was looking forward to our round together, so I could speak to him about that.

My cell phone chirped and I took it from my belt. I didn't recognize the number on caller ID.

"Mr. Austin, this is Terry McCarthy. I feel bad calling you . . . "

It wasn't even 7:30 yet and he sounded troubled. I'd told him to call if he needed anything. "It's good to hear from you, Terry. What's up?"

"I'm in my dad's workshop . . . "

That was where he'd found the stanozolol. I braced.

" . . . because I need to be alone to do this. I was headed to a tournament this morning but my mother told me . . . " His voice cracked. I'd anticipated bad news, but I sensed Terry had been the one to learn something troubling this morning. "I don't want my mom to know I'm calling to ask for . . . Mr. Austin, you said if I needed . . . "

"Terry, do you need the entry fee for the tournament?"

"Yes."

"How much is it?"

"A hundred and forty."

"Do you have a credit card?"

"Visa."

"Charge it and I'll send you a check."

"I'll pay you back."

"Finish in the top five," I said. "That's good enough."

"Mr. Austin, thanks. My mother says we're going to move."

I didn't say anything. Beside me, Will Arlington finished tying his spikes and slapped my back when he stood to go. "I don't blame you if you did tell Richie to keep his mouth shut," Arlington said. "He's hard to take seriously."

"Hold on, Terry," I said. Then to Arlington: "I told him to

keep his mouth shut, *unless he had proof.* That was what I said. He didn't have proof until the suicide note."

Arlington shook his head, slapped me on the back again, and headed to the range.

"Terry," I said, "play well today."

"You too," he said.

It made me smile. I wouldn't have reason to again for a long time.

· · ·

I waited until we reached the fairway at the 424-yard par-four fourth hole. I was even par on my round, Richie was one under, and the third member of our group, Tom Lehman, was even. The right side of the fairway on No. 4 was lined with bunkers. I'd played safe off the tee, hitting a three-wood. Lehman had hit a driver and split the fairway, leaving no more than a nine-iron to the green. Richie had pushed his drive into a fairway bunker.

Richie cursed as we walked to his ball. Lehman, the Ryder Cup captain, was across the fairway waiting to go to his ball. Silver and Richie's caddy were several paces behind us. I'd held my tongue for three holes, an hour and a half. Only a handful of spectators were following our group, none within earshot.

"Don't criticize me in the media again, Richie."

He didn't stop walking. "Did you just threaten me?"

"No," I said.

"Oh, because that sounded like a threat."

"Really," I said. "Then, let me be more clear. If you criticize me by name in the media again,I'll rip your head off."

"I see," he said.

"I hope you do."

"Actually, Jack, I didn't criticize you," he said. We were fifteen feet from the bunker in which his ball lay. As we walked, he turned to look at me. "In fact," he said, and smiled broadly, "I just quoted you."

I looked at him. "Four guys are dead and you're as happy as can be, huh?"

He shrugged. "The game is clean again. I like knowing I had something to do with that."

"You held a press conference in a parking lot and made blind accusations. The right thing to do was go to the Tour and lobby for testing or more research on beta-blockers."

"If you want to take a stand, you have to go public."

"No. You go public if you want to make a name for yourself. You had people suspecting Padre Tarbuck of using beta-blockers. The guy busted his ass to get better."

"Whatever," Richie said.

We reached the bunker and stood at the edge. Richie folded his arms across his chest and stared down at his ball. "For a long time, Jack Austin has been the Tour's golden boy, the guy who stopped that gambling ring Hutch Gainer was involved in. Well, this time, the game needed you and you turned a blind eye. If you're feeling guilty about that, don't take it out on me."

"That's what this is all about, Richie, isn't it?"

"And what's that?"

"Personal glory," I said. "Four guys are dead and you're worried about being a hero."

"Those guys got what they had coming."

"Two of them had families."

"Spare me," he said. "Like I said, if you feel guilty about not being there for the Tour, don't take it out on me."

I looked at him for a long time. For weeks, I had witnessed one tragedy after another. It occurred to me now that not everyone had lost. I dug my hands into my pockets and looked at the spectators. Behind us, Silver and Richie's caddy chatted.

"I don't feel guilty, Richie, unlike some other guys this week."

"Are you talking about Paul Meyers? Guilt can make people do crazy things."

"So can greed," I said, "and the desire for fame."

As I walked away, I looked over my shoulder. As expected, Richie was staring at me.

43

At 10:35 P.M., the lights were out in my hotel room. Darcy had been in bed for two-and-a-half hours. I had gone to sleep thirty minutes earlier. Lisa had worked at the desk under a solitary lamp until 9:45, researching statistics, making phone calls, and typing notes. If I was right, she'd have the biggest story of her career. She'd been asleep for nearly an hour and always slept like the dead. She never heard the ring.

The call wasn't expected, only the impending conversation.

"Yeah?" I said.

"Jack," the voice said, "can we talk?"

I was awake instantly. I took a deep breath, covered the receiver, and exhaled slowly. "Sure," I said, as easygoing as a door-to-door salesman.

When I hung up, I made one other call on my cell phone. Then I waited twenty minutes before leaving.

. . .

This car was no Kia. This late-night meeting took place in a Mercedes E500. As soon as I got in, the car started moving.

"You didn't say anything about going anywhere," I said.

The car accelerated quickly. The speedometer hit fifty in a matter of seconds.

"What do you want?" I said.

No answer.

We turned left out of the parking lot and sped to make the first traffic light. That accomplished, the car slowed to fifty in the thirty-five zone.

"You cold?" he said.

"I was asleep," I said. "I threw on jeans and a windbreaker. What do you want?"

"You said something today that disturbed me."

"Yeah? What?"

"You don't remember?"

"No."

The inside of the car was dark. Occasionally, a passing streetlamp offered momentary light. He wore a dark sports jacket over a button-down shirt and jeans. This wasn't the plan. We weren't supposed to leave the parking lot. The radio wasn't on and I could hear his breath, which seemed to rasp. His anxiety made me nervous. So did the sports jacket. The .357 would be under it.

"You called me greedy. What did you mean by that?"

"Just what I said, Richie. I think you did what you did for the glory. I think your 'good-of-the-game' talk is bullshit."

"Do you mean my press conference?"

"No, I don't."

"Then what did I do?"

"We both know what you did."

"What, Jack? Tell me what you think."

"Where's your bodyguard? That was a good touch."

"Tell me what you think," he said.

"Somehow you found out about the steroids and you killed them all and left the suicide note pinning the whole thing on Paul Meyers."

He was quiet. We had slowed and, in the passenger's-side mirror, I saw several cars behind us.

"You invested a hundred grand in Nichols Golf," I said. "You got burned like the rest of them. But you got to know the principal investors—Ron Scott, Hurricane, and Meyers. Ron went to California to train with Pete Sandstrom. When he got back, he introduced Hurricane and Meyers to Sandstrom."

Richie never looked over. He just drove. He didn't speak and that was a problem. Things were not going as planned.

"Somehow, you got wind of the steroids. They probably offered to set you up with Sandstrom."

"And Hollis," he said. "Sandstrom thought he was hot shit. But Hollis was the guy they needed. He got the stuff. And you're wrong, Jack."

"What about? Was Brian, the bodyguard, the shooter?"

"No, he didn't do that. You're wrong about why I did it. I was one under today, when you called me greedy."

"You ended up shooting seventy-five."

"That drove me fucking nuts. Still does. I did it for golf. How can I compete if guys are using steroids?"

We were back to where this started in a Scottsdale parking lot—with Richie Barter talking about Richie Barter.

"Why not just blow the whistle?" I said. "Why'd you kill them?"

"First, because they cheated. The game can't have that. You weren't about to do anything. No one was. So I did. But they also took me for a ride. Ron Scott built a fucking mansion and I paid for it."

"You?"

"I lost more than a hundred grand. It was over a million. Ron Scott said he had a can't-miss stock. Then the business goes under, but he builds this fucking monstrosity of a home?"

"You think he stole your money?"

"Think? In the alley, he told me he did, offered to pay me back." He shook his head, remembering. "Christ, he even paid the broker off to keep his mouth shut."

I thought about Schmidt's anonymous source. How much, if any, had been invested? Schmidt said he never saw the portfolio. Sherry McCarthy had been unable to tell me what stocks the money had been invested in. It all made sense.

"I think he took Hurricane's money too," Richie said, "but Hurricane was too stupid to put two and two together."

"So you killed them all?"

He turned to me and nodded as if I'd asked if the sky was blue. "Of course," he said. "They all had it coming. That rumor about me? Where do you think that began? Meyers and his new endorsement deals. McCarthy acts like he's a good putter. And, of course, Ron Scott was a cheater and a thief."

He put on his blinker and we turned into an empty parking

lot. The cars behind us drove on. This was not how thing were supposed to go. Richie parked facing a closed convenience store. The windows of the store were barred. Beyond them, I could see an unlit Miller Light sign.

"I want to show you something," Richie said. "Let's take a walk."

"I don't think so. This is your personal car. You won't do it in this."

"Do what?"

"Fuck you," I said.

"Get out, Jack." He reached under his coat and pulled out a .357, his gun of choice. The first .357 had been wiped clean and left with Paul Meyers's corpse.

"Get out," he said, again.

I shook my head. "Let's see you explain the blood in this Mercedes. You made a mistake, Richie. Should've taken the courtesy car."

"I said get the fuck out!" He unlocked the doors and slid closer to me. With his right hand, he jammed the barrel of the .357 in my left ear. With his left hand, he reached past me and opened my door.

I could feel warm blood run down my cheek. I didn't dare fight him. The gun could go off during the struggle. He pushed me out and, as I went, shoved me hard. I stumbled to the ground. He followed me out before I could scramble to my feet and stood over me. He looked around quickly and cursed. Then he reached down, grabbed my shirt collar, and dragged me to my feet.

I had nothing to lose. I hit him in the face with all the right hook I had.

He staggered back three steps but didn't go down. "I might not hit like Pete Sandstrom," he said, "but I can take a punch."

He had found out a lot before he killed each one.

He was bleeding from the nose but didn't seem to notice. Instead, he stood staring at me. "What were you doing in this section of town, Jack? What were you thinking? Sandstrom told me how you'd already been mugged once. And then you come here, lose your wallet, and get shot?" A thin smile emerged as a trickle of blood ran down his chin and onto his shirt.

He raised the .357.

Instinctively, my hands went up. I turned and stumbled forward ludicrously as if I could outrun the bullet. There was thunderous boom and the sudden and momentary buzz of a gnat near my left ear. Then a thud and a groan, followed by silence. The pavement seemed to leap up at me and my face hit hard, the forward momentum scraping my nose on the tar.

I heard a second blast and glass shatter.

"Jack!"

I recognized the voice and rolled over. Inexplicably, I didn't check for bullet wounds. Instead, my hand went to my stinging nose. There was blood on my fingers.

"Jack, are you hit?!"

I was trying to piece it all together and didn't answer. There was a sound like a sandbag being pulled along the pavement. Then Perkins kicked the .357 away from where Richie Barter lay motionless. The car door was still open, casting a small stream of light. I could see what had once been Richie's boyish face. Perkins's shot had entered beneath Richie's right eye. The bullet hole was small and looked like an old penny. The blood streamed down his cheek like ink in the shadowy light. My mind raced to another shooting, when a pair of blood-splattered hands wouldn't relinquish the steering wheel.

"Jack!" Perkins yelled again. He let the cane clang on the ground and leaned over to look at me. He slapped my face. "Hey! Hey! Snap out of it!"

"I'm not hit," I said. "There were two shots."

"I shot him," he said. "I think his gun went off as he was twitching."

I flinched at the image.

"You were lucky you weren't hit," he said.

Behind me, the window and the Miller Light sign were shattered.

"Where were you?" I said.

"I followed you. When he turned in, I drove a little past. I was about fifty feet away when I took him. I wanted to get closer, but then I saw the door open and you fall out. I knew I had to take the shot." He reached down, ripped open my windbreaker, and tore free the microphone taped to my chest. He reached into his pant pocket and withdrew a cassette. "This would've been worth four life sentences," he said.

I lay back on the tar and exhaled deeply.

At 8:30 Friday morning, Perkins and I were in my hotel room, sitting on the loveseat, sipping coffee. Darcy was on the floor playing with her Polly Pockets. On the television, the screen was split. On one half, Lisa was standing near the practice green at Mirasol; on the other, *The Early Show* host Charles Donald once again sat on a stool in the New York studio. Lisa had just recounted the events of the previous night.

"This PGA Tour Security man, Darcy Perkins, shot over Austin's shoulder?" Donald said. "That sounds like something out of a movie."

"Mr. Perkins is a highly skilled professional," Lisa said, "a former homicide detective and investigator."

The screen cut to a professional photo of Perkins.

"Jesus Christ," I said. "Your head won't fit out the door."

"Daddy," Darcy said, "potty word." She went across the room and returned with her piggy bank. I reached into my pocket and dropped a quarter into her bank.

"And Mr. Perkins is in possession of a taped confession?" Donald said.

"The tape has been turned over to local authorities."

"Have you listened to the tape?"

"Yes," Lisa said.

"And it indicates that Barter killed four people for the good of the game?"

"I don't know if we can speculate as to why he killed them," Lisa said. "Clearly, he was not a stable man, Charlie."

"Oh, good play, Lisa," I said, and raised my coffee cup.

Perkins tapped it with his. When the television went to a commercial, I turned it off and we sat quietly for a while. Darcy was playing ventriloquist with her dolls, assuming one voice, then another.

"You did a lot of the work," Perkins said. "Actually, most of it. They barely mentioned you."

"You made the shot that saved my life—again," I said.

He drank his coffee.

"What happens to Liz Scott," I said, "and all that money Hurricane lost? I had to give Terry McCarthy a loan yesterday."

"Billy Peters says Illinois State Police is looking into the financial aspects of this thing. If someone looks hard enough, the numbers won't add up."

"When I first went to her house," I said, "Liz told me the house cost more than she thought they could afford. When I asked her how much of their money Ron lost investing, she said she didn't know."

Perkins shrugged. He looked tired. His blond hair was disheveled beneath the TaylorMade cap I'd given him and he had bags under his eyes. My ear was cut and hurt where Richie had jammed the .357 in it.

"All I want from her is for the McCarthy family to get their money back."

"I don't know how that will turn out," he said. "I'm sure Billy Peters will push the State guys. Hell, it might even go federal since the money crossed state lines."

"FBI?"

"Bet your ass," he said. "This is high profile."

Darcy walked over. "Uncle P, potty word."

Perkins leaned forward, put a hand on the coffee table, and struggled to his feet. He took a quarter from his pocket and handed it to Darcy. Her face lit up and she went back to her dolls.

"You're teaching the kid to be a money-hungry spy," he said, as he sat down again.

"Linda and Jackie sleeping?"

He nodded.

"How are things?"

"I've got a lot of apologizing to do. Linda wants me to talk to someone."

I didn't say anything. I took his cup and went to the pot on the desk and poured us each another cup. I added sugar to mine; Perkins took his black. I went back to the sofa and we sat quietly for a time, watching and listening to Darcy play.

"Thank you," I said. "That was a hell of a shot. Not many guys could've done it."

Again, he only shrugged.

"Not many would've had the balls to do it either."

Perkins continued to watch Darcy.

"She's named after you, you know?" I said.

"I know," he said.

"The leg didn't bother you last night," I said. "You made the shot when you absolutely had to."

He turned and looked at me. After a few seconds, he nodded. "It's time to go home."

. . .

That afternoon, Silver and I were in the middle of fairway on the twelfth hole, a 588-yard par five. I was two under on my round, even for the tournament. But the projected cut was −2.

"You hit a monster drive," Silver said, "but you still have two sixty-eight to reach the green. You've been steady all day. Lay up with a five-iron, then play a wedge to the green."

The TaylorMade staff bag stood between us. I reached for a club I hadn't hit all day, pulled the headcover off, and took a practice swing.

"That's not even your club, Jack. Don't take a gamble."

The previous night, I had stared into the barrel of a .357. I hadn't played well in weeks. And I was over the cut line. It was just Tom Lehman and me now and our gallery was thin. The Florida sun felt warm on my back as I held up the four-wood and examined it. THE HURRICANE was printed along the bottom of the clubhead. I thought about Hal "Hurricane" McCarthy. Was he a cheater? Yeah. Had he hurt the game? No question. But he was also among the best fathers and husbands I ever knew. A lot of people had gotten tangled up with Nichols Golf and the steroid scandal—Ron Scott, Richie Barter, Paul Meyers, and maybe even Liz Scott. All of them had sought money, fame, or both. I'd never condone Hurricane's actions, but I still couldn't condemn the man.

I brought the four-wood back slowly and made a smooth pass at the ball, my right elbow tucked tightly against my side. The contact was crisp. The ball rose against the pale-blue sky and landed softly on the putting surface. I handed the four-wood back to Silver and said, "It's our club now."